# THE DISSENT
# OF
# ANNIE LANG

## Ros Franey

MUSWELL
PRESS

First published by Muswell Press in 2018
This paperback edition published in 2019

Copyright © Ros Franey 2018

Ros Franey asserts the moral right
to be identified as the author of this work.

Typeset by M Rules
Printed and bound by CPI Group (UK) Ltd, Croydon CR0 4YY.

A CIP catalogue record for this book
is available from the British Library

ISBN 978-1-99961-352-5

Muswell Press
London
N6 5HQ
www.muswell-press.co.uk

# CONTENTS

# PROLOGUE

## *1932*

My story starts and ends at railway stations, though of course I can't know this yet as I clamber off the boat train at Victoria that warm May afternoon. Through the clang of shunting, whistles, the shouts of porters and the sharp smell of coal from the tenders, it's suddenly a tremendous relief to catch sight of Beatrice. She is standing in a pool of yellow light shining through the sooty glass roof, her grey eyes scanning the throng from behind new circular horn-rimmed spectacles, a slight frown breaking into a smile as she sees me a moment after I see her.

'Annie! Phew! What a crush. I thought I'd missed you!' Her gloved hands catch mine for a moment, and then she grabs my suitcase and joins the queue jostling for the barrier. 'Goodness, girl, what on earth have you got in here?'

I laugh and take her arm. She's wearing a white dress with blue roses and a little blue-grey bolero, smart grey shoes, grey-blue gloves that match her eyes and a dove-grey leather bag.

'Gosh, Beatrice, you look so ... elegant!'

We're standing at one of the bus stops in front of the

station. Beatrice smiles shyly and raises a critical hand to her hair, which has been cut in a bob, held at the back with a bow. I've barely seen her since she took up her job in London. People say she's not a beauty – though, to me, she's my beautiful sister – but there's no doubt about it: Beatrice has style. I feel a scruff in comparison, with my plaid cotton dress, its starched white collar probably coated in smuts from the journey, my creased summer coat, sensible brogues and tangled hair from sitting on deck for most of the crossing. Beatrice surveys me, taking all this in, and says nothing.

Later, after supper at her digs in Bloomsbury, I tell her a bit about France and my ten months studying in Bordeaux, holding on to it fiercely to stop it slipping away. Beatrice is ironing a blouse for next morning and I tease her about the care she takes with her wardrobe. She says seriously, 'The secret is to buy *well*, Annie – quality, not quantity.' She is a secretary to two of the ministers at the G-Pom. 'It's all right for you; you're a student,' she adds wistfully.

'When will you start your training, Bea?' I ask her. I don't want her to feel I'm putting on airs because of going to the university. Beatrice's dream is to be a missionary.

She avoids my gaze. 'I don't know yet. I'll have to see. It depends.'

'On what?'

She concentrates on the ruffles of her blouse, pressing the iron against each one with precision. 'Oh, you know ... on my vocation, I suppose.'

'Oh ... I see.' This is a part of her life into which I can never enquire. 'I thought you ... I mean, well, you've *got* a vocation, haven't you? You've always had it!'

'I don't know, Annie. It's more complicated than I used to think. You have to be called,' she explains gently. 'It's not up to you.'

'Oh,' I say, very much hoping no one will call me.

There's a short silence. She finishes the blouse and stands the iron on a trivet to cool. 'But, listen, that's enough about me. What have you heard from home?'

'Oh, you know. Nothing much.' I'm still thinking about Beatrice and how annoying it must be to have to hang around waiting for God. I turn my mind to her question. 'Nothing's happening at home, is it? Daddy's worshipful whatsit of the lodge by now, I suppose. Golly, I hope that doesn't mean I'll get dragged off to ladies' evenings!' I pull a face in mock horror. 'I say, d'you suppose Mother has to go? I can't see it, can you? Imagine – she'd have the Bagshaws singing "The Old Rugged Cross" within half an hour!'

We both smile uneasily.

'Anything to report on that front?' I ask after a moment.

'On Mother? No. But Annie—' Beatrice has folded up the ironing board. She comes to sit down. 'They haven't mentioned Fred?'

I throw myself on the slippery counterpane of her bed, levering off my shoes without untying the laces. 'Fred? What about him?'

'He's not been well.'

I stare at her. 'How d'you mean?'

Beatrice sighs. 'Oh dear. Listen, before we talk about it, let me make you some cocoa.'

I shake my head. 'I want to know about Fred. What's the matter with him? Is it serious?'

'Quite serious, but it's not' – she looks at me meaningfully – '*physical*.'

'You mean it's like last time?'

Beatrice nods. 'But worse. "Nervous exhaustion", they say.'

'Where is he?'

'Mapperley.'

'*In*, or as an outpatient?'

'He's in there, Annie. He's been there a few weeks.'

'And they never told me!'

We look at each other as I take this in. The hospital is a great brick lunatic asylum from my childhood; girls at school who lived nearby called it The Building. They'd threaten to lock you up in it if you did something stupid. If you walked past, it was like ambulances: you had to hold your collar until you saw a dog. And now our brother is inside. 'What about his work?' Daddy had found Fred a job as an insurance clerk through one of his Masonic chums.

'Well, he couldn't cope,' says Beatrice. 'You know? Couldn't concentrate. Found it hard to be there on time. Forgot things. . .' She tails off. It's not the first time this has happened: he dropped out of college two years ago, but he could never talk about it at home; couldn't explain to any of us what was wrong.

'I always thought it was that stupid school,' I say. 'He was never quite himself after they sent him away.'

Beatrice shakes her head. 'Whatever it is, he's poorly. They're saying complete rest is the only thing that will help. There's some new electric treatment in America, I've heard, but it hasn't come here yet.'

'Can I see him?'

'They're a bit funny about visiting. They think it may upset him more. . .'

'Is that what *she* says? Well, I'm going to see him!'

Beatrice throws me a warning look. 'Just watch it, will you? You know what you're like!'

'Why didn't they tell me, Bea?'

'They won't have wanted to worry you, Annie, when you were so far from home.'

\*

4

But as the train pulls north out of St Pancras next day, I feel further from home than ever. I think about Fred and the world I'm going back to, and realise, of course, that the story doesn't start here at all. It began long ago, and what I can't recall I can read – because I wrote it down when I was twelve.

# Part One

## 1926

# ONE

These are the secrets of Annie Rose Lang, in which I write the history of my hidden thoughts and all the things I can't say to anyone, not even Beatrice, except I do say some things to her. I am twelve and a half, the daughter of Harry Lang, manager of Roebuck's Biscuits and some other things, and of Agnes Mary Lang my beloved mother, not of Agnes Ada Lang who is my mother now.

I can see from our photograph album that Our Own Mother and Daddy had a wonderful wedding with trails of flowers and cousins in white. Beatrice says they are in the garden of the big house at Mapperley Top where Grandfather still lives. Grandfather is there looking not too religious for once, and beside him Auntie Grace in a hat like a cake towers over my little parents, Daddy very handsome and twinkly, Mother looking alarmed. And that's all I know about that, because of course Beatrice wasn't there either, so she can't tell me.

The first thing I have to recount is what happened to my mother Agnes Mary when I was six years old, and this is difficult because I remember only a few things. Sometimes it is hard to know what I actually recall and what Beatrice and the others have told me since. I would prefer not to write anything I don't know for myself, but there are a few things I learnt, or thought, later. This can't be helped, for they need to be put down as well.

One of my earliest own memories is where it all started. *Faster than Fairies, Faster than Witches, Bridges and Houses, Hedges and Ditches.* We were reading *The Child's Garden of Verses* at bedtime. On that particular night instead of Mother coming to read to me, Maisie came. I remember thinking it odd because Maisie should have gone home. I asked, Maisie, where is Mother? And she answered very quickly that she would read to me tonight and where had we got to? It's poems, I said. You don't get to anywhere with poems, you just read them. This was rude, but I didn't want to read 'From a Railway Carriage' with Maisie because Mother was more fun. *And Charging Along Like Troops in A Battle, All Through the Meadows of Horses and Cattle . . .* Mother used to pretend the bed was the railway carriage and *bounce* as she read it, and I would laugh out loud. Maisie took up the book and leafed through it like someone who is not used to looking at poems.

'Here's one,' she said: '"To Mother".' I waited. Maisie sat very still. She didn't bounce on the bed. She jammed her knees together, I could see the shape of them under her pinny, and read it in a sort of flat-reading voice, almost like in the Mission. I won't copy it out here because it makes me cry.

'Where *is* Mother?' I asked again, when she had finished.

'Go to sleep now,' she said. 'Mother's lying down.'

'Where's Beatrice? Where is Fred?'

'Beatrice is in her room.'

'Where's Daddy?'

'Hush,' said Maisie. She put her scaly palm on my forehead. 'It will all be better in the morning, duckie.' After a few minutes in which I shut my eyes and pretended to be asleep, she left the room, leaving the door ajar as Mother would have told her to. This was a good sign.

As soon as her feet had gone downstairs I jumped out of bed and crept to the place where the gaslight fell across the corner of my room from the open door. In our rooms we had electricity but in those days the landing and the hall light was still gas that hissed a bit with a greenish smell. There was a funny sound about the house, like a doom, but no people. I tiptoed back for Little Sid, who goes everywhere with me, and then out along the corridor to see my sister Beatrice. She was lying on her bed, reading, winding her long hair in her fingers like French knitting.

'Annie, you're supposed to be asleep!'

'Mother didn't say goodnight,' I announced.

'You've got to be a good girl tonight.'

'I want Mother to come and do "From a Railway Carriage".'

'She can't,' Beatrice said. 'Maisie's stayed late instead.'

'Maisie can't do poems.'

'Daddy says Mother's a bit poorly. If you go back to bed she'll be better in the morning.'

'Little Sid doesn't want to go back to bed. He wants to stay here with you.'

'He'll go if you go with him. Here—' She jumped off her own bed and took my hand.

'Can we go and see Mother?'

'Mother's very tired. She's sleeping.' Beatrice and I and Little Sid crept back along the corridor. 'Mind that bit,' Beatrice whispered as we got to the creaky board, as if I didn't know. A door opened downstairs and we heard Daddy's voice. He was speaking to Maisie. We held our breath but the door closed again and we heard Maisie down in the hall.

Beatrice hurried me back into my own room and tucked me up in bed.

'Night, night Sleepyhead,' she murmured. It was what Mother used to say. 'Have you said your prayers?'

'Sort of. No.'

'Well say them in bed. Say them for Mother.'

'Why?' I demanded.

'No reason. Just to be on the safe side. I've said mine.' Beatrice has always been better at prayers than me. She left the room then.

I lay in bed and curled my toes into my nightie to warm them up and clutched Little Sid very tightly. I don't know what prayers I said, probably God Bless Mother and God Bless Daddy and God Bless Nana and God Bless Beatrice and Fred and Maisie and Little Sid and then at the end God Bless Mother again, to make sure he jolly well did.

I hoped it would all be better in the morning, but it wasn't. For a start, Daddy didn't go to his office down in the town, very peculiar. Maisie seemed to be creeping up and downstairs a lot with pans of something and towels and medicine that smelt dismal in a cup. Dr Martin was away, so another doctor came. I remember his big overcoat and his bulging shoulders as I watched through the banisters. It was the holidays and we didn't know what to do. Beatrice played the piano, *Scenes of Childhood* and *Für Elise*, then she tried to teach me Halma, one of the games in the box on the bookshelves in the drawing room. I just remember everything being jumpy and not concentrating. No one took any notice of us and I had the butterflies in my tummy. Fred came in – although he was younger than Beatrice, he was a boy and always out. Maisie said we should put on our coats and go into the Oaks with Nana, but although she was only two in those days Nana knew something was up and hung back with her tail between her legs. Fred had to drag her by the collar up to the reservoir. Beatrice and I did skipping and Fred got bored and wandered off again with Nana.

This went on for several days, until Sunday. Sunday in our house is different because of the Mission and we all have to go. You have to go at least three times, morning and evening and Sunday School, which is Bible Story in the afternoons. But Mother said I was too little and I only had to go twice. When we are older and baptised with the total immersion, we shall have to take the pledge, as in the foreswearing of alcohol, and go to the Mission even more. It is important to go to the Mission because it was founded by our grandfather, William Eames, who is the Pastor there, and so we have to set an example. It is known as the Golgotha Mission, after the Crucifixion. The other people who go there have to name their children after us because of Pastor Eames being our grandfather. Well, maybe they don't have to, but a lot of them do it anyway and there are all these Freds and Beatrices and Annies running round in the Sunday School class. I hate it. Why can't they think up names for themselves? Anyway, on this particular Sunday a whole lot of prayers were said for the sick and Our Dear Sister Agnes Lang and it was awful afterwards when everyone came up to us and wanted to take us by the hand and look pityingly at us, as if she was dead or something, which they couldn't have known she was going to die. I hung on to Beatrice with one hand and kept the other clutched around Little Sid in my pocket, so I didn't have a hand free and they couldn't touch me. I was glad Auntie Vera wasn't there to see me: she is very fierce with people who put their hands in their pockets, especially in the Mission.

Once (though this was later) I forgot my gloves when Auntie Vera was visiting and spent the whole service in an agony of not knowing whether it was worse to keep your hands in your pockets, or to reveal to the entire congregation you had no gloves on. In the end I tucked my hands under *The Hymnal*, on the grounds that if she caught me with my hands in my pockets she would discover, on making me remove them, that I was committing not one sin but two. I tried to walk out at the end with my fingers concealed in the folds of my coat, but she spotted me anyway. In Auntie Vera's view not wearing gloves is as dreadful as not wearing knickers, especially in church. I had to learn a whole chunk of Isaiah: *And in the year that King Uzziah died, I saw the Lord sitting upon a throne* . . . But that was lucky because I had learnt it in school the previous term, though I didn't let on. Oh, I must record that I have never, *ever* forgotten to wear knickers at the Mission.

On this occasion I *was* wearing gloves, because on most Sundays it is too cold in there not to. Of course it's rude to shake people's hands with your gloves on so I would have had to take them off and feel all that sympathy coming at me through the skin of the congregation. And Auntie Vera wasn't there to see me, so I stuffed my left hand in my pocket and my right hand into Beatrice's left. Beatrice is four years older than me and always knows what to say. I wanted to run away but I couldn't because I'm afraid of Grandfather Pastor Eames who is very fond of going on about the Wrath of God, and giving you even bigger chunks of the Bible to learn, and I still am scared even now when I'm twelve and so much older. I don't like Sundays, but that Sunday was the second worst I can remember.

That night it was the end of the holidays. I was supposed to be starting at Mundella in the juniors but no one had made any preparations. Daddy said Beatrice should take me, but Maisie told him I couldn't go if I didn't have a uniform or pencils and Daddy didn't argue. There were things that

Mother had to do, but how could she? Mother was lying in the high twin bed in the big front bedroom and I don't remember anything more about that. I stayed at home and the house became very quiet. Little Sid and I took to spending a lot of time in the breakfast room with Nana when Fred and Beatrice were at school.

One day, when Maisie was out and Daddy doing other things, I sneaked in to the bedroom when Mother was alone. It didn't seem the right thing to bounce on the bed, so I stood as close to her as I could and recited softly, '. . . *All of the sights of the hill and the plain Fly as Thick as Driving Rain; And ever again in the Wink of an Eye, Painted stations whistle by.*'

I waited. She seemed to be very far away from me, on a distant journey of her own. But she stirred a bit and opened her eyes. They were deep in her face, much deeper than usual, but they were smiling. She whispered, '*Here is a cart run away in the road Lumping along with man and load; And here is a mill and there is a river. Each a glimpse and gone for ever.*'

'Oh Mama,' I said. It was my special name for her. But she had closed her eyes again and actually I was glad because my chin was wobbling and I couldn't stop it. I wanted to take her hand but her hands were under the bedclothes in the tall bed, so I stretched out on tiptoe and could just reach her nose. I think she smiled. Then Maisie walked in and I was told to leave.

The strange doctor came again. He was upstairs a long time, and Maisie with him. I saw Daddy out in the yard. He seemed to be looking at the flower tubs with great attention. I saw the doctor go out and speak to him before he left the house. They both had their heads bent as if the doctor was interested in the flowers, too. Sometime after that, I was passing the open door of the sitting room and I heard Daddy crying, the only time before or since. Now this is a terrible thing for a little girl to hear in her own father. He was crying in big sobs and my whole world went head over heels and broke. *Each a glimpse and gone for ever.* I ran into the breakfast room and threw myself down beside Nana's basket. I remember the rolled-thick bristly hair at the back of her neck as I hugged her desperately, and her dear, smelly breath and her worried nose. I wished Beatrice would come home, and then she did – early – and that was worse. *God Bless Mother and God Bless Daddy and God Please, Please, Please don't let her die.*

But He did. That was where it all went wrong. And Grandfather and the whole Mission droned on about it being God's Will and God in his Mercy and Wisdom Gathering Agnes His Child unto Himself. Whenever they spoke like this I did not know what to think. I would watch Daddy look at his toes and say 'hmm'. I don't know what he meant by this 'hmm', but as I grew up, I wondered. As I have got older I think more and more, what is Merciful or Wise about God gathering Mother, for goodness sake, when He has all His other children in the whole world who He can Gather and do whatsoever else unto them He wisheth? How *unthinkably selfish* to help Himself to our mother when she's the only one we've got. Then Beatrice told me that someone let on Mother had died of a stupid thing that no one's meant to die of. I asked whether, if Dr Martin had been there, he might have cured her and stopped God doing it, at which Beatrice's eyes went as round as saucers and she said that was blasphemy and I must wash out my mouth. Of course, if God wanted to gather Mother He would have seen to it that Dr Martin wasn't around. He's clever like that and all-seeing, so He thinks of everything. His will be done. *Hmm.*

And so began life after Mother. Whenever I open the photograph album all the after-Mother pictures fall out because there is no one to stick them in any longer, so I always start at the beginning where everything is neatly in its place, secured by the thick black photo-corners that taste funny and curl up when you lick the back. First there is the drawing of Grandfather's mill, four storeys high with a flag flying above the roof that says 'Eames Eureka Flour'. Around the bottom of the building there are tiny horses and drays and outbuildings and men bustling about in top hats and frock coats; and floating in the sky there is a second picture entitled 'London Office'. I have a miniature rolling pin, china with wooden handles and 'Eames Eureka Flour' in blue writing, but that is the only thing left. Fred says Grandfather gave all his money to the Lord when he built the Golgotha Mission and he doesn't own the factory any longer. Fred says our Grandfather went bankrupt, but honourably, on account of saving the souls of all the little Beatrices and Annies: Pastor Eames is also a Freemason and much revered in the city and we must hold our heads high. Some boys and girls have tea with their grandfathers on Sundays, but of course ours was always busy, and at Christmas and Easter, too. So it may have been to do with that, or it may have been what Fred said later: our grandfather thought children were a nuisance. Whatever the reason, we didn't see much of him outside the Mission. To me, he was always Grandfather Pastor Eames in his pulpit.

All the same, I'm glad he didn't lose so much of his money that he had to give up the house at Mapperley Top. There is a photograph of my grandmother (whom I do not remember) and a maid in a long white apron and a frilled cap, and my mother and Auntie Vera as young women standing at the front door with their dog who was called Major. I know every inch of the picture of the beautiful wedding party in their garden, but there is another photo I love even more: it must have been taken much earlier. Mother is sitting in the same garden between her sisters Grace and Frances, whom we call Auntie Francie. (Auntie Vera isn't there, I'm pleased to say.) They are all very young, just girls, Mother not much older than Beatrice is now, and the person taking the photograph must have told a joke because she has just exploded in giggles. In all her other photos Mother looks serious or startled, but in this one she is herself: thick curly hair falling around her shoulders, the long full sleeves of her blouse more stylish than those of her sisters, and a big grin. That is how I like to remember her.

Sometimes I ask where Mother used to keep those photo-corners so that I can stick the new pictures in, but the others have all got more important things on their minds. The first picture to fall out is of Daddy with the three of us in the yard at Corporation Oaks, which is where we live. I am very close to him, holding his hand. Beatrice is sitting on the kitchen stool which proves it was a proper, posed family photograph because the kitchen stool is never normally allowed out in the yard. Beatrice has one leg crossed over the other and her hands folded on her knee like a grown-up. Fred is standing slightly apart from us. I think he is trying to look as if it's all the same to him if his mother is alive or dead. Next in the pile is the photo of me in my Chinese costume. I look very sweet and am clasping my hands together in the way I've been told Chinese mandarins do. The costume is, of course, a present from Auntie Francie, who isn't in the wedding photos because of being a missionary. She lives in China now and goes around on a bicycle unbinding the feet of the women and making sure they are Saved. She lives in Shansi Province in a place called Tai Yuan-Fu. She's always been there, even before I was born. Every Christmas she sends presents to England, and our house, Grandfather's house, Auntie Vera's and Auntie Grace's are all full of vases and jugs and plates and teapots and incense burners and silk dressing gowns and embroidered slippers and bendy teaspoons with a funny taste – all sent by Auntie Francie. Beatrice says she wants to be a missionary when she grows up and go to China with the God's Purpose Overseas Mission which we call the G-Pom, but Beatrice is anxious just going to Mablethorpe for the Summer holidays so I don't expect she'll get to Tai Yuan-Fu. I'd like to go to China, but I don't want to be a missionary so I can't.

There seem to be quite a few family portraits in the two or three years after Mother died, which is odd because I can't find any photos of us all when she was alive. Maybe they didn't feel the need for them when everything was still all right; perhaps Daddy thought that with Mother not around any more he ought to get the family together and make sure we all knew the rest of us were still there. Daddy is not very tall but you don't know that when he's sitting down. He has a cheerful face, lots of dark hair and a walrus moustache. The thing you notice most in all the photos of him is his wide blue eyes which are very smiley. I am on his knee, my hair tied with a big ribbon. In one photo I'm wearing the velvet party frock I loved so much, with its scalloped lace collar. The dress was royal blue, though of course you can't tell that from the photo; nor can you see that Little Sid is sitting in the gathered pocket – but I know he's there. The collar was made, I believe, by Maisie's sister who works in the Lace Market where they make the Nottingham lace that is world famous. Maisie sometimes tries to teach me how to begin with simple stitches, but it's all I can do to manage doubles and trebles in crochet. Fred, dressed in a sailor suit, stands beside Daddy's chair and looks serious. Beatrice, the oldest, is behind him. She has long hair and a misty look about the eyes, which some people may find fascinating, but I know comes from not wearing her spectacles; she needs them all the time now and does so hate herself in photographs. None of us looks like Mother.

After the family portraits in the jumbled pile comes the first photograph of the other Agnes.

# TWO

When life began without Mother, I realised that everything and everyone I knew – Eames Eureka Flour, the Aunties, China, the Mission and Grandfather Pastor Eames – was to do with her family. I know nothing about Daddy's family at all. I suppose that's because he came from somewhere else, so there were no grandparents or places or cousins to grow up with from his side; the only thing was Auntie Vera saying that our father 'had a good war'. From the way she said this, which was not quite approving, I thought perhaps he didn't fight in it, but he did do *something*. Whatever it was, he never told us about it, and I suppose we never asked him. I don't even know if Daddy was religious to begin with. If he was, I had the feeling he didn't throw himself into it with quite as much *fervour* as Mother's side of the family. (*Fervour* is a word Grandfather Pastor Eames is very keen on in his sermons.) I mean, Daddy had taken the pledge and came to Sunday morning services and so on, but the things he did outside work, mostly with the Mechanics' Institute and the 'Masons, were nothing to do with the Mission. Fred said Daddy was a businessman and liked cars, and that was all we knew when I was little.

It didn't matter, though, because Daddy was very jolly; a lot more fun than Auntie Vera and Grandfather Pastor Eames, anyway. He liked dance music and we were one of the first families I knew to get a wireless and listen to music on the BBC. Sometimes he used to dance with Beatrice and me around the armchairs in the sitting room. He was a very good dancer. If you couldn't do the steps, he would guide you so surely that you got it right – and you could almost believe you had done it by yourself, which was thrilling. The music bubbled through him when he danced and he loved it, too, grinning from ear to ear and telling us we were 'doing fine'. I'm too young to remember him dancing with Mother, but Beatrice said they used to go to Ladies' Evenings at the Lodge. Mother had some beautiful dresses which still hung in the wardrobe as if she might be coming back for them: my favourite had a rich satin lining in peacock blue. Of course, after she died, there was no more dancing for a while, and later, when it was all right to dance again, things had started to change.

One of the first things to happen after Mother's death was that Maisie spent more time at our house and Elsie arrived. Maisie called her the Scullery Maid. Elsie slept in the little attic bedroom above Fred's room and got up early to light the fires. We don't have fires in our bedrooms, of course, but once she had done the stove Elsie would wake us, so we were able to go downstairs to a warm kitchen. I can still hear her sing-song voice calling up the stairs,

'Come and 'ave yer break-fast, duckie.'

I hated porridge, but if she had time and the fire was glowing and not flaming she would make me toast on the toasting fork with the Chinese monkey at the end of the handle, another present from Auntie Francie. This she spread with dripping from the big green enamel bowl, the same one we have now but not as chipped. The toast and dripping was a secret; Maisie would not have approved, but it was what Elsie said she had at home. We had other secrets, too. In the corner cupboard was a large clear bottle of disgusting yellow cod liver oil with a sticky cork. I was supposed to have a big spoonful every day. Each morning Elsie would go to the cupboard, take down the bottle and give me one of her looks. And I would say *Oh Elsie,* and screw up my face and she would hesitate a moment before putting the bottle back in the cupboard again. 'Least said, soonest mended,' she would tell me. I never knew what this meant. From time to time she would pour some of the bottle down the stone sink so Maisie wouldn't suspect, and look at me, and wink, and that was that.

'You've got Elsie round your little finger,' Beatrice would say.

'So?'

'It's not fair, Annie. She could get into trouble.'

'What for?'

'You know what for.'

'Elsie'll not tell.'

'That's worse. She'll have to tell a lie and then she really will be in trouble.' She meant, with God of course, not with Maisie.

I wanted to think God would understand that the lie was in a good cause, but after Our Own Mother and everything I knew God was not on my side. He would strike Elsie down very probably. This made me feel guilty, so I said nothing.

The truth was that in those days, meaning eight months after my mother's death so they had stopped making allowances because I was a poor motherless waif and stray, people found

23

me argumentative and were always saying things about me, such as, 'Annie, you are growing increasingly troublesome.' That's what Miss Battersby, our headmistress, said, and she was not the only one. Maisie would shake her head and mutter, 'Too clever by half', which I wasn't sure was a compliment.

I remember overhearing a conversation between Auntie Vera and Daddy one Sunday teatime. I was playing with Irene and John, my cousins, in the yard and had been sent inside to fetch the skipping rope. Passing the drawing-room door, I heard voices and immediately knew they were talking about me.

'... out of control,' Auntie Vera was saying. 'No discipline.'

'A bit of a madam,' he answered.

I stopped and put my ear to the door-hinge in an effort to hear through the crack, but they were speaking softly and I could only pick out the odd word: 'insubordinate', 'highly strung', 'cheeky'. Then Auntie Vera must have moved because I began to hear her voice more clearly.

'... really can't carry on like this, Harry. Dear Agnes would have wanted ... Children need a moral structure ... discipline.'

I swallowed hard. If Auntie Vera were our mother we would certainly have had that. Cousin Irene confided in Beatrice once that poor John still wet the bed like a baby, he was so frightened of her.

'I suppose you're ... Had thought of ... housekeeper,' Daddy was saying. He sounded doubtful. His voice dropped at the end of each sentence in a hopeless-sounding way, so I couldn't hear. But what was he talking about? We already had a housekeeper: we had Maisie!

'... some good woman,' Auntie Vera told him. '... Golgotha.'

*From the Mission?* This was an appalling prospect. My mind ran swiftly through a few candidates. Mrs Rancid; Hilda Barnes? I found myself shivering. Maybe Madge Grocott who taught us Bible Story at Sunday School. We must have our lives interfered with by a stranger from the Mission, and all on account of *me* being 'insubordinate'. I was still reeling from the awfulness of this when the sound of Auntie's sharp heel on the floorboards at the edge of the carpet brought me to my senses. I fled.

For weeks after that conversation I made a huge effort to behave well. I was courteous and polite, did what I was told, tried not to speak unless spoken to, wore gloves at all times and even forced myself to swallow a few spoonfuls of cod liver oil – believing that if I did lots of unpleasant but virtuous things God would stop Daddy bringing in a housekeeper. I tested this theory on Beatrice, who didn't think much of it. 'That's what Catholics do,' she said. I was secretly thrilled. Catholics were greatly disapproved of at the Mission. If Catholics did it, I thought I might be on to something.

I also kept a close watch on the grown-ups. I hung around their conversations and lurked outside doors in the hope of picking up some titbit of information. Whenever Daddy was late home in the evening I dreaded that he might be calling at the houses of Grandfather's parishioners on the lookout for a housekeeper. I envisaged him tramping round the streets off the Woodborough Road where many of the Mission's congregation lived; streets of flat, grimy red-brick houses strung together, with ranks of front doorsteps that got scrubbed every morning and backs with washing lines. It was not an encouraging picture: there were no trees in those streets.

But Beatrice's response was practical. 'He might find

someone who can cook dumplings and treacle pudding,' she said. Maisie was a wonderful cook, but she went home after lunch on Saturday and never worked Sundays. Elsie was not allowed to cook, thank goodness, apart from the porridge.

Fred said, 'Daddy will never replace our mother.'

'No one's suggesting he will,' Beatrice assured him. 'He's looking for a housekeeper, not a wife.'

'But we've got Maisie!' I protested.

'Well,' explained Beatrice. 'Maisie started doing it because she was sort of here already. She's not really a housekeeper.'

'Perhaps the new one will read us stories, like Mother used to,' I suggested hopefully.

Fred grunted. He was reading his own stories now.

'She could test you on Horatius,' said Beatrice. Our class was learning 'The Keeping of the Bridge' by Lord Macaulay. I had been reciting it all over the house.

I closed my eyes and took a deep breath.

'Now look what you've started!' Fred groaned.

> 'And, like a horse unbroken
> When first he feels the rein,
> The furious river struggled hard
> And tossed his tawny mane—'

Fred threw the coal-glove at me. I dropped my voice to a whisper, thumping Nana's large head in time to the rhythm as I recited:

> '. . . And burst the curb and bounded,
> Rejoicing to be free,
> And whirling down in fierce career
> Battlement and plank and pier,
> Rushed headlong to the sea!'

Nana beat her tail on the ground. 'This housekeeper'd better like Nana, too,' I added fiercely.

At the end of the verse, Fred heaved a loud sigh and went back to his book.

'Come on, Fred,' said Beatrice. 'You love the tiger poem.'

'Poetry's for girls,' he muttered.

'Horatius isn't girls' stuff!' I threw him a challenging glare, but all he said was, 'Tiger's different. Mother taught it me.'

I pushed my fingers into my chin because I suddenly wanted to cry. We ought not to need a housekeeper or Auntie Vera or any of them.

Fred jumped up. 'Come on, Nana,' he said harshly. 'Let's go out. This is dreary.'

After a few weeks, and no housekeeper in sight, I started to get bored with spying on the grown-ups. Make no mistake, I was still watchful; I knew that as long as I kept an eye on things it would be all right, but if I dropped my guard completely a housekeeper could be sneaked in under cover. To this end, whenever Daddy was later home than usual I would ask Maisie, 'Where's Daddy, Maisie?'

'You always ask me that, Annie. He's a busy man, your father.'

'Did he say he was going to be late?'

'He'll be home for his tea.'

'Has he gone to see someone?'

'I don't know, lovie, do I?'

'He might have said.'

'Why should he tell me?'

'But Maisie, it might have a big important effect on all our lives!'

The first couple of occasions I said this, she just laughed. But when I wouldn't leave it alone, she became uneasy, I could tell. 'You're a rum one, you are. What are you on about, Annie?'

'I think you know more than you're letting on,' I grumbled.

'Know what? What is there to know?'

'About a certain thing, a certain person.'

She stared at me.

'Beginning with H ...' I said darkly.

'H? What d'you mean H? H for himself is all I know.'

This was a favourite of mine, and I forgot all about the housekeeper in an instant. 'Oh Maisie, say it, say it!' I begged.

'A is for 'orses.'

'B for mutton,' I chimed in.

'C for yourself,' we chorused.

'What's D for?' I asked. 'E for brick.'

'F for pheasant; G for police!' We spun round. My father stood in the kitchen doorway. He laughed his big laugh and spread his arms wide.

'There you are, you see,' Maisie said. 'She wasn't half going on about you being late, Mr Lang.'

'Were you, Annie?'

'Not really,' I said. I was cross because I'd been outwitted by Maisie.

'Well, I'm here now.' He ruffled my hair as he walked past me into the hall to hang up his hat and scarf.

I asked grumpily, 'What's "I" for, Maisie?'

'I for tower.' She went out to the scullery to get her own coat; she must have been waiting for Daddy to come home so that she could leave. All I knew about Maisie's life was that she lived somewhere in Hyson Green with a husband she always called Mr Brown. I thought of him as Old Mr Brown, the owl in Squirrel Nutkin – *Mr Brown paid no attention whatever to Nutkin. He shut his eyes obstinately and went to sleep.* I imagined Maisie and Mr Brown living halfway up a tree in Hyson Green, two tubby people with kind hearts. There had been some little owls, too, but they had flown before we knew Maisie. Poor Mr Brown must have waited ages for his tea night after night since our mother died, but I never thought of that in those days, because I was only small.

Maisie came back into the breakfast room, adjusting her hat with a pin. She knew what H stood for all right; she had her crafty smile on. I felt slightly sick. 'YZ for young shoulders,' she said darkly and let herself out of the back door.

That Sunday, Auntie Vera came and met me from Sunday School. This was unusual; Fred and Beatrice usually waited after the big children's class and we walked home on our own.

'What did you do today?' she asked.

'Loaves and fishes.' I kicked at a pebble.

'Don't scuff your boots, Annie. What hymns did you sing?'

'"There's a Friend for Little Children" and "Jesus Bids us Shine".'

'I love that one.' She sang in her quavery voice, *'Jesus bids us shine with a cool, clear light, Like a little candle burning in the night . . . something something something* – how does it go?'

'Can't remember, Auntie.' I didn't want to sing stupid hymns with Auntie Vera. I wanted to go home for tea.

'At your age you should remember all the words.'

'Well, *you* can't remember them!'

As soon as I said this I knew it was a terrible mistake. All my hard work to improve over recent weeks collapsed in an instant. *'You in your small corner, and I in mine,'* I chanted loudly.

*'What* did you say?'

'I'm sorry, Auntie, I didn't mean it.' I looked up at her. I could feel the anguish tightening my face all over.

'How *dare* you speak to me like that!'

'It just sort of— I'm so sorry, I'm so sorry. I didn't mean it.'

'Your mother is up there in Heaven and she watches over you. But when she leans down towards her little girl, what does she hear?'

I didn't want to see my mother leaning towards me from Heaven. I looked down at my buttoned boots. We were still walking up Robin Hood Chase. The boots swam below me, left, right, left, right.

'Well?'

'She hears me being rude, Auntie.'

'Are you snivelling?'

'Yes, Auntie.'

'Where's your handkerchief?'

I fumbled in my pocket, extracted the handkerchief and shook it to open it out.

'Not with your gloves on!' snapped Auntie Vera.

I tried to remove the glove from my left hand by pulling at each finger as she had taught me – and dropped the handkerchief.

'Oh, for goodness' sake. Insolent and clumsy with it! Well, pick it up, girl!'

I stooped. I was crying in gulps. I was up there with Mother, leaning out of Heaven watching me make a mess of everything. Then deep inside me I suddenly heard Mother say, *Lay off her, Vee, she's only seven years old.* I picked up the handkerchief, wiped my eyes and blew my nose. I looked up at Auntie Vera at last. 'I'm sorry, Auntie,' I said. 'It was terribly rude. I didn't mean it.'

She sort of made a noise like *harrumpgh*, as they write it in books. 'Well,' she said, 'it just goes to prove that you are out of control. I don't know how your mother ever put up with you. I'm glad to say that from today, things will be different.'

I stiffened. 'Will they?' I asked.

'When we get home, your father's new housekeeper will

30

be there to meet us. This has all taken far too long, I must say. From now on, you children will have a firm hand to guide you.'

It had happened. 'Oh,' I said. My feet slowed. My tears were forgotten. *A firm hand.*

'Come along!' exhorted Auntie Vera. 'Beatrice and Fred will have met her already. There'll be no scones left.' We tramped on up the hill.

My first glimpse of the lady who was to be housekeeper was in our sitting room. I had taken Little Sid out of my pocket as I entered, for courage and so he could meet her too. I say 'first glimpse' but it wasn't, because as soon as I saw the pointed angles of her profile, I realised I knew exactly who she was: Miss A. Higgs, as it said on the Mission noticeboard, played the harmonium at the Mission. She played 'Onward Christian Soldiers' and 'He who would valiant be' and I had often wondered what it must be like to sit up there sideways to the congregation with all eyes on you and pull out the mysterious stops and buttons and dance your feet on the pedals beneath. She could make snorting noises like trumpets and wobbly sounds like ghosts. I had always thought of her as something of a magician and when I saw that it was she who was to be our housekeeper I felt a huge rush of excitement. She was a musician. *I* played the piano. Perhaps it would be all right, after all. Miss Higgs was seated at the table behind the silver teapot with her back to the window, as tall and grave as she sat at the keyboard. I had never seen her face close up and I could not look into it now.

Auntie Vera had swept into the room before me. 'Miss Higgs,' she announced, 'this is Annie, the youngest.' She said *youngest* with a hiss as if to nudge the new housekeeper with a you-know-the-difficult-one dig in the ribs. I dropped my eyes and was faintly aware of brown bar shoes poking out from slender ankles. I could feel the penetrating gaze on me.

'Annie, say hello to Miss Higgs.'

'Hello, Missiggs. This is Little Sid.'

She recoiled. 'Errgh. What is that?'

'Not now, Annie,' Auntie Vera interrupted.

'It's Little Sid,' I repeated. I held him out for inspection in the palm of my hand. 'He's a panda. From China,' I added meaningfully, hoping she would know that *China* meant Auntie Francie the missionary, and win approval. 'Well, obviously not a real-size panda. He goes everywhere in my pocket.'

'Oh!' She scrutinised him cautiously. 'Does he need a good scrub? You made me jump. I thought it was a mouse.' Miss Higgs gave a sort of breathless sigh that might have been a laugh and might not. 'Go and wash your hands for tea, Annie.'

Auntie Vera gave me one of her looks. I left the room and went to the kitchen sink, reaching up to sit Little Sid on the mantelpiece above the range out of harm's way. Good scrub, indeed! I returned to the sitting-room.

'What did you learn in Sunday School today, Annie?' asked Miss Higgs.

'Loaves and fishes,' I muttered.

'Loaves and fishes, Miss Higgs,' hissed Auntie Vera.

'Missiggs,' I echoed.

'Annie, please look at me when you speak to me!' she said.

I jerked my head up and gazed at her. The light was fading and her features were in shadow but I could make out grey eyes in a rather long, flat face, a neat, straight nose and lips in a line. I am trying hard to write what I thought about it that very first time, now it has so many layers over it that came with knowing her. But I truly think I liked her. She had the distant air of a maiden in a fairy tale, rather stately with her hair in a bun, waiting to be rescued by St George. Her hair was not dark like mine; it was brownish, between colours. But I liked her calm expression and I thought that any moment her eyes might smile at me. She looked like a person who would stick the photos into the photograph album and bring order to things.

'And we sang "There's a Friend for Little Children",' I finished, aware I had been staring at her rather rudely and hoping she would not guess what I was thinking about her face. Also because I knew from years of Auntie Vera and the rest of them that this question always came next. I waited for her to tell me to recite it, but after a few moments more of silence in which she looked at me with an expression I could not fathom, she asked, 'Did you wash your hands?'

'*There's a Friend for Little Children Above the Bright Blue Sky*—'

'I asked if you had washed your hands, Annie.'

'Yes, Missiggs.'

'Let me see.'

I held up the palms of my hands for inspection, as if I was offering her a baby bird.

'And your nails!'

I hastily turned my hands over, dropping the bird.

'Do you bite your nails, child?'

'No, Missiggs.'

'Are you sure about that?'

'No, Missiggs. I mean, yes Missiggs.'

Beatrice had entered the room behind me. She said softly, 'She has to keep them short for the piano, Miss Higgs.'

'You play the piano?'

I was thinking, *Like you. You play. I know who you are! We can be friends!* But she made it sound like a sin. 'I'm just

33

learning.' I looked up at her again. 'I can play for you after tea, if you like.'

'On a Sunday?'

'I can play "Where E'er You Walk",' I said quickly, hoping it would sound religious. She played the harmonium on a Sunday, after all.

This seemed to go down better. 'You're young to be playing that,' she said. I glowed. Beatrice passed me on her way to the sofa, giving me a reassuring touch on the arm as she went. I didn't know what I was supposed to do next. Our new housekeeper said nothing so I edged towards Beatrice a little, hoping to escape further questions.

'I suppose you will have milk,' Miss Higgs said.

'Oh tea, please,' I answered, and immediately encountered a hard look from Auntie Vera who was standing to one side observing the inquisition.

'You drink tea?' The housekeeper looked shocked. 'Does your father allow this?'

I wasn't sure what was supposed to be wrong with drinking tea, so I bit my lip and said nothing. Beatrice came to my rescue again. 'Mother always allowed us to drink tea if we wished,' she said, sounding very polite so no one could accuse her of answering back. 'Annie takes one sugar.'

'I'm not interested in what Annie takes. Today she will take milk.' She poured some milk into a cup and handed it to me. I took it and retreated to the sofa, the cup trembling in its saucer. I hate milk. 'The scones have been taken away,' said Miss Higgs. She pronounced them 'scoans'. There was no further explanation as to who had taken them or why I was to have nothing to eat.

I plucked up courage to make an ally of Auntie Vera. 'Would you like me to fetch you a *scon,* Auntie?' I asked, unable to resist the emphasis.

'Oh no, thank you, Annie,' Auntie Vera replied. I looked covertly at Beatrice who shook her head imperceptibly: *Don't try it,* said the look. But Miss Higgs rose to the occasion. 'You may fetch a scone from the kitchen if you would like one, Annie,' she said. I put the cup of milk carefully to one side. Yes, she was a princess that first day. As soon as the door shut behind me I slid down the shiny hall tiles in my Sunday shoes.

# THREE

For the first few weeks, we all tiptoed around each other carefully. It reminded me of the fish tank at the Arboretum in which each fish goes about its business opening and closing its mouth, being polite to the other fish but never bashing into them. I was relieved that there was no sign of Maisie leaving; she still spent weekdays with us so whatever the job of housekeeper was supposed to be, Miss Higgs must have been doing something else. Looking back, I don't think she quite knew what was expected of her, but she seemed anxious to do the right thing. She took Elsie in hand with the housework and introduced a few touches to the décor that, while I didn't much like them, were not offensive. She hung a picture called *The Light of the World* outside her bedroom door. Beatrice said it was meant to be Jesus, but it didn't look much like him to me; it was just a fellow with a lamp. At least Miss Higgs seemed to understand that it would not be a good idea to interfere with our mother's style of things. We were grateful for that.

'Did you know our mother, Missiggs?' I ventured to ask her one day.

'I knew who she was, of course,' she answered. 'I saw her at the services every week. I didn't know her, as you might say, *well*.'

I told her I always watched her there at the harmonium, pulling out the stops and doing the pedals. Sometimes she'd move her hands really quickly – in between verses. 'I'd love to have a go,' I said. 'All those different sounds you get. It must take lots of practice.'

'Well, I'm in good hands.'

Even then, I knew when Mission people spoke like that, they were talking about Jesus. I had a sudden vision of the Light of the World standing behind Miss Higgs at morning service. 'Did you see me, Missiggs, on Sundays?' I blurted out. It sounded a bit bumptious; with her having the Light of the World to bother about, she'd not have time to look out for Beatrice and Fred and me.

'The grandchildren of our dear Pastor Eames must always sit at the front,' said Miss Higgs gravely. 'So yes, I saw you. I knew who you were.'

I wondered if she might have a family of her own and took a deep breath, steeling myself to ask. But her face was turned away from me and I had a strong sense that this was not a conversation she was enjoying, so I breathed out again and said nothing.

The curiosity stayed with me, though, and I returned to the subject one day when we were folding sheets. Elsie boiled the sheets in the copper with the blue bag and put them through the mangle; they came in from the washing line rather board-like, as if starched, with wrinkles along the creases.

'Ends together. Now pull ...' instructed Miss Higgs. I leaned backwards, putting my weight on the sheet to stretch the creases out. We repeated the action and then advanced towards each other; I carefully gave her my two ends and as

I did so my hands brushed hers. The skin of her fingers was dry and tight, a little shiny with carefully trimmed cuticles. I picked up the new, shorter end and backed away, stretching it as before. When the sheet was a manageable size she took it from me and finished it off herself, laying it neatly in the ironing basket for Elsie. She seemed to be well practised at the art of sheet-folding.

'When you did this at home, before you came here, Miss Higgs,' I asked, 'who did you do it with?' Sheets could not be folded by one person. I used to sometimes do them with Mother if Maisie or Beatrice were not around. She looked at me curiously, not understanding the question. Then she said, 'Are you asking me who I lived with at home?'

I was immediately on my guard. This could well be construed as rude. 'Not exactly, but, well yes, perhaps sort of,' I replied.

'In that case,' she said evenly, 'you should ask what you mean to ask and not ask sly questions.'

'I was just thinking of how difficult it is to fold a sheet without another person,' I answered, adding, 'I'm sorry. I didn't mean to pry.'

She considered this and must have decided she believed me, which was good because it was true. I hadn't meant to be nosey; but I was curious.

'I fold sheets with my sister,' she answered. 'We lived together before I came here.'

'Is she far away?' I asked.

'Not far.' She hesitated. 'Beeston.'

'What's her name? Does she live on her own now?'

'She is called Gwendolen. Gwen.'

'Gwen.' I repeated it. It sounded like a quill pen going into an inkwell but I did not say this. 'Does Gwen play the harmonium, too?' I asked.

'Gwen plays the piano. As do I.'

'Will you play for us, Missiggs?'

'Perhaps. One day.'

After a couple of conversations like this, I thought she might start to be nice and not always think of me as a bad child. I wanted to be friends with her. Mostly I wanted to be friends with her so she would help me with my arpeggios, which I was just beginning.

'Missiggs,' I started, the next time we were together. 'You know C-minor? I always make a mistake going from the G when you have to get your thumb on to the C above.' I tried to demonstrate on the kitchen table tucking my thumb under my palm. 'I sort of miss. I can't do the stretch. Does that happen to you?'

'No.'

'Did it used to? When you were my age?'

'I really couldn't say.'

I looked at her sideways. 'I wonder how you learn . . .?' I so wanted her to help me. Also, I'm afraid to say, I wanted to make it quite clear that it was *arpeggios* I was doing, not just silly old broken chords.

'You practise. And if at first you don't succeed—'

'Yes I know . . . but sometimes I just can't.'

'There's no such word as can't.'

I sighed. 'It's not so bad coming down. It's going up that's hard.'

'It won't happen on its own. You need to work at it. How long do you practise?'

'Quite long . . . but I need to get on to my pieces.'

'Then you need to practise arpeggios and scales for longer, so you need to spend longer altogether.'

'But I have homework this term . . .'

'Then it's simple: you get up early in the morning and do it then.'

I began to regret this conversation. Getting up early, specially in Winter, was not my favourite thing.

Miss Higgs went on, 'I've told Elsie to start earlier as she can't seem to do her jobs before breakfast. She can wake you at six.'

I stared at her round-eyed. 'But she won't have done the fires at six!'

'Don't moan, child. You'll soon warm up with the C-minor arpeggio.'

Next morning, Elsie tiptoed into the room at 6.15. 'Annie!' she whispered. 'Sorry, me-duck, I daresn't leave you sleeping any longer. She gave me instructions.' I swung my feet dizzily on to the lino. It was pitch dark and my toes ached. Elsie lit the oil lamp rather than dazzle me by switching on the electric bulb overhead. 'Don't worry, lovie, I'll have the fire lit downstairs by the time you're finished.'

I poured icy water into the bowl on the wash-stand and dabbed it on my face, neck and fingers, then I grabbed my clothes and dived back into bed to dress. When I crept downstairs to the drawing room, where the piano was, some of my fingers were white at the ends and my chilblains, almost healed at the end of Winter, came back to life and throbbed.

There is something I need to say about the drawing room. It is the smell. It's always there, of course, but I think I noticed it more in my nose that first morning of the early piano practice because it was so cold and dank. The drawing room doesn't get used very much; they never light a fire in there and the sun doesn't shine through its windows. But the smell isn't because of that: it's because the drawing room is over the cellar. It is a smell partly of damp, and partly of something worse which I shall come to later.

Anyway, what with the smell, the aching cold and the chilblains that morning, the arpeggios did not go well. I played them holding down the soft pedal because I dreaded *her* listening to me in the silent house. I could see my breath in the Spring dawn, least I think I could. After half an hour, when it was light enough to see the music without the electric light, I started on *Für Elise*, jerkily, my fingers folding on the keys. Suddenly the door opened to reveal Miss Higgs. My hands flew into my lap. I stared at her.

'Well, Annie. Have you practised your arpeggios?'

'Yes, Missiggs.'

'I didn't hear them.'

'I did. I played them.'

'Begin again.' She advanced on the piano. She was carrying a metal ruler, tapping one end softly into the palm of her hand. I had heard some teachers would rap your knuckles if you got the notes wrong. I thought, *I'll show her.* I blew on my fingers and rubbed them against my cardigan to try and make the white ends pink. Then I started to play, clumsily at first, trying to imagine she was not in the room. Thankfully, the arpeggios sort of behaved themselves this time, thumbs and fingers cascading and tripping but more or less hitting the right notes.

'Elbows out. Fingers UP.' She stood behind me, listening. I imagined her ruler at the ready; it made my spine go funny. After a while she left the room, saying as she went, 'Your technique is sloppy. I shall speak to your teacher, but you have a good touch.' For a little moment my heart sang: a good touch! Mother used to say that when I very first started to play. At the end of an hour, I was told I could go and have breakfast.

*

'The Keeping of the Bridge' and other poems were to be performed by our class at parents' evening a few weeks later. It was a shock to hear from Maisie that Daddy had asked Miss Higgs to go with him.

''S none of her business, parents' evening!' Fred said. I agreed with him. It gave me an odd feeling that Miss Higgs should go with Daddy.

'Specially when she's only just arrived,' Fred continued. 'She knows nothing about us.'

'Well, I'm sure Mr Lang thought it would be a good opportunity for her to learn more about you,' Maisie told him. 'She only sees you when you come home from school. She doesn't know what you get up to all day.'

'That's the trouble!' Beatrice muttered. 'Perhaps we'd rather she didn't find out.'

'Heavens above,' said Maisie. 'You little angels have nothing to worry about! A sight too well behaved, if you ask me!'

Maisie!' I took her hand and stared into her face. 'Didn't you know, I'm BAD? Really, seriously BAD? Auntie Vera says God will strike me down!' I did an evil spirit's dance around the scullery.

'It's true though,' said Fred a bit later, when Maisie had gone. 'Miss Higgs knows nothing about us, and we know nothing about her. Has she got a proper home of her own?'

'She told me she folded sheets with her sister,' I chimed in. 'But we don't know – she might have a husband.'

'She can't have a husband, silly. She's a miss. Anyway, how could she look after him and us?'

'Maisie does.'

'Maisie doesn't live here,' Fred pointed out.

This was true, of course. I thought of Maisie up her tree with Mr Brown, the owl.

'Well, where does Miss H go on her half-day off?' Fred

asked. 'Hey, we could follow her. We could be Emil and the Detectives.'

'Supposing she turned round and saw us? We'd have to take Nana to protect us.'

'We couldn't take Nana. She'd give the game away. We'd have to go in disguise. I could wear a handlebar moustache and Daddy's trilby hat. What about you, Bea?'

Beatrice wasn't listening. 'D'you think she'll come to Mablethorpe with us this summer?' she asked.

'Ugh no. Mablethorpe's a holiday. We don't want her around.'

'I wouldn't mind,' I said.

'Just because she said you have a nice *touch*,' Fred taunted, 'you're sucking up to her all of a sudden.'

'I am *not*,' I retorted. 'But I think she's trying. She just doesn't know what children want. I'm going to make friends with her, then she'll find out.'

'Good for you, Annie,' Beatrice said.


One sunny Saturday afternoon we were in the yard and Miss Higgs was teaching me how to thin out seedlings in the tubs. It was early for sowing, she said, but it was good to get a grip on things. She sighed as if to say there was a lot to get a grip on. I sighed, too. I liked to watch her with the trowel, gently coaxing and firming the stronger plants in the soil, pinching out the weaker.

'Where do they go?' I asked. I pointed to the limp pinched-out ones lying on the ground.

'What do you mean? They go in the ash-pit.'

'But they'll die!'

'Yes.'

'Couldn't you plant them somewhere else?' I asked.

'They wouldn't grow, Annie. They wouldn't survive.'

44

'You could give them a chance.' It seemed a waste of flowers to me. 'They all belong to Jesus, don't they?' I added doubtfully, unsure where this would take me.

She shot me a look – to see if I was being insolent, I suppose, but I just felt sad for the flowers. I picked the tiny stems from their hard grave on the floor of the yard and held them in my hand. 'Go to Heaven and flower for my Mama,' I whispered to them.

Miss Higgs continued her twitching and tidying; I watched her, wondering if I would ever be able to give her a hug, but her mouth was in its straight line. After a few moments, she put down her trowel. 'You're a fanciful child, aren't you?' she said.

I dropped my gaze. 'I don't know.' I would have liked her to explain or ask me a question or something, but she didn't seem to know what to say next. At last she resumed her work with the seedlings. 'Your mother was a good woman and a lady,' she told me. 'That's what we always thought.'

So I really did try with Miss Higgs, but as the weeks passed and turned into months we sort of got stuck. It was hard to have conversations with her, and this wasn't helped by her talent for sniffing out small misdemeanours along the way, which meant I always had to be on my guard. In her reorganising of Elsie, she spotted at once that a system requiring Elsie to dose me with cod liver oil was open to cheating. One morning, she stood and watched as Elsie, with shaking hands, poured cod liver oil into a teaspoon, spilling some of it down the side of the bottle.

'Come along, girl,' Miss Higgs instructed. 'Pull yourself together. You're behaving as though you've never done this before' – which, of course, Elsie hardly ever had. Poor Elsie started to shake uncontrollably and spilt more cod liver oil, while I shifted from foot to foot eyeing the teaspoon.

'Oh give it to *me*!' Miss Higgs took the bottle from Elsie and poured a deft spoonful. 'Open wide, Annie.'

I obeyed, screwing my eyes shut while she approached me with the horrid spoon, jamming it so far back in my mouth that I started to gag uncontrollably.

'Well, swallow it!' she commanded, as I stood there goggle-eyed.

I gazed at her, unable to speak and equally unable to swallow. I could feel nausea rise to the top of my gullet. Knowing I would be sick, I launched myself past her, almost knocking her flying, and retched into the sink, greenish yellow oil and bits of porridge dripping from my hot face. 'I'm sorry,' I was crying. 'I'm sorry, Missiggs, I'm terribly sorry – I didn't mean to—' I hunched over the sink waiting for the punishment I was certain would come, but instead I heard her say,

'Well, that was a bit of a shock, wasn't it? I never liked cod liver oil, either, Annie, but I made myself get used to it.'

'Yes, Missiggs.'

'So clear up that mess before you go to school and tomorrow we'll try again. Elsie, don't stand there gawping. *I* shall give Annie her cod liver oil in future.'

Accordingly, each morning after breakfast I would take a deep breath and accept the spoonful of cod liver oil from Miss Higgs. Then I would calmly leave the kitchen, closing the door behind me, gallop upstairs to my room and throw myself down beside the cupboard where the dolls' clothes were kept. Day after day, their little dresses and coats absorbed mouthful on mouthful of cod liver oil. In one of those peculiar lapses of very efficient people, she never noticed that I neither spoke nor breathed nor swallowed after my dose of oil. She never demanded I say thank you, as she normally would, nor stopped me leaving the room. Each day I promised myself I would take the dolls' clothes out of the cupboard and wash them in secret, but somehow there were always better things to do.

# FOUR

About the next thing that happened in my memory of all this is that Fred had his ninth birthday and was sent away to school. You'd think that nothing ever happened in our family except in Winter time, and I know it must seem odd. The truth is that all my little scraps of memories before Our Own Mother died were of the Summer, and everything that happened afterwards seems like Winter, which is called pathetic fallacy. This is a thing invented by John Ruskin, as we learnt last week. Of course it wasn't really always Summer or Winter but according to Ruskin and this pathetic fallacy, it seems that way. Which proves I am not writing a True Account at all, and this is bothering me. I write my memories as they seem to *me* to be true. But if I pretended that what happened next was Summer, I would be making it up, and that would be wrong also. So whatever I write is wrong.

All I can say is that Fred was born on Christmas Day, which is why his middle name is Noel: Frederick Noel Lang. At the beginning of New Year after his ninth birthday it was definitely Winter, and that's when he went away. Beatrice says he would not have been sent if Mother were alive because she didn't agree with it, but everything had changed now. I remember going into his room a few days before the end of the holidays. He was crouched on the floor running his new London and North-Eastern Railway engine past a signal our cousins had given him for Christmas. On the bed, laid out in neat rows, were stacks of vests and socks and white shirts, each marked with his name tape; Maisie had been stitching them in for weeks. I gazed at the array of clothes. A big printed list lay on the eiderdown to one side. '*Three prs games socks grn,*' I read aloud. '*Three prs college socks bl. 24–36 plain white handkerchiefs.* Golly, they obviously expect you to have loads of colds.' Fred said nothing. I picked up Desmond, who is a floppy white dog with Fred's pyjamas inside, a present to him from Mother the last Christmas she was alive. 'Are you taking Desmond?' I asked. I knew Fred cuddled Desmond in bed every night.

'Come and look at this,' said Fred.

I stroked Desmond's velvet nose. 'Desmond's not a teddy bear,' I said. 'He's a pyjama case. It'll be all right.'

'Look, the signal works!' Fred said. 'Watch!'

I squatted down beside him, still holding Desmond. To be honest, I'm not very interested in signals, but I liked the beautiful engine. The black and white signpost bit of the signal was operated by a lever at its base. Fred pulled the lever and the signal rose and fell, just like on a real railway line. 'Who works the lever?' I asked.

'The signalman walks up the line.'

'I thought he stayed in the signal box with some levers connected to wire things.'

'That's the points, silly. It's the de luxe version,' said Fred huffily. 'They don't sell it in Jessops. You have to go to London for that.'

'Well, it doesn't matter. This is just as good.' I knew he

was unhappy about going away. 'When are they coming for the trunk?'

'Dunno.'

'Can you take all this?' – I indicated the train set, its lines and tunnels; the shunting yard and station with painted trees. But I guessed he wouldn't be allowed to.

'Goodness no. She sent me upstairs to pack it away.'

'You've got another two days, haven't you?'

'She said I've to do it now.'

We both sighed.

'It'll be all right,' I told him. 'When you get there.'

'Oh I can't wait,' he said and smiled a tight smile so as to make me think he meant it.

'You'll get away from her for a bit!'

Silence.

'Wish *I* could go to boarding school!'

'No you don't.' His voice was wobbly.

'You will take Desmond, Fred, won't you? You'll need something to remind you.' I didn't want to say, *remind you of Mother*. 'I bet the other boys will all have teddy bears!'

Fred wiped the back of his hand across his nose. 'Course they won't,' he said.

'Desmond will miss you,' I told him, smoothing the dog's ears.

'He's a pyjama case, for heaven's sake,' whispered Fred fiercely.

I was suddenly very glad I am not a boy. I thought for a moment. 'It'll be more fun there.'

'Oh yes.'

'Lots of sports and stuff. Lots of boys to play boys' games with.' The grown-ups were always saying how terrible and *unhealthy* it must be for poor Fred to have to endure life with mere sisters.

'Yes.'

'No Mission!'

'S'pose not.'

'No Auntie Vera.'

He said nothing. Then, 'Look after Nana for me, Annie.'

'How can you ask? I love Nana!'

'I take her for more walks than you do.'

'I'll take her for as many walks as I can, Fred, I promise.'

'I'll miss her, Annie.'

'You won't miss Bea or me, though!' I gave him a dig in the ribs and he lost his balance. That made him laugh at last. He turned back to the railway, picking up the engine lovingly. 'It's the Flying Scotsman,' he said. He cradled it in his hands for a moment and then placed it gently in its box.

I didn't think that Fred's departure would make a great difference to life in Corporation Oaks, which sounds unfeeling, but truly his days as a boy had been different from mine, despite our closeness in age. He didn't have to get up early to do piano practice for one thing. And it was Beatrice I had always turned to for wisdom and comfort and with whom I shared stories and poetry. Fred's things were all slugs and snails and puppy-dogs' tails and it wasn't till some days after he had gone that I realised there was a hole. For a while I couldn't put my finger on what exactly had vanished. And then came the unpleasantness over the cod liver oil, and I understood.

I had arrived home from school with my head full of the spinning towns and the weaving towns, because we had a test next day, so I was off guard as I washed my hands at the scullery sink, when suddenly I heard Miss Higgs's foot on the stone step behind me.

'Annie, I want your presence upstairs. In your bedroom. Now.'

I frowned. 'Hello, Miss Higgs. I just got home.'

'At once.'

'Yes, Miss Higgs.'

I dried my hands and followed her obediently upstairs with a falling feeling in the pit of my stomach, racking my brains for what I might have done wrong. As soon as I entered the room, however, it became clear. The door of the dolls' clothes cupboard was open and a heap of jumbled dresses, tiaras, trains and dolls' pram blankets lay in a heap on the floor. Over them, stood Miss Higgs, an expression of extreme distaste on her face. A faint fishy smell rose from the heap.

'Annie, how do you account for this?'

'Er ...'

'And don't pretend you don't know to what I am referring.'

'No, Missiggs.'

'To what *am* I referring, then?'

I wondered if there was any chance at all she hadn't tumbled to my cod liver oil activities. 'Well there was a bit of an accident,' I mumbled.

'An accident? An *accident?* Annie, I hope you are not going to compound your crime with a lie!'

'No, no, Missiggs.'

'So how, pray, do you explain this—' She bent and picked up a doll's white dress with yellowish sticky stains on it.

I looked at my toes. The stains on the dress were truly disgusting. 'The cod liver oil made me feel sick, Missiggs, so I, so I ...' My voice tailed off. Bury, Oldham, Rochdale, Burnley. . . The spinning and weaving towns were careering through my brain in nightmare disorder.

'I'm waiting, Annie!'

'I sort of wiped it—'

'You *spat* it, you mean!'

She almost slapped me with the word. 'No. Well, yes,' I said. I couldn't look at her.

'When?'

'Last week.'

'How often, Annie?'

'Sometimes. When I felt sick. When I couldn't swallow it.'

'Not sometimes. Every time.'

'No, no. Sometimes I managed to sw—'

'You're lying.'

'Most times,' I admitted. I forced myself to raise my eyes to her. 'I just hate it,' I said.

'Hate is a terrible word, Annie. God is a wrathful God, but He does not hate.'

'Not hate. I mean, I really *really* don't like it.'

'Then you must learn to like it, mustn't you?'

I said nothing.

'First. Pick these up and follow me.'

I did so, trooping downstairs with sticky dolls' dresses tumbling from my arms, the smell of it making me close to retching again. She led the way into the kitchen and opened the back door.

'Take them down to the ash-pit. Place them inside the bin.' I looked at her. It was now quite dark outside with a wet fog slippery on the steps. We never went down to the hated ash-pit in the dark. '*Now,*' she instructed. I stumbled out into the gloom, grateful for the light from the kitchen. But barely was I down the kitchen steps into the yard when she closed the door behind me and I was truly in darkness. Unable to reach out for the banister with my hands full, I edged forwards, feeling with the toe of my shoe for the first slimy step, the sick smell of cod liver oil mingling with the foetid garbage from below.

By the time I returned to the kitchen, I was damp from the mist and starting to shiver, my gymslip stained from the wet brick walls and my shoes scuffed. I was instructed to sit at the kitchen table and did so, although part of me was suddenly up in a corner of the ceiling, curious to see what would happen next. Miss Higgs took the bottle of cod liver oil and poured a cupful, which she set in front of me. 'And now you will learn not to *hate*,' she said. 'You will drink it. You will savour each mouthful, brought to you by the kindness of your family and the bounty of Our Lord. And when you have finished it you will go to bed and reflect on what you have done.'

She had chosen her evening well. Beatrice was at a Junior Bible Fellowship class and would not be back till eight. Maisie had gone home. It was Daddy's night at the Lodge. There were just the two of us. Miss Higgs never left the room but stayed silent nearby, darning thin places in socks. I sat at the table from half-past five by the kitchen clock above the mantelpiece to half-past seven, two hours, forcing cod liver oil drop by drop down my throat and during most of that time my memory is that we did not speak, which is a long silence. I was painting a scene in my head, which grew and became elaborate with all kinds of details and consequences both major and minor, in which I had stumbled on the ash–pit steps and crashed to the ground below breaking a leg – well perhaps that would be a little too serious, an arm would do – and she would have let me lie there and I would have caught the pneumonia, or perhaps just a cold as pneumonia might be life-threatening, well – no, pneumonia would be best, except perhaps I wouldn't need to have pneumonia *and* a broken arm. Anyway, something awful. And Daddy would have come home from the Lodge to find Doctors and Danger and me in the Children's Ward, or maybe I wouldn't have to go to the Infirmary because that would be too horrible, but then again it ought to be hospital because the scales would have to fall from Daddy's eyes, as they say in the fairy stories, and he would need to say to her: 'Miss Higgs, how could this happen? How could you send her cruelly into the darkness, a small child on a Winter Night?' And she would leave at dawn next day in shame, her small suitcase packed and The Light of the World under one arm, and we would not have to have a Housekeeper any more. This make-believe went on and on and grew to such dramatic proportions in my head that suddenly I found myself Dying, and that was not the point at all, so I forced myself to leave it alone and think of something else.

I say we did not speak, but towards the end Miss Higgs laid aside her darning and took up the Bible. She started to read aloud. She read from Isaiah about the person who would be Jesus – though of course Isaiah was Old Testament so couldn't exactly know that yet – and how he would be spurned and how God would make him go like a lamb to the slaughter, because through his wounds and whippings and bruisings he would take on our sins and die for them. Then she closed the Bible and explained that it all came to pass at the Crucifixion, and his suffering healed us. And so it followed, she went on, that just as God punished His Son to set us free, punishment was part of God's Plan for all little children because that's how we would become good. So we must bear it in silence, just as Jesus did. Her voice was low but her words burrowed into my head. From time to time she would look over to see how I was taking it, and I couldn't meet her eye but stared down into the fishy depths, willing her to stop.

The only other memory I have of that dreadful evening is that Nana, who had been lying warily between us, occasionally raising one eyebrow and opening an eye to make sure I was all right, got to her feet at one point, plodded over to the table and lay beneath it with her great head on my shoe. And I loved her so much I wanted to cry for that. Though I honestly don't know if it happened, or whether it was just another bit of Mr John Ruskin's pathetic fallacy, so perhaps I shouldn't even write it. But when the last drop of cod liver oil was gone and I finally stood up to leave, I knew why I missed my brother. It was a shock, because we had never spoken of it: Fred was the only one who shared with me the boiling anger inside.

I was lying in bed later, feeling miserable and rather peculiar, turning these thoughts over in my mind, when the door opened and Daddy came in. He sat down on the bed with a sigh and looked at me with a sort of sorrowful expression. 'So, Annie, Miss Higgs tells me you've been naughty.' He paused. 'Again.'

I looked at him, praying he hadn't been told about the dolls' clothes in *detail*. 'I'm sorry, Daddy.'

He sighed. 'Yes, well, you see, it's all very well saying sorry afterwards, but you make it very difficult for Miss Higgs,' he began.

I buried my head in the pillow and spoke to Little Sid who was in bed beside me. 'She makes it difficult for *me*.'

'She has a lot to get used to, coming into our family. It's hard for her.'

'I know, Daddy. I do try.'

'You see, she thinks – well, I think too – that you're rather out of control. I suppose it's my fault in a way. I probably didn't keep a firm enough hand over you this past year or so.' He gazed sadly out into the room. 'I've had too much on my mind, I suppose, and being without a mother's guidance has gone to your head a bit.'

I had taken my face out of the pillow and was looking at

him properly. It sounded as if no specific crime had been mentioned.

'You've got a bit, well, full of yourself. It's um, well Agn— Miss Higgs expresses it in terms of vanity.'

I stared at him. 'What did you call her?

'. . . The sin. She says, you know, the sin of vanity. It's pride.'

I bounced out from under the bedclothes and faced him, kneeling upright on the eiderdown. 'Daddy!'

'Listen, Annie. Pride, as you know, is one of the seven deadly—'

'*Daddy!*'

He paused.

'You called her Agnes! That's Mother's name!'

'It's her name,' he said quietly. 'Miss Higgs's Christian name is Agnes, too.'

'It can't be!'

'It is, Annie.'

'She can't be Agnes! You called her Agnes!' I threw myself face down on the pillow again.

He rubbed my back through the thick calico yoke of the nightie. 'There you go again, you see. It all has to be such a drama with you, doesn't it?'

'It's awful,' I wailed into the pillow.

'Well, you'll just have to get used to it.'

I turned over and looked at him. I desperately needed him not to go. 'Daddy, read me a story. Please.'

He sighed, hesitated and picked up the book from my bedside table, *Lamb's Tales from Shakespeare*.

'Very well. But remember what Miss Higgs said.'

It was better then. But later, before I dropped off to sleep, I remembered what had really upset me. He had called her Agnes.

*

It was sometime deep in the dead of night that I woke up and knew there had been a mistake, and for once it wasn't mine. Not that this was the first thought in my head at that horrible moment; it was only next morning when the doctor had gone and I lay in bed shivering and listening to the strange sounds of the day in which, to my great relief, I had been ordered not to take part that I began to understand what was going on. The proof came at lunchtime when Maisie appeared with dry toast and the bottle of kaolin clay. 'Maisie, I can't,' I told her. Even the sight of the toast sent a wave of pain through my stomach.

'Doctor said you were to try.' She shook the bottle ominously. 'And dry toast is the best thing for a tummy upset.'

Desperate to distract her from the greyish stuff in the bottle, I whispered, 'Did she tell you what happened?'

Maisie looked blank. 'What d'you mean, lovie?' Clearly, as with Daddy last night, it seemed nothing had been said.

I turned away. 'It doesn't matter.'

'Miss Higgs thought you must have eaten too many liquorice allsorts.'

I swivelled my head back on the pillow and stared at her with big round eyes. 'Is that what she told you?'

'Or aniseed balls,' said Maisie.

I laughed. It came out as a kind of grunt. *Did she now?* I was trying to think straight.

'But don't worry, Annie,' Maisie went on. 'She isn't cross with you.'

'No,' I said. 'She wouldn't be.'

'What d'you mean?'

'It wasn't liquorice allsorts or aniseed balls,' I said darkly.

'Well you'd have had to eat *tons*,' Maisie laughed. 'I told her that. I said it was just a germ. Our Muriel had it.'

'And?'

'Oh, Miss Higgs agreed,' Maisie said. 'That's why she's not angry. You can't help getting a tummy upset. Now, just one little swallow for me . . . and then you can have a spoonful of *this*!' And from her capacious pinny pocket she produced with a great flourish a jar of my favourite strawberry jam.

When Maisie had gone, I lay in bed talking about this very quietly to Little Sid who was of course in bed too. If Miss Higgs hadn't *told*, then she didn't want it known, I explained to him. In fact, she had made a suggestion to Maisie that was a lie, which I think was not very Christian of her, but I couldn't talk because I might have done the same. The day dragged on. At least I had missed the geography test (I've never been able to tell the spinning towns from the weaving towns from that day to this). It got very boring and Little Sid went to sleep. I tried to read from *The Playbox Annual* but my mouth was dry and my head hurt. The light through the curtains turned dull after a while and I could tell it was coming up for teatime. At length, Beatrice arrived home from school.

'What happened?' she asked, plumping down on the bed. 'You missed frogspawn, you lucky thing.'

I winced. 'Shush!'

'The teachers got jam with it, but we didn't. Edie Ellersby missed half of maths because she couldn't swallow hers and they made her sit there till she'd finished it. She said the eyes were staring up at her.'

'Beatrice! Be quiet about frogspawn.'

'I thought she was putting it on, though, because she can't do algebra. So what's up with you?'

'Dunno,' I said. 'Tummy upset, I s'pose.' I had been wondering whether to tell her the dreadful events of last night, and thought I probably would. But when the moment came it was too awful about the yellow sticky mess on the dolls' clothes and I just couldn't. The worst thing about yesterday was that *Miss Higgs* had discovered my terrible secret. Of all the people in the world, I minded that she knew this thing about me. And I couldn't face telling Beatrice because it was just too shameful. Bea in any case would not have sympathised because she quite likes cod liver oil. Also her dolls are beautifully neat and she brushes their hair a lot, just like she brushes her own. Beatrice has beautiful hair. Actually, by this time she didn't play much with dolls any more, being eleven, but when she *did*, she would never let me touch them.

If I couldn't tell Beatrice, then I certainly couldn't tell Daddy. I would die rather than confess about the dolls' clothes to Daddy. The plot I had slowly hatched over the afternoon collapsed the instant I realised this. It meant Daddy wouldn't be able to give Miss Higgs the sack, because he would never know what she had done. For ever after, Miss Higgs and I shared a shameful secret that bound us together in a loathsome way. And very soon I would come to regret terribly that I hadn't got rid of her when I still had the chance.

# FIVE

In the months since Miss Higgs had become our housekeeper, she had continued to play the harmonium at the Mission. This meant that on Wednesday evenings, which was her practice night, and for much of every Sunday, she would be out of the house. On the first Saturday of each month she also had a day off when she would visit her sister in Beeston. In the hours of these absences I fancied the house was actually lighter, which was impossible of course, but I certainly felt lighter inside and everyone from Daddy to Nana seemed more jolly. I was particularly watchful of Daddy's mood on these occasions. From the night when he had referred to her as Agnes, I had cherished a shocking secret fear that he might *marry* her, which is what they all seemed to do in the Brothers Grimm – you know, when it's glaringly obvious to absolutely everyone that the housekeeper is a wicked witch, but the Man of the House marries her anyway, which of course means his children have a wicked stepmother to inflict misery and evil spells upon them.

After the cod-liver-oil incident, which I did recount to Beatrice (though, forgive me, I sort of glossed over the disgustingness of the dolls' clothes), I interrogated her frequently on the likelihood of Daddy marrying Miss Higgs.

'It won't happen, Bea, will it?'

'Oh Annie.' She groaned. 'Not again. How do I know?'

'You're older than me. You ought to see the Signs.'

'You know Daddy. He's always cheerful and friendly to people. I'm sure that's all it is.'

'So you *have* seen Signs?'

'I'm saying you can't *tell*.'

'He was cheerful and friendly to Gladys Hughes when she came to collect for the Miners' Welfare, but he said afterwards he could see her – what did he call it? – sizing up the joint, he said.'

Beatrice burst out laughing. 'Annie, he didn't!'

'He did so! I said you couldn't see the joint because it was in the oven and he told me not to be smart!'

'Well it just proves that he is always cheerful and friendly and his attitude to Miss Higgs is no different.'

But I wasn't convinced. 'Bea, suppose he does marry her?'

Beatrice looked at me and sighed. 'If you could see your little face, Annie, and those big worried eyes!' She reached out and stroked my hair.

'I hate her!' I wailed.

'Not hate,' corrected Beatrice. 'You know what happens when you talk about hate. God doesn't hate.'

'I'm judging her, then!'

'Annie, that's wicked to put yourself on a level with God and you well know it.'

'She sent me down the ash-pit steps. God wouldn't have liked that!'

'That was weeks ago. Just pull yourself together,' said Beatrice crisply. 'Self-pity has always been your most unattractive feature.' She said she was going to call it *S-P* from

64

now on, and I'd get a sharp dig in the ribs every time I fell into it.

'Why do people marry their horrid housekeepers?' I asked her.

Beatrice sighed. 'I don't know. I suppose everyone wants him to marry again. She lives with us ...' She shrugged.

'Who's everyone? What's it got to do with them? It's what Daddy and us want, isn't it?'

Beatrice hesitated. 'Perhaps Daddy does want it.'

'How on earth can he *want* to marry an old stick like her?'

'Perhaps because he's lonely,' said Beatrice. 'Like – like Mr Rochester.'

'But it's not fair on our mother!'

'She's not here, though, is she?'

'She's in Heaven! She's watching us! She'd *know.*'

Beatrice stared out of the window. 'Maybe she wouldn't mind,' she said softly. Then she turned back into the room. 'What are we on about?' She laughed. 'It's probably not even going to happen!'

But it did. It happened at Spring half-term, when Fred was home from school. It was a Wednesday night and I was waiting for Miss Higgs to go out to her harmonium practice as usual when it dawned on me she wasn't going. This was odd. I was playing Snakes and Ladders with Fred, who didn't bother to disguise the fact he was bored. Everything seemed to bore him since he came home from school; the only thing he liked talking about was how 'super' it was there, a word he would definitely not have used before he went. I noticed he had laid out his train set upstairs, though, and Desmond was still curled up on his bed.

'Shall we go and play with your trains?' I asked him. I didn't want to be in the same room as Miss Higgs.

Fred whooshed up a big ladder. 'It's all right,' he said. 'We'll finish this if you like.'

'I want you both to stay down here,' Miss Higgs told us. 'Your father will be home soon and he wants to talk to you.'

I darted a look at her. What was this? 'Beatrice isn't back,' I said.

'Beatrice is with your father.'

'Is this why you aren't going to the Mission tonight?' I asked.

'Curiosity killed the Cat,' she replied.

'Sorry, Missiggs.' I swung my legs under the table. *Satisfaction brought it back,* I echoed silently to Little Sid in my pocket.

'Oh crumbs, you're on that big snake!' cried Fred, who was counting ahead of me.

'No I'm not – I got a five.'

'Five gets you to the big snake.'

'Oh no, does it? Rats!'

'Annie!' warned Miss Higgs.

'Sorry,' I said. ' Is Rats a bad word, Miss Higgs?'

'Don't be insolent,' she snapped.

I could feel the demons rising within me. Sometimes I just can't stop them. 'Li–i–ike. . .'

I was going to say *Crikey* but Fred shot me a fierce look. *Crikey,* which I can't even write down what it means, would have got me sent to bed and I was desperate to know what Daddy was going to talk to us about. Fortunately, Miss Higgs let it go.

About ten minutes later, when Fred had won Snakes and Ladders by miles, the door opened and Daddy came in, followed by Beatrice. Bea wore an air of Importance. She wouldn't meet my eye. I sat up very straight. This was serious.

Daddy crossed the room to the fire where Miss Higgs was sitting and warmed his hands at it. I couldn't see whether he smiled at her or anything like that. Then he straightened up on the hearthrug and turned to face us. Beatrice sat down on the sofa with her hands folded in her lap. Fred swivelled round from the table where he had been packing up the Snakes and Ladders board and looked at Daddy expectantly.

Daddy cleared his throat. He was smiling. 'It's Wednesday,' he began. 'And on Wednesday evenings Miss Higgs usually goes to practise the harmonium at the Mission.'

We waited.

'She isn't going tonight because Miss Higgs will not be playing at the Mission any longer.'

This was a surprise. 'Oh!' I said. I stared at her. Miss Higgs was sitting in the fireside chair with her face turned away, looking into the flames.

Daddy continued, 'She won't be playing at the Mission any longer because she will be a married woman.'

I felt dizzy. I closed my eyes. In the fraction of a second that followed I had time to make-believe she might be marrying an undertaker and moving to Worksop and we'd be free of her for ever.

'Children, Miss Higgs and I are to be married. She will be your new mother. You may call her Mother from now on.'

I had known it, of course, the way one always seems to know really, really bad news. I forced myself to keep looking at Daddy and I hoped he would not see that my eyes had gone glassy with tears. I dared not reach into my pocket for my handkerchief.

None of us spoke. There was nothing to say. My throat ached trying to hold down the sobs and I terribly needed to sniff. I couldn't imagine what Fred would be feeling; I daren't catch his eye. Daddy filled the silence by going on about how this was a happy day and would bring joy to Corporation Oaks and how grateful he was that she, he called her Agnes, had consented to take him on, and his three children, and how it was a huge honour and we were really lucky and God was smiling and ... he didn't say whether Our Own Mother would be smiling or not. Beatrice said she would make a cup of tea and I fled to the kitchen to help her, so as to blow my nose. Not a word was spoken as I assembled cups and saucers with a lot of clattering because my fingers were twitching in shock. Bea warmed the pot and boldly added a plate of biscuits from the Roebuck's Biscuits Christmas Celebration tin, which were not generally permitted on Wednesdays. I suppose we drank our tea in the sitting room but I can't remember any more. I went to bed. Oh, I hung around in the room for a bit because I didn't know what to call her. I felt I ought to curtsey or something. She sat by the fire looking regal, sort of serene, Beatrice said later, but I thought she just looked smug.

'Goodnight Missmm ...'

'Goodnight, Annie,' she said. 'Don't forget to say your prayers.'


I'm not going to talk about the wedding because I can't remember it. All I remember is that there was no cascading white lace dress like my mother wore in the photograph album. I know what she looked like though, because – like Our Own Mother's wedding – I have seen the photo of Miss Higgs and Daddy that day many times. Miss Higgs was married in a suit. You can't see in the photo but I remember it as a sort of blancmange colour which is not quite white, with a long straight jacket and a neat white blouse peeping through the fox fur around her neck. The suit skirt was straight to below the knee and then gathered into little pencil pleats, quite modern even for Jessops at the time, falling to just above her ankles in a continuous line, not balloony. She wore flat shoes with bars across and round toes; I thought the suit would look better with heels but Beatrice pointed out that she would then have been taller than Daddy, which would not have done, as they walked down the aisle or in the photographs. Her hat was a sort of custard cloche with a little net veil and behind it her long pale face looked grave and rather dignified as she gazed over the photographer's shoulder to a point in the distance. For the first time I could see why she might be thought of as beautiful in a way. What you can't even see in the photo, of course, is her hair which is probably her best feature. She generally wears it smooth and pulled back with a black Alice band; it's fastened in a bun at the nape of her neck. In the photo of his wedding to Our Own Mother, Daddy is looking very handsome and jolly. In the marriage to Miss Higgs he looks serious, like her. I said to Beatrice, Look, he's not smiling this time, and Bea replied that it wouldn't be right for him to grin from ear to ear with it being his second marriage and his poor beloved first wife sadly deceased and everything. So I was really pleased about this and agreed that it was fitting. I'd have looked serious if I was marrying Miss Higgs.

I began to watch for ways in which life might change now she was no longer a housekeeper but the Lady of the House. At first I could notice nothing; life went on much as before, for which I was grateful, except we had the sitting room redecorated in sort of pale beige wallpaper with something Beatrice called a 'self pattern' of leaves and ferns. There was also a new curtain to pull across the bay, shutting out the table on Winter nights. It was made of green prickly wool and cascaded to the floor from large round wooden rings that clicked along the metal curtain pole with a comfortable clack-clack. I thought it was like the theatre: a whole new world could happen behind that curtain and you would never know.

But the first real change was nothing to do with life at home. When Miss Higgs stopped playing the harmonium at the Mission, her job was taken over by a new person, a girl really, called Mildred Blessing. At first, I thought she must be very holy on account of having a face like the little angels on Christmas cards and a name out of the Bible, but Beatrice explained this was not necessarily so; it was just a name, like ours was Lang. Miss Blessing was very young, only a few years older than Beatrice herself, and she played the harmonium beautifully; after service she would sometimes play tinkly, intricate pieces, which Mother had never played when she was Miss Higgs. I used to love sitting along the pew at the far right so I could watch Miss Blessing play.

One day, to my utter awe and astonishment she came to service not in the usual black buttoned boots that we all wore, but in a pair of blue high-heeled shoes. Well, not very high, but with heels that definitely raised the back of her feet off the ground, with a little flourish that went in and out, like the turned legs of our fireside stool. I watched her feet, transfixed as she manipulated the narrow wooden pedals, terrified one of her heels would skid off and get stuck in the gap between, launching a terrible drone or clarion call – for, like the stops, the pedals did strange and wonderful things, producing angel trumpets from the heavens, and from the deep, other sorts of noises like boiling sulphur and moans of torment. But Miss Blessing's feet stayed deftly in control with never a slip. She had a lot of lightish, brownish hair, over which she wore a hat with a bunch of silk forget-me-nots pinned to the hat-band, and the blue of the flowers exactly matched her shoes.

She was more like a fairy from Fairyland than a girl from the Golgotha Mission.

Miss Blessing sometimes taught Sunday School, and the week after the Shoes first appeared I was excited to know whether she would wear them again. My disappointment when she walked in in the usual old boots was impossible to contain.

'Oh Miss Blessing,' I said. 'You aren't wearing your wonderful shoes!' It just came out before I could stop myself. Luckily there were no other grown-ups in the room. Some of the girls giggled. I scarcely dared look up at her, thinking she would be angry, because people were always angry whenever you spoke out of turn. But Mildred Blessing was smiling a little ruefully.

'I know, Annie. It's a great shame. I couldn't help wearing them once, because they were new!'

'But you must wear them again!' I cried, emboldened by her smile. 'There's no point having blue shoes if you can't wear them for your Sunday Best!'

'I don't think it was right to wear them to Mission,' she said firmly. And a deep blush spread over her cheeks and her large dark eyes clouded for a moment and then flashed with a *something*. 'Now, children,' she went on briskly. 'Open your Bibles at St Luke chapter fifteen, verse eleven. Today we're going to hear the story of the Prodigal Son.'

I stared at her. I knew that expression. It was how my own face looked when I got into trouble. It was completely obvious to me that someone must have had words with Miss Blessing about the Shoes. She had been reprimanded. And now she was the Prodigal Son and had returned to the fold. I shook my head and tried to concentrate. But then there was the last bit of the expression – the most important bit: it was defiance. She wanted to wear those blue shoes to Mission, and she wouldn't have swallowed the cod liver oil, either: we were alike, Miss Mildred Blessing and me. Each Sunday service I tried to sit at the end of the row and observe if she ever dared wear the Shoes again. But Daddy wanted us to have the best seats near the middle aisle and would stand back for us to file into the centre of the pew and *he* took to sitting at the far end, though the blue shoes would have been lost on him. So I never did find out – or at least not till later.

About the first event in my life after the wedding was the Mundella Easter Pageant. On the day of the casting, I rushed home with important news. I so wanted Daddy to be there, but of course he wasn't.

'It's *Midsummer Night's Dream,*' I told Miss Higgs. 'I'm the First Fairy.' I said it in capital letters so she would know how very important it was. *'Hail Fairy, wither wander you?* – That's Puck. He says that.' Then, leaping across the room to be me, *'Over Hill, Over Dale, Thoro Bush, Thoro Briar, Over Park, Over Pale—'* Miss Higgs, who I shall call Mother from now on, was drying her fingers on the roller towel. I broke off when she turned and I saw her face.

'We'll see about that,' she said.

'We did it last term,' I babbled. 'I know it already almost. *I do wander EVERYWHERE, swifter than the Moon-es sphere.'* I knew I ought to stop, but some demon inside me wouldn't. 'You have to say "*Moon-es*", you know, because of the rhythm, the meter: *The mountain sheep are sweeter but the valley sheep are fatter, we therefore deemed it meeter to carry off the latter.'*

'Annie! Come and wash your hands for tea.'

I went to the sink and picked up the slithery cake of green carbolic.

'Easter Pageant,' Mother said. 'I'd like to ask Mrs Spencer

what it has to do with the death and resurrection of Our Lord, all this carry-on.'

'It's only one scene – 3C are doing Moses in the Bullrushes.' I shot her a sideways look to see how this went down.

'That's another matter,' she said. 'Tableaux are another matter. This is ...' She hesitated. She didn't seem to know what it was. 'A *play*.'

'Not the whole play, just—'

'A scene. A scene with words.'

I finally came down to earth at that point. Maybe she was going to stop me doing it or something. '*Shakespeare,*' I reminded her in a little voice.

'The author is immaterial, Annie. You know my views.'

I knew them. I sat down at the tea table in silence. 'Please may I start?' I asked.

'You'll wait for your sister. Where *is* Beatrice?'

'She had to go and see Mr Remington about ...' I didn't want to say. Beatrice had to go and see Mr Remington about *her* part in the school pageant. 'Something,' I mumbled. 'She won't be long.' I didn't want to discuss it further. Better save it for Daddy first.

But Miss Higgs, Mother, was in her element now. She started on about the theatre being the 'espousal' of vanity and this seemed to be my fault, 'getting above' myself, she said. 'What makes you think Our Lord wants to see you making an exhibition of yourself on a stage?'

I looked down at my plate, at the friendly faces of the little pink and white flowers crowding across it, May Medley by Royal Standard. It always came back to this, the sin of showing-off, the sin of pride. Why, after all, should *anyone,* never mind the Lord, want to hear me going on as the First Fairy? 'Don't know,' I muttered.

'*Blessed are the meek,*' she intoned. 'Why?'

'*For they shall inherit the earth.*'

'Don't mumble. Repeat.'

I did so. I didn't want to inherit the earth. I just wanted to play First Fairy.

'Continue.'

'*Blessed are . . .*' I could only do the whole thing on a run. '*The merciful?*'

'Wrong.'

'*Blessed are.*'

'*They which*—' Mother prompted.

'*They which do hunger and thirst after righteousness because*—'

'*For.*'

'*For they shall be filled.*'

'You can read St Matthew chapter five after tea. You clearly need to refresh your memory.'

'I've got equations,' I wailed. Another mistake.

'In that case you can get up an hour early and read it before piano practice.'

I glared at the potted meat sandwiches. Mother always did this, popped your balloon with her hatpin. But then I had this thought: 'Mother?'

'Yes, Annie?'

'You know when you used to play the harmonium at the Mission . . .'

'What about it?'

You see, this is what happens: I say things. I walk into it. I can't stop myself. A chasm opened up between the plate of sliced tongue and the fish paste. 'It doesn't matter.'

Mother shot me one of her looks. 'Finish your sentence, girl.'

'I – I'm not saying he, that is *He*, the Lord, considered you playing the harmonium a vanity or anything like that, but – might the Lord accept *me* doing Shakespeare not as vanity but, sort of, as an offering – you know, in praise of Him?'

Mother's eyes were like glass needles.

'So each to his own . . .' I blundered on. *'If I were a shepherd, I would bring a lamb* . . . if you see what I mean, Mother?'

But before she could reply the kitchen door flew open to reveal Beatrice, glowing. 'Oh Mother,' she cried. 'We're doing Pandora's Box and I'm to play Hope!'

# SIX

In the end, Daddy said we could perform in the school pageant. He said something about Talent being a gift from God, after all. Beatrice hugged him but I was trying very hard not to crow in front of *her* so I said 'thank you' politely and got out of the room and shut the door as quietly as I could. And then I raced upstairs two at a time to take down the pink crepe paper Mrs Spencer had given me, which I'd had to hide on top of the wardrobe.

So nothing more was said on the subject and life at Corporation Oaks went on quietly, with Beatrice and me leaving most of ourselves in the classroom and doing just demure things at home, like needlework and cutting roses out of the pink crepe paper but taking care not to drop *bits*. My dress had been Marjorie Bagshaw's bridesmaid's frock: it was cream net over a long cream taffeta skirt, trimmed at the hem, neck and sleeves with Nottingham lace, of course. The crepe-paper roses were to be stitched to the overskirt and I was to have a pink sash from Mrs Spencer's daughter, Kathleen. The question was: who would do the stitching? My own needlework was dismal. My embroidered coal-glove had been the class joke and the invisible hemming on my needlework folder so visible that it was constantly being ripped undone by the teacher. It had taken a term and a half to hem, by which time everyone else had finished their woven egg cosies and were starting on their sampler.

After dropping various hints to Maisie, which she never seemed to take, I screwed up my courage to ask Mother if she would sew the roses on to my dress. We were playing a game after tea while Mother did some needlework.

'D'you like sewing, Mother?' I began.

'I have satisfaction in a good job well done,' she replied.

'*A stitch in time saves nine,*' Beatrice chipped in smugly. Honestly, what a thing to say. I ignored her.

'So Mother, you know my dress, for the pageant. You know the roses: the crepe paper we were cutting out?'

I paused expectantly. Mother said nothing. Bea hunched over the Halma board trying to look as if she were somewhere else. 'Please would you sew my roses on for me, Mother?' There. I had asked her.

A long silence fell. At length she said, 'We'll see, Annie, but I think it is unfair of you to ask. One day you will understand just how unfair it is.' Something about the way she said it made me feel small.

Later, when we were upstairs, Beatrice told me exactly what she thought of me. 'She's very religious. Much more religious than us. We need to respect that. If it was up to her we wouldn't be taking part in the pageant and you're really stupid because if you're not careful she'll talk to Daddy and get us barred from it.'

'No she won't. Daddy won't let her.'

'Don't be so sure, Annie! You always go too far. You don't know when to stop.'

'Well she's no business being in this house anyway. Our

Own Mother would have sewn my roses on. I wouldn't have had to ask her.'

'*S-P!*' flashed Beatrice and gave me a dig in the ribs.

She was right of course. There wasn't much I could say to that.

But the next day when I came home from school and looked in the wardrobe, my cream First Fairy dress had five small crepe-paper roses sewn neatly on to its net skirt: two at the front, one at each side-seam and one at the back. I hope it doesn't sound ungracious if I admit they weren't quite as ... abundant as the ones I'd had in mind when I cut them out, but they were *there*. I raced downstairs and arrived breathless in the kitchen where Mother was helping Maisie to roll out pastry.

'Mother! Thank you! Oh, Mother, you are wonderful, thank you, thank you!' I threw my arms around her and hugged her legs. Nana, sensing there was something to celebrate, lumbered out of her basket and wagged her feathery tail and barked. I felt Mother stiffen. It was like hugging a lamp post.

'Annie! Stop it! What are you doing, girl? Can't you see you'll get covered in flour? And make that dog behave!'

Maisie chuckled. 'Well you did the right thing there, Mrs Lang. You've got a friend for life now.'

Mother disentangled herself from my arms. 'There's no need to get overexcited about a few roses,' she told me. 'Take that dog out into the yard. Then go and do your homework.'

I took Nana and went away happy. Mother wasn't such a bad old stick. I was starting to learn that 'we'll see' sometimes meant 'yes'.

\*

I loved my dress with a passion, tried it on in secret, balancing on the dressing-table stool and doing a twizzle to see it go swish, and whispering my lines.

Beatrice's dress was nice, but I'm glad I didn't have to wear it. Being classical times it was straight, a tunic, cut from white material in Jessops' sale. Bea called it damask but it just looked like curtains to me. I think it was a bit left over because it only came just below her knees. Beatrice was to be packed into her box with the Spites. She said there would be seven of them altogether, which was giving Mr Makins a problem because he had to build the scenery.

'We all have to crouch down behind these desks,' Beatrice explained. 'They'll put a canvas over, painted like Auntie Grace's big oak chest or something. I'm at the bottom because of course I have to come out last.'

I didn't understand what they were all doing in the chest in the first place. Beatrice said, 'Oh Annie, you must remember! Our Own Mother read us the story.'

I said she never read it to *me* and I thought it was a stupid story.

Then Beatrice sighed that sigh that means she's worrying about me. She said I must have been too young and touched my hair. But I can't stand it when she's all sorry for me, Little Orphan Annie, as if she's going to hug me or something ridiculous, and I jerked my head away. *'Don't!'* I get this lumpy feeling in my throat when she goes like that.

But on the first day of Spring, March 21st, it went really cold like mid-Winter. I was doing E-flat minor and in my early-morning practices my fingers were flabby and whitish all over again, like tripe when you've just unwrapped it from the greaseproof. The scales came out in clumps. Beatrice and I both got colds and had to do inhaling over the scullery sink with the Friar's Balsam, disgusting, and Mother's primulas went brown and slimy overnight with the late frost. The hooves of the coal horses trying to pull the cart up St Ann's Hill went slithering on the cobbles and I watched them snorting and heaving at the load of greasy coal sacks, and the clang of metal on their shoes echoed round the yard. The coal man yelled at them, as if it was their fault, poor things. I yelled at him, but he didn't hear.

We took no notice of Lent in our family. There was nothing to give up, what with the grown-ups all signing the pledge and not smoking or playing games on Sundays or committing any sins at all as far as I could tell. When Beatrice and I asked Mother to test us on the Litany, which we had to do at school every Friday prayers, she muttered at its being Popish, which must be wrong because if Mundella was Roman Catholic they'd have us out of there before we could say 'knife'. (That's an expression of Auntie Grace's, but I don't know why 'knife' rather than 'cat' or 'gusset'.) Anyhow, Mother said she would test us because she was pleased we were learning the prayer book rather than Shakespeare or Thomas Love Peacock. I wish I was called Annie Love Peacock rather than Annie Lang.

So we were well into Lent and the Litany and the Friar's Balsam what with the late frost, when Mother announced – it was eleven days before the concert – that the weather was too cold for the wearing of flimsy dresses. We were walking back from the Mission at the time, which has a special coldness that goes deep into your bones when Pastor Eames is doing the sermon. Mother was walking just ahead of us, with Beatrice and me tagging behind and she sort of threw it over her shoulder. She knew it wouldn't be popular. I clenched my fists deep in my pockets and mouthed at Beatrice, 'I'll kill her!' Bea shot me a look of warning and said, 'Mother, perhaps we can wear our flannel vests under our costumes?'

Mother stopped and waited for us to catch up because you don't talk about underwear when you're crossing the Woodborough Road, especially on a Sunday after Mission. 'You're wearing flannel vests already. It will be too much of a change in temperature.'

'We'll wear two!' I said. I was desperate. 'And our long coms!'

Now it was Beatrice to get upset. She gave me a sharp pinch. 'I can't wear my long coms!' she protested. 'They'll show. I'll wear two flannel vests and – and a liberty bodice.'

But Mother had made her mind up. Flannel vests, liberty bodices *and* long woollen combinations would be worn for the Easter concert.

I felt awful. 'Beatrice, I'm so, so sorry,' I told her when we were in her room later that day.

'It's all right for *you*. Your dress comes down to your ankles almost.' She raised her face from where it had been buried in her arms. She'd been crying.

'Well, Mother was on the point of saying we couldn't wear our costumes at all,' I pointed out. I picked up Bea's coms, lying in a heap on the floor. They were thick and pink and hideous. But maybe – 'Hang on,' I said. 'Let's try something. Put these on a mo.'

'What for?'

'Just put them on. I've thought of an experiment.'

Beatrice reluctantly pulled the combinations over her black stockings and I started to roll one of the legs up from the ankle. 'It won't. It's too bulky,' she groaned. 'I tried that already.'

But after a lot of pulling and scrabbling we managed to roll them up to mid-calf length, where they stuck. Beatrice shook her head. 'They're really tight. They'll cut off my circulation. I won't be able to stand up, let alone leap about the stage.' On her release from the box Hope was to do a dance indicating the conquest of the Spites. So then I made her take them off again and we bunched them like a concertina and heaved, and this time we got them just high enough to be invisible above the tunic. Beatrice plodded round the room. 'It's everso uncomfortable,' she complained. I couldn't help laughing because she looked like a duck. She took the combinations off and dropped them on the floor again in a heap.

Then suddenly I had a brainwave; it was absolutely the only thing to do. 'Mother won't come to the pageant, will she?' I asked. 'She told Maisie she'd never let down the Lord by going to a play or something.'

'She came to the Poetry,' Beatrice said. 'And the Christmas carols.'

'Yes, but that's like church and music and stuff. She doesn't approve of this one. Specially with it being Maundy Thursday.'

'So?'

'So we just don't wear them!'

'How d'you mean? How can we tell her that?'

'Beatrice, we wear them when we leave the house and then we . . . take them off.'

Bea stared at me. 'How can we?'

'When we change our frocks.'

'Are you saying we *lie*?'

'No, of course we don't lie. We're not expected to come home and say, *Oh Mother, it was so good wearing our long coms in the school concert*! We just don't mention it.'

'We lie by omission!'

'No we don't! It's not omission if it just doesn't come up.'

'We disobey.'

This was it, of course. I rolled Beatrice's combinations

into a ball and put them carefully back in her drawer. 'Well, in a way.'

'What d'you mean *in a way*? We deliberately disobey our Mother!'

'Well we wouldn't have to if she didn't make stupid rules!'

'Annie, I worry about you, I really do. How can you even suggest such a thing?'

'Daddy'll come, but he won't notice. He'll just imagine we've rolled them up.'

'*That's not the point!*' She was really angry. She went on about it being a moral thing.

'Listen,' I burst out. This was something that had been dawning on me all day. 'Mother isn't thinking of us and our colds and all that. She doesn't approve of the concert or Shakespeare or your tunic or my vanity or anything. She can't stop us doing it because Daddy's told her. So she's finding a way to spoil it for us. Don't you see?'

'Annie, that is nonsense. We've both had bad colds. We could have a shadow on our lung. We could have the TB if we get chilled. She's right!'

'No she's not! It'll be warm in the hall with the lights and the people and it's only for a short time. No one else's mothers will make them wear their long coms. You'll see!'

'But that makes no difference. She's trusting us to do what she tells us. It's dishonest if we betray her trust.'

'Well, I'm sorry if that's the way you see it, but I'm not wearing mine.'

'*Yours* won't show. Mine will!'

'So take them off, Beatrice!'

I was sorry because it makes me sad when there is a space between Beatrice and me and this argument made a big hole. And I felt guilty because whichever way you looked at it, I

84

*was* being dishonest and I don't consider myself a dishonest person. I thought about it a lot over the next few days. I stood on my dressing-table stool and did another twizzle to see if the long coms showed beneath the dress. It seemed to be all right as long as I didn't do a *big* twizzle. I went into the yard and looked to see if the daffodils were growing in the hope that the weather was getting warmer. I asked Marjorie Bagshaw would she be wearing *her* long coms and she said was I daft? I told her Mother was making us wear ours and she shrugged and said, well they won't show under the brides-maid's dress, will they? This made me feel worse. It didn't seem to occur to anyone else to disobey. Beatrice and I didn't talk about it again but I could feel a cold draught across the space between us and I wished I hadn't started it.

On the day of the concert we both wore our long combi-nations, so I wasn't dishonest in the end, except in thought which some say is as bad. I had hitched them up a bit and tied them with pink ribbons, so that if they showed I hoped they would look like part of my petticoat. My scene was a big success and Mrs Spencer gave me a hug afterwards to her ample bosom. But I don't want to talk about that because when it was time for Pandora's Box, and Beatrice and the Spites had been stuck beneath Mr Makins's canvas 'chest', and Nora Porter and Joan Gadsby had gone around stinging Pandora and Epimetheus and flown off to attack the rest of the human beings in the world and at last it was Beatrice's turn, a terrible thing happened. She came out of the box with Miss Wise playing sort of hopeful music on the piano and it was very tingly and dramatic. And Bea began her dance, a bit carefully at first, I could tell, and we know why. But then just as I thought it was going to be all right, the music sort of swelled. She had to do this little run across the stage, and the long woolly combinations started to slide just a little (and perhaps only I watching from close by would have noticed them at first) but then, as they got lower down, they kind of gathered speed until there they were in their full pink horror, cascading to her ankles.

From where I was standing by the side door I could see most of the audience and I looked desperately for Daddy because I knew he would do the right thing, whatever that was. He was sitting about seven rows back and I saw with a pang that he hadn't noticed; he was smiling at some blonde person sitting next to him, as if she had just made a joke that was nothing to do with Beatrice and the long combinations. Then some nasty girls in 4D started to snigger and there was a terrible wave of giggles all over the hall, and I sank to the floor and my cheeks were hot and I couldn't watch my dear sister because I knew that honesty had got her nowhere. And I was angry that Mother was not present to witness the humiliation of Beatrice and our entire family that was All Her Fault. And I think that was the second time I stopped believing that Jesus is a friend to little children, because even when they are honest and pure like Beatrice, He just is not.

Truth to tell, this episode made me worry more than ever about my soul. Of course, we're brought up to believe these things without question. Beatrice believed it, so I couldn't talk to her, and Fred would just have snorted if he'd been there, which he was not. So the following Sunday after Sunday School, when Beatrice had gone out to tea and I was to go home on my own, I hung around waiting for Miss Blessing so as to walk to the bus stop with her.

'I wanted to ask you,' I began, 'about Jesus.'

'Oh dear!' She gave an uneasy little laugh. 'I'm not sure I'm the best person to speak to, Annie. I'm not an expert, you know.'

'But you teach us Sunday School. And you're *Mission*, aren't you?'

'Well, my father was, and my mother kept up with it for his sake, but the rest of our family aren't in this congregation, you know. I don't think they're quite as, well, rigorous about it as you are at Golgotha.'

I noticed two things about this answer: first, she had spoken of her father in the past tense; secondly she had said, 'as *you* are at Golgotha', as though she was outside and not part of it.

'But you do belong to the Mission, don't you?'

'I came here because they wanted someone to play the harmonium, and it's very good practice for me. So yes, I joined the congregation, but I may not know all that much about Jesus Himself.'

I was intrigued. 'What do you have to practise for?' I asked.

'Oh ... well.' I felt she was wondering whether to tell me and hoped it wasn't an impertinent question. But she went on, 'You see, I'd really like to be a piano teacher. I love the piano and I'm taking Grade Eight next year, but we can't afford for me to go to the Royal Academy in London, or anything, so I'm practising for my LR, if you know what that is – LRAM?' She broke off and looked at me, her eyebrows raised in a question. Then she went on, 'When I leave school, I'm hoping to get a job that'll let me study music part-time ... But I don't know why I'm talking about me! What did you want to know about Jesus?'

I had stopped bothering about Jesus. I was deep in the information she had given me. Grade *Eight* – when she must only be six or seven years older than me! And she wanted to be a piano teacher, which was a marvellous thing. 'I don't see why you need to come here for that!' I said in wonder. I didn't know what 'LR' was, but it sounded very grown-up.

'Oh, I get nervous playing in public,' she said with a laugh. 'So playing at the Mission really helps me with that. Then they asked me to do the Sunday School.' She shrugged. 'So here I am. But I'm not exactly an authority on Our Lord. I just know the stories.'

I remembered what I ought to ask her. 'It's just . . .' I began, 'that we're told Jesus protects the little children, but we also have to be punished so we can be saved, and – and things keep happening to our family which make me wonder if Jesus can do both things at once.' I hoped it didn't sound blasphemous.

'What sort of things?' she asked.

I couldn't tell her about the long combinations because that was too shameful, so I said, 'Well, one thing is our mother dying when we were little.' I tried to say it in a very offhand sort of way, like a report in the newspaper, so there would be no hint of the *S-P*, which would have been just awful.

'I'm sorry about that, Annie,' she said softly. 'I mean, I did know, of course – because that's how I come to be here. I took over from Miss Higgs when she became Mrs Lang.'

I thought about this. 'So . . . Mother dying and Miss Higgs marrying Daddy and you coming to the Mission could all be part of God's plan for us, couldn't it?'

Miss Blessing looked uncomfortable. 'No, Annie. The tragedy of your mother dying is far greater than the good fortune of my getting this job. I'm sure God didn't plan it that way.'

'But it's true we're just little, aren't we, Miss Blessing, in a bigger Plan? And we have to accept that we need to suffer, and we can't always have what we want?'

'Well,' she said after a short silence. 'I think that's a very grown-up way of looking at it, Annie. My father died in the War. I don't have many memories of him, and sometimes I get so angry I think I'm losing my faith. I never really knew my poor father, but I miss him enormously! Do you remember your mother?'

'A little,' I mumbled. I kicked at a pebble.

'Well sometimes,' she said, 'I get very cross with God and I can't see I'm part of any sort of plan.'

No one in my family had ever said they got cross with God. I thought no one but me ever did, and here was my Sunday School teacher admitting to it! 'So what d'you do then?' I asked. 'D'you pray?'

She didn't reply for a moment, then she said carefully, 'I think I've decided it's all right to be angry.'

'With God?' I looked at her round-eyed.

'Yes.' She was thinking about it. 'I mean, if we're taught that we're a family with God as our father, it's natural, isn't it? We all get cross with our families sometimes but it doesn't mean we don't love them.'

'Oh,' I said. I thought about how I got cross with everyone in my family. 'Yes, I suppose so.'

'Perhaps you and I are angry with God because we're sad, aren't we, about losing our parents?' she went on. 'Being sad is quite reasonable under the circumstances. If we tried to pretend we weren't sad, weren't cross, we wouldn't be honest with God. And I suppose God knows that.'

'You mean, being sad is part of His plan for us, to help us be saved?' It didn't sound like a great plan to me, but I liked the way she said 'you and I'.

She nodded slowly. She seemed to be working it out in her own mind. 'Maybe,' she said. 'At the moment. I hope not for ever.' She smiled down at me.

'So ... maybe in the end, in the long run, Jesus may be being kind to the little children after all?' I asked doubtfully.

'Perhaps,' she said. She didn't sound too sure. 'I hope so,

anyway. But I suppose I'm not far enough along the road yet to know.' We had reached her bus stop. 'So all I can do in the meantime is to try and have faith,' she finished. She must have seen my disappointed expression because she added quickly, 'Of course, it's not as simple as that and I often still get angry and upset, but I'm trying.' She gave me an anxious look. 'Oh dear. I don't think that's helped you at all!'

'Yes it has, Miss Blessing.' I shifted from foot to foot, wanting to get away now. 'I'm going to have to go and think about it. But thank you.'

I walked up the hill, turning over what she had said. Whoever you talked to, it always came back to faith. Bea's was absolute and it cheered me up that Miss Blessing's was shakier, more like my own. Perhaps mine would sort of arrive as I got older. Meanwhile I was stuck with the anger. But just before I dropped off to sleep that night I remembered what made me angriest of all: it was Daddy sharing a private joke with that stranger, unaware of Beatrice in her moment of need. When I grow up, I hope I will pay more attention than that to the people I love.

# SEVEN

On Saturdays and Sundays we had tea in the sitting room, spread out on the table behind the new green curtain. It was high tea with ham and lettuce and sometimes pork pie and bottled fruit. Tins of cooked meat and bottles of damsons and plums from Grandfather Eames' garden were stored along the shelf at the cellar head. It was a spidery place where grit rained constantly down on the jars and they had to be wiped with the dishcloth before Maisie opened them. Sometimes I was told to go and find such-and-such a thing from the cellar head and it was an errand I loathed. If you were lucky it would be just inside the door and you wouldn't have to go down there, but mostly the Thing, whatever it was, would be further along the shelf, lost in the gloom. With each step, you had to go down a stair-tread, of course, so with each step you were groping higher and higher and there would be a fear of falling into the abyss, as I imagined it from Bible study. I had never been right down into the cellar, but I knew that's where Elsie had to go for the coal, the large, craggy lumps for the fire grate in the sitting room and the anthracite for the range. She would heave the coal scuttles up, panting and coughing. 'Lord,' she'd say if I met her in the hall. 'That place is like the pit of Hell, Annie. It's that scary, I tell you. Evil things down there, I shouldn't wonder.'

'What evil things, Elsie?'

'Heaven alone knows. No good can go on in a place like that.'

'What's it like then?' I'd ask, with a dread fascination.

'It stinks, for one thing. Dank and evil. There's a draught from the North Pole, yet the air is ... sort of, you know, poisonous. Breathe it and you choke. See my hands?'

She'd hold out her chapped fingers, grimy and damp to the touch. 'Ghosts in that cellar, my girl,' she'd say darkly.


One day in September I was sent to the cellar head for a jar of beetroot for Sunday tea. As usual, I turned the large key in the lock (that was a mystery in itself – what was down there that they had to keep from breaking out?), then I took as deep a breath as I could muster and plunged through. No beetroot among the first three or four visible jars. I retreated back outside the door and switched on the Bakelite switch; then I gingerly took a step down. As usual, the clammy cold enfolded me and the smell washed up my nose, even though I wasn't breathing. It was the same smell that seeped into the drawing room above, where I did my piano practice, but down here it was much stronger. Shipham's bloater paste; tinned pilchards; ham; pickled eggs; a jar of something greenish ... I descended another step, resting my fingers on the flaking whitewash at the edge of the shelf which was now at the level of my bulging eyes. Piccalilli. Tongue. Can't breathe. Mustn't breathe. I launched myself back out into the light and took a couple more lungfuls of good air at the very moment Mother appeared out of nowhere. I jumped.

'Annie, what on earth are you doing?'

'Nothing,' I said. 'I just couldn't find it so I was, um, just taking a breath.'

She gave me a funny look and I thought she was about to go down past me to get the beetroot herself, but she hesitated. 'No, *you* go.' She gave me a little push. 'Don't be so feeble, child.'

To my relief she stood there as I ventured down again. On the third step, my groping hands found the beetroot. I lifted it gingerly down, blew off the coal dust and returned to the hall as fast as I could without dropping it. As I placed the grimy jar in her hands, our eyes met and I saw in hers a kind of – I can only call it a *dawning* look. I suddenly knew she had found something out, and it terrified me. I turned quickly away to lock the door.

Cousin Irene and Cousin John were coming to tea that day because their parents, Auntie Vera and Uncle George, had to go somewhere else; the house felt almost jolly for a Sunday. Irene and John didn't have to go to the Mission. For some reason to do with Uncle George, who wasn't part of our family, they went to the Church of England, which I thought sounded wonderful because they were allowed to read stories and even play Pit and draughts on a Sunday, unheard-of in our house. They wouldn't have to have the total immersion when the time came, either, or sign the pledge, or anything. I envied them.

There were rather too many of us to sit at the table, so we younger children were allowed to have the nest of tables and sit together on the sofa. When she returned to the sitting room after washing her hands, Irene had failed to shut the kitchen door so Nana, invariably banished at mealtimes, trotted in after her and for once no one noticed. I gave John my milk, because he didn't seem to mind it, and concentrated on the pork pie and salad. I like pork pie when it is spicy and the crust is crisp. I don't like the jelly round it, though; jelly is all right when it's red or green in puddings, but not when it's see-through in pork pie. I waited till the grown-ups weren't watching and slipped it quietly to Nana, who understood the need for secrecy and managed to eat it from my hand without slurping.

It wasn't for twenty minutes or so that anyone noticed the pink spots. They were appearing, as if by magic, on the new wallpaper behind us. Beatrice saw them first. She jumped up and came closer to examine them carefully.

'Beatrice—' Mother looked up. 'Where do you think you're going?'

'What are these, Mother? Look!' cried Bea.

We were all staring now as more and more bright pink spots materialised on the walls around us.

'It's magic!' I squeaked excitedly. 'It's the pink fairy!'

Mother did one of her withering looks.

Irene and John gazed at the wall entranced, too shy to speak.

Then Daddy burst out laughing. 'I know what it is! See, all of you!' He was pointing at Nana, who stood by our little tables with a big grin on her face, so pleased to be included in the family tea, her tail swishing from side to side, dipping into the vinegary dish of beetroot and sending it like a joyful painting over the new beige wallpaper. Taking our cue from Daddy, Irene, John and I chortled and squeaked and threw our heads back and laughed as I can't remember laughing in that room for a long time. Even Beatrice was grinning and Nana, who loved to cheer us up, wagged her tail all the more.

Then Mother ordered, 'Harry, get that dog out of here!' and instantly I stopped laughing. I knew that voice.

Daddy stood up from the table. 'Come on, old girl.' He led Nana out of the room by the collar.

'Into the yard,' Mother called after him.

'It's not her fault,' I murmured.

'And trust you,' snapped Mother. She was dabbing at the spots with a napkin. 'Beatrice, fetch the borax and a pint of warm water.' To me, she said, 'You are so predictable, Annie. I can't tell you how infantile it is, your constant moaning.'

My face burned. I could feel Irene's anxious eyes upon me. 'Please may we leave the table?' I asked, as politely as I knew how.

'You can do better than that. You may go to your room. It will soon be time for your cousins to leave, in any case.'


'It's all my fault,' wailed Irene, when we were safely in my bedroom with the door closed. 'Spats always has tea with us. I didn't realise Nana wasn't allowed to.'

'It's my fault too,' I consoled her. 'If I hadn't given her my pork-pie jelly she wouldn't have wagged her tail so much. Don't worry – it's only *her*, Mother, who's brought in that rule. Daddy never used to mind. You saw him. He thought it was funny.'

'It won't come off, you know,' said John, who was always inclined to be gloomy. 'We did it in chemistry.'

'Did *what*, John?' asked Irene sharply.

'The master was testing common household substances. It's a pretty fast dye, is beetroot juice.'

'It's only a bit of . . . *salad*,' I said. 'Nothing to get worked up about. It's just 'cos she chose the wallpaper and she hasn't been Mistress of the House very long. It'll blow over.' I wanted to make Irene feel better, but inside I feared for what would happen next.

'Personally,' commented Irene, 'I thought it was an improvement!' and we all laughed at that.

'Can't wait to write and tell Fred about it,' I said. 'He adores Nana.' I went to the window and stared down into the yard. In the dusk I could see her huddled between two flower tubs, her chin resting watchfully on her paws.

Nana was allowed back to her usual bed in the scullery that night. But next day as I left for school, I saw Mr Holley, who does odd jobs for us, unloading wood on the back hill, very ominous. By the time I got home, there it was, the hateful thing – my worst dread. The yard smelt of creosote. I wrinkled my nose, but said nothing. Tea passed with a sort of veneer like that thin icing with cracks in it. No one said a word about the Thing in the yard. That's what's weird about our family; there it was, where there had been nothing yesterday, and no one so much as sighed, or raised an eyebrow or said something like, 'Well now . . .' I knew Mother expected me to start on, so I willed myself to stay silent. Nana lay with her head on my feet under the kitchen table as I did my homework; *she* knew what it was all right.

At bedtime, Beatrice and I trooped upstairs and still not a word spoken. When I interrogated Beatrice about it, she said she knew nothing *and best to shut up about it.* I lay awake in the dark, listening. I don't know what I was waiting for – barking, a scuffle, perhaps, when they tried to shut Nana outside – but my eyes fell asleep before my ears . . .

The next thing I knew, it was deep in the middle of the darkest hour of night and I was suddenly wide awake. What was it? A *something* had woken me up. Not a whine. Not a whimper. I held my breath and listened. Nothing but the sighs of the old house in the darkness, except . . . yes, a *something,* very quietly, like a spider trampling a leaf: *scritch scritch*, then silence. After a moment, I heard it again. I lay listening, agog, willing the sound to stop. I couldn't bear for it to be what it undoubtedly was, because if I heard it and did nothing, it made me a traitor. *Scritch scritch*. I swung my toes to the floor and groped for my slippers. Pulling my Winter dressing gown around me, I tiptoed to the window avoiding, as ever, the third floorboard from the wall. The yard was in deep shadow, no starlight to distinguish the hateful black of the new kennel from the darkness around it, but the noise was unmistakable, quiet and persistent. It could only be Nana.

With extreme care, and my vast experience of the geography of our house, its cracks and creaks and bottomless pits, I reached the kitchen soundlessly. And there was the noise: a named noise now, on the outside of the scullery door, not even a scratching, more a *wiping* of a heavy paw over the panels. I reached for the key. Then, leaning against the door with all my strength to avoid a sudden *clack* as the mortise opened, I turned it in the lock. The scratching had stopped. I willed her not to squeak in greeting, but Nana knew better than that. The door opened. She was sitting at the bottom of the two steep steps leading down into the yard, her head on one side, expectantly. For a moment we looked at each other, then she was in my arms, tail swinging in the night. I hugged her to say sorry, Nana, sorry for the horribleness of the grown-ups, and you know it's not my doing, Nana; I would never, ever do this to you if I were to live a thousand years and it wasn't your fault about the beetroot – all this without a sound, my silent tears buried in the thick white ruff of her neck. Nana knew about caution. After a while she drew back and looked at me, awaiting instructions: *Do we go in now*? I had no idea. The sense of outrage that had carried me downstairs gave way to dismay as I considered what to do. If I let her in, we would both be doomed. If I led her back to the kennel and tried to settle her, she would very likely not be able to resist whimpering or – my stomach lurched – *howling* at my betrayal. There could be only one course of action. It had the satisfying advantage of not incriminating Nana, while allowing me to atone for the terrible injustice done to her.

I stood up, reached around the open door for the key, locked it, just as gingerly as I had unlocked it but this time from the outside, and joined the bewildered dog in the yard. Thankful now for the extreme darkness, and trying to ignore the cold lapping around my ankles under my nightie, I groped my way past Mother's flower tubs, under the shivering clothes pegs to the hulk by the far wall. *Would I fit through the doorway?* I hadn't examined the horrid thing before. Nana was a tall dog, but narrow. Feeling cautiously for the opening, I knelt and ran my fingers around the splintery edges, softened by damp and creosote. Then ducking my head and wriggling sideways, I clambered in. Nana stood outside, her head cocked uncertainly. 'Come on,' I whispered, and gave her collar a tug. After a moment, she obeyed, squeezing through the doorway with what must have been a look of great puzzlement. There was no bed, of course. I might have known they would provide nothing for her to lie on, but Daddy must have taken pity on her because, feeling around, I found a couple of old newspapers thrust into a corner. We scrambled around each other, Nana and I, as I tried to spread the papers underneath us, curling up finally in a sort of ball, with my feet under her tummy for warmth and my head against the pillow of her neck, where I could breathe in warm dog and not the damp and stinking night.

Waking in the early dawn, queasy from the stench of creosote and sensing the hour from birds twittering in the darkness and the metal crunch of cartwheels down St Ann's Hill, I spoke to Nana sternly. I told her I must go now; that she must make no sound *at all* and that I would think of a way out of this, but at the moment we would have to go along with the grown-ups and do whatever they wanted. If we did not, it would be worse for both of us. Then, easing my numb feet from under her, I levered myself out of the kennel and back to the kitchen in the grey light, unlocking and locking the door quietly, as before. Stopping in the hall to examine the solemn ticking grandfather clock, I could just make out that it was almost six. This was cutting it fine. I fled as fast as silence would allow back to my room and dived shivering into bed. There I lay, straining my ears for noises from the yard. The birds were louder now. A motorcar climbed in low gear up Woodborough Road. But from Nana there was no sound.

Next day, I made my plan of campaign. From the dressing-up box I pulled an old plaid rug which they would never miss. Then I found a couple of mothy velvet cushions and lifted down the spare hot-water bottle from the back of the dresser cupboard. It was kept there for visitors, who never came to stay. That night after dark I lit the gas under the kettle and turned it as high as possible, not letting it boil for fear Mother would hear it. I placed the stone bottle in the sink for safety and poured the water in, holding the heavy kettle with both hands and blowing softly to peer through the steam when it should be full. Wrapping it in my oldest jumper and the tartan rug, I stole out of the kitchen door and hid everything inside the kennel, then returned for the cushions.

That night, after they had all gone to bed, down I went to the dog kennel, dressed this time in my thickest socks, a cardigan over my nightie, and a pair of long combinations underneath. The kennel was dank but the jumper and the rug were dry enough and the hot-water bottle lukewarm (I decided not to bother with it in future). Once more, Nana played her part without a sound. We snuggled up together with the tepid hot-water bottle digging into my shoulder blade and I thought I would sleep quickly, what with the exhaustion and everything. But somehow my head took a wrong turning and instead of falling asleep I found myself wide awake in that miserable box, its damp soaking into my bones. My jagged brain screamed at the nonsense of what I'd chosen to do. But, too tired to move or to sleep, I lay on under a spell, starting at every small noise, every spider and toad, in a night that lasted for ever.

And sometime in the middle of it a strange event took place. I had almost persuaded myself to kneel upright and squeeze out of the opening and go back to bed, and was actually about to do it, when I fancied I heard a new sound: as if it were heavy feet climbing the ash-pit steps from St Ann's Hill. At first, I couldn't be absolutely sure that they *were,* but then Nana was suddenly awake beside me; I could sense her head alert as we held our breath in the dark. The footsteps were crossing the yard now. What if they came to the kennel and looked in? Was it a burglar who could hit us over our head? What would Nana do? I tightened my arms around her as we waited, ears on wires . . . but now I could hear nothing at all. Perhaps the burglar had got into the house! Nana sniffed the air, as if to make sure this was not a sound to be barked at, waited a moment more, then put her head gingerly back on her paws.

I breathed out. My tummy hurt. The creosote fumes were like fingers reaching down into my lungs and throttling me. But any thought of making a break for the kitchen was out of the question now; for all I knew, the burglar could still be outside, *waiting to pounce.* In vain, I lay there telling myself that Nana had not barked, and burglars do not have keys. I might almost have believed I'd imagined the footsteps, but for Nana: she clearly knew they were real, on account of being practically a person herself. Yet if she hadn't barked, surely it could only be Daddy walking round to the front ... except why would he, when I had plainly heard him going along the landing to bed last night? After what seemed like many more hours, it was a wonderful thing to be rescued again by the song of the first bird of the morning. I needed to get back to my room, but was still too terrified to move. Dawn was breaking as, shivering and sick, I finally crawled out of the kennel, barely making it upstairs before Elsie got up to light the fires.

At breakfast, no one said anything about a burglar. I explored Daddy's face secretly for clues as to whether it might have been him. I thought he looked as if he needed a shave, but I couldn't be sure. He said barely a word, but there was nothing odd about this: he rarely spoke at breakfast.

Mother remarked, 'I can smell creosote.'

My head jerked up guiltily. I had wondered about this. But before I could come out with an excuse, Beatrice said, 'I washed my hair with Coal Tar soap, Mother. It's probably that.'

'Well it's very strong,' Mother observed. 'I fancy I smelt it yesterday.' Her gaze fell on me, and I hastily scooped up a porridge lump.

'Mr Holley left his brushes to soak at the top of the ash-pit steps,' Maisie chimed in, turning from the gas stove with the oven glove on her hand. 'It's probably blown in on the draught.' It was a source of wonder to me that still no one had ever spoken the words *dog kennel* in my hearing.

This seemed to satisfy Mother. She said only, 'You're pale as a ghost, my girl. You want to get more fresh air. You're too soft.'

'Yes, Mother,' I mumbled and poked at another lump of porridge, wishing Maisie could make it and not Elsie, who always seemed to get the lumps.

After that wretched night – and spelling 'occurred' with one r in the spelling test, which was obviously humiliating and got me an odd look from Mrs Spencer – I knew this state of affairs could not go on. That day, it rained a needling rain, as if to say Autumn is coming and Something Must be Done. And I decided I would have to tell Beatrice about my nights in the kennel, which would also mean I could consult her about the burglar. As I pushed my nose against the cold pane and stared into the garden, thinking with dread about the coming night, the prospect of unburdening myself to Beatrice made me feel better at once.

'We've got to do something about Nana,' I announced, when we were in Bea's bedroom after tea.

'What about her?' Beatrice looked up from a stocking she was darning.

I was sitting on the floor with my hands clasped around my knees. 'We can't just leave her out there day and night,' I said. 'Got to do *something*.' I gave her a sideways look.

Beatrice frowned. 'Did you put those things in the kennel?'

I turned and looked at her properly. 'What things?'

'The tartan rug and the cushions? Was that you?'

'So you looked in there, then?'

'What if I did?'

'So you care about her, too?'

'Of course I jolly well care,' said Beatrice crossly. 'It's cold. She's not an outdoor dog.'

'We've got to do something, Bea.' I grabbed hold of her arm. 'She'll die if she has to live outside in the Winter.'

'Her coat will grow thicker. I suppose she'll get used to it.'

'But she won't. She'll die and Mother will be pleased. It's what she wants.'

'Don't be silly, Annie. Of course it's not.'

I ignored this. 'Mother's hated Nana ever since she came to live here. We can't let her do this, Beatrice. Nana was here first! We've got to get Daddy to help us. You're the oldest. *You* talk to him.'

Beatrice sighed.

'In the meantime ...' I rocked forwards and backwards, searching her face for clues. 'We'll have to do something.'

'What sort of thing?'

I hesitated. The moment had come. I felt breathless. 'Well, a sort of *rescue* thing ... Bea, I've got something I want to tell you ...'

But Beatrice didn't hear this last sentence because she had put down her mending and cut across me with, 'Annie, it's not worth it.'

'What d'you mean?'

'I know you. You'll do something mad and get into trouble, and it will be serious. It's not *worth* it.'

'Nana's worth it!'

'I know she is. But—' Beatrice took off her spectacles and rubbed her eyes. 'You know you've got into hot water before. She thinks you're Trouble. You'll make life even more difficult for yourself.'

'I don't care,' I said. 'I'll talk to Daddy, if you won't. It's not right she should have to live her whole life outside. Jesus said ...' I fished around in my head for what Jesus might have said on the matter, '... I dunno. *Suffer the Little Children to Come Unto Me.*'

'Annie, she's a *dog*.'

'It doesn't matter. He meant all innocent helpless creatures, Bea. I bet He did. I – I mean – I'm sure He did. Like in that picture with the birds flying around His head, and lambs and things. And Nana's our faithful friend. We can't betray her!'

But even as I said this, I knew I could not tell Beatrice about sleeping in the kennel, or the burglar, or any of it. Why, to protect me she might even have gone to the grown-ups. And the pain of locking it away was a physical pain; the knowing that Beatrice would not help me and I would have to deal with it by myself.

That night, I read three extra chapters of *The Secret Garden* to try and keep myself awake until they had all gone to bed. When the house was quiet at last, I pulled on my dressing gown and thick socks and tiptoed downstairs, as before, to the kitchen door. The rain had slowed to a drizzle and the yard was full of fog that caught the back of my throat like a mouthful of soot. I clamped my fingers to my neck to stop from coughing. Nana was hunched on the rug in the kennel. She looked really cold. This time, instead of clambering in with her, I leaned forward and gave instructions. She was to come with me. But quietly. She raised her head and cocked it slightly to one side as if considering this. I grasped her collar and gave it a tug. It took some coaxing but she came, at last, cringing backward as I led her through the kitchen door. I wanted to cry, seeing how quickly she had come to regard her home as a place of danger. Once inside, I put my hands on either side of her head and whispered, 'Silent, Nana. Very quiet now.' We moved noiselessly over the kitchen tiles and into the hall, but once on the stairs it was dangerous; this was where the creaks began. All was well until we reached the landing where her claws made a clip-clop like three cart horses, but finally we reached my bedroom door. I turned the latch. We entered. I closed the door as softly as I knew how. We waited, listening. Silence. I had made a bed for her on the hearthrug and, obediently, she flopped down with a deep sigh and a small beating of her tail. I crawled into my own bed and fell asleep at once.

For the next three nights, this ritual was repeated. Somehow my inner fear woke me unfailingly before dawn and I returned Nana to the kennel each morning without arousing suspicion. But my ghostlike appearance deepened, and at the Mission on Sunday I actually fell asleep in the Second Lesson. Beatrice had to jab me in the ribs. I sat bolt upright for the rest of the service and listened closely, terrified Mother would catch me nodding off. This did me no good at all because Pastor Eames, our grandfather, chose today of all days to preach about punishment and how good it is for you. His text was from Proverbs and made me feel a whole lot worse because it took me straight back to Miss Higgs and the night of the Cod Liver Oil: *Withhold not correction from the child: for if thou beatest him with the rod he shall not die. Thou shalt beat him with the rod and deliver his soul from hell.*

As I sat there I could hear Miss Higgs's voice going on about Jesus suffering for our sins, and I could taste the cod liver oil again and I thought I might be sick.

'What on earth is the matter with you?' asked Beatrice when we were walking home ahead of the grown-ups.

'Nothing. Really. I'm just a bit tired.'

'You look awful. They'll be marching you off to the Doctor's if you're not careful. You'll get Dr Wampole's Pills, or Beecham's Powders, or Worse.'

I didn't want to get caught with Nana and beaten, even if the beating did deliver my soul from Hell. I decided it was all the more urgent to persuade Daddy to bring Nana indoors again, so I wouldn't have to sin in the first place. The opportunity to speak to him came after Sunday School that afternoon, when Mother was out and had taken Beatrice with her. He had a visitor of his own, but no one I knew. He didn't get involved with Parish business, so it must have been someone from Roebuck's, which was peculiar on a Sunday. I waited a respectful minute after she left before going quietly into the sitting room. He was leaning back in his chair by the fire dozing, with a copy of *The Masonic Record* draped over his head. I crept in and sat on the footstool at his feet, noticing with relief that John was wrong: the beetroot stains had responded to the borax and Nana's misdemeanour had been expunged (indeed I had seen Maisie working her way around the walls expunging it shortly after the fateful tea).

'Daddy.' I paused. 'Are you asleep?' It wouldn't do to put him in a mood, though I knew he couldn't be very fast asleep.

'Mmm,' he grunted.

I raised a corner of *The Masonic Record* and caught the gleam of an eye. 'Well if you're asleep,' I said, 'I could talk in your sleep, couldn't I?'

'I don't know,' came the response. 'Isn't it *me* that's supposed to talk in my own sleep?'

'Well if *I* do it, it'll save you the trouble. All you have to do is listen.'

'How can I, if I'm asleep?'

'You can hear me *as in a dream*,' I replied poetically.

'Oh, I see.'

I waited a moment. 'So Daddy.'

A snore came from under the newspaper.

'Daddy, I'm serious, I want to talk about Nana.'

The snoring stopped. Silence.

'Daddy, it's Winter. We can't let her sleep outside. I think that now Maisie's cleaned the beetroot off the walls and Nana's done her punishment, she ought to be allowed to live indoors again and sleep in the kitchen like before.'

I waited.

'Because she's our dog and she's part of the house. And it isn't right. Daddy.'

Silence.

'Please?' My voice broke. 'She'll die.'

'That's nonsense, Annie. She won't die.'

'But it's not fair.'

'Life isn't fair.'

'But *why*?' I burst out. 'Why does she have to stay outside?'

'Because she's a nuisance.'

'She's not a nuisance. She was never a nuisance before.'

'Before what, Annie?'

'Before—' I waved my hand at the beetroot-free walls. I took a deep breath. 'You know what I mean.' *Before her. You brought her into this house. We didn't want her. We didn't need her. She's cruel and she doesn't love children or Nana or anyone. So it's your fault. It's your responsibility. It's up to you to sort it out.* But of course I didn't say any of this.

'Annie, your mother has a very difficult job. She has come into this house with children in it who have had their own way for a while, and they are headstrong. She has to make this house her home, too. And if the presence of a large dog makes life more difficult, then she has to solve the problem her way. You must learn to see things from others' points of view as well as your own.'

I pulled the paper off his head. I needed to look at him as he delivered this speech. He was staring at me, not smiling, and behind the words his blue eyes were cold, saying something new that I didn't understand.

# EIGHT

I can hardly believe it now, looking back, but having failed to
get Daddy on our side and reinstate Nana in her rightful home,
I sort of settled into a pattern and during the Winter months
anyway – which, as you know, was most of the time in our
house – this thing with Nana became normal. I would read
in bed and then, as soon as the grown-ups were asleep (and
they luckily went to bed early), I would tiptoe down to the
back door and Nana would hear the key in the lock and slip
into the house on muffled paws. We never faltered. We were
past masters of deceit, experts in the art of silence. She would
stay with me till the dark morning when I got up for piano
practice. At 5.45 sharp, I would go downstairs and let her out
of the back door before returning to the drawing room. I did
get a bit sleepy at school, but made up for it in the holidays.

Then one morning, crossing the hall with Nana on our
way back outside, to my utter horror the front door opened
and Daddy came in. It was like the Night of the Burglar all
over again, but this time it was worse. We froze. For long
moments we all stood and stared at each other: Daddy, Nana
and me.

Then he spoke with a sort of a false jolliness. 'Good Heavens, is that the time already?'

'Daddy.' It was the only thing I could say.

'I probably made you jump,' he said.

I nodded. He was peering at my face in the gloom, not looking towards Nana, who stood stock-still.

'Well. I just. Went out for a morning walk. Nice morning.'

I couldn't reply. In the darkness I could see the stiff white shirt, the black bow tie against it. 'I'd – I'd better ...' I whispered.

'Yes, yes. Better go and do those scales.'

For a moment, I hesitated, torn between the logic of making for the drawing room and the necessity of getting Nana out of the house. I edged a step towards the kitchen and he turned to hang his hat and coat on the hall stand. At that, I fled to the scullery, Nana before me, and turned the key in the lock with fingers trembling lest he come and catch me – though I told myself it was all pointless: the game was up. He must have seen the dog. Even in the gloomy hall with dawn barely breaking, you couldn't *not* see Nana; she was simply too big. When I pulled the door open, a draught of rain and mist surged in ('nice morning', indeed!). Nana trotted silently out and I locked the door as usual. The scales were hopeless that day. My hands trembled uncontrollably; even if Daddy were not to tell her, Mother would hear my guilty secret loud and clear from the piano. I sat there, shoulders hunched, forcing my fingers on to the keys, braced for the torrent of anger, the punishment, fearful for poor Nana, terrified for myself.

He must have been choosing his moment to tell her, though, because nothing happened during piano practice and nothing at breakfast. I heard him leave for work as usual, his footsteps on the hall tiles and the front door click shut. Mother had not appeared, so breakfast was supervised by Maisie, but this was not unusual and I left for school with a strong sense that the reprieve was only temporary. I lingered after classes with Marjorie Bagshaw, dreading the thought of going home.

In those days, Marjorie Bagshaw was my best friend at school. I knew her because our fathers were in the 'Masons and they must have decided between them that we should both be sent to Mundella. It was quite a journey to get there, so right from the start we went on the same bus. Most of the girls in our class, who didn't come from our part of town, seemed to know each other already, which was another reason we were thrown together. But the fact was that deep down we weren't best friends really. I don't like saying it, but I didn't always trust her – and with a real friend you'd never have to think twice about that. Sometimes I didn't even like her very much and I don't think she liked me. But I suppose she found me a bit of a curiosity because of the Mission and everything, and I was drawn to her because she was nothing to do with any of that. Her family weren't even Christians from the sound of it. They never went to church anyway.

'You all right, Annie?' she asked. 'You look a bit peaky.'

I said I was fine, but that I was scared to go home because of Mother being cross. I had wondered whether to tell Marjorie about Nana, but had never told her anything because it was too big a secret to share. I scuffed my toe against a kerbstone, not looking at her.

'She's a weird one, your stepmother, isn't she? My mother says—'

'What?' I looked up, interested.

'Nothing. I didn't ought to say.'

'No, go on. Tell me.'

'It's nothing. She just can't understand . . .'

'What?'

'Why your father had to go and marry her.'

I smiled. 'That's what *we* said!'

'I mean, she's not exactly—' She broke off.

'Not exactly what?'

'His ... sort of ... well his *type,* is she?'

I looked at her. 'What d'you mean?'

'It's just what me mam says.'

'What *does* your mother say? What *type*?' I didn't understand, but I was curious all right.

Marjorie was blushing. She looked over my shoulder. 'Well ... me mam says—' I could see panic in her face. I wondered what she was so afraid to tell me. I could feel her fishing around for words. 'Take your real mother,' she said at last. 'I mean, she wasn't a bit like her, was she?'

'No,' I said with feeling. '*No.* So?'

But Marjorie would tell nothing more.

As I walked home, doing fairy steps to make it longer till I got there, I knew that wasn't really what Marjorie's mother had said. I wondered whether to tell Beatrice about this conversation. Bea might know what it meant, but she didn't think much of the Bagshaws anyway and would go on at me for listening to Marjorie. Then my thoughts turned to Daddy. What had he been doing out all night? Because surely he hadn't been for a morning walk in his evening shirt in all that drizzle. For some reason it was linked in my mind with a thing Fred had said about Roebuck's Biscuits being in trouble. I didn't know what that meant, except that it might require unusual behaviour, like the managers staying up all night smoking cigarettes and talking about what to do. I decided this is what must have happened, and of course Daddy didn't want to worry me – though whether Roebuck's Biscuits was in trouble or not didn't bother me nearly as much as what would happen when he told Mother about

Nana being indoors at night. As I turned into Corporation Oaks and started the slow descent to our house, the sickness came back to my stomach and I stood outside for a moment, searching the big dark windows for clues about what would happen next.

First I went quietly through the side gate, as I usually did, to see Nana. As I approached her kennel the sickness was boiling into panic – supposing Mother had had her taken away as my punishment?

'Nana?' I called, very softly, frozen suddenly, unable to walk round to the front of the kennel and look in. My relief was tremendous when her dear old sooty head came through the opening, and her half-floppy ears. Glancing up at the sitting-room window to make sure Mother wasn't watching, I threw down my satchel and hugged her, and she beat her tail against the sides of the kennel in a silent greeting. Then I backed off, smoothed down my coat and gymslip, picked off a couple of dog hairs, took my satchel and walked sedately into the house. Nana and I both knew that we must not display too much happiness, otherwise *she* would think of a plan for taking it away. In the kitchen, Maisie was making shortbread, my favourite, and the butterflies almost departed as I smelt the delicious sugary baking smell.

'Where's Mother?' I asked casually, as I washed my hands at the sink.

'Your Mother's poorly, lovie. She's got one of her bad heads.' Maisie nodded towards a medicine bottle with its cork stopper, sitting with a glass and a spoon on a tray covered by a lace doily: calcium lactate, as I came to know it later. 'It's a bad 'un. She can't even swallow that today. You've to be very quiet and settle down to your homework.' She winked at me. 'No piano practice this evening.'

And that's how it went on. Not that night, nor the next

day – when Mother reappeared looking paper-skinned and tired with the dark circles beneath her eyes – nor in the days afterwards, was anything ever said about Nana. I couldn't believe Daddy hadn't seen the dog. It could only mean that he had decided to keep my secret. Dear Daddy. He was my friend and my defender, like all the Knights of the Round Table. I was especially nice to him for at least two weeks after that, plumping up his cushions, laughing at his jokes, handing him his newspaper before he even asked for it. If he noticed, he never said. After a couple of days when I left her outside, Nana and I dared to go back to our routine and life returned to, well, to normal.

When Fred came home and saw the kennel for the first time, he dropped to his knees in horror. 'Nana! How could they?' he breathed, and as soon as he said it I knew I could let him into my secret.

I sat him down and told him what I had been doing every night, and I won't forget the look he gave me when I had finished. *Not bad, for a girl.* He immediately said he would do it, too. He had no choice: she was his dog, after all, and he was a boy; of course he was brave enough! I made him swear not to breathe a word to Beatrice, who couldn't bear any kind of deception. We paced out the routine together, the noisy back-door lock, the floorboards to steer clear of, the creaks on the stairs. His room was closer to the staircase than mine, and further from Mother's, so it wasn't quite so dangerous for him, but of course I knew better than to point this out.

So during school holidays, whenever he was home, Fred took responsibility for Nana; but he was mostly away and it fell to me. It was good for my piano playing because I never missed a practice and got a distinction in Grade Four, which they said I was young to get it. I knew it wasn't a patch on what Miss Blessing had done, but I kept that to myself. Anyway, it was just the way we lived now.

One day at the end of the following Summer, so Nana had been living in the yard for a whole year, I walked her as usual after school, swishing up the Oaks through the dead leaves. It was one of those warm, late afternoons when you think Winter is still a long way off. The sky was pink over the city and I counted, as I had started to do recently, *ten more years and then I can leave home.* It was an age, five times as long again since Our Own Mother died. Mother's grandmother had been French and Beatrice said I looked like her: she had shown me the miniature from Mother's jewellery box, and although I couldn't see any resemblance, I was excited to believe it might be so. If I went to France I would become very good at French indeed. I decided at that moment France would be my escape. Then I remembered Nana, trotting loyally beside me and felt guilty. Of course, I couldn't leave while Nana was with us because I was the only person who could protect her. 'Don't worry, old girl,' I told her. 'I'm not going anywhere for ages and ages.' She looked round at me gratefully and wagged her tail.

I realised we were quite far from home by this time and had almost reached the Arboretum. Suddenly two figures emerged through its gates, girls deep in conversation, and I saw immediately that one of them was Miss Blessing. I waved and quickened my step towards them.

'Hello Annie,' she said. 'What brings you out here?'

I felt suddenly shy, and hesitated a short distance off, fiddling with Nana's lead. She was my teacher, after all; her confessions over the blue shoes and being angry with God somehow made it complicated. But if I was uncertain, Nana was not. She wagged her tail and pulled me forward as if to greet an old friend. And in a moment Miss Blessing seemed to recollect herself; turning to her companion, she said, 'Eddie, this is one of my Sunday School pupils, Annie Lang. Annie, this is my sister.'

I examined Miss Blessing's sister curiously. She was a few years older, but had the same auburn curls, the same direct brown eyes as Mildred and the same sweet smile. 'Hello,' I said.

'Hello, Annie. My sister doesn't know how to introduce us properly. I'm Edwina, but you can call me Eddie if you like.' She held out her hand and I shook it, clumsily, because there wasn't time to remove my glove first. Auntie Vera would have been scandalised, but Eddie Blessing didn't seem to notice.

'We love coming out here,' said Mildred. 'Gives us the chance for a good old gossip.' She turned and smiled at her sister and squeezed her arm.

'Weekdays, we might come here to the Arboretum, and then sometimes at weekends we go to the flicks,' said Edwina.

I looked from one to the other, mystified.

'The pictures,' Mildred translated, seeing I hadn't the faintest idea what they were talking about.

'Oh we *do,*' Edwina said. 'It's our great Saturday-night treat! My, but we live it up!'

I was in awe at the idea of these sisters, arm in arm at the Mapperley Park Essoldo, or whatever it was called. Oh, how free and wonderful their lives must be!

But Edwina had turned her attention to Nana, standing by my side. 'And who is this?' she enquired. 'Please will you introduce us?'

'Oh this is Nana,' I said. 'Nana is my dog, well Fred's originally but mine since he went away to school.'

'Nana!' Edwina bent towards her and held out a hand for inspection. Nana sniffed it and gave it a small polite lick. 'Oh Nana, you are beautiful. You remind me of our dear Wendy.'

Mildred explained, 'We lost our beloved dog last year and our mother is too sad to get another just yet.'

'Nana – Wendy's dog from Peter Pan,' said Edwina. 'That's a coincidence, Millie, isn't it? It must be lovely to have a real Nana to take care of you.'

I breathed in sharply. 'W–well,' I stammered. I suddenly felt breathless. The sisters looked at me. And then, after months of bottling up my horrid secret, the words came tumbling out before I could stop them. 'I – well, she can't, that is, she's not allowed in the house any longer. She has to have a kennel in the yard now – just like Nana in the story.' I bit my lip. No one outside the family knew about Nana's banishment, and no one *inside* ever discussed it.

Both Miss Blessings looked at me with concern. 'She has to live outside all the time?' asked Edwina. 'All Winter? But that's terrible.'

I suddenly felt I had betrayed a family secret. 'Well I suppose lots of dogs live outside,' I said, regretting my indiscretion.

'That's one thing!' cried Edwina. 'But a dog that's grown up a house dog, forced to live out in the cold – it's not right! Goodness me. We'd have her, wouldn't we, Millie? It'd be so good for Mother, wouldn't it?'

Mildred said, 'Steady on, Ed. She's Annie's dog. Annie doesn't want to get rid of her!'

My hand dropped protectively to Nana's head. 'No. That is – I make sure she's all right, you know. I love her very much.'

'Of course you do,' Edwina said. 'But all the same, if things ever get too difficult – she'd find a good home with us. We'd take care of her.'

'Ach, don't listen to her,' Millie interrupted, giving her sister (I noticed) a sharp nudge. 'Anyway, Eddie, you're not even going to be here if Canada comes off! I'm sure Nana can look after herself, can't you, Nana?'

Nana wagged her tail. I wondered what 'Canada' meant, but didn't like to pry. Edwina cast Mildred a sideways look. '*If*,' she muttered.

'Eddie's applying for a teaching job in Canada,' Millie explained. 'She's very modest about it, but I think she's going to get it. We'll miss her terribly.'

Canada. How glamorous! I wanted to tell these beautiful sisters everything; how I had slept in the kennel, just like Wendy's father in Peter Pan, and how I risked my neck to smuggle Nana upstairs at night. But I knew I would do so at my peril; it was something that could never be told. Anyway, it all paled into insignificance beside *Canada*! They would scarcely be interested in my woes. I was suddenly aware that the light was fading fast and there would be more trouble if I stayed out after dark. 'I must go!' I told them. 'They'll be looking for me.'

'Are you all right, Annie? Would you like us to walk home with you?' asked Edwina. 'We could explain to your mother that you met us.'

I thought I saw Mildred shrink back a little and throw her sister an anxious glance, so I guessed she must have had experience of Mother's critical tongue when she took over as harmonium player. The prospect of the two Miss Blessings speaking to Mother seemed somehow impossible; they were my discovery and I didn't want her to spoil them. Besides, I had said too much about my family already. 'That's very kind of you, but really it's quite close by,' I told them, 'I've Nana to protect me.' I tightened the lead. 'Come on, old girl!' Turning back to them, I said, 'Goodbye . . . When I'm older, can I come to the flicks too, please?'

As I left them I realised that it was indeed almost dark and hurried across Mansfield Road and up Elm Avenue, thinking furiously about the adventure I had just had. There was something nagging at me about it, something said or not said . . . I was just on the point of recalling it when I suddenly saw the headline: it was a hoarding outside the paper shop on the corner of Cranmer Street: *City Girl Missing.* I quickened my step. I didn't want them to think I had gone missing, too. As I slipped around to the yard to leave Nana in her kennel, Beatrice came to the back door and stared out at the darkness. I called to her.

'Annie, where have you been?'

'Has Mother said anything?'

'Mother's in the sitting room. Come quickly and wash your hands for tea and with luck she won't notice.'

As I ran upstairs to brush my hair, I thought again about Our Own Mother's French family. I was sure there'd be none of this creeping around, always scared of getting into trouble with *them*! For a start, I bet they weren't Mission people, or have to be saved or get the total immersion the way we did. In France it would be warmer, the light brighter than the Midlands and the houses not red brick. They wouldn't have to eat porridge or tinned pilchards or beetroot, tongue or suet puddings; they would eat – I tried to think what they could eat: garlic on strings from the onion man's bicycle, and big sweet tomatoes because of having more sun than us, and . . . oh yes – I frowned – *white sausages*. It had come up in a *dictée* at school. But I hope I wouldn't have to do that. I thought: ten years till I can leave home! I couldn't wait.

# Part Two

## 1926 and 1932

*From the Nottingham Journal, 1931*

# FRENCH SCHOLAR

## LOCAL GIRL'S SUCCESS IN ALL-ENGLAND EXAM

Unknown to the majority of East Midland people, a Nottingham girl, Miss Annie Lang, younger daughter of Mr and Mrs Harry Lang of Corporation Oaks, came eighth in all England in the competitive examination – the "Grand Concours" for all English Universities – of the Société Nationale des Profésseurs de Français en Angleterre. The first twelve are awarded free courses abroad, and Miss Lang is to study at the University of Bordeaux.

Miss Lang, 17, who, on her return, will be enrolling for a BA in French at University College, Nottingham, is an Old Mundellian where, in addition to gaining her hockey and swimming colours, she took an interest in literary and dramatic work and attained distinction in her Grade 7 piano examination. Her father is Worshipful Master-elect of the Basford Lodge.

# NINE

## *1932*

**Wednesday, June 1**

'You look as if you've been through a hedge backwards,'
Maisie greets me cheerfully, as I heave my suitcase past the
guard at the barrier at the station and out into the booking
hall. 'Heavens, Annie Lang, you've *grown*, my girl!'

I want to hug her, or at least kiss her on both cheeks like
the French do, but we just beam at each other. 'Oh Maisie,
I'm glad it's you!' I say.

She gives me a sideways look. 'Well you know how your
mother is with anything about travel. Sets off her nerves.' It's
probably meant to be an apology, but I don't care that Mother
isn't here to meet me. I need to adjust to one thing at a time.
I make to turn out of the station to the bus stops, but Maisie
pulls me towards the forecourt. 'We've to get a taxi. Mr Lang
said – with the suitcase an' that.'

My eyes widen; this is luxury indeed. 'Yeah, well, business is a bit better these days,' Maisie says, noticing my

expression. 'All over the Midlands, it's starting to pick up. Our Albert's got work. They've been taking people on at Raleigh.'

'Bet they're not eating more *biscuits*, though,' I tease her.

'Makes no difference, Annie. When folk get work they can afford the little luxuries. Oh and your dad's getting a new car!'

'Is he? Shame he didn't come and meet us in it then!'

'Wolseley. It hasn't come yet, but he showed me a picture. My, it's smart. It's a sort of silvery-grey with a black stripe on the side, I don't know what they call them stripes.'

'Will he teach me to drive in it, d'you think?'

Maisie snorts. 'You'll be lucky. Besides, he's that busy, is Mr Lang these days. I tell you, Annie, it's a rare sighting if I catch him coming home before I leave of an evening.'

'Late nights at Roebuck's, is it? That sounds familiar.'

'That and Lodge business, mostly. Oh, and the Mechanics', of course. He's doing a good deal of charity work.'

We have reached the front of the taxi queue and nothing more is said till we're driving up Woodborough Road. Staring out of the windows, I'm thinking that, boom or not – and even on a bright summer day – how grimy and poor the city looks. People on the streets are much paler than the French, sort of suet-coloured. I think about the food in Bordeaux.

'And how's Mother?' I ask at last.

Maisie doesn't reply for a moment. Then she says, 'Oh, Mrs Lang's keeping well enough; her usual self. You know.'

I turn back from the window and look at her. 'How d'you mean?'

'Well . . .' Maisie isn't meeting my gaze. 'She keeps herself busy. She runs a sewing circle at the Mission.'

'And?'

'Well, there's the garden. And her Bible study. She does a lot of Mission work for the Pastor, your grandfather. She does get tired.'

'Does she go and visit Fred?'

Maisie raises her eyes and looks at me now. 'How, d'you mean, duck?'

'Beatrice told me,' I say impatiently. 'You don't need to hide it, Maisie.'

'Mrs Lang said—'

'Yes, I can imagine what she said. There's not nearly enough gets talked about in this family! It's not your fault, Maisie. Beatrice told me last night.'

Maisie sighs. 'That poor lad.' We both think about him for a few moments. She looks as if she wants to say something further. I wait. 'Well, since you ask,' she goes on guardedly, 'Mrs Lang thinks it's better not to disturb him, though your father *would* go . . .'

'But?'

'But Fred won't see him.' Maisie gazes at me, her eyes troubled. 'It's his illness, Annie. Fred's not himself. He told Mr Lang . . .' She falters.

'What did he tell him?'

'Oh,' she shakes her head. 'Some nonsense.'

'Have you been?' I ask her.

She hesitates. Then she gives a little nod. 'I take him a cake sometimes. He used to like my Dundee, and I always say it's got the goodness. Food's grim in that place . . . But I don't let on that I go,' she adds with a warning look.

I reach over and squeeze her hand.

We have arrived at St Ann's Hill and the taxi turns into it, bumping up the cobbles. 'Eeh, Annie, I don't fancy our chances getting that suitcase of yours up the steps,' says Maisie loudly, one eye on the taxi driver.

The driver grins. 'Don't worry, duck, I'd have carried it up for you anyway.'

'There's a nice man for you,' says Maisie, beaming at him. 'And since it's Mr Lang's money, you'll get a nice tip an' all.'

I climb the steps slowly, following the taxi driver: past the ash-pit with its rank-dank smell and up into the yard. Mother's tubs are blooming with summer flowers, nasturtiums, sweet William and little blobs of white alyssum and blue lobelia alternating around the outsides, the way she always plants them. Behind them stands the house, smaller than I remember, its red brick more soot-blackened, its windows dark against the sunshine outside. In the place where Nana's kennel used to be, there's nothing now except a slightly darker rectangle where its frame touched the ground.

I follow Maisie into the scullery. Like the rest of the house, it has shrunk. I hadn't realised how cramped it is, and dark, the small window above the stone sink letting hardly any light through. Perhaps Maisie notices it too, because she says, 'Seems wrong to be bringing you the back way like this; you ought to be walking in the front door.'

I smile. 'Then I'd feel like a visitor,' I say. I lug the suitcase through the breakfast room and out into the hall, stopping from habit to listen for clues. Daddy would not be at home; but Mother? The house is silent, the hall dark and cool, a square of crimson light from the stained glass in the front door falling on the tiles beside the hatstand. I go into the front drawing room; even on this warm afternoon it gives off a chill and, when I enter, there's that smell again, of damp coal dust and something dead rising up through the floorboards from the cellar below: it takes me straight back to that most dread night. Need to break the spell. I tiptoe to the piano. Someone has shut the lid; it was never shut in the olden days. I raise it. The keys look wan and unplayed, yellowing. Poor piano. I sit down, think for a moment whether to disturb the quiet of the house and summon a genie. Then I play, as softly as I can, the first *Arabesque*, my latest passion; I've brought the music home from France but I know it by heart. The piano is flat. Some of the notes are sticking. With Beatrice gone and me gone, there's no one to care. Yet Miss Higgs (for I still think of her as that) is a good pianist. Why doesn't she play? Our own mother would never have let the piano go flat. Our own mother would have met the train. Fred would not have had the 'nervous exhaustion' if our own mother were alive. I play more loudly ... and raise the genie.

'So you're here, Annie!'

My hands fly back from the keys mid-phrase. I jump to my feet. She is standing in the doorway, wearing a long, thin navy dress, by which I mean the shape beneath the dress is thin, her face more angular than ever. Her eyes are like pale stones.

'Just this minute. Hello, Mother.'

'What are you playing?'

'I'm sorry. I hope I didn't disturb you.'

'I don't think I've heard this piece of music.'

'Oh, I'm sorry. It's Debussy. His first *Ara*—'

'Debussy. Yes. I might have known.' She turns away. 'Get that suitcase out of the hall,' she says as she leaves the room.

Daddy comes home at six o'clock, bearing a pork pie and sliced ham.

'... In your honour, Annie! I was over in Melton today. This pie was walking round the pig-sty two days ago, mark my words.'

We eat it with beetroot, lettuce, tomato. I consider offering to make a vinaigrette, but decide it would not be diplomatic on my first evening. Daddy is in a jolly mood. 'Quite brightens up the house, doesn't it, Agnes, having our little Annie home with us again?'

'You're looking a better colour in any case, Annie,' Mother acknowledges.

I smile at her. I would like to have said the same to her, but it wouldn't be true. Mother seems to have aged in the past year, little pouches visible around her mouth and a strained new set to her jaw.

'Annie's blooming!' Daddy says. 'Eighteen years old, eh? Quite the little *Madam-oiselle*! Make lots of friends over there, did you, Annie? Chic young ladies from the university?'

'A few, yes, I did,' I say, hoping I won't have to talk about them. Bordeaux is precious. Bordeaux is mine.

'And your French has come on in leaps and bounds, I expect!'

'I hope so,' I say. 'It was hard at first doing all the classes in French, but when I got the hang of it, it helped a lot.'

'I should hope it did,' Mother remarks drily. 'After all the fuss and expense of going there.'

'Well it was a free place, of course,' Daddy reminds her. 'A scholarship, really. Hats off to our clever girl for getting it!'

I catch the look on Mother's face and swiftly change the subject. 'It was lovely to see Beatrice in London. She met the boat train. I would have been lost without her!'

'How is she?' Daddy asks. 'We haven't seen her since – Whitsun, wasn't it, Agnes?'

'Oh, she's frightfully well,' I tell him. 'Have you noticed she's got awfully—' I'm about to say 'fashionable' or 'smart' or some such, but I think that might not go down too well, so I say, 'Awfully sort of grown-up. She was wearing a very nice frock. She says you have to be neat for work.'

'Of course you do,' Mother agrees. 'She's working with some of the most eminent figures in the country. She's a very fortunate girl.'

'Well, I think they're lucky to have her,' I say. 'I'm sure she's terribly efficient and practical and keeps them all in perfect order.'

'I doubt if they need Beatrice to keep them in order,' Mother remarks. 'They've got first-class minds of their own.'

'You stayed the night there, didn't you?' says Daddy. 'Are her digs all right?'

'She's got quite a decent room and an armchair and a gas fire, and a view over a little park. There was a bird singing out there in the middle of the night. One of the other girls was away so the landlady let me sleep in that room; she was very kind.'

'It sounds expensive,' says Mother. 'Don't you think she'd be better off in the YWCA, Harry?'

'Well . . .' he begins.

I'm kicking myself. 'Oh the room's not all that *big*,' I say hastily. 'It's up in the attic and you have to walk up lots of stairs and . . . and the bathroom's two floors down . . .'

'That'll do, Annie,' Mother says. 'It sounds vertiginous.'

I laugh and throw her a grateful look, but I don't think she was joking.

Then, taking advantage of the softer mood, I breathe in a deep breath and say, 'Um, Beatrice said something about Fred.'

Mother pauses, a forkful of pork pie halfway to her mouth. 'What about him?' She puts down her fork and waits.

'Poor Fred. I understand he's not well.'

'He needs rest. He needs to be left in peace.'

Daddy says, 'He's getting the best possible care.'

'How is he?' I ask. 'Have you seen him, Daddy?'

'I have been in there, yes.' My father stirs his tea vigorously. 'It's – well – it's an old building, of course, but they keep it cheerful.'

I can't resist asking, 'How often do you go?'

'Just the once.' Daddy isn't looking at me.

'They have a very clear policy,' says Mother. 'The doctors firmly believe that he needs to be kept away from his usual surroundings.'

Daddy throws her a glance. 'As your mother says, they've got this idea that it's better not to visit. But I know about it, as well, from the Mechanics', you see.'

'The Mechanics' Institute? What have they got to do with it?'

'Well, we organise a few things for them, outings for some of the patients; and there's a staff choir and we send in visitors, too. It's a lively place, believe it or not. Very forward-looking.'

This is interesting. 'Oh,' I say. 'So it's not bad for *everyone* to have visitors then?'

'Oh ... well, Annie. You can't generalise about these things, of course.'

'But for some patients it's good to have visits from outside, is it?'

'Annie,' Mother cuts in, 'we need to talk about your *arrangements* for the summer. Have you any thoughts of what you intend to do? Because I have several suggestions.'

'Of course, Mother.' I drag my mind away from the subject of Fred. 'Actually, there's one thing: please can I have piano lessons again? I'd like to start working for Grade Eight. Please may I?'

Daddy says, 'I don't see why not, if you can fit it in with your studies, don't you agree, Agnes?'

Mother sighs. 'That's generous of you, Harry.' But turning to me, she says, 'I do hope that now you're home, Annie, you will cease to live to please yourself, as you have been during your lucky year in France, and apply yourself to the good of others.'

'Yes, Mother,' I murmur.

'You will, of course, be visiting Pastor Eames at your earliest opportunity,' she goes on. 'And I took the liberty of suggesting to him that you might share some of my duties visiting the sick. I find it exhausting, and it would do you good to see how some of our congregation have to suffer.'

I take a sip of tea. It's good, strong English tea with fresh milk and I missed it in France. 'I shall be glad to visit the sick,' I tell her. 'And – with your blessing – I should like to start by visiting my sick brother, though not, of course, until after I've been to see Grandfather Eames.'

Mother's eyes narrow.

'Annie . . .' Daddy half-raises his hand towards my arm.

'What I mean, naturally,' I hurry on, 'is that I should like to visit the hospital and ask the nurses and doctors whether they might permit me to see Fred once in a while.' I look from one to the other. 'Do you think, since I've been away for a year, that perhaps I'm not too closely connected to the state of mind that brought on his illness? I would like to *ask* them, at least,' I finish, with what I hope is a placatory glance towards Mother.

There is a short silence. I jump up and go to refill the teapot with boiling water.

'I've been meaning to ask you, Annie,' Mother says as I sit down again. 'As a young person, perhaps you can enlighten me: what kind of world is it we now live in, in which someone who comes *eighth* in a competition should win a scholarship? In my day, eighth was mediocre. Where is the virtue, would you say, in rewarding that?'

'Oh I say, Agnes,' Daddy breaks in. 'She was eighth in All England – out of the whole country!'

'I'm aware, Harry, of what All England means. I'm interested in Annie's opinion.'

She waits.

I stare at my plate. It's Miss Higgs triumphant, as ever. There is no satisfactory answer I can possibly make.

'I'm very thankful to have been given the opportunity,' I mutter at last. It sounds more honest than saying something about God's will, but still horribly lame. 'Imperfect as my achievement was,' I add. I raise my eyes and look at her.

She regards me for a moment. 'Is that the best you can do?'

'Mother, I don't know what you want me to say. I will visit the sick with you. I will do my best.'

And that's all I can remember about coming home. With a single swipe she has reduced me to eight years old again.

# TEN

## *1926*

Of all the trouble I have ever got into with Mother, the most serious was when I was eight years old. I do not like to think about it, but it's what happened next, so I shall write it fast and then it will be over.

I'd been on at Marjorie Bagshaw to let me go with her and her mother to Goose Fair, which is our world-famous three-day fair every Autumn, nothing to do with geese, but there are dodgems and coconut shies and candyfloss and mushy peas. Marjorie's mother said yes, if I had the permission. And Mother said she 'supposed so' as long as I was back by half-past four. I could tell Mother wasn't all that pleased about this outing, probably on account of Marjorie's family not being Saved, but Daddy gave me sixpence and we had a lovely afternoon. Marjorie's older sister Iris came too.

Mrs Bagshaw was a jolly sort of mother and I liked her because she was a bit dramatic. She enjoyed dressing up and for the Fair she was wearing a rather dashing crimson costume with a purple hat. She let us go on the carousel and I chose a black horse with a beautiful blue bridle and many-coloured ribbons to ride on; Marjorie's was white with silver stars in its ears. Iris said she was too old for all that; she'd rather go on the dodgems, which Mrs Bagshaw said she couldn't. Mrs B. hugged us both when we jumped off our horses and ran back to her. It felt funny and I pulled away because we don't do hugging in our family, but immediately I wished I hadn't. There was a man on a tightrope with a long stick walking high in the air between two roofs and we had toffee apples which splintered into smithereens when you crunched into them and you had to stuff your mouth really full in order not to drop it all.

But then a terrible thing happened. While we were concentrating on the tightrope man who was nearly at the end of his walk and had stopped to twizzle the stick over his head, which made him wobble, Mrs Bagshaw suddenly let go of our hands and jerked away and shouted something angrily at the top of her voice. By the time I realised what was happening, she had left us and was plunging through the crowd screaming, 'Stop him! Stop that man – he's stolen my purse!'

Marjorie and I huddled close to Iris and watched in horror as the crowd surged around and swallowed her up. There were shouts and confusion and a policeman blowing a whistle and when Mrs Bagshaw reappeared her eyes were blazing angry and we had to go to the Station and it was all the most enormous fuss, quite exciting at first. I tried to tell them I didn't see anything because I was watching the man on the high wire, but no one seemed interested. Iris stayed with her mother but Marjorie and I were sent outside into the corridor where people were hurrying up and down with important-looking notebooks and files. There must have been all sorts of crimes committed at Goose Fair because the police station was crowded to bursting. After a while, a man in handcuffs was bundled up the corridor and taken into the room where Mrs Bagshaw and Iris were talking to the constable. Marjorie dug me in the ribs: 'Look, that must be him!' she whispered excitedly.

But watching the clock above the desk, I saw with alarm that time was passing at great speed.

I tugged at her sleeve. 'Marjorie, I've got to go. Mother said to be back at half-past four.'

'Well you can't go, can you? Mam's in with the constable.'

'D'you think she'll be coming soon?'

'I don't know, do I?'

'Shall we ask that man behind the desk?'

'Give over, Annie. Your mother can't mind – it's not your fault if you're late home.'

But I knew better. I began to wish I'd never come. Before my horrified eyes, the hands of the clock positively whizzed towards half-past four; I swear I could see them moving.

At about quarter-past, my prayers were answered when the door of the inner room finally opened and Mrs Bagshaw came out, looking grim. Iris was grinning from ear to ear. 'They've got him!' she announced.

'I hope he goes to prison for a long time for that,' said Mrs Bagshaw tartly.

'Was it him that we saw, then?' Marjorie asked.

Mrs Bagshaw waved her purse in triumph. 'Look girls, the power of the law!'

'That's wonderful!' I said. 'Mrs B—'

'So now, girls, we celebrate! Let's go and have tea.'

I was jumping from foot to foot. 'Mrs Bagshaw, I've got to be home at four-thirty. Mother said!'

'Nonsense!' replied Marjorie's mother. 'You're not going

anywhere. Your afternoon's been spoiled and now I'm going to make amends.'

'But—' I wailed.

Iris, who had been watching me closely, turned to her mother. 'Better get her home, Ma. That stepmother of hers is a right dragon, so I've heard.'

I nodded gratefully. But Mrs Bagshaw was having none of it. She stopped and looked at me a moment, taking in my distress. 'Little Annie,' she said seriously, 'that stepmother of yours will just have to wait for once. Don't fret yourself. I'll explain it all to her.'

So we went for tea at Jessops and had fingers of buttered toast, my favourite, but it stuck in my throat because I could just imagine Mother pacing the floor at home. True to her word, Mrs Bagshaw came with me to the front door in Corporation Oaks. Saturday was Maisie's day off, so it was Elsie who answered the doorbell, her face a picture of dismay. Over her shoulder I could see the grandfather clock in the hall: it was half-past five.

'Please can I speak to Mrs Lang?' Mrs Bagshaw asked. She had a new sort of voice on – determined. 'I know Annie's a little late home, but we had a mishap and I can explain everything!'

Elsie shook her head, her eyes shining with anxiety. 'I'm so sorry, ma'am. Mrs Lang has gone out to her Women's Fellowship Meeting and won't be back till eight.'

'What about Mr Lang then?'

'He's not home yet,' replied Elsie. 'He's at the Works,' which is what they sometimes called the Biscuit Factory.

Mrs Bagshaw turned to me. 'Well, Annie, you'll have to explain it to them yourself, lovie. You must tell them they can talk to me if they like. You know where we live.' Turning to Elsie, she drew herself up and said, 'I shall write Mrs Lang a note to inform her I have been the victim of a felony this afternoon at Goose Fair, though I am happy to say that the thief was apprehended and my purse restored. You must please tell your mistress that we have been detained at the Police Station where the pickpocket was under arrest.'

'I'm very glad to hear you had a happy outcome,' Elsie told her. 'But I must tell you that Mrs Lang is extremely angry with our Annie for being late and I fear there will be consequences.'

I burst into tears.

'This is nonsense!' protested Mrs Bagshaw. 'The child is absolutely not at fault. She had no choice but to come with us to the Station. There was nothing else for it.' She snapped open her handbag and took out a pencil and a piece of paper, which she tore from a small notebook. Elsie invited her in and fetched her the pastry board to rest on, and Mrs Bagshaw wrote the note – it was very short – and folded it.

Iris was shifting from foot to foot, looking uneasy. 'Didn't you ought to say a bit more than that, Mam?' she asked.

Mrs Bagshaw hesitated. Then she handed the note to Elsie and said, 'Please tell Mrs Lang, she can apply to me if she wants the details.' And so saying, she turned on her heel and took Marjorie by the hand. I was still snivelling on the doorstep when Iris turned and gave me a look as they strode towards the garden gate. It said, *I'm really sorry about my mother, Annie. If it were down to me this wouldn't have happened.* For a moment my heart went out to Iris Bagshaw, but then the garden gate clicked, and they were gone.

Elsie sighed and patted my shoulder. 'Come on in, duckie. I'll do me best with 'er, but I'm out tonight – it's my sister's birthday.'

'Tell my dad, Elsie, please,' I begged.

'I will,' she replied sourly. 'If he's home at any respectable hour. Come on, ducks, I'll do you a boiled egg.'

Mother said, 'Take your hands out of your pockets, girl.'

I did so. They were shaking and I put them behind my back so she wouldn't see.

'What's that in your pocket? What have you got in there?'

I looked up at her. 'Nothing, Mother.'

'Don't be insolent. It can't be "nothing".'

It was in fact Little Sid. I put my hand back in my pocket and pulled him out to show her.

'That disgusting bear. I might have known.'

'He's a panda,' I whispered, keeping my voice as quiet as possible for the politeness.

'Give it to me.'

I did not want to give her Little Sid.

'Give it, Annie!' She held out her hand.

I hesitated. 'Please', I said. 'Don't do anything with him, Mother.' I held him out to her. I had no choice.

'You're far too old for something like this.' She took him as though he was a mouldy sandwich. I looked at him fiercely in her pale hand, willing him not to come to harm.

'Can I explain to you?' It was the second time I had tried to do this.

'No.'

'Mrs Bagshaw had a—'

'I said *no*. Do I have to tell you again?'

It was ten past eight. Elsie had left as soon as Mother came home. I heard her say, 'You want to read this, Mrs Lang. Mrs Bagshaw's left a note explaining about our Annie.' But Mother had pushed it away without looking at it and Daddy had still not returned. Beatrice was at choir practice.

'Mother, I couldn't help it.'

'I'm not interested. You broke your word. That's like breaking a promise to God.'

'But God *knows* I didn't!' I insisted. 'God knows everything!'

'Don't you try and tell me about Our Lord, my girl. Follow me.' She turned and stalked along the hall. She had reached the cellar door before I realised where this was leading.

My hand shot into my pocket, but Little Sid, my comfort and protector, was no longer there, of course. 'No!' I pleaded. I shrank back but Mother grabbed me by the neck of my cardigan.

'*Yes.*'

'I can't!'

'No such thing as *can't.*' She tweaked me upright, still holding on with her right hand while her left unlocked the door to the cellar head.

'*In.*'

I was shaking uncontrollably. 'No, Mother. Please, Mother. Please don't.'

'Oh don't be so feeble!' She pushed me on to the top step where the jars and bottles were stacked along the shelf. 'If you don't want to be punished, you must think ahead about the consequences of disobedience. It's all so simple. An *intelligent* child would have worked it out.' And so saying, she closed the door firmly and locked it. I heard her hard shoes clacking along the hall.

First, I did that pointless thing that heroines do in books: I tried the door and rattled the doorknob furiously. Of course it did not open. Then I sank down on to the step and clasped my arms around my knees, burying my nose and eyes into the folds of my skirt to blot out the spidery darkness. I knew all too well that the light switch was on the outside. The dank reek of the cellar smothered me like a blanket. As my head stilled, I began to hear the sounds of it, too, a dripping and a pattering on the gritty black floor somewhere deep below. Straining my eyes, I tried to make out the bottom of the cellar, a place I had never been. For all I knew, the steps on which I was sitting could have gone down and down to hell itself, a hell not of flames, which might at least have been cosier, but a bottomless stinking clammy pit, full of the ghosts that Elsie had spoken of. I felt in my pocket again for Little Sid. But Little Sid's gone, stupid. *She* made sure to take him off you first. And a great howl came from someone that I barely recognised as me, and sobs and screams that at last spilled out from all the times I had had to bite my tongue and not answer back, and the rage and the sorrow and, yes, the awful *S-P*, too, of course. I don't know how long it lasted, but when it was done I did feel somehow – it sounds funny to say it – *cleaner*.

For a while I sat without moving, listening in the blackness for whether she might have realised what a terrible thing she had done, and relented and come to get me. I tried the door again, but it was still locked. And that's when I became aware of something else, a greyness, a different, lighter place in the gloom. It was when I turned my head to find its source that a *something* brushed my cheek. I screamed again, thinking it would suffocate me, stuffing my knuckles into my mouth to keep the Thing out. Then I spoke to myself sternly, like Mother Miss Higgs spoke to me. *Don't be ridiculous, girl, it's just a spider's web.* Fred had told me spiders were our friends. He never killed them. He fetched a glass and slid a postcard beneath and carried them gently out into the garden. Then I remembered Robert the Bruce and the spider, which we'd been told about in Transition class during needlework. All this I tried to think of very calmly, knowing at the same time that the only person who was going to look after me was *me* myself. Not Daddy. Not Beatrice or Fred. Not Our Own Mother, who was just dead and miles away in Heaven. Certainly not God, who was the God of Miss Higgs, not the God of little children or nice people; all these things rushed through my mind at once, jumbled up, not clear as I write them now. I closed my fingers carefully around the back of my neck to keep the spiders out; friends they might be, but there was a limit.

Little by little, my breathing slowed and I remembered the greyness again. Trying not to move my head in case of spidery fingers, I searched the void with my eyes wide and found it; I should say I felt it first, because I gradually realised there was a draught of clean air coming from somewhere. Further along the shelf, where the jars and bottles sat, I could now make out a grille I'd never noticed before in my occasional errands to the cellar; and the grille was a window without glass. It must have been two feet long and about nine inches high protected with iron bars, and if I moved towards it, I could breathe without the sulphurous fumes of coke dust. And there was light, too, from a gas lamp out on St Ann's Hill; if I strained my eyes I fancied I could see shapes out in the yard. The tiny link to home made me feel better ... yet – what was I thinking of? – this terrifying prison *was* my home. I moved gingerly along the step in the darkness towards a place where I could sit with the draught on my face and tried to blot out everything else.

Amazingly, I must have slept, because I definitely know I woke up. How much later it was I have no idea, but it felt like the very dead of night; my body ached with being scrunched up as tight as possible and with a seeping cold that I had never felt before, colder even than Nana's kennel. For a few moments I thought I had wakened in a nightmare, and hoped I was really still asleep; when it was obvious that I wasn't, the terror returned. But then I realised it was a noise that must have woken me because I heard it again: a kind of whimpering, grunting, breathing – ghosts in the darkness; devils from the void. I gulped a mouthful of air to scream, but something stopped me: the sounds weren't coming from the depths below but from the window grille. I lurched to my feet, clasping the edge of the shelf for support, and peered out, but what I saw there is something I cannot explain. Silhouetted in the lamplight, half hidden behind a jar of pickled onions, close up against the grille itself, I saw . . . feet. I looked again. There seemed to be two of them – I strained my neck around the onions – no, *four*: two had ankles, two were covered in trousers. They seemed to be facing in different directions and not in two pairs, as you might expect, but muddled up and shuffling around. This was extraordinary. My first thought was to reach through the grille and poke my fingers at the feet to let them know I was here. Whoever it was, they must be people who could ring the doorbell and tell Daddy to set me free. I wiggled my hand up to the grille and tried to stick my fingers through, but the space was too narrow and I could only reach as far as the joint on my middle finger. There was nothing for it: I would have to shout at them and risk waking Mother. But suddenly the feet began to move more definitely, swaying and staggering, and the moving went with the noises, which had started again and were louder now and not like human noises, except suddenly there was a sob and groaning, which was very human indeed. Then it was just noises again and I couldn't tell what they were. One of the feet was now so close to the grille that I could almost touch it, and it was at that point I recognised them: the blue shoes.

By what magic I got out of that place, I can scarcely repeat: it seems too peculiar. My only explanation is that the vision of Miss Mildred Blessing's Sunday Best shoes at the dead of an Autumn night set my mind on such a crazy journey that I thought I must be caught in a dream, and in the way of dreams I decided I must therefore not be locked in the cellar after all. Stiffly on cramped legs, I clambered the three steps to the door and turned the handle again. When it opened, dream or not, I had to stifle a sob of surprise and relief. I groped my way, half crawling, along the hall, up the stairs and at last into my bedroom. I lay shivering in bed in the dark, covered with every jumper and eiderdown I could lay my hands on, for the cold was real enough, and thought back over what had happened. I knew with absolute certainty I had tried the door when Mother shut me in, and later too: it had been locked.

As I eventually began to warm up and was finally able to fall asleep, I fancy I heard someone creeping up the stairs and past my bedroom door. But whether I really did, or just dreamed I did, I do not know.

# ELEVEN

## *1926*

Elsie had to wake me in the morning.

'Annie!' She was shaking me. 'You'll be late for Mission, duckie. I've called you three times!'

I sat up with a jolt. 'Oh no!'

'Yer all right, if you hurry; Beatrice and your mother went out early.'

I stared at her, trying to take this in. I was still half asleep.

'Come on, Annie. I've your porridge on the stove. Blessed if I know what's got into you this morning.'

She left the room and I swung my feet to the floor. There, facing me on the bedside table, sat Little Sid. With a cry I snatched him up and cuddled him. How did he come to be there? Had *she* put him there last night? If so, why hadn't I seen him when I came to bed? I stood up unsteadily. Could it be . . . that none of this had *ever happened*? Had it really been a nightmare? Mother, Little Sid, the cellar, the door locked and mysteriously unlocked, everything?

And the *blue shoes* out in our yard?

I tottered over to the washstand and poured water into the bowl – dear Elsie, she had brought me warm water today. Splaying my fingers over the surface I looked at my nails, no more than averagely dirty. But when I turned my hands over, I thought I could distinctly see a few clinging specks of coal grit from the cellar windowsill and a fragment of something that might have been a spider's web. I lifted the palms to my nose and sniffed – and, yes, the musty reek of the cellar, of damp and coke dust, was there, unmistakably. This slender evidence was peculiarly comforting: perhaps I was not going mad.

Nothing further was said about my late return from Goose Fair. I did try to explain to Daddy, because I couldn't bear the thought that he would blame me. The conversation went something like this:

ME: Daddy, can I talk to you about Goose Fair?
DADDY: *[reading the paper]* Hmm.
ME: Daddy, I'm sorry to disturb you but you probably heard I was late back.
DADDY: Were you, Annie? That wasn't very good, was it?
ME: Well, we had some trouble. I couldn't get home because we were at the police station.
    *[I pause for effect]*
*Without looking up from his paper, Daddy says:* Oh, I see.
ME: Mrs Bagshaw had her purse stolen by a pickpocket.
    *[Daddy stops reading at that point]*
    . . . But she shouted out and chased him through the crowd and a police constable arrived and they got him and we had to go to the Station. But there were lots of crimes and all these people and

we had to wait ages. And I said to Mrs Bagshaw that I was afraid I would be late, and she said you leave that to me, I'll explain. Only Mother was out and she didn't read Mrs Bagshaw's note and... [*I pause guiltily. I have not mentioned tea at Jessops.*] And Mother was cross and she said I'd let her down, only I didn't mean to.

*I stare at him anxiously. I'm wondering whether to tell him about the cellar, but something stops me. I'm not sure why, but I can't say it. Maybe the Cellar didn't happen. And as for the blue shoes . . .*

Daddy looked at me for a moment and then he took a deep breath. 'Annie, why are you telling me all this?'

I felt panicky and helpless. If he didn't understand, how could I explain? Maybe I wanted to tell him, *Because I want you to know how horrible Mother is,* but you can't say things like that. 'I didn't want you to think I'd broken my promise,' I said at last. It was a sort of whisper.

He thought about this. Then he went back to his paper. 'It's all right, Annie. You can run along now.' I stayed where I was for a moment, staring at the headline at the spot where his face had been: *Second Girl Goes Missing,* it said (but I only remembered that later). I really needed him to say something more, or maybe just give me a hug. But he was deep in the paper again. It was as if we hadn't spoken. I stood up and softly left the room.

After that, I had a sort of dread feeling in my stomach. Everything felt upside down. I terribly needed someone to tell me that they understood, they had made a mistake and it wasn't my fault; but no one spoke of it. Although I knew I hadn't, I felt I had done wrong and I was ashamed.

On the Monday morning, Marjorie Bagshaw said, 'My mam wants to know, was your mother all right about Goose Fair, then?'

'She was angry,' I said.

'And? Did she read the note Mam left?'

'I didn't see her read it, no.'

'So what happened? Were you punished?'

'Yes.'

'Oh no! What did she do?'

I fiddled with the lid of my pencil case. I still don't understand why I just couldn't say, *Well actually she shut me in the cellar and locked the door and I was there half the night.* It sounded unreal and unbelievably dramatic. Marjorie'd think I was making it up. I mumbled, 'She took my teddy away.'

'Took your teddy? Did you get him back?'

'Afterwards, yes.'

'Well that was all right then, wasn't it.'

'S'pose so.'

She didn't ask me anything else, and I didn't tell her.

But the dread feeling lingered. I couldn't face being alone with Mother and would make an excuse and leave the room whenever I could. I was longing to talk about *it,* but terrified of talking to *her.* I felt I was being squeezed until I couldn't breathe properly. That night and the next, I stopped going downstairs for Nana. I had lost all my courage. Walking her round and round the reservoir at the top of the Oaks one mild afternoon after school, I whispered the whole story to her. We met a lady in a fox fur who luckily I didn't know, and I had to bend down and pretend to adjust the lead on Nana's collar so the lady wouldn't see how much I was crying. Then I put my arms round Nana's neck and sobbed. I told her why I'd stopped going down to get her at night-time. I told her I loved her just as much and begged her to understand. Nana leaned against me. We stayed like that a long time.

After a couple of days, Beatrice noticed something was up.

'You're looking peaky,' she said. 'What's the matter?'

I took a shaky breath and tried to tell her. When we got to the bit about the cellar, she stared at me, appalled. 'I can't believe this. You're saying she locked you down there. Are you sure you're not making this up?'

'It seems impossible now, Bea, but it happened, I promise. I tried the door,' I told her. 'You were at choir. Daddy was out.'

'Daddy's always out!' she said.

'She locked the door. I swear to God—'

'You mustn't say that,' she flashed. 'It's blasphemous.'

'I'm sorry. But she did lock the door. I was down there hours.'

'How'd'you get out, then?'

'I fell asleep in the end. When I woke up the door had been ... unlocked.'

Beatrice looked at me warily. 'How d'you mean the door was unlocked – did some fairy come and unlock it? Are you sure you didn't dream the whole thing, Annie?'

I shook my head desperately. 'Beatrice, I swear – she must have thought better of it and come down and unlocked the door in the night or something, and not told me.' *Because she's evil*, I added silently, but you can't say things like that to my sister.

Beatrice was shaking her head. 'I'm sorry. It doesn't make sense. Why wouldn't she tell you? I don't know what to believe.'

And that was the end of that, really, except I did tell one person: I told Fred when he came home for the holidays. Fred knew how I felt about Miss Higgs and he felt the same, so I knew I could tell him what had happened in the cellar because he would believe me and would keep it to himself. And I just sort of went on and told him about the blue shoes as well, though I didn't think he'd be interested. But Fred listened carefully, which was not like him as a rule. Later that day he came back from the Oaks with Nana. I was cleaning my boots on the back doorstep. Fred walked past me into the kitchen, and seeing no one was around, he came back and sat beside me on the step.

'I've been thinking about that Thing,' he said after a few moments.

I knew immediately what he was talking about. I turned and looked at him, but he was staring straight ahead. 'About the cellar?' I whispered.

'Yeah. About the blue shoes.'

I waited, a blob of black polish poised to rub into the toe of my boot. Fred said softly: '"The curious incident of the dog in the night-time".'

'What?'

'Hang on a sec.' He jumped up and ran into the house again, returning a few moments later with a book.

'Sherlock Holmes,' he explained. 'Have you read it?'

'Fred, you know we're not allowed.'

'I read it at school,' said Fred softly. 'There's this story about a racehorse which goes missing. And Sherlock Holmes, who – as I'm sure you know – is a *very* clever detective, solves the mystery immediately, because he notices that on the night of the disappearance the dog that lives in the stable *doesn't bark*. Listen—' He found the place. 'The racehorse owner asks what's on his mind, and Holmes replies:

". . . The curious incident of the dog in the night-time."
    "The dog did nothing in the night-time."

"That was the curious incident," remarked Sherlock Holmes."'

Fred looked up triumphantly. 'What does that tell you, Annie?'

'I dunno.' What was he on about?

'*Think!*' His voice had dropped to a whisper. 'Nana was in her kennel, wasn't she? If Miss Blessing was in our yard outside the cellar, Nana would have heard her.'

I hadn't thought of this. Nana had become an excellent guard dog since being banished from the house. She barked at the dogs down in the street, the cats on the neighbours' walls and everyone who came to the back door. A familiar sense of unease started to well up from my stomach. If Nana hadn't barked, maybe I *had* imagined it after all. 'So what are you saying?' I hissed. 'You think she wasn't here? That I'm making it up?' I felt I might faint if not even my own brother could believe it.

'You might be making it up,' said Fred lightly. 'But there's also another explanation.' He laid his hand on my arm for a moment. 'Listen. In the story, Sherlock Holmes realises that the person who stole the racehorse must be someone the dog *knew*, because it didn't bark when the thief entered the stable.'

I thought about my night in the kennel when Nana didn't bark at the burglar. 'So?'

Nana, hearing her name, had wandered over to Fred and stood listening with her head on one side. 'So Nana must know whoever was in our yard. The person must have been here other times, too. Eh, Nana? Isn't that right, old girl?'

'But she doesn't. She hasn't! Miss Blessing's never been here. Why would she be in our yard at all, Fred? That's what I can't understand.' Then even as I said this, I remembered how when we met Mildred Blessing and her sister near the

Arboretum that time, Nana had gone up to her, wagging her tail almost as if they were old friends. That was the thing I was trying to recall afterwards, the odd thing about our meeting. I reached out and stroked one of her floppy ears. Nana knew everything: the dog that didn't bark in the night.

But comforting as it was to know that Fred took my strange vision seriously, this did little to get rid of the Dread. I felt I was in a small dark box. Everywhere I turned, there was silence and nothing. If I cried out, my voice came back to me in a whisper. Lying in bed at night, I tried to tell my real mother about it, but I couldn't get near her. Heaven was just too far away and smothered in foggy clouds, like the sausages of cotton wool in the top of the milk of magnesia tablets. So instead I began to make up stories about things that were going to happen to Miss Higgs, as I had gone back to calling her. They were terrible things. At first, they were about witches and evil demons dragging her into the burning fiery furnace like Shadrach, Meshach, and Abednego. But that didn't work because, of course, Shadrach, Meshach and Abednego didn't burn in the furnace on account of being delivered by Our Lord; Miss Higgs was a very devout Christian so presumably He would deliver her, too. Next, my mind turned towards things that were more practical, like putting glass in her dumplings, so she wouldn't realise it until the dumplings were digested and the glass ripped up her insides. Or I read that you could kill people by dropping ball bearings on a staircase and the person would tumble down to the bottom and die. We didn't have any ball bearings, except in my skipping rope, but we did have silver balls that Maisie used for decorating the Christmas cake, and in my mind it would be the perfect crime because the silver balls could have fallen by accident. Why, if you timed it right, you could even *eat* the murder weapon afterwards! I tried taking a couple of silver balls out into the yard and treading on them experimentally, but they squished under my boots so that was no good. Next I considered turning on the gas taps and then leaving her alone in the kitchen, but when I tried it on the quiet, the gas came out with a sinister popping hiss and the reek of it was so strong that I knew she'd smell it before it did her any harm. So after considering all these things darkly in my heart at night, I decided the only thing would be for me to expose her in her True Colours and I began to watch, and to plot, how this might be achieved.

Days passed, and Miss Higgs did nothing. She must have been minding her Ps and Qs. We circled around each other politely. She even tested me on my G. K. Chesterton without making any reference to the fact that he was a 'Papist', which is what she had said last year. However, this display of good behaviour on all sides made me feel no better, and again the box enclosed me. One night after supper when Beatrice and I were knitting blanket squares for Auntie Francie's mission in Tai Yuan-Fu, I could bear it no longer.

'Beatrice,' I said. 'D'you think Mother is really Saved?'

Beatrice replied that yes of course she was, because she had had the total immersion and entered into His kingdom.

I said darkly, 'I don't think Jesus would have done what Miss Higgs did.'

'Mother,' Beatrice corrected.

'She's not our mother. I'm going to call her Miss Higgs from now on.'

'She is our father's wife, Annie. We call her Mother.'

We knitted in silence for a few minutes. 'Anyway,' I went on. 'I don't think Jesus would have done it. It was a cruel thing to shut a child in the cellar.'

Beatrice looked up sharply over her spectacles. 'What have I told you about the *S-P*?' She reached across to jab me in the ribs with her knitting needle, but I dodged.

'I don't care,' I retorted. 'I'm just saying the truth.'

'Well we know the truth now, so you don't need to go on about it.'

'You still don't believe it happened, do you?'

'I do if you say so.'

This was not good enough. If I couldn't even make Beatrice see the truth, how was I to open the eyes of Daddy and The World? I cast around desperately for something to say that would convince my sister. I needed bruises. I needed scars. I needed proof. When Beatrice went for more wool, I stabbed myself experimentally with the knitting needle, but I was too scared to do it properly. I ought to have hurled myself down the cellar steps to the bottom and been discovered half dead next morning by Nana, briefly allowed into the house to search for me. Nana could have saved me, condemned Miss Higgs and won her way back into the household at a stroke. I realised I had missed an opportunity.

But then I remembered there was still something I hadn't told Beatrice. Sticking my needles into the blanket squares and letting them fall to the floor, I began to explain what I'd seen through the grille at the cellar head, finishing with the blue shoes of Miss Mildred Blessing. I knew this was a detail too ludicrous to make her believe in the rest of it, but the suffocating feeling was rising up inside me demanding to be let out. As I finished, I shrank away from my sister and examined the white bits in my thumbnails, waiting for the torrent of derision that must surely follow. But there was silence. After a few moments I raised my head and looked at her.

Beatrice was sitting with her needles in mid-air staring at me fixedly. She had gone as white as a sheet and I saw that at last, and for the first time, I had her full attention. Laying the knitting aside, she breathed, 'Who have you told about this?'

'No one.' I shook my head. 'I've told nobody.'

'You said nothing to Daddy?'

'I told him about being late from Goose Fair and tried to explain it wasn't my fault, and why.'

'Did you tell him about the cellar?'

'No. He didn't want to hear any of it anyway. He wasn't interested.'

'You said nothing about Miss Blessing?'

'Of course not! Miss Blessing in our back yard in the middle of the night? – I could scarcely believe it myself, Bea. I thought maybe I dreamed it, but I didn't. I *didn't*.'

'Shut up!' Beatrice leaned forward and put her fingers on my mouth. 'I never said you did.' She was silent again. Then, in a little voice I barely recognised as hers, 'Annie, I'm scared.'

I was so surprised by this, I didn't know what to say. 'Why?' I asked.

Beatrice said nothing. She was suddenly looking at her knitting very carefully. 'I don't know.' After a moment, I saw a large tear drop on to her clenched hands. She wiped it away. 'Annie,' she whispered fiercely. 'You're to tell no one about this.'

'About Miss Blessing, you mean?'

'Don't even say her name in this house, not to Mother, or Daddy or anyone.'

'Why not?'

'Or Marjorie Bagshaw. You didn't tell *her*, did you?'

'She's no idea who Miss Blessing is. I didn't tell her anything.'

'Well, *don't*.'

I shook my head. But I was still waiting for an explanation.

When none came, I asked, 'Miss Blessing's not a bad person, Bea, is she? She's our teacher!'

'I'm not saying she's bad. We've just got to not talk about her. I mean it, Annie.' She looked at me fiercely.

'All right. But I wish you'd tell me why.'

'I can't. It's a secret. Well, I don't know really. I just know we mustn't.'

A sudden thought popped out before I could stop it. 'It's nothing to do with Roebuck's Biscuits being in trouble, is it?'

Beatrice looked at me with her what-on-earth-are-you-on-about face. 'Why ever would it be?'

'Dunno.' I shrugged. I didn't know why I'd said it. 'Except that's a secret too, isn't it? We're not supposed to know that's why Daddy has to keep coming home so late.'

Bea's face relaxed. She wiped her tears. 'Yes, that's a secret, too. But I promise you . . .' She stared hard at me again. 'There is absolutely no connection between Roebuck's Biscuits and Miss Blessing. D'you understand?'

I said I did, but I didn't. What on earth was the secret, then, about Miss Mildred Blessing?

# TWELVE

## *1932*

### Thursday, June 9

Just over a week after my return from France, I'm walking through the iron gates of Mapperley Hospital, past a sort of cottage, which is the gatehouse where I give my name to a person in uniform, and up a wide driveway towards a large Victorian gothic red-brick building. I'm clutching a paper bag full of grapes, which is already going soggy. The main building has three floors and there's a tower, four storeys with a steep roof and a turret higher still, topped by four small pillars. It ought to have bells in it, and I wonder if it has. I'm doing this, counting the storeys and the pillars, to take my mind off what's ahead. I have been approved by Sister Bellamy, who seems to be a very important person, and at last I'm going to see Fred. Maisie (who knows everything) told me who to write to, and almost by return a note came back informing me that if I attended between half-past one and two-fifteen any weekday, I would be able to visit him. But will Fred want to see me? The fact he won't see Daddy suggests his mind is very disturbed. Mother has kept me on a tight rein of sewing circle and sick-visiting, but here I am at last: eight whole days since I got home. With so many questions to which I need answers, this delay is hugely annoying.

I reach the front door, which is under an arch, and ring the bell, a long lever with a handle that sets off a jangling somewhere inside. After a minute, the door is opened by a nurse in a cream uniform and a complicated cap. She looks at me expectantly and I hand her Sister Bellamy's note.

She stands back and I edge past her solid apron into a wide hall with maroon and grey tiles and stained glass. There's a large fireplace with a polished copper jug standing in the hearth.

'Wait here,' instructs the nurse. She wheels around with a jangle of keys and sails away, holding the precious note before her: the note that opens doors.

The hall is cool. Well, no, it isn't cool; there's a creeping chill despite the summer sun outside. Somewhere in the interior, a bell rings. I become aware of a distant clatter of knives and forks and the mixed smells of cauliflower and carbolic. Five minutes pass; it seems like an hour. I nibble a grape and rub at the goosebumps on my arms. A cleaner comes through the hall. She's wearing a shapeless grey smock and carries a mop and bucket.

'Yer all right, duck?' she asks. 'Did you get to Goose Fair?'

'Not yet,' I say, laughing. 'It's in November, isn't it?'

'Aye, but it *was,* though.' She shakes her head. 'And them meat pies. I haven't been since 1919, of course. Too busy, you see, in here. Me mam threw me out for it. But I were a good girl really.'

I look at her again, a small woman with bright brown eyes. She could be thirty-nine? Fifty? I'm no good at ages.

'Said he'd only just been discharged from the army. Never clapped eyes on him since,' she says. 'Have *you*?'

I wonder if they've forgotten me and am on the point of asking her if she knows Sister Bellamy, but there's something . . . Anyway, at that point the nurse returns. 'Run along, Carrington. Don't go bothering the visitors.' Then, turning to me, 'You may follow me now.'

She flaps off down a long corridor, cap bobbing dangerously on the back of her head and her formidable apron creaking in the draught. I can barely keep up. We turn down two side corridors, past a poor soul in a grey shift like Carrington's, on her knees silently polishing the tiles. 'Let you loose with the jumbo, did they, Bennett?' the nurse calls to her as we swish past. I'm wondering if I'll ever find my way out, when she turns abruptly up a flight of stairs and pauses at a brown-panelled door at the top. Deep in the bowels of the building, another bell rings.

We enter a bare room with brown lino on the floor, the bottom half of the walls painted brown, the top half sludgy green. There are some wooden benches and a few scattered Windsor chairs, three of which are occupied by people who, I imagine from their identical baggy suits, must be Fred's fellow patients. They glance up as we enter, then two look away again and the third, a pale middle-aged man, continues to stare. A vase of cornflowers on a table in the centre gives the room a welcome splash of colour. My nurse goes to an open door on the far side and shouts, 'Lang. Visitor.' I follow her, as much to avoid the staring man as out of curiosity. Peering around her headgear, I can see a large dormitory with beds up each side, a small locker and a chair beside each, perhaps twenty beds in all. From the far end, a figure stands, raising his arm like a schoolboy in class, eager not to be passed over. He is halfway down the room, hurrying but shambling in his grey uniform, before I recognise that it is really Fred. His hair is short, shaven high above his ears. His face, pale with dark circles beneath watery blue eyes, has bones and hollows I have never seen before. My heart cries for him.

'Fred.'

'Annie! You're here? You're really back?'

I cannot stop myself: I throw my arms around him and hug him tight, partly (I admit) so he can't see me weeping. 'I've come to see you,' I mumble unnecessarily.

'Oh Annie,' he says. 'You don't belong in this place.'

I pull back and look at him. 'I'm not sure you do, either.' I don't care if he sees I'm crying.

He grins ruefully. 'Oh, I belong all right. If only ... But it's so odd to see you here. I can't believe you're real!'

I take his hand and lead him to a bench. We sit down. Like so many things since my homecoming, he seems to have shrunk.

'Twenty minutes,' says the nurse. I've forgotten about her. 'And don't upset him. I'll be back.' She hands me Sister Bellamy's precious note and leaves the room. I glance around for signs of a member of staff on the ward – not that the still figures dotted around the room would seem to pose much of a threat. There is just one: a male attendant sitting at a desk in the corner, apparently writing notes. He pays us no attention.

At first it's easy. I chatter away about France, trying to keep my voice low. I tell Fred Maisie helped me arrange the visit, told me what to do. 'But they seem fine about visiting. Mother and Daddy said the hospital don't like it, but the Sister was all right.'

'Of course that's what they *say*.' He's nodding vehemently.

'All part of the plan, Annie. After all. After all . . . what's a nice boy from a nice family doing in a place like this? Lock him away, I say! Oh, if only. . .'

He's not bothering to lower his voice. One of the figures on a nearby chair grunts in agreement.

Fred's anger is disquieting. 'I thought there was a rule here that visits are upsetting for patients – for the people in here,' I tell him softly. 'But that doesn't seem to be the case for *you*.'

'Why would it be? It's not upsetting for anyone *here*, is it, Mr Soames?' he calls over to the attendant in the corner. 'It's upsetting for Mr and Mrs Harry Lang, worshipful Grand Master of the Basford Lodge! A mad son! How perfectly frightful!'

The attendant in the corner glances up and says, 'Quieten down, lad,' but Fred is in full flood. 'That is, ladies and gentlemen, Mrs Harry Lang the Second,' he announces to the room at large. 'Not to be confused with Mrs Harry Lang the First. Ha! *If only if only if only . . .*'

I'm conscious I'm doing exactly what I've promised not to – I'm 'upsetting' my brother – and for a moment I wonder if there's some wisdom in Mother's edict. 'I mean, they think it's not good for you to see people from home,' I press on. 'Not good for your recovery. They only want the best for you, Fred.'

At this, the fight goes out of him. He looks at me dully. 'Do they, Annie? Is that what they really want?'

'It's what we all want.' I take his hand again.

'But what's the point?' He asks. 'What's the point of *wanting the best for me,* when it's no one's fault but mine? *I'm* the problem. I'm the son, the great disappointment; the son with the awkward truths.'

'It's no one's fault *at all*,' I tell him. 'You're not well. No one's to blame.'

'Oh, but they are,' he says softly. 'You have no idea, Annie. There are people who are very much to blame, and I know who they are.'

I sense the precious minutes ticking away and that this is not a fruitful line of thought. So I ask him questions about life in the hospital and after answering for a few minutes in a desultory way, as if it were nothing to do with him personally, he suddenly launches into a recitation: 'Six a.m.: First Bell. Patients to Rise. Eight a.m.: Bell: Patients' Breakfast. Eight-thirty: Bell: Patients go out to work. (That's not me, by the way, I'm too ill. *Tee-hee.*) . . .'

This is all so unlike Fred that I can't help asking, 'What about treatment? Are they giving you medicine?' Perhaps that's what's affecting his mood.

There's a long silence. I think maybe he hasn't heard me; he's staring into space. After a deep sigh, he says, almost in his normal voice again, 'When I came here they thought I was a raving lunatic, you know. Ha! Well I probably was. *Schiz O'phrenic.*'

I look at him in alarm and he repeats the word with a little flourish, as if presenting a rather larky Irish gentleman.

'And are you?' This is surely more serious than anything I've been told.

He ignores the question. 'So they have a treatment for *schiz-o-phrenics* called *Convulsion Treatment*. They like labels, you see. Label, label.' He savours the word, rolling it around his lips.

I try to keep my voice steady. 'And what does this treatment – what happens?'

He is staring into space again. Then he says, 'Did you say you brought Dundee cake?'

I shake my head. 'I'm so sorry. I brought grapes.' I've forgotten the grapes; the bag has now collapsed on the bench beside me, grapes falling out of the bottom. 'Do you have—?' I glance around looking for a plate or a bowl, but it's pointless to ask. The room has nothing at all: no games, no pictures, no books – not even a Bible – and certainly nothing like a plate.

Fred stares at the grapes. 'Ah,' he says. 'Grapes for the sick. Is that what Mother takes to her parishioners, do you think, or does she just take the Gospel? Hmm?'

'She doesn't take grapes,' I tell him. 'I know that, because she's had me visiting the sick every day since I've been back. You wouldn't believe how many sick people there are in St Ann's!'

'St Ann's, thou art sick!' Fred intones. 'You know she told me Blake was unhealthy? Blake the Apostate! (Or is it heretic?) See, this is my problem, Annie: a boy with two mothers. One teaches him "The Tiger", the other bans Blake! What to do?'

I shake my head. The two mothers seem to be a recurring theme, but before I can say anything, he's off again: 'Whole of benighted St Ann's is sick, Annie, none more so than every member of the congregation of the Golgotha Mission. The Invisible Worm that flies in the night. Oh yes. Blake knew what he was talking about.'

I've never known Fred quote poetry since he was at the elementary school. Clearly, I've missed out on some important features of my brother and I want to get to know this grown-up Fred; it upsets me all over again that he's locked up in here. 'So – this treatment?' I prompt him gently, sensing the Mission is another subject to be avoided.

'Yes-yes.' Fred snaps back into his hospital-routine delivery. 'With Intravenous Cardiazol.' In the distance, another bell rings. 'Hark! The Convulsion Treatment with Intravenous Cardiazol Bell. Ah, but it doesn't work, you see.'

'What happens? What do they do to you?'

'. . . For schizophrenia. No, no, no. But it *does* work,' his face falls. 'Well, they *say* it does, for melancholia.'

'So you don't have schizophrenia after all?' I really want an answer to this question.

'Pay attention, little sister. This is what I'm telling you. If the treatment doesn't work for the condition you have – *hey presto!* Change the condition, of course, and keep taking the medicine! *Melon-Colia*. Sounds like orange squash, doesn't it, but oh dear me, it's not. If only . . .'

'Tell me about this treatment.'

'Don't want to talk about that, thank you.' He pulls a face.

But I need to know. 'It makes you sick?' I prompt him.

After a moment he recites, mechanically, half to himself,

> '. . . *The Invisible Worm*
> *That Flies in the Night*
> *In the howling storm,*
> *Has found out thy bed*
> *Of crimson joy;*
> *And his dark secret love*
> *Does thy life destroy.'*

He thinks for a moment and then adds, conversationally, '. . . Does *my* life destroy. All our lives. You know, when the No Blake rule came in, I learnt a couple of his poems off by heart. He couldn't strip those away.'

I'm trying to keep up. 'You mean *she* – Mother?'

He sighs in exasperation. 'No,' he says. 'Not Mother. Neither Mother: our Father, Annie.'

I stare at him.

'Our father which art in Hell.'

I recoil. 'Fred, how can you say that?'

'All right,' Fred concedes. 'Maybe he's not there yet, but he will be one day.' Then after another pause, he whispers, 'Burning, like a fiery river.'

'Burning? Where?'

He brushes his hands up his arms, over his chest and stomach. 'Before the convulsions come. You're ... pulled ... out of yourself. You can see them,' – he indicates around his head – 'the nurses and the doctors, but you're in another place. And your brain ... *shakes*. Afterwards,' he pauses, shudders, turns his head away.

From the back of the room, the attendant calls out, 'Five minutes, Mr Lang.'

A wave of irritation passes over Fred's face, but he ignores the attendant and smiles and says to me, 'So much to talk about, little Annie.' He takes my hand. 'Please believe me: I'm not mad.' His eyes search my face pleadingly. 'Not mad, my dear. Just very ... sad, and so much to say. You don't know the half of it.'

My eyes fill with tears again. I smile back at him.

'Don't cry, don't cry. If only ... Were we ever happy, Annie? What was our childhood? What was that? I can't remember any of it and it's gone. We had fun sometimes, did we – even after our own mother died? D'you remember? We did. Please say we did.'

I can't speak. I nod.

'D'you remember the engine, the Flying Scotsman? That was my best present *ever*. But by the time I was home for the holidays again – *pouf*! It was too late. And dear Nana ... I miss her, Annie. I miss her so much. If only we hadn't had that blessed beetroot for tea that day. I lie awake at night sometimes and cry for her. She was the only one who under-stood. Imagine that.'

'If it wasn't the beetroot it would have been something else,' I tell him sadly.

He's not listening. 'D'you remember—?' He breaks off. '"The dog that flies in the night"? No, that's wrong, isn't it?'

'"The dog that didn't bark in the night"?' I smile. 'Yes, I remember.'

'That's *it*! Oh Annie, I'm so glad you're here! It's been bothering me for days!' My heart leaps up to see him smile at his own mistake. 'Well, I was right about that.' His face darkens. 'All those whispers in corridors. Those conversations breaking off when I went into a room. *They* knew.'

'Mother? Daddy?'

He snorts. 'Mother, Daddy, Nana, the World. Even Beatrice knew: I got it out of her in the end. Only *you* didn't. You knew nothing, little sister.' He sighs. 'Poor Nana.'

The door opens again and my nurse bustles in. 'Say good-bye now, Miss Lang. Time to go.'

I make to stand up, but Fred clutches my hand. 'She's here, you know, Annie. I see her in chapel on Sundays.'

'Nana?' I've been starting to catch glimpses of my real brother, but now he tells me he's seeing *our old dog* in here?

Fred lets out his breath in a kind of despairing sigh and pushes me away. 'Go,' he says. 'You can't begin to understand.'

And then I have a thought, though it seems barely credible. 'You see – *who*, Fred?'

'I told you not to upset him,' snaps the nurse.

I look at her urgently. 'Please let me just—'

'*No.*'

'I'll come back very soon, Fred. I promise,' I tell him. 'As soon as I can get away.'

Fred shrugs as if it's all the same to him. And then the nurse, jangling her bunch of keys in her left hand, grips my arm with her right and marches me to the door. I manage to turn back for one last look, and he's sitting staring into space again as he starts to eat the grapes.

I can't wait to get out of the place, so I can let myself cry all the way home on the bus.

# THIRTEEN

## *1932*

**Thursday, June 23**

Reading back over my first visit to Fred, I don't know why it upset me so much. The Fred of that first day was positively chatty in comparison with the poor, withdrawn figure of my two visits since. My main objective is to find out why he's so angry with Daddy – angrier even than with Mother, it would seem; and what is it the whole world knew, according to Fred, except me? Then who is he seeing in the chapel?

On my next visit it's immediately clear there's no chance of discovering any of this. Draped over one of those miserable hard forms, jacket hanging loosely from his shrunken shoulders, he can barely muster an 'If only . . .' and my every question is met with profound sighs: 'You don't understand, Annie,' his principal refrain.

He has started to rub at his neck and twist his head awkwardly. I ask him, 'What's the matter, Fred? Does it hurt?' and he moves his head from side to side and says, 'Treatment.'

'Your neck hurts from the treatment?'

Silence.

'What is the treatment, Fred? What happens?'

'My own fault. If I'm quiet, I won't have to have any more.'

'Is that why you're barely speaking to me?' I joke. 'Is it so horrible, the treatment?'

'It took four of them last time.'

'Four of whom? To do what?'

'There's no point in discussing it, thank you.'

'I'm sure they know what they're doing. You have to give it a chance.'

He looks at me sharply for the first time this visit. 'You've changed, Annie. You're becoming one of them. You'd never have said that before.'

I can't meet his eyes. How do I know if what they're doing is any good? It seems to be making him quieter, but in a way that's worse. If I try to speak of outside things, hearing my own voice reedy and trite, he drags everything back to himself.

'We had a letter from Beatrice; she's been on a river trip to Greenwich.'

Silence.

'She walked through the park and visited the place where the Meridian is. You know: Greenwich Mean Time.'

Silence.

'She went with some of the girls from work; they took a picnic. It sounded very jolly.'

'If only . . .'

'I know, my dear. But when you're better we can go and visit her. We can both go. She can show us the sights.'

'I'm never going to get better.'

'Fred, of course you are. You just need to rest in here for a while.'

'It's all my fault – so what's the point of it? You don't understand, Annie.'

'There *is* a point. Fred, we're young. You've got your whole life. . .'

Silence. Deep sigh. 'If only . . .'

By the third visit, I realise it's counterproductive to challenge these expressions of hopelessness, so I just hold his hand and say, 'I know.' To which he replies, 'No, you don't.' I have by now a long list of taboo subjects and unwise questions, such as, 'How are you?' or, 'Do you remember when we used to . . .?' These two unleash the deepest sighs of all. If this is melancholia, it's grim indeed. I even start to long for the quick-fire retorts of O'Phrenia. I try teasing him. I try agreeing with him – 'Yes, you're right, it *is* pointless!' – but neither seems to work. Of his treatment, I can learn nothing further. On my third visit, Fred is still complaining of a crick in his neck from 'the treatment'.

I approach an attendant to ask about it, but he says only, 'I'm afraid, Miss, you will have to ask the doctor.' I enquire if there is a doctor on the ward, knowing full well there is not. I say, 'Mr Lang has hurt his neck. He says it's the treatment. Please will you tell the doctor? Or write it in his notes. Or something?' I glare at him as fiercely as I can. The attendant says he will. I hope he does.

As our third, painful visit draws to an end, Fred looks at me properly for the first time and says, 'Will you come to chapel with me on Sunday, Annie?'

I'm startled. 'Here?'

'Of course, here. I'm not going anywhere else, am I?'

'Am I allowed to?'

'Just come!' He giggles. 'Wear a sack. They'll think you're a patient.'

173

Sunday is a problem, of course. We have to go to the Mission on Sundays; I shall not be able to get away. But his sudden eagerness, the first he has shown all week, prompts me to say, 'I'll try, Fred. But no promises: you know how it is.'

'You can do it, Annie. You've lived in *France!*'

I can't help laughing at this, mostly at the relief of seeing a flash of the brother I know.

'I want you to come,' he explains, 'because I want to prove I'm not seeing things. It *is* Miss Blessing in the chapel! I want *you* to see her, too.'

## Sunday June 26

By Saturday, no plausible reason has occurred to me for skipping morning service at the Mission next day, and on Sunday I wake too early, worrying about how to fulfil my promise to Fred. *He won't remember,* I tell myself, plumping up my hot feather pillow and trying to turn over and go back to sleep, but the possibility that Miss Mildred Blessing might be working at the hospital is too intriguing to be missed and I lie awake in the dawn resolving to get to the chapel some-how. I have no plan. It's only when I come down to breakfast, bleary-eyed and cross, and see the bottle of calcium lactate on the kitchen table, that there's a glimmer of hope: is Mother having one of her sick headaches, then? She doesn't appear, and as I boil Daddy's egg – Elsie is having a rare weekend off – I start to think it may be possible after all.

'Your mother says can you take the basket of clothes for China to Nora Dyer,' Daddy tells me.

'How is Mother?' I ask. 'I saw the medicine bottle.'

He grunts. 'Poorly.' He's reading his paper. There's a short silence. Then he recollects himself as if perhaps feeling he ought to show more concern. 'She takes on too much, does Agnes. Your own poor mother was just the same. She'll be right as rain by teatime. Rest'll do her good.'

I take a deep breath. 'Daddy, Fred asked could I go to chapel at the hospital with him today. That would be all right, wouldn't it?'

He looks up at me. Our eyes meet. We both know Mother would not have allowed it. 'How much do you see of Fred, then?' he asks.

'Oh, not a lot. He's very . . . withdrawn.'

'So they're not bothered about you visiting, then?' It's as if in Mother's absence we can talk about it for the first time.

'They seem pleased I go to see him. There's no restriction, Daddy.' I hesitate. I want to add, *so I don't know where Mother got that idea from*, but I don't. I say, 'You could go too, perhaps, when you've a moment?'

'Perhaps I will.' He stares ahead in thought. 'Fred's troubled, poor boy. Never been strong. Took it the hardest of all of you when your mother died. You were just a nipper; you barely noticed. But it's harder for boys.' He sighs.

There's not much I can say to this. I bring my teaspoon down on top of my egg with such venom that little pieces of shell fly across the table and Daddy looks at me in surprise. 'Best eat your egg, Daddy,' I tell him, 'before it gets cold.'

'I have a feeling,' my father goes on, 'that this is what it's all about, this business with Fred: your mother's death. You go and see him: what do you reckon?'

I'm startled. I don't think he's ever asked my opinion before. 'Perhaps it is,' I say. 'He's certainly very sad about something, poor Fred.'

He shakes his head. 'Bad business. Should never have happened.' I imagine he's talking about Fred, but then he says,

'She wasn't ill seriously, you know. It was just a silly thing; should have been treatable – an infected hernia.'

'Treatable?' Beatrice said something of the kind when we were children. *So why, then, why was it not treated? Was it the doctor's fault? Or her fault for not telling anyone? Why did my dear mother have to go and die of something silly and small?* But this isn't the time for any of that. He eats his egg in silence, then returns to his newspaper, giving it a businesslike shake.

'Can I go then?' I ask after a while. 'To morning service, I mean, at the hospital?'

'You've to get that basket of clothes to Nora What's-her-name, mind.'

So I take that as a 'yes'. 'I'll drop it off on my way,' I promise him.

He finishes his breakfast and dabs at his moustache with his napkin. 'Your stepmother is a remarkable woman,' he says, giving me a sort of hard stare. Then he picks up his newspaper and leaves the room.


As soon as I've done the dishes I gallop upstairs and put on the dress I've been planning to wear: plain grey with starched white collar and cuffs; it's not exactly the same as the patients' uniforms, but I hope I'll blend in and not be noticed. By this time, the journey to Mapperley is familiar and, after running down the hill to Miss Dyer's house with the basket of clothes, I set off back up Woodborough Road at a brisk pace, though I've still time enough to get there. I realise as I reach the hospital, feeling rather hot in the flannel dress, that I haven't thought how I'm going to sneak in without having to explain where I'm going. I've no idea if visitors are allowed into the service, but luckily I reach the main door as a family in their Sunday best are being ushered through for a visit, and manage to slip in behind them, unnoticed.

I've seen signs pointing to the chapel from the main corridor and set off confidently, defying anyone to ask me where I'm going. As I approach, I can hear the harmonium playing something tinkly, just as it would play for people arriving for a service at the Mission. I slow down and watch as a crocodile of patients is shepherded by nurses and attendants through the double doors. How will I ever find Fred? As the last of them files in and the attendants turn away, I follow on the end, scanning the faces of those already seated for a sign of him. The chapel is lofty and dim with stained-glass windows and rows of chairs, and I stand by the wall towards the back from where I can see the doors. More patients arrive, filling the rows from the front, ward by ward, I'm guessing – now older women; now younger – and then I catch sight of one of the men from Fred's ward and there, three or four paces behind him, is Fred himself. I move forward and take a seat directly behind my brother, feeling conspicuous, as this part of the nave seems to be exclusively for men. But to my relief, the next ward to enter is a female ward, and I stand to make way for them to pass me, which they do without curiosity. Fred has knelt to pray and I wait until he sits up again before I kneel also, a position from which I can just reach forward and poke him in the back. He turns instantly and his face lights up; he makes to say something, but I notice a sharp-eyed nurse at the end of my row, and place a finger on my lips. She is staring at me. I lower my head in prayer. The important thing is that Fred knows I'm here.

This is not a familiar service – the altar is grander and the robes more ornate than at the Mission, and I don't know some of the hymns. Everyone recites the Creed, which we don't say, though I recognize it from hearing it in French at the Protestant church in Bordeaux. My familiar world rocks a little when one or two patients make the sign of the cross and I imagine what Mother would have to say about that! But otherwise it all proceeds much the same as morning service at Golgotha.

At the end, the chaplain disappears into the vestry and after a few moments, the harmonium, which has accompanied us throughout, strikes up with the voluntary. The patients have sat through the service more or less in silence (not counting the one who shouted 'It's all so boring!' in the middle of the sermon and another who wept loudly throughout), but now they start to fidget and chat and some stand up to leave. But I sit transfixed: the music is *Sheep May Safely Graze*. The business of getting here, of dodging Mother, finding my way to the chapel and meeting Fred, has eclipsed the reason for coming in the first place: I look over to the harmonium, its straight back obscuring the face of the accompanist. But there can only be one accompanist who would have chosen this music today, one of her favourite pieces. Can it be true, then? Has Fred found our Sunday School teacher, Mildred Blessing?

As if in answer, Fred turns around now. 'See?' he asks. 'Didn't I tell you? At the harmonium!'

'Is it Miss Blessing? Really, Fred?'

'Course it is.'

'What's she ... Is she working here?'

He frowns in disbelief. 'Hardly!'

The music has stopped and the chapel is emptying out. Women are queuing to pass me; I turn and file into the aisle with them and wait for Fred.

A hand on my arm. I turn: it is the sharp-eyed nurse from the end of my row. 'I must ask you,' she demands, 'what you think you're doing here? This service is for patients and staff. As far as I can see, you are neither.' She turns to look accusingly at Fred.

'She's my sister, Nurse,' he says meekly, staring at the ground.

'You have no business—'

I won't have my brother spoken to like this. 'Nurse,' I cut in, 'I'm sorry. He very much wanted me to come today. I didn't realise it wasn't allowed. I thought it would *help him*.' I give her a meaningful stare.

'I shall have to report you to the dean,' says the nurse. 'This is a flagrant breach of the rules. Your name will be struck from the visiting register.'

'Nurse Bleakley!' Through the departing congregation, someone is coming towards us. 'I see you've met Miss Annie Lang.'

I stare at the woman who has joined us. The voice is Miss Blessing's, but not the pallid face or the diminished figure under the baggy grey smock, a patient's smock.

'Well, Miss Lang has no business to be here,' the nurse insists. 'I've told her—'

'Ah, but I think Miss Lang is interested in working here as a volunteer,' says Miss Blessing. 'Didn't the dean put out a notice that he is anxious to expand our force of volunteers, Nurse?'

I can say nothing. I look at Nurse Bleakley and nod dumbly.

My brother stifles a snort – it's the first time I've seen him laugh since he's been in this place. 'That's it, then, Nurse, isn't it?' he says, with a flash of insolence I find reassuring.

'I'm sorry,' I add. 'I didn't know the rules.'

The Nurse examines me coldly; she's been thrown off balance by Miss Blessing. 'Well, in that case,' she says haughtily, 'I suppose I would be prepared to let it pass. Just this once.'

'Nurse Bleakley!' A very senior and august-looking sister in an alarming headdress has appeared at the chapel door.

'Nurse, your women need you; they're straying all over the corridor. Take them straight back to the ward at once.'

'Right away, Sister Bellamy. I'm sorry I was detained—'

'I'm not interested. Off you go.' And the mighty Sister Bellamy – for this must be she who approved me as a visitor – turns on her heel and out of the chapel, followed by a scuttling Nurse Bleakley.

We look at each other, Fred, Mildred Blessing and me. For a moment, we're smiling in relief and astonishment, not knowing how to begin; then I remember where we are. 'I never thought to see you here,' I tell her, and immediately feel it's the wrong thing to say.

'Nor I you,' she returns. 'But oh, how you've grown up, Annie! I wouldn't have recognised you but for your brother. How long is it? *More than six years?*' She closes her eyes for a moment, shutting them out. I wouldn't have recognised her, either. Where is the spirited young woman I knew? But she manages to recollect herself and turns to Fred. 'I've seen you around the hospital once or twice, Mr Lang. How are you?'

'Fred,' he says awkwardly. 'Please. We're all in the same boat here, aren't we?'

'Can we go outside?' I ask suddenly, hating the place. 'It's a lovely sunny day. Can we, please?'

'You go,' Mildred says. 'Can you, Fred? I ... can't.' She indicates a figure hanging back near the harmonium. 'I've got my jailer, you see.' She shrugs with a laugh, but there is no humour in it.

I don't understand. 'Why?' I ask.

'Oh, Doris is all right. She gives me a lot of slack. But I need to get back now.'

'Back – where?' I look from Mildred to Fred. I am completely perplexed.

'Are you . . . detained, then?' he asks.

She nods. 'For my own protection,' she explains to me. 'I might run away. Escape.' She smiles, and for a moment I catch sight of the old Millie.

'So you are a patient, then?'

'Oh, most certainly.'

I can't stop myself. 'What for?' I burst out. 'They let you play for chapel? You can't be very ill. Why are you here?'

'My privilege for good behaviour – and they need an accompanist, so it suits them. I thank the Lord for it; it keeps me sane.'

I look at her, but there's no irony in what she's saying. 'Can I visit you?'

She thinks for a moment. The attendant near the harmonium has begun to move towards us. 'Almost certainly not,' she says hurriedly. 'They won't permit it. But you can, you *really can*, come in as a volunteer – if you've the stomach for it. Ask for the female long-term ward.' The attendant has nearly reached us. 'I must go. If you tell them . . . tell them you're interested in . . . becoming an almoner, or some such, they might let you in to work with us. We can talk then.'

'Ready, Blessing?' Doris wears a different uniform. It isn't that of a nurse; she looks more like a policewoman. She is brisk, not unkindly, but her use of Miss Blessing's surname without 'Miss' in front is peculiarly shocking.

Mildred holds out her wrist. For a horrible moment I think she's going to have to wear handcuffs, but the woman merely grasps her wrist and starts to lead her away. As they go, she pulls back a moment. 'Annie,' she says in an undertone. 'Please don't tell – anyone at home – that you saw me. And if you do apply as a volunteer, don't mention my name . . . *anywhere*. If you do, they'll never let you come.' She looks at me intently.

I nod. 'I will apply,' I say. Fred and I watch as she is led from the empty chapel.

This extraordinary encounter leaves me in a state of shock. Fred explains that he only has something called 'hospital parole'; he isn't allowed outside, either. So we go to his ward and sit talking until the dinner bell rings and I'm shooed out. I notice he seems much more himself, and more animated, than on any of my previous visits. He explains he has heard that some of the long-term wards are locked, with certain patients detained against their will; he knows little of these wards, only that some inmates are said to be raving mad, confined in padded cells with nothing in them at all for fear they might do damage to themselves or others. It is rumoured a few even need to be kept in straitjackets. But other patients from the locked wards, he says, he has seen in treatment rooms under supervision of people like Doris, and they seem perfectly normal, meekly allowing themselves to be led by the wrist as Miss Blessing did. It's hard to believe these poor people are a threat to anyone, I say, so why are they locked up? Fred shrugs. He has no idea, but he has heard from other inmates that some have been in the hospital for years – women in particular, he tells me. No one knows much about them because they're segregated and never discussed. He says it's as if they don't exist.

And why should Miss Blessing have joined their ranks? What is her illness? How long has she been here? I resolve to find out, and contemplate the possibilities: since it seems Daddy has connections to the hospital through the Mechanics' Institute, the easiest route would be to apply to them, via him, as a volunteer. Miss Blessing's name need not be mentioned, and Mother could scarcely object to such a saintly ambition, since she's the one who's been urging me to live for others instead of myself. For a few hours I'm sure this is the way forward, and decide to broach it with Daddy at the first opportunity – even tonight, if Mother is still in bed with her headache.

Yet I hesitate. The truth is that meeting Miss Blessing again has raised unquiet spirits from the past.

# FOURTEEN

## *1926*

I remember the first time I heard Miss Blessing play *Sheep May Safely Graze*. It must have been a whole year after my night in the cellar because it was Winter again, and smoke hung in a yellow blanket over the city. One Saturday, Mother took me with her to buy vests. We were to stop off at the Mission on the way because she had to see to something. I said I'd wait outside; it was not my idea of fun to go into the Mission, with the chill that crept down inside you and the smell of damp hassocks – I had quite enough of that on Sundays. But Mother would have none of it, of course; no leaving me in the evil streets of St Ann's, though they always seemed quiet and harmless to me, just horse manure, and paper bags blowing, where the girls with no stockings picked their way between the cobbles.

Mother instructed me to stay in the chapel porch on a pew by the door. 'No slouching. You can practise sitting nicely, for once. Remember that means no closer than four inches from the back.' She said this before Mission every

Sunday and it seemed unfair she had to say it on a Saturday as well.

As soon as she had disappeared towards the vestry I squirmed around to try and count the inches between me and the wooden pew-back, but it was hopeless. My feet almost touched the floor these days. I was definitely growing.

Suddenly, from the depths of the chapel came the quavery notes of the harmonium: someone was practising for tomorrow. I jumped up and opened the heavy swing door a crack. This door was peculiar to the Mission; I couldn't imagine one anywhere else. It had a Mission clammy feel, and was covered in cold brown material like car seats, but not leather, hammered down with brass studs. Peering round it, I could see no sign of Mother so I slipped inside, leaning on the door to make it close with a quiet swish, not a *thwack*, as when latecomers hurried through in their embarrassment. The harmonium, as I have described before, was on the far side beneath the pulpit by the front pews. I slipped around the back in the shadow of the gallery and tiptoed up the side aisle. As I had suspected, the harmonium player was Miss Blessing. I waited, listening. I knew the piece and loved it: *Sheep May Safely Graze*. I had found the music for it myself inside the music stool at home. I fancied Our Own Mother played it and it made me think of green hills and sunshine in the Derbyshire Dales and the woolly white sheep tugging at the grass with no one to bother them, in the days before she had gone and died. I could manage the beginning; it wasn't very hard, just two flats. But quickly it went into big split chords in the left hand with accidentals, and some of the chords that weren't split had four notes and I couldn't reach them all.

Miss Blessing was concentrating on a difficult bit and didn't notice me at first; when she did, she jumped back with a little frown and her fingers flew off the keys. 'Annie Lang!

Gracious. You gave me a fright. How long have you been there?' She seemed different. Her voice was snappy.

'Only just now,' I said, not wanting her to think I'd been spying. 'I like that piece.'

'Well it won't be ready for tomorrow. There are tricky bits.' She sounded annoyed.

'I know,' I said, 'I can't play it.'

'Well, you will in good time,' she promised me. She had stopped playing and was looking at me with slight impatience, as if waiting for me either to ask a question or go away.

'Please play some more,' I begged her. My thought was that Miss Higgs would notice she had stopped and would hear us talking.

She pulled a face, her lips set tight. Then she seemed to relent, patting the bench on which she sat. 'Come and play with me. You can pull out the stops when I tell you.'

I hopped up beside her and she went back to practising, while I experimented with 'tuba' and 'flute'.

Glancing down at the pedals I saw she was wearing her old button boots: 'You're not wearing your lovely shoes, even though it's Saturday!' I had said it before I realised.

She was silent, her face set hard as she played. Then she said flatly, 'I don't wear those any more.'

'Oh', I breathed. This was sad news. 'Why not?'

'I just don't.' She spoke it quite harshly, and in a manner so abrupt that I realised she was definitely not happy with me and I wondered what I'd done wrong. For a moment I wanted to burst into tears – I had always felt we had a special bond with her beloved father and my mother dying when we were small – but just as unexpectedly, she seemed to realise she was being unfriendly and said, 'Actually, I gave them to my sister. Pull out the trumpet stop, will you, Annie? We'll try the ending loud.'

I searched for the trumpet stop, my mind aflutter. I had not considered that there could be more than one wearer of the blue shoes. I tried to imagine Beatrice ever giving me a pair of *her* shoes: no chance! 'But surely,' I faltered, 'they can only be worn by you!'

'Me and half the City!' she said bitterly. 'They were in Timpson's sale!' The trumpet stop blared out the final chords of *Sheep May Safely Graze*. Clearly I would need to revise my whole notion of Miss Mildred Blessing; it suddenly seemed far less likely that it had been *her* dancing in our garden that night. Why, it could have been half the City! Disappointment flooded through me. I slithered off the harmonium stool. 'I've got to go,' I told her. 'And anyway you shouldn't use the trumpet stop: it's meant to be *ppp* at the end.'

She must have caught the dismay in my voice, because she turned to me in surprise. 'Oh Annie, what's the matter? It was just our joke. Just a bit of fun. Don't rush off; we'll play it properly now.'

'Mother's waiting,' I said. 'I'll get into trouble. Goodbye, Miss Blessing.' I needed to be away from her with her change-able moods. I needed to think. I could sense the regret in her eyes as I scuttled irreverently in front of the altar, the quickest way to the door.

As I passed the vestry, which was off to the side beyond the pulpit, I could hear a murmur of voices from behind the dark green vestry curtain. It was Mother, and she must have still been talking to the Verger, which was a relief; maybe she hadn't heard Miss Blessing on the trumpet stop or realised I'd disobeyed her. I was about to creep out to the chapel porch when something in their conversation stopped me. It was a note of doom in the Verger's voice. I couldn't help it, I stood and listened: 'And now another young girl ... Police on the doorstep ... disappeared.'

Miss Higgs, somewhat louder, responded, 'Well, Mr Wilkinson, I trust that. . .' Her voice dropped and I couldn't hear the next bit. '. . . That's where they are: believe me, I know.'

The Verger murmured something in an undertone; I caught the words, '*three of them* . . .' Then Miss Higgs said briskly, 'And now, Mr Wilkinson, I can't stay here tittle-tattling—'

I didn't wait to hear more. With a sympathetic thought for the poor Verger, put firmly in his place, I shot through the door, leaned against it so it would close softly once more and sat down on the pew where Miss Higgs had left me, trying to take deep breaths in the hope she would think I'd been there all along. Could Mother really know where the missing girls were? I didn't have time to consider this fully before she came bustling along to find me.

'Mother,' I ventured as we turned down St Ann's Well Road towards the centre, 'is it time for me to have a new pair of shoes, do you think, for the Winter?'

She looked at me critically. 'What for?' she asked.

'Well, you know, my feet are growing.' I held one up for inspection, hoping the boot on it would look suitably tight.

'I'll be the judge of that. Walk properly, girl.'

Somehow I had to get to the window of Timpson's and see if the blue shoes were still in the sale. 'Sort of pinches,' I said. 'I think they're getting a bit small.'

'Don't moan, Annie. If they are, Beatrice has grown out of her size threes, which are perfectly good.'

'I'm not ready for a three, Mother. These are twelves. I'm still on children's sizes.' I could hear myself sounding petulant, which was really all to do with feeling upset about Miss Blessing being so peculiar.

Mother said nothing. We walked in silence for a few

moments. 'We could go and look at my feet in Timpson's new Pedoscope! Marjorie Bagshaw had it done,' I suggested – immediately regretting it, because Marjorie Bagshaw must for ever now be associated in Mother's mind with *that night* after Goose Fair. Besides, I no longer had the stomach for this fight, and she could tell.

'I'm the one who decides what we're doing, Annie, not you – and we are not buying boots. We're buying vests. Good gracious, I hope you girls aren't going to grow up with huge ugly feet!'

That stung, of course. She certainly knew how to get at a person. Auntie Vera always said graceful young ladies had small feet, and I fervently hoped that mine would stop growing. For the rest of the afternoon, as we crossed the city centre to and from Jessops in King Street, I forgot about the shoes and kept my eyes peeled for newspaper hoardings that might throw light on my newest piece of knowledge from the outside world: the mystery of the three missing girls and *I know where they are*. But it was Saturday afternoon and there was nothing on the billboards except 'Forest Final', which is all about football and not in the slightest interesting.

'Beatrice,' I asked that night when we were marking the readings in our Bibles for tomorrow's service, a weekly ritual introduced by Mother to stop us riffling through the pages and making a disturbance during the lesson, 'do you know anything about young girls *disappearing*?'

'Oh *no*,' said Beatrice, who wasn't paying attention, 'it's not the Parable of the Talents again! I'm sorry, but I have great difficulty with Jesus about this. *For unto everyone that hath shall it be given, and he shall have abundance: but from him that hath not shall be taken away even that which he hath.* And then the people with nothing go and get thrown into everlasting fire. How can it be fair, Annie?'

I shrugged. I didn't know why things like this bothered her so much. God was unfair and I didn't understand why Bea couldn't see that. But I didn't say it, because I loved her. I just looked at her with pity and waited for an answer to my question.

She put the marker in Matthew 25 and snapped her Bible shut. 'Sorry. What did you ask me?'

I told her about the conversation I'd overheard at the Mission.

'You shouldn't have been earwigging,' said Beatrice, unhelpfully.

'It's not my fault I was there. Anyway, it's in the papers.'

'I don't know,' she concluded.

'Haven't you heard about it? There are three missing girls, and Mother told Mr Wilkinson she *knows where they are*. D'you think she's going to tell the police?'

'Search me,' said Beatrice. Honestly, what's the point of an older sister who's so busy worrying about the Parable of the Talents that she doesn't listen to ordinary decent gossip?

Then I remembered something else I needed to know. 'Beatrice?'

'I don't want to talk about it, Annie!'

'It's not about that,' I said quickly. 'Are your feet still growing?'

'I don't know,' she replied absently. 'Probably.'

'I thought I needed new shoes and Mother said we might end up with clodhoppers. I don't want big feet, Bea.'

'Mmm.'

Then a thought came to me. 'In China it wouldn't matter if your feet grew big, would it, because you'd bind them anyway.' Perhaps this was the solution: I could maybe bind *my* feet if they got too big. I thought about it for a few moments. 'Beatrice, if you were Auntie Francie bicycling around China unbinding the women's feet, d'you think they'd want you to? Maybe they'd rather have little feet?'

Beatrice looked up. I knew I was annoying her, but serve her right for not knowing about the missing girls. She thought for a moment. 'I don't think so,' she said. 'They'd probably be glad. In the end. Maybe not straight away.'

'Why not?'

'Because it would hurt, wouldn't it? If your toes have been bent up underneath you since you were a little girl?'

I stared at her in alarm. 'Is that what they do? What *do* they do?'

'They . . .' Beatrice hesitated. 'I don't really know,' she said.

'Do they break little girls' toes, Bea? *Do* they?' I realised I was whispering; it was too horrible a thing to say out loud.

Beatrice looked stricken. 'I – I'm not sure,' she said.

'Why do they do that?'

Beatrice shrugged. 'Well, I suppose if your feet are bound you can't walk very far. You can't dance, or anything.'

'You can't run away, you mean?'

'I suppose. Yes.'

'How awful.' I had a sudden vision of the little girls of China queuing up in their clean white cotton socks and a man coming down the line with a hammer . . . I shuddered. 'Then what does Auntie Francie do?'

'I dunno, Annie. Unbinds them, I suppose. I'm sure she's very gentle.'

'So are they all right after that? Once it stops hurting?'

'I don't know,' said Beatrice miserably. 'I expect so.' But she didn't sound very sure.

We hunted through out Bibles a bit more, in silence. Then I asked, 'So will you do that, Bea, when you're a missionary? Go round on your bicycle and unbind the little girls' feet?'

Beatrice looked at me for a moment, then she said kindly, 'It doesn't happen here, Annie, does it? So you haven't to worry about it any more.'

I curled my own toes inside my black lisle stockings. I said nothing.

I remained in the dark about the disappeared girls for almost a week. Then it suddenly came up in domestic science, of all places. We were making pastry for our jam tarts. As usual, mine was stuck to my fingers.

'You know what, Miss, they found those girls, Miss!' said Edith Jelley.

'They never,' corrected Marjorie. 'They only found the place they'd been kept.'

'They found the cellar,' Edith admitted. 'But the girls must be round there somewhere.'

I was all ears, but Miss Pollard, the domestic science teacher, was having none of it. 'Edith, you want to concentrate more on the pastry and less on the gossip,' she remarked. 'What are you going to do with that, girl? Plaster the kitchen?'

Everyone giggled.

'Lightly,' Miss Pollard went on. 'Use the tips of your fingers lightly, like playing the piano, Grace Wiggins, not like kneading clay.'

'Is mine all right, Miss?' Marjorie asked, pausing in mid-air with her elbows sticking out.

'Just keep at it, Marjorie. And I do have a name you know.'

'We've been doing it for ages, Miss,' Edith moaned.

'We've been doing it for ages, Miss *Pollard*,' Miss P. corrected her. 'And you can do it for a while longer. Annie, more flour.'

Later, when Miss Pollard left the room for a moment, the tarts in the big hissing ovens and the domestic science room starting to smell all fragrant, I whispered to Marjorie, 'What cellar?'

'Cellar in Beeston. Imagine! They found *traces*.'

'Traces of what?' I asked.

'Of them, of the girls that disappeared.'

'How did they know it was them?'

'Search me.'

'What sort of traces?' asked Grace Wiggins, who was leaning against the sink.

'Body parts!' said Edith, and snorted, trying not to laugh.

'Don't be daft! I dunno, maybe bits of clothing or summat. A teddy bear.'

I thought of Little Sid and let out a small cry.

Marjorie turned on me. 'I don't know, do I, stupid?'

'How many girls?' asked Doreen Noakes.

'Loads, I should imagine. At least five!'

'*Three!*' chorused Edith and Marjorie, and glared at each other.

'How did the police know they'd all been down there?' Grace wondered.

Edith shrugged. 'Guesswork, I suppose. *Fingerprints*, maybe?'

I suddenly had an image of my own fingers, slightly greasy and with that smell on them from the coal dust, spread out over the basin of water the morning after my night in the cellar.

'Whose house was it? Where are the girls now?'

Nobody knew.

'*Beeston?*' I repeated.

'Aye, "The Black Hole of Beeston", so it said in the *Evening Post*.' We all looked at each other uneasily, not quite knowing whether to find it funny or not. Then the tarts were cooked and Miss Pollard bustled back into the room and I think we were all very pleased to forget about it. But walking home from school through the Oaks, I went over the conversation again and filed it away. A cellar in Beeston. Miss Higgs said she knew where they were. She also knew about cellars. And Beeston was where she'd lived with her sister.

It was a few nights after this that my Nana routine went wrong. Had we become careless? I have wondered about this, but I don't think so. Whatever the reason, I had just returned from collecting her and was dropping off to sleep with the rain whipping against the windows when I suddenly started wide awake. Beyond the sound of the rain came another; the unmistakable tread of Mother in her hard slippers along the landing. Perhaps she suspected; perhaps she did not and was just on the prowl as she had been before. But in a flash, and thankful I had decided it was too dangerous to make Nana a proper bed on the hearthrug, I lifted the heavy counterpane that hung around my own bed and Nana, instantly knowing what was expected of her, shot underneath with a speed I would not have thought possible in one so large. A second later, the door opened and Mother entered.

'Annie?'

I pretended to be just waking up. 'Mother?' I asked sleepily.

She snapped on the light and her eyes darted round the room, taking everything in. 'Did I hear a noise coming from this room?'

I looked at her blearily. 'Noise? No . . . I don't know.'

'Are you sure?'

'I didn't hear anything.' A gust of wind blew a shower against the glass. 'The rain—?' I suggested, blinking at her.

She advanced on the bed ominously. 'Have you been up to something?'

'No—oo,' I groaned. 'I was asleep.'

With one practised flick of the wrist she wrenched the bedclothes back. I lay there with Little Sid tucked in beside me, shivering in my white flannel nightie. From Nana there was no sound, or perhaps her breathing was drowned by the wind and rain, for after a moment Mother, who seemed unsure what to do next, leaned down and grasped my toes. 'Your feet are cold. Have you been out of bed?'

'No, Mother. I am cold. It's *cold*.' I wanted to tell her to give me back the bedclothes and get out and let me go to sleep, but I knew this would be fatal, so I bit my tongue and waited.

'Don't moan, child. You should be wearing bedsocks,' she said after a moment. Then without pulling up the bedclothes she turned and left the room, switching off the light, without a word.

'Good night, Mother,' I said softly to the closed door. 'Sleep well, Mother. Sweet Dreams.' Then I rearranged the messy bed and snuggled down. Lifting the counterpane again, I felt beneath for Nana. I heard her tail beat just twice on the lino. She gave my fingers a small lick, but stayed exactly where she was. I lay wide awake, my heart hammering against my ribs. On the following night, Nana hung back and I had to pull at her collar to get her through the kitchen door. She took it upon herself to sleep under the bed every night after that, and I'm glad to say nothing else went wrong for ages.

Then one Monday, when I came home from school, Beatrice – who had stayed away that day with a poorly chest – came into my room and sat down carefully on the bed. I looked at her. I could tell she had *news*.

'Good day at school?' she asked, delicately disentangling one of Nana's hairs from the counterpane.

'S'all right,' I said. I watched her intently. 'Did Doctor

Martin come?' As I've said before, poorly chests were to be taken seriously, what with *shadows on the lung* and worse.

But Beatrice shook her head impatiently. 'Oh it's nothing. He says it's not congested. I've just got to stay off this week and do the Friar's Balsam.'

'So what, then?'

'Well, I—' She was picking at the counterpane again. She didn't seem to know how to start.

'What's up, Bea? Look at me!'

She sighed. 'I don't want to alarm you . . .' Her voice tailed off.

'You don't want to—? You *are* alarming me! What is it, Beatrice? What's happened?'

'Trouble is,' she grumbled, 'you'll get the histrionics and it won't help.' She looked up at me for the first time. 'Will you promise to be sensible about this, Annie?'

'I don't know, do I? Depends what it is!' If this was her idea of keeping me calm, it wasn't succeeding.

'All right. Listen. It's something I heard this afternoon. . .'

It seems that after the doctor's visit, Daddy had come home for lunch and Beatrice had been sent to lie down. She'd forgotten her book and come back downstairs to get it, passing the partly open door of the sitting room where Mother and Daddy were having a conversation. What caused her to stop and listen was Agnes saying, '*That dog.*'

My hand flew to my mouth as I listened to what she had to tell me: 'I couldn't hear it all,' Beatrice shook her head in frustration at the memory. 'These were the snatches I heard.' She frowned, trying to remember them in order. 'Mother saying, "Winter coming on again . . . Mess in the yard . . ." And Daddy saying something about "house dog".'

'What mess in the yard?' I broke in. 'She makes no mess! We take her out all the time — poor Nana, stuck out there.

If she doesn't want a mess in the yard, that's simple! Bring her back into the house where she belongs! And what does Daddy mean by *house dog*? Does he mean she ought to be in the house, or that she does a useful service as a house dog, barking and stuff?'

'Shush, Annie.' I could tell Beatrice was quite cross. 'What did I tell you about histrionics? Now shut up and listen. Then Mother said, "Dog's not getting any younger ... Gets on my nerves, Harry ... Need to do something." And he said, "Difficult ... Children ... ask Mr Holley." And she said, "See to it, Harry."'

I had to take this in for a moment. Then I said, 'I hate her.'

For once, Beatrice let it go.

'Nana's not old,' I burst out. 'She's only five!'

'Six,' Beatrice corrected. 'She came two years before Mother died.'

'Well six isn't old.'

'She probably meant it wasn't fair to make her stay outside another Winter.'

'Well bring her in then!' I exploded.

'*Calm*, Annie,' reminded Beatrice.

'So what will Mr Holley do with her?' I asked. 'He doesn't want a dog, does he?'

'Well ...' Beatrice took a deep breath. 'He ... might not keep her.'

'So what will he do? Will he give her away?' The idea of Nana going to strangers was unbearable.

'I don't think he'd find a home for a six-year-old dog, Annie.'

'So what will he do with her, then?'

Beatrice was silent for a moment. 'I remember Fred telling me last time he was home that Mr Holley's got a gun.'

I stared at her.

She couldn't look at me. 'I'm not saying ... but that's why I'm telling you this. We need to do something. I need you to be very grown-up, Annie, and help us decide what to do.'

My mind was in complete uproar: for one thing, Beatrice had never, ever asked me to help her decide anything. This was the very first time. Secondly, I hadn't realised she cared so much about Nana that she would even consider going against our parents' wishes. It must be difficult for her, and I had no doubt she was doing it for Fred and me. I also knew her to be scrupulous and that the words she had recalled would have been the correct words; unlike me, she was never prone to exaggeration – not that I *fib* about things exactly, but perhaps I sometimes make them out to be more dramatic than they really are (that's what people say, anyway). So if she was even mentioning Mr Holley's gun, it could only be that she had heard more than she let on. Perhaps they had spoken about shooting Nana and Beatrice had wanted to spare me that. As this idea grew, I became convinced of it and I was deeply grateful to her for confiding in me, and for saying that we were in it together and must find a way through it – together. She was right: this was too serious to waste time weeping and wailing. Nana was our dog and we must save her. I must prove myself a sister worthy of Beatrice's trust.

# FIFTEEN

## *1926*

And it was this problem with Nana that led us right into the middle of the mystery of Miss Mildred Blessing. The day after Beatrice had told me about Mr Holley, and I don't want to say anything more about the gun because it was just too dreadful, Marjorie and I were taking a shortcut back to school after hockey practice. I had briefly considered asking Marjorie if their family could take Nana, but it didn't feel like a good solution; they'd probably think nothing of keeping her in the coal-hole. So I decided not to say anything about our dog dilemma to anyone at school. Besides, Beatrice thought that with her being at home, ill and everything, Daddy probably wouldn't do the horrible deed, because it would be just awful for Nana to have to go with Mr Holley if Beatrice were watching. So she reckoned we had a few days – until she was back at school, anyway – to think of a plan.

Marjorie had led us down Exchange Road past the Kingdom Hall and as we approached it, I wondered again what it would be like to be a Jehovah's Witness. When I first heard about the Bible Student Movement I thought it sounded rather like us: I discovered they had the total immersion, but much bigger – on football pitches in America, they told me – and I thought about Nottingham Forest, which was so huge I had only glimpsed bits of it between the houses, and imagined the whole pitch transformed into a celestial swimming baths, with their Pastor, like Grandfather Pastor Eames, floating about in the middle, dunking the queues of believers backwards under the water, one, two, three. But Mother put me straight on the Bible Student Movement. She said they weren't like us at all, not one little bit, because they hadn't been saved. She said they *thought* they had, because at Armageddon they believed the whole world would be turned to rubble with just them alive in it, but they were wrong about this because it wasn't them who were getting saved – it was us. She told me I had to be grateful I was not one of them because they had to do the Ministry on the doorsteps and anyway they didn't believe in Christmas or birthdays, so it was no fun. Well, she didn't say it was no fun – that's what I said to Beatrice afterwards. 'And imagine having to go and knock on people's doors and tell them they've got to follow their Jehovah if they want to survive Armageddon,' I told Beatrice. 'I'd just *die* if I had to do that.'

'Well, you're not, so you don't have to,' retorted Beatrice. 'So don't worry about it.' She didn't seem to find the Bible Student Movement a bit interesting.

'I'm glad I go to the Golgotha Mission,' I confided. 'Fancy doing the total immersion on the football pitch and everything, and spending hours at the Kingdom Hall thinking you're going to be saved, when you aren't saved at all, and you don't even get birthday presents.'

Beatrice had given me a withering look and I shut up.

Trouble was, I was thinking to myself as I walked down Exchange Road that afternoon, if I didn't believe in God the way Beatrice did, maybe *I* wasn't saved, either. God would know, of course. There's no pulling the wool over His eyes. But then another thought struck me, a thought that was very probably blasphemous and could get me *un*-saved on the spot, even if I wasn't already: how were we to know that we *were* God's chosen? Supposing Grandfather Pastor Eames was wrong and it was the Jehovah's Witnesses all along? I didn't want to think about that, so I came back to the present with a bump, walking down the road with Marjorie Bagshaw after hockey, worrying about Nana – and then I saw them.

At first I thought I was dreaming because it was so peculiar to see people together, like you see them in dreams, when they belong to quite separate bits of your life: but there they both were, Daddy and Miss Mildred Blessing, walking slowly and talking together just ahead of us on the street. I stopped dead in my tracks, clutching the sleeve of Marjorie's coat.

'What's bitten you?' she asked loudly, her gaze following mine to the two of them

'Shut up!' I hissed. 'That's Daddy with my Sunday School teacher. They're not even friends.'

'Eh, well you're obviously wrong about that!' said Marjorie. 'Here—' She dragged me behind a billboard outside the Kingdom Hall. WHAT IS MISSING IN THIS CH—CH? it asked, and underneath, the letters: UR. 'You want to wait for them to go.'

'What for?'

'Because they probably don't want you walking up to them.'

'I don't see why!'

'Oh well, go ahead then, go and disturb them. But it looks to me as if they're having a very private discussion.'

'It must be about the Mission,' I said. 'Miss Blessing plays the harmonium there.'

'Miss *who* did you say?'

'There's nothing wrong,' I told her. 'What could be *wrong*?'

'You tell me!' Marjorie pulled a face. 'Stories we hear about your dad, I'd say you wouldn't want to bet on that.'

Marjorie had hinted at this before. 'What stories? What about my dad?' I asked her crossly.

'Oh nothing. Just that he's a bit of a charmer.'

I looked at her for a moment, unsure what this was supposed to mean: *snake charmer*? 'Who says?'

'Our Iris went to a Ladies' Evening at the 'Masons with Dad and your dad was there. She says he's got an eye for the girls.'

Ever since that terrible day at Goose Fair I'd had a soft spot for Marjorie's sister Iris, but Beatrice would have said Bagshaws were not to be depended on – and in any case I was aware I had to defend Daddy's honour. 'Well I don't care,' I said. 'I'm going to go and speak to them. Come on!' I started off down the road at a brisk trot with my shoe-bag and hockey stick knocking against my legs, and Marjorie rather reluctantly in tow. This was unlike her; she was usually much bolder than me. As we got closer to them, I could tell that Miss Blessing and my father were indeed having a very earnest conversation. From behind, they both looked serious (I know you can't see a person's face from behind, but I could tell). I've said before that Daddy is not very tall, and as Miss Blessing is a good deal taller than – well, me, for instance – she did not have to look up to him very far.

'Daddy!' I called, when I was close enough to speak without shouting, which would have been rude.

His head was sideways on to me and for a split second he

seemed to hesitate, his eyes on Miss Blessing's face, before turning around to me. 'Good heavens! Hello, Annie.'

'Hello Daddy! Hello, Miss Blessing.'

'Well what a surprise,' he said, beaming his good-mood smile. 'What are you girls doing here?'

I remembered to introduce them to Marjorie, hoping as I did so that I had got it the right way round, something I always forget. 'Miss Blessing, Daddy, this is Marjorie Bagshaw.'

'How d'you do?' Marjorie whispered, peeling and unpeeling the rubber at the top of her hockey stick.

'How's your father, Marjorie?' Daddy asked.

'Very well, thank you, Mr Lang,' mumbled Marjorie.

'We're just on our way from hockey,' I explained.

'Well, well. I believe you know Miss Blessing?'

'Oh yes,' I said, suddenly feeling shy. I stole a glance at her. She was looking strained, I thought, and not her usual self at all.

'Hello Annie,' she said. 'Fancy that.' She sounded sort of formal, different; it reminded me of the way she had been that day at the Mission. There was a slight hesitation before she went on, 'I was just—'

'We were talking about Miss Blessing's family,' Daddy broke in. He smiled at Miss Blessing.

'Oh – I hope they're quite well?' I asked her.

'Yes, thank you,' she replied. 'My sister is teaching in Canada now.'

There was a short pause. 'We've got to go,' said Marjorie. 'We'll be in detention if we're not back, Annie.'

'Really?' Daddy looked surprised. 'Goodness. Strict discipline at Mundella, then. That's what I like to hear.'

I shot him a curious look. This wasn't what he would normally say; he sounded like the father in the *Dick and Jane* books – not like a real daddy at all. He just stood there beaming at us in a sort of cardboard way, and I suddenly wanted to be gone. "Bye then, Daddy. See you later,' I said. 'Goodbye, Miss Blessing. See you on Sunday.'

'Goodbye, Annie.'

Then Marjorie was practically dragging me down the road.

'So there you are, then,' I said as we turned the corner. I hadn't dared look back at them.

'There I am – *what?*' asked Marjorie. 'That was just about the most embarrassing thing that's ever happened to me in my whole life, Annie.'

'No it wasn't! What's wrong with it?'

'What's *wrong* with it? Did you not notice, Annie Lang, that they were dying of embarrassment.'

'Not specially. It was just a bit of a shock.'

'It was written all over them! I wanted the pavement to swallow me up! You should have done what I said and stayed out of sight!'

'What for? I've nothing to hide.'

'You've nothing to hide. What about *them?*'

'Marjorie, my Dad goes to the Mission every week – he must know her. She plays the harmonium – that's what my stepmother used to do.'

'Oh Annie. You're even more innocent than I thought you were! She probably doesn't even have a sister.'

I rounded on her, 'Of course she has, if she says she has. Besides, I've met her sister. So.'

'Well I was watching her, and she definitely didn't want you coming up and finding them talking like that.'

I was almost crying with frustration. 'Marjorie, he's my father. He takes an interest in people. What's so mysterious about it?'

Marjorie said nothing. We hurried back to school in silence. I was remembering how Beatrice had made me promise never to mention the name of Mildred Blessing to Mother or Daddy under any circumstances. But our chance meeting had given me an idea: of course Miss Blessing was the solution to our Nana problem! The Blessing family loved dogs! Edwina had just about offered to rescue ours! Surely her mother would give dear Nana a safe home.

I wanted to tell Beatrice about my idea as soon as I got back to the house, but to my surprise Daddy was home early and we all sat down together. The suspicions stirred up by Marjorie made me decide to say nothing about our meeting and I was hugely relieved when Daddy raised the subject himself. 'Little Annie's getting very grown-up these days,' he remarked as Mother poured the tea. 'I bumped into her in town – near Trent Bridge, no less.'

'What were you doing down there, Annie?' asked Mother.

'Walking back from hockey with a friend,' I said. The name of Marjorie Bagshaw was still taboo where Mother was concerned. I looked at Daddy. I didn't want to go on.

'I was talking to Miss Blessing,' he said. 'You know, Agnes, one of the people who took over from you at the harmonium. Her brother Eric has been trying to get an opening at Roebuck's.'

I was watching Mother closely. Did her hand falter on the teapot? No. She responded, 'Oh, I didn't know she had a brother.'

It was news to me, too. I thought they had been talking about her sister going to Canada.

'Yes, she does. He'd had his application rejected and wanted to find out why.'

Mother was looking at him intently now.

'I told her to suggest he tries again next year. I wanted to give her some hope for him.' Daddy smiled at me as he said this.

'Too many poor young people without jobs,' Mother murmured, half to herself. 'What's to become of them all?'

I had heard about this. It worried me that Elsie had left us very suddenly a few weeks ago. I said, 'Will Elsie get another job, Mother?'

At this, Mother and Daddy both stiffened. 'I wouldn't spend time worrying about Elsie, Annie,' Daddy said. 'She's only herself to blame.'

'What for?' I asked.

'Because she's no better than she should be,' Mother put in quickly, addressing the tea cosy rather than me. I didn't know what she meant, but it was clear I needed to drop it. Elsie had always seemed all right to me, and I was sorry for her. I hoped she would have somewhere to go.

'Don't worry your head about Elsie,' Daddy repeated, in a voice that said the subject was closed.

'So will you try and find a job for Eric, then?' I asked him. 'Who?'

I stared at him. 'Miss Blessing's brother.'

'Oh yes, Eric Blessing. Yes. Well, I'll see what I can do.'

I wished Marjorie Bagshaw could hear this. Trust Daddy not to brag to us in the street about trying to help Eric Blessing. His good spirits came back after tea. He even played Pit with Beatrice and me and chortled as he called out, 'Corner on Oats!' and suchlike. I think he enjoyed the game more than me, actually, because I find it pretty boring trading in things like barley, flax, hay and stuff. When I asked Bea about the job thingummy afterwards, she said it wasn't just Roebuck's Biscuits in trouble; it was all over the country.

'And what about Elsie, then?' I asked. 'Why did she leave if there's no jobs?'

'I've no idea,' answered Beatrice, in the sort of offhand voice that made me think she had a pretty good idea, but wasn't going to say.

'Well I hope she's all right,' I said. 'I know she made lumpy porridge but I liked her. I don't see why she had to go.' Then I took a deep breath and reminded Beatrice she had told me before that I was never to mention the name of Mildred Blessing at home.

'Did I say that?' She was sounding deliberately vague again.

'You did, Bea. I thought it was strange. It was after that time when I thought I saw her outside – when I was in the—'

'I know when it was,' said Beatrice quickly. Like me, she hated any reference to my night in the cellar.

'You said I wasn't to mention her!' I was staring at my sister. How could she have forgotten? I needed her to explain, but all she said was, 'Well, you must have misunderstood.'

I hadn't. But I thought it prudent to leave it at that. Besides, we urgently needed to work out our Plan. Beatrice had said yesterday she wanted us to ask for Nana to go to our cousins' in Mountsorrel – but that was miles away in Leicestershire. I would never be able to see her, except when we visited for tea at Whitsun or something. Besides, I argued, Auntie Vera wouldn't want as big a dog as Nana in her tidy house; she already had Spats and he was tiny in comparison. And weren't they talking of moving to Southbourne? We'd never see her if they did that!

'Let's at least ask them!' Beatrice pleaded.

It was the sensible thing to do, of course, but now I was bursting to tell her my brainwave after bumping into Miss Blessing this afternoon. First, I described my meeting with her and Edwina near the Arboretum after Nana was banished to the yard, and how they had fussed over her (though I may not have said that Edwina was in Canada now). 'Their mother lost a similar dog called Wendy – imagine, Bea, it must be *meant*! They said they would take her. Nana would be happy; Mrs Blessing would be happy; and I'd be a little bit happier because I could at least visit Nana! They actually offered, Beatrice!'

'Are you sure, Annie? Really?'

'Yes. They loved her.'

'*Why* did they offer? You weren't giving them a hard-luck story, were you, about us?'

I fidgeted uncomfortably. 'No. It wasn't long after it first happened, that's all. Come on, Bea, would I want to get rid of her?'

Beatrice looked at me hard. 'I suppose not,' she admitted. 'But you mustn't go blurting our business all over town.'

Because it was urgent, and we had no way of actually getting to Mountsorrel to ask Auntie Vera, Beatrice finally agreed we could try the Blessings first. The problem was that I had no idea where Miss Blessing and her mother lived. They weren't from St Ann's. They lived a long way away, I thought, which was no help at all.

But Beatrice knew what to do. 'The Mission will have a record. Of course they will! She plays the harmonium and teaches Sunday School. It'll be in the register. We'll go and look tomorrow.'

The following evening after homework, we slipped out of the house and made our way to Golgotha. Beatrice had to be wrapped in two flannel vests and a muffler because she still wasn't supposed to go out on account of the *shadow on the lung* situation, but we had no time to lose: Mr Holley might come for Nana as soon as Beatrice was well. It was Wednesday and lights shone through the thick diamond panes of the Mission windows. Beatrice said there would be Senior Bible Study, so we could sneak in unnoticed.

We climbed the steps to the side door. 'Follow me,' Beatrice instructed. 'Don't speak unless you're spoken to, and whatever you do, don't gasp or titter or anything. I may have to be' – she smoothed down her coat and straightened her hat – '*inventive.*' Then she pushed open the door and we marched in.

The nave was lit by a single light from the chancel, making it even gloomier than usual. From a small room off to one side, we could hear the murmur of voices. Beatrice turned left and walked up towards the vestry, where she knew the records were kept. Behind the heavy curtain at the vestry doorway, a second light was burning and we entered to find Mr Wilkinson, the Verger, seated at the vestry table, bent over some papers. What was he doing here at past six o'clock? I could feel Beatrice hesitate in her step. This was not what we had bargained for.

'Good evening, Mr Wilkinson,' she said. I noted with admiration that her voice had its usual even, friendly tone. 'How are you?'

The Verger looked up in surprise. 'Ooh, Miss Lang,' he said, as startled to see us as we were to see him. 'And Miss Annie, too. Good gracious. Are you here for the Bible Study?'

'Not this evening,' replied Beatrice firmly. 'As a matter of fact we've come on a little quest.'

'A quest, eh?' He removed his spectacles and peered at us more closely. 'And what sort of a quest would bring two young ladies to the Golgotha Mission so late on a Wednesday evening?'

Beatrice smiled and removed her gloves. 'Well, it's like this,

Mr Wilkinson, we need to see Miss Blessing, and we don't know where she lives.'

'Miss Blessing? The young lady who plays the harmonium? Ho well.' He seemed to fall into a reverie. 'I played the harmonium myself, once,' he told us. 'Said I could do it again when our good Miss Higgs became Mrs Lang and was unable to fulfil her duties in that respect. Such an excellent woman, Agnes Higgs. I remember her when she was Miss Blessing's age, when the family lived around here, you know. She and her sister nursed their mother single-handed until she died. It was a sad business, a very sad business. I was pleased the Good Lord called her to marry Mr Lang, a happy outcome to her afflictions.'

'Well ... that's why we need to speak to Miss Blessing now,' said Beatrice gently. 'On account of ... of playing the harmonium.'

'I told them I could do it,' he repeated. 'But the good Pastor Eames said no. He said "young blood", he said.' The old man's expression clouded. '"Mr Wilkinson," he told me, "There is a time to play the harmonium and a time to be silent." Ha ha. He meant well, I'm sure. I felt the Good Lord call me to play the harmonium again.' Mr Wilkinson thumped his gnarled fist against his waistcoat buttons. 'But Pastor Eames saw differently. Well ... Then the Lord sent us the sublime Miss Blessing.' He gazed mistily ahead of him and sighed.

'I wonder,' Beatrice began again, 'whether you could possibly help us to look in the Mission register, Mr Wilkinson?'

'The register?' Mr Wilkinson recollected himself and focused on Beatrice. 'Miss Lang wants to consult the Mission register, does she?'

'If you would be so kind?' said Beatrice, and dropped her gaze demurely.

'The harmonium is the domain of Miss Blessing. But the Mission register is the domain of the Verger,' pronounced Mr Wilkinson distinctly. 'Miss Lang, granddaughter of Our Founder, Pastor Eames, wishes to consult. She must seek my permission.'

'Of course,' Beatrice murmured. 'That is why I am here, Mr Wilkinson. If you would be so kind. As I said, it's – it's about the harmonium.'

'You may speak to *me* about the harmonium.'

Beatrice gave him a level stare. 'N-not this harmonium, Mr Wilkinson. It's to do with a kind offer Miss Blessing made about playing, er—' I could see panic briefly cross her face, '. . . somewhere else. For charity,' she added, hopefully.

He glared at her. 'And what would you have done, Miss Lang, had I not been here at six o'clock on a dark Autumn evening?'

Beatrice said nothing.

'Ha! It cannot be that you came at six o'clock in the hope that you might be able to consult the Mission register without asking? *Unimpeded*? Eh?'

I was getting fed up with this. I thought about 'unimpeded', a word I had not heard before, and had a picture of centipedes and millipedes crawling across the Mission register. Then I heard myself say with as much politeness as I could muster, 'We had to have tea and finish our homework first, Mr Wilkinson. We didn't mean to come so late. It just took that long.'

They both turned and looked at me. Mr Wilkinson seemed to focus on me for the first time. 'We're very sorry to have disturbed you,' I added hastily, remembering I wasn't supposed to speak. 'We don't want to waste your time.'

'Of course not,' said Mr Wilkinson. 'Of course not.' He fumbled in his pocket and took out a bunch of keys large and small, from which he slowly selected the very smallest and fitted it into the table drawer. The register was a large, shabby green ledger with dark crimson edges to each page and thumb indentations down the side for the letters of the alphabet. Mr Wilkinson's knobbly finger faltered its way to the 'B' slot and he turned to the opening page. The register must have reached right back to the beginning of time, as it contained many Bs, each of which had to be considered as he ran his finger slowly down the list, whispering the names to himself as he did so. On something like the eighth page, and almost the last B on the list, he came to Miss Mildred Blessing. We, peering over his shoulder, were ahead of him and I had almost memorised the address before he found it. Miss Blessing lived in West Bridgford, I saw with dismay – right on the other side of the City. Beatrice took a pencil and paper from her pocket and wrote down the address at Mr Wilkinson's dictation. After listening respectfully to a further homily about the necessity for this information to be kept in confidence under lock and key, delivered as he peered at us over the top of his spectacles, he informed us that had we not been the grandchildren of the good Pastor Eames he would never have divulged the address so readily. We were duly grateful, standing with our hands clasped in front of us and our heads bowed. Then we left, and walked sedately out into the street, not speaking or breaking step until we were safely out of sight of the Mission.

'Holy mackerel!' exclaimed Beatrice as we clutched each other in triumph, wheeling around the pavement and almost collapsing into the gutter. 'That was an effort – even for me!'

'The sublime Miss Blessing!' I imitated Mr Wilkinson's quavering voice.

'Dirty old man!' expostulated this entirely new sister of mine.

Then we recollected ourselves and walked briskly off into the night. So far, so good.

For the rest of that week, I hurried home from school each day with my heart in my mouth, fearing that I would find Nana gone. But whether because of Beatrice's theory that nothing would happen while she was off school, or perhaps Daddy was taking his time 'seeing to it', to my enormous relief she was still with us on Friday evening. Each night since Beatrice's catastrophic news I had been down to collect her after the family had gone to bed. I had paid her the greatest attention, wanting to seal every detail of her into my memory, from her old fur-coat smell to the scratchy, rough pads on her paws. But I didn't cry for her: I was too intent on saving her life for that.

On Saturday afternoon, Beatrice and I sat nervously in my bedroom, studying a map of the city. She had drawn me a sketch-plan of the roads I must walk down from the West Bridgford bus stop to Miss Blessing's house. At first she had wanted to come with me, but I managed to persuade her that I was more likely to succeed if I went alone.

'I'm older,' she argued. 'Miss Blessing and her mother will take me more seriously.'

'But I *know* her,' I said. 'I'm sure she'll believe me because she trusts me. And her mother might feel we're being too pushy if we both turn up on her doorstep.'

Beatrice reluctantly accepted this, though I was less certain of it myself. I couldn't get out of my head the impression, the last couple of times I had seen her, that Millie Blessing had gone off me for some reason. She had clearly been making an effort not to show how annoyed she was; yet in all our earlier dealings I had felt easy and at home with her – as if we were allies. It was in this spirit I would appeal to her now. I felt, with Fred not at home, that Nana was my dog and that I alone must save her – which wasn't really fair, because I would never even have found out where to go if it hadn't been for Beatrice. Anyhow, this part of the Plan was my job. Bea was to guard the fort at home and say, if asked, that I had extra hockey.

'You've got the address?'

I nodded.

'Which buses are you getting?'

'The 40 down St Ann's Well Road. Number 5 to West Bridgford.'

'Where do you change?'

'At the centre.'

'Dog biscuits?'

I held up my games bag. 'I'm carrying them in this,' I told her proudly, 'to make it look more like I'm going to hockey. Oh . . . and I took her rug from the kennel. I don't want her to be without anything she knows.'

Beatrice pulled a face. 'I hope it's clean.'

'It's all right. It's got to have her smell on it.'

'If they're not there . . .?' Beatrice looked at me. We hadn't considered this when we made our Plan.

'I can wait awhile,' I said, after thinking for a moment. 'I'll keep walking around the block.'

'Don't wait too long. You mustn't be coming home on your own in the dark. You won't have Nana with you then. Find a phone box. I'll stay here this afternoon and I'll be sure to answer if you call.'

I nodded, stifling a horrid sad feeling at the idea of coming home without my beloved dog. Writing this now, I don't think either of us considered the possibility that the Blessings might say they couldn't take Nana. I suppose we just had to deal with one thing at a time.

When there was nothing more to be said and the whole wretched journey couldn't be put off any longer, Beatrice and I took Nana's lead, and went down into the yard.

Nana stretched and wagged her tail in a circle when she saw us, and yawned with her special creaky excited throat noise, which she made whenever she saw people with her lead and their coats on. I hooked the lead on to her collar as I had so many times before and we trooped down the back steps and turned left. The plan was for Beatrice to wait with me at the bus stop and then return home, but as the Number 40 came into sight she suddenly announced she would go with me as far as the centre. I was more grateful to her than I cared to say.

The journey was uneventful. Beatrice took me to the second bus stop to make sure I didn't get lost. Then she crouched down, put her arms around Nana and told her to be good, turning away very quickly after that with a wave of her hand. Nana and I went on alone and all too soon, it seemed to me, we were walking down West Bridgford streets whose names I had learnt by heart. As we approached the Blessings' road, I suddenly felt panic in my stomach. I took smaller and smaller steps in a kind of daze, only realising I had slowed to a crawl when I caught Nana looking up at me with a definite question on her face. The road was running past a small park at this point and I suddenly swerved into it, letting Nana off the lead when we were inside, murmuring to her that at least I could give her one last run before we said goodbye. She stood beside me for a few moments, scenting the unfamiliar air, then ambled off at a brisk trot to investigate the trees and the grass. I stood and watched her, tears falling down my cheeks. I mopped at them hopelessly. How was I ever going to manage to give her away to strangers? I turned and walked off down a wide avenue, kicking at leaves and trying to pull myself together. Of course, Miss Blessing wasn't a stranger. And Mrs Blessing had loved her dog Wendy so much that she mourned her loss for ages. These must be kind people. Then I fell into a sort of fantasy that perhaps I wouldn't have to give Nana up for ever. Perhaps, on losing her, my parents would realise how much they loved and missed her and after a time, when Mother had recovered from all her griping, she would agree to have her back. Not only back, I decided, but Nana would be allowed to come into the house and spend the second half of her life in the breakfast room in front of the warm range and even by the coal fire in the sitting room, and sleep on a rag rug, which I would make for her. This dream got me all the way round the park, which was not much more than a recreation ground really, Nana sometimes trotting at my heels, sometimes chasing imaginary rabbits – which we both knew to be imaginary because she sort of lolloped more than running. Eventually, I came to and told myself sharply that's what it was: a dream. And now I must find my way out of the park at the same place I had come in, because Beatrice's map showed only the streets between the bus stop and the Blessings' road: I could easily get lost. This proved to be the case, and I had to walk almost twice around the park before I found the right way out. Hooking the lead back on to Nana's collar, I led her on our way.

As we approached the house, a church clock struck four; it was later than I thought and the sun was dropping. I double-checked the house number from the address in my pocket, pushed open the gate and after taking a long shuddery breath, left over from the crying, I walked up to the front door and rang the bell.

There was no one at home.

After ringing twice more and rat-tatting at the letterbox in case the doorbell wasn't working, I stepped back to look up at the windows and realised all the curtains were closed. It was a two-storey semi-detached house with a gate at the side. I walked around to this gate and pushed at it, but it was locked. The top half was a kind of latticework painted in peeling green paint and I could see that ivy growing on the garden wall had threaded itself into the lattice. The gate was not in use. Returning to the front door, I realised I was being watched over the wall dividing the front garden from next door. I rang the bell again, without any hope at all that someone would come.

As if in answer to my thoughts, the old woman watching me over the wall called out, 'It won't do you any good, duck. They've gone.'

I turned and went a few steps towards her. 'You mean they're out?'

'They won't be back, mark my words. She said she wouldn't be back.'

'Mrs Blessing?'

'Aye. They've gone. Left.'

'You mean – they don't live here any more?'

The woman shrugged. 'Always kept herself to herself. You a family friend, are you? I'm surprised you don't know.'

'Don't know what?'

'That's not for me to say. But there's trouble, as I heard.'

My mind was reeling. I stared at her. 'Where have they gone?'

'So sudden, like. She never left a forwarding address. Landlord'd know, I suppose.'

I was struggling to take this in, ask the right questions: 'W-When did they leave?'

'Few days ago, maybe? Never said goodbye. Reckon she wasn't the sort to do a moonlight flit, though. Been here years. Nice family. Hate to think who we'll get next.'

But I had seen Mildred Blessing just last week in the street. I felt dizzy. 'What about – what about . . . the other daughter? Edwina?'

The neighbour shrugged. 'She's the one gone to Canada, teaching, isn't she? I don't know about her.'

'You haven't her address? Or the son's address – Eric?'

The neighbour shook her head. 'Don't know owt about any son: Edwina and Mildred is all I know. Anyway, I can't be standing out here. You'd better get home to your family, young lady. We don't want another one disappearing. Maybe your mam can find out where Edwina is in Canada.'

She turned and shuffled back inside her own house. Numbly, I made my way out of the front gate and retraced my steps to the bus stop, the bag containing Nana's rug and dog biscuits dragging now at my shoulder, and she still trotting beside me, none the wiser as to how her life had almost changed for ever. All the way home on the two buses, I stood crushed against shoppers and men returning from the football match, trying to shield Nana from their feet and their bags. Of course it was wonderful still to have her with us, but how were we going to save her now? The neighbour had said there was trouble. Was Miss Blessing's mother in some sort of difficulty, then? Was that why she and Daddy had looked so serious last Tuesday? All I could hope for was that Millie Blessing would turn up at the Mission tomorrow as usual, her mother having moved house for some reason. Yes, surely that would be it. Then Beatrice and I could maybe speak to her on the quiet after Sunday School when Mother wouldn't be around; everything could still be arranged before Bea went back to school on Monday.

But Miss Blessing was not at morning service. The harmonium was played by Mr Wilkinson, which was upsetting in itself — to know that he must be quite pleased about her not being there. Nor did she appear at Sunday School. I sat and listened for the umpteenth time to the Raising of Lazarus with a double sense of dread. What could have happened to the family? Where had they gone? And who would help us rescue Nana and be our Good Samaritan now?

# SIXTEEN

## *1932*

### Tuesday, June 28

That brief meeting with Millie Blessing after hockey all those years ago is the last time I saw her – until our meeting in the hospital chapel. And the more I think about it now, the more uneasy I am about asking Daddy for help with my plan to become a volunteer. If her name is still forbidden, and Mother and Daddy somehow know what has happened to her, might they not block my scheme on the grounds I could bump into her around the hospital? And besides, Miss Blessing herself has told me I mustn't breathe a word... I will speak to Beatrice because she will know what to do. As luck has it, she's coming home for a few days' holiday next weekend. I must be patient and wait till then.

But by the time of Beatrice's visit, I'm so suspicious of my entire family that I decide it's too dangerous even to mention to *her* about Miss Blessing being in Mapperley Hospital. I'm afraid Bea will tell me I mustn't have anything to do with going in there to find out why she disappeared. So I simply explain that in visiting Fred I've become interested in the patients and, since Mother wants me to do some good works, I've decided to volunteer.

Beatrice gives me one of her looks. 'This isn't your usual style, Annie.'

'What d'you mean? What *is* my usual style?'

'I wouldn't have said it's visiting the sick, for one thing!'

I ignore this rather insulting remark. 'Well, I don't have much choice, do I? Mother keeps on at me. She's already got me doing lots of boring stuff in the parish; if I volunteered at the hospital it'd get me out of some of that.'

This seems to ring true with Beatrice. 'So have you asked her?'

'Not yet. I wanted your advice: how do I approach it so she doesn't say no?'

Beatrice laughs. 'I'm not a clairvoyant! How do I know?'

'Oh . . . you're good at these things, Bea. You know how to make it sound all right.' I test out Miss Blessing's suggestion. 'Shall I tell Mother I'm thinking of becoming an *almoner*?'

Beatrice wrinkles up her face. 'No,' she says, after a moment.

'Why not? Isn't it a good thing to be?'

'Yes, but not for you!' She bursts out laughing. 'You're not the type, Annie. She'd smell a rat.'

'Why am I not the type? What is the type?'

Beatrice sighs. She thinks for a moment and doesn't answer

the question. 'Listen, you're about to go to university and study languages. If you start telling her you want to be an almoner, she could see a way to stop you doing your degree. You don't need French and German to be one of those.'

This is the thing about Beatrice. She can be prissy and bossy and sometimes a bit religious, but she's wise. 'All right,' I agree. 'So what do I say?'

'Tell her the truth, Annie. She's not going to eat you; she's perfectly reasonable. Tell her you've been visiting Fred—'

'She only thinks I've been there once! I go on her Bible study afternoons.'

'. . . Tell her you've visited Fred, then, and one of the nurses at the hospital told you they're looking for volunteers and you thought it would be a good idea to—'

'Broaden my outlook?' I suggest brightly.

'No, that will alarm her no end!' Beatrice is giggling. 'Tell her you're a daft prima donna and you want to visit raving loonies because it's more dramatic than visiting the ordinary old sick of St Ann's!'

So then I throw a cushion at Beatrice and realise I'm going to have to think up my own reason.


In the end, it's one of those conversations that's simpler than I think it's going to be. I tell Mother that when I visited Fred I'd met a sister who had mentioned they were looking for volunteers, and I thought that in my endless free time before starting my university course, it would be a worthwhile thing to do. And she considers for a moment, and says that would be acceptable, but that I must take care not to be influenced by some of the godless attitudes I might encounter in the hospital – by which I think she means that they might not all be practising Nonconformists. I promise her I will hold fast to my faith, and that's that.

Far more problematic, as it turns out, is how to get into the long-term ward. I decide to approach Sister Bellamy, because fearsome as she is, she has already given me permission to visit Fred and has saved me from the bossy nurse in the chapel. This time, my note is answered with an invitation to attend for interview, and I find myself sitting on an uncomfortable leather armchair in front of her shiny desk.

Sister Bellamy asks what skills I think I have to bestow on the unfortunate patients of Mapperley. I have no skills. I am lost for words. I can feel the back of my frock sticking to the leather chair. There is a silence so long and terrible that I almost blurt out about being an almoner but manage to stop myself. Beatrice was perfectly right: Sister Bellamy would see straight through it.

'Cat got your tongue, girl? You must think you have something to offer, or you wouldn't be here!'

'I – I can listen,' I say falteringly.

'You can *listen*?' She glares at me. 'And what does that mean, pray?'

My mind is blank. I don't possess a single quality of the slightest use, apart from listening. I want to run away. 'My brother—' I begin, and tail off into silence.

'What about him?'

'He. Um, I think. He finds it helpful to . . . to talk.' I look at her hopefully.

'Go on.'

'Poor Fred.' To my intense annoyance my eyes have filled with tears. I can't speak.

'You're not going to be any good if you blub over the patients,' says Sister Bellamy.

'I'm sorry.' I dab my nose with a hanky. 'It's because he's my brother and I love him, Sister. I wouldn't be so hopeless with the others. But I think it helps him to talk and have me listen, and we can sort of get back in touch. . .' (What's this drivel? But she's listening now.) 'I mean, even if we're just talking about silly things, I feel he's better when I leave than when I arrive and – no, I'm sorry, that sounds arrogant. I don't mean that, Sister.'

'I know what you mean, Miss Lang. And because you know your brother, knew him before his breakdown and see him now, you have some insight into what can happen to someone when they become ill. Is that it?'

I nod gratefully. 'Something like that, Sister. Not understand everyone, of course – I wouldn't presume to – but perhaps I could help others. A little.'

'So maybe you could visit other patients with short-term problems similar to your brother's, you mean?'

I am glad to hear Fred's problems are considered short-term, but this is not what I mean at all. 'Oh,' I say. 'I don't think it would make a difference, short-term, long-term; in fact, perhaps if some of them have been here for a *long time* and maybe don't see many people, it could be helpful to visit them . . .?'

Sister sighs. 'My dear, this is very laudable, but I don't think you have any concept of what it means to be a long-term patient in this hospital. We deal with some of the most disturbed creatures it's possible to encounter anywhere in the system. Talking and listening doesn't arise.'

'But not for all of them, surely?' I ask, a little too sharply. Is Miss Blessing a 'disturbed creature' in Sister Bellamy's book?

After her recent thaw, she seems to freeze over again. 'You're very young and you have no idea what you're talking about, Miss Lang.' She places both hands flat on her desk to indicate our interview is over. 'I am, however, persuaded that you could be useful in some of our milder wards. I am happy to refer you to the relevant authority.' She glances down at the ledger in front of her. 'We have your address. We shall write to you shortly. Thank you for coming to see me.'

She nods a dismissal. 'Thank you, Sister,' I say as humbly as possible. I stand up to leave. 'It's very kind of you, Sister. Goodbye.'

## Monday, July 25

So for the past ten days I've been taking around cups of tea and talking to patients in the female equivalent of Fred's ward. Sometimes we're even allowed to walk in the hospital grounds. I have to admit it's quite different from visiting the sick of St Ann's. For a start, they're depressed and sometimes a little delusional, while the sick of St Ann's are depressed and all too realistic about what's wrong with them, which is mostly that they're poor and can't afford the medicines they need for themselves and their children. I like the Mapperley patients for the fact their illnesses tend to make them less bound by the rules of good behaviour, and also I don't have to read the Bible or pray with them or any of that. Best of all, I can forget that I'm the granddaughter of Pastor Eames. All that Lady Bountiful stuff is loathsome and makes it all so false and stilted when I have to go to St Ann's with Mother – or even on my own – because the Mission parishioners are so deferential to me, a mere stupid girl who knows nothing, that I sometimes want to give them a good shake!

But much as I like going to this ward in Mapperley, it is not where I need to be. I am keeping on the lookout, and trying to see a way of getting myself transferred to the long-term women's ward. So far, I haven't the faintest idea how I'm going to do it, and precious time is passing.

## Monday, August 1

Then suddenly it happens. We volunteers have a little room called 'Sister's room' in which we leave our coats and lock our bags in a locker. There is a noticeboard in there with news for the volunteers, notices of open days and appeals for people to make cakes, and so on. Today, there's a new notice:

### DOES ANYONE PLAY THE PIANO?
### ACCOMPANIST WANTED URGENTLY

For staff choir concert on Sept 10th.
To take over from their usual accompanist for
the concert itself; handover during August.
Please apply to Staff Nurse Jennings,
LT Women's ward.

It's the last line that holds my attention: the long-term women's ward is Miss Blessing's ward; surely she must be their 'usual accompanist'. I go to the nurses' station on my own ward.

'Excuse me,' I ask Sister Jones. 'I wonder if you can tell me how I can contact Staff Nurse Jennings?'

The sister looks up from her writing. 'Ooh, Miss Lang, it's not about the piano playing, is it? Do you play?'

I tell her I do, as long as it's nothing too enormously difficult.

'I'm in the choir myself,' she tells me. 'We've been left in the lurch by our usual accompanist who has decided to take a holiday, if you please, at the very end of August!'

This is disappointing news: I was so sure the regular piano-player must be Miss Blessing, but I listen politely. 'So this person will teach me the music before he or she goes away?' I ask.

Sister shakes her head. 'I'm sorry, Miss Lang, I'm not explaining very well: our *regular* accompanist, for the rehearsals you understand, is a patient on the long-term women's ward. She's awfully good, but of course she can't possibly perform in the concerts so, as a rule, Mr Beamish takes over for the actual event. It's Mr Beamish who's going on holiday, not the long-term patient,' she adds unnecessarily.

I can't help asking, 'Why could the patient herself not accompany for the concert?'

Sister Jones looks a little taken aback. 'Well, naturally not. She's a *patient*. On that *particular* ward. It would be out of the question.'

I have a brief mental picture of Miss Blessing sitting on the platform during the concert wearing an elegant evening dress and her blue shoes, chained to Doris the security guard. 'I suppose it would,' I say.

'But, Miss Lang, she's not violent and perfectly under control. You'd be absolutely safe with her, if that's what's worrying you. Truly,' she gives a tremulous smile, 'you'd be doing us an enormous favour. We have been quite at a loss . . .'

'That's fine, Sister. I'd be happy to do it,' I tell her.

Sister Jones claps her hands. 'What a brick you are! Just wait till I tell Muriel Jennings. She'll be thrilled!'

'Just as long as I can meet the patient and go through the music with plenty of time to practise.'

'That isn't a problem at all. You can meet Nurse Jennings and Blessing – that's the patient's name, you know – the next time you're in.'

And that will be very soon! It feels, at last, as if I'm about to go through a door that's been closed since I was a child. I start to think more about what happened in those days; how much I knew, and how much I did not.

# SEVENTEEN

## *1926*

The Monday morning after our failure to give Nana to the Blessings, Beatrice and I said goodbye to her with heavy hearts. But no sooner had I reached school, than I had a shock that knocked all thought of our beloved dog out of my head. Under cover of her desk-lid as we were tidying our desks before lessons, Marjorie hissed at me: 'I heard your Miss Blessing's gone missing.'

I was truly shaken. Marjorie was not a member of our church; where had she heard such a thing? 'Who says?' I whispered fiercely.

'Our Iris is seeing Ernest Wilkinson. He says his dad had to play the harmonium Sunday. He said it were embarrassing,' she smirked.

I didn't want to tell Marjorie what I had discovered at the weekend. 'I've no idea where she's gone,' I said.

She gave me a look. Then she added, 'If you ask me, she's been kidnapped, same as those others.'

At that moment Mrs Spencer came into the room and we

all had to shut our desks and stand up. 'Good morning, Mrs Spencer,' we chorused, and that was the start of the normal school day. We were doing the Wars of the Roses, but I couldn't concentrate. Perhaps it was true that Miss Blessing had been kidnapped – but if so, why would her mother have to move house? The neighbour said it was sudden and there was 'trouble', and *We don't want another one disappearing*, but you wouldn't move house if your daughter was kidnapped – why would you? I was worrying about this so much all day that I almost forgot to worry about Nana and it was only when I returned home from school that I saw to my immense relief that she was still there.

Later, when Beatrice came home, we compared notes. 'In my class they're saying another girl's gone,' she told me.

I nodded miserably. 'Same here,' I said. 'Marjorie Bagshaw thinks it's Miss Blessing. D'you know, Bea, her sister Iris is friends with the son of the Verger, weird Mr Wilkinson. Imagine!'

'Well, there's a reliable witness!' said Beatrice huffily. 'I think the two things are getting muddled. Maybe another girl has gone missing. Then a family leaves town and people jump to conclusions. It's obvious, isn't it? Miss Blessing has disappeared because her mother's had to move away for some reason. Nothing more sinister than that. Trust the Bagshaws!'

But, rumour or not, there was no getting away from the fact that Miss Blessing had apparently vanished. Her name was all over our class next day and everyone seemed to assume she had been taken by the mysterious abductor. Marjorie Bagshaw was parading around that morning like Princess Alice on account of having met the latest Missing Person, and 'being almost the last to see her alive', as though she was dead or something. Of course, I knew Miss Blessing far better than she did, but something stopped me from saying so and Marjorie was quite happy to soak up the attention.

After break, when we were changing our shoes in the cloakroom, she said, 'Bet the police will be round your house, anyway.'

I looked at her, startled. Did she suspect Mother of being somehow involved with the missing girls? 'What for?' I asked.

'Well . . .' Marjorie paused dramatically, pulling her shoe-laces tight. 'They'll be wanting to speak to everyone who knew her, won't they?'

'My mother didn't really know her,' I said. 'She's just part of our church.'

'I'm not talking about your *mother,* silly.' She took her left foot off the bench and stood to attention with an air of drama. 'It's your father who knew her, isn't it? It's him they'll be wanting to interview.'

*Interview?* I suddenly felt very scared. 'My dad doesn't know Miss Blessing.'

'Doesn't he, now?' Marjorie's eyebrows shot up. 'Unless my memory's playing tricks on me, Annie, that was your father walking down the road with Miss Blessing the other week, just before she disappeared, wasn't it? Why, I believe you went and spoke to them, you even introduced me to them, and to my way of seeing things, they weren't very happy about being caught together!'

'They weren't "caught together" – that's nonsense,' I told her, but I didn't like the catch in my voice. 'I *told* you, Marjorie, he was trying to help her brother get a place at Roebuck's.'

'And we know why,' Marjorie sneered.

I ignored this. 'He *told* us: that night at tea, he *said* it. He told Mother and Beatrice and me. He wouldn't have done that if it wasn't true, would he?'

'Course he had to explain it,' said Marjorie. 'He had to say something, didn't he, because he knew you'd seen them together! You might have *told* on him.' She looked at me for a moment. 'Maybe you wouldn't of, though. Because maybe you knew there was something fishy about it and you didn't want to get him into trouble!' And without waiting for an answer, she turned on her heel and stalked out of the cloak-room. This disturbed me very much and I spent the next few days feeling sick every time I saw a policeman, wondering if he was on the way to arrest Daddy.

Of course, it was no big event in our household that Miss Blessing had gone: why should it be? She was just another member of Grandfather's congregation. Mr Wilkinson continued to play the harmonium and made a mess of 'Onward Christian Soldiers', but otherwise it was never mentioned, because it wouldn't be Christian to indulge in gossip. So life went on as before.

Or did it? After Marjorie's accusations, I couldn't get it out of my head that although I was sure Daddy hadn't been involved, Mother might have been, and I was still pondering this suspicion when something happened that seemed to confirm it.

The week after my conversation with Marjorie, sometime after ten at night, I was tiptoeing past the kitchen window on my way to collect Nana as usual, when a dim light fell across the yard – a motorcar stopping on St Ann's Hill below our house. I hesitated, wondering whether to creep back upstairs in case it was Daddy home late again, though why he should come in the back way was a mystery. As I watched, a shadowy figure emerged at the top of the steps and before I could escape, I heard the clack of the old lock in the scullery door. Without a moment's thought, I dived under the table, thankful for the long oilcloth that hung down from it, silently tweaking my dressing-gown cord out of view and breathing as quietly as I could, though I suddenly seemed to be out of breath and gasping.

But this time, the feet that entered the scullery and came through into the kitchen were not Daddy's; it was a woman's step. My first thought was that it must be Maisie, who had forgotten something so urgent that she needed to fetch it before tomorrow morning. Instead of switching on the electric light, which would have flooded the room with brightness, the person turned up the lamp, which had been left burning low, and to my alarm approached the table under which I was crouching. Something heavy seemed to be heaved on to the oil-cloth, and as the light intensified I saw with horror that the shoes, just inches from my own clenched toes, were not Maisie's but Mother's. If I'd been half a minute earlier we'd have bumped into each other on the doorstep, and this thought alone made my heart beat so loudly I thought she must hear it. The feet then retreated, moving around the kitchen, and I could hear cupboards being opened and closed. Then I heard things being shifted around in the large cupboard where they kept dustpans and brooms and the Hoover. After a few moments of this, the feet returned to the table and I heard the heavy thing above my head being dragged off and dumped down, and there was more jostling and bumping, presumably to make room for it. I was shuddering now, hot and cold with terror. If she found me, it would be the cellar again; and besides, what deadly secret would she think I had uncovered? – for certainly, whatever she was doing had an air of being furtive in the half-light.

After an age, but it was probably no more than a minute or two, I heard the cupboard door close. The feet crossed and re-crossed the room a couple of times, as if she were uncertain of her hiding place. I prayed she would not change her mind and start moving whatever it was again, but after another few moments she turned down the lamp and went out into the hall. I could picture her removing her hatpin and coat by the pegs opposite the front door, but when I peered out from under the table I could see that she had not switched on the hall light and must be feeling her way upstairs in the darkness, just as I did when I climbed up each night with Nana. This was extremely odd. What reason had she, a grown-up, to tiptoe around her own house in the dark, if not to deceive us, who were supposed to be her family? Whatever she was up to in the kitchen must have been a secret deed, and therefore very likely an evil one. I sat on, under the table, hugging my cold knees, considering this. Long after the house was quiet again, I crept out, standing up gingerly for the pins and nee-dles. By this time I had decided it would be too dangerous to go for Nana tonight and wished for nothing more than to be safely in bed; but I also knew that here, at last, lay a possible clue to the Mystery of Mother. I had to investigate the Heavy Thing.

I turned up the lamp a little and opened the tall cupboard, with excitement and dread at what I might find. There on the floor, barely concealed by the ironing board, was a large bag I had never seen before. This must be what she had hidden. It was fastened with straps like a Gladstone bag and by heav-ing it just half way out of the cupboard I was able to undo them. On top, there was a garment of some kind in which was wrapped a hard object – I lifted it out carefully and set it on the floor; the object was a cut-glass vase. Beneath, there were books. With extreme care, stopping every few seconds to listen for sounds from upstairs, I picked out each in turn: The Complete Works of Shakespeare, a rather beautiful one in a leather cover printed on India paper; Palgrave's Golden Treasury (a different binding from the one in our book case); a novel by Mrs Gaskell, but not *Cranford* which we were reading at school; a book with a long title that I can't remember but something to do with the Rights of Women; and lastly a book called *The Gardener's Friend*. And that seemed to be all. I wish I could say these mysterious titles and the vase revealed a dark secret but truly, if they did, I had no idea what it was or why Mother should be creeping about at night hiding them in a cupboard. Disappointed, and suddenly anxious again that she might return, I started to repack the bag.

But as I replaced the first book, my fingers caught at something else at the bottom: a paper folder. I lifted it out: it was the cover of a mounted photograph from a photographer's studio, like the ones Auntie Vera had insisted Daddy must take of us a few years ago, and inside it there were two other loose photos. I carried them carefully over to the light: the first was of a man in army uniform, very upright; the second was of two little girls in party frocks; and the third, the mounted photograph, larger than the other two, was a posed portrait of a young woman who I did not know, but who looked slightly familiar. And then with a lurch of my stomach I realised, although I had met her only once, that I did know exactly who she was. I snatched up the other photo again, the one of the two little girls, and held it tilted towards the lamplight for a better view. The girls were about six and eleven, the eleven-year-old almost certainly the same as the young woman in the portrait, and although I had not known them as children it was perfectly clear who they were: sitting on a wide bench in their party frocks with the Nottingham lace, just like mine – Edwina and Millie Blessing.

\*

I couldn't bear to keep this discovery to myself and the very next day wrote to Fred and told him about Mother and the mysterious bag. All his letters to and from school are read by the teachers, so I wrote in the code he had taught me, the one based on noughts and crosses. It took me ages, and I bet everyone knows that code anyway, but I thought they probably couldn't be bothered to decipher it all since they must have trillions of letters to read every day. Fred wrote back (in code) and said this was an important clue and I must keep a careful watch and if possible follow Mother if she went out again with the bag, to discover where she took it, or who she gave it to.

For the next two days, I made frequent visits to the cupboard to see if the bag was still there. I wanted to tell Beatrice about it, but I didn't want to have to explain what I was doing sneaking down to the kitchen at the dead of night, for Fred and I had still never told her of our nightly ritual with Nana. By the afternoon of the second day, I had thought of a way around this and planned to show the bag to Beatrice as soon as the grown-ups had gone to the sitting room after tea. But when I got home from school and checked the cupboard again, it had gone – just as mysteriously as it had arrived.

This worried me greatly. I realised I might now be the only witness to the misdemeanours of Mrs Agnes Lang the Second, a terrible responsibility to bear. Marjorie Bagshaw's words had also left their mark and, for the sake of justice and Miss Blessing, I started to think I must go to the police. I imagined a long scene, played out over and over in my head, which began with me entering the police station, just as I had with Mrs Bagshaw after her purse had been stolen at Goose Fair, and having to wait a long time because they'd have lots of crimes to deal with. Then it'd be my turn to see the Sergeant and I'd say, 'I've come about the missing person, Miss Mildred Blessing, and maybe the others,' and the Sergeant would say, 'Step this way please, Miss,' as they said to Mrs Bagshaw. And we'd go into a room, a small room with no window. Or maybe it would have a window, but it'd be high up in the wall, with bars across it like a prison cell, and this would make me very nervous. I always got stuck at this point because in my imagination I was back in the cellar again and the window was the grille through which I had seen the blue shoes ... If I managed to get on to the next bit, the Sergeant would be writing notes in his notebook and I would give him my name and address and my age, and he would say, 'Does your father know you're here?' And I'd reply, 'No, because it's a secret.' And the sergeant would say, 'So what have you come to tell me?' And before I could answer he'd say, 'And this is a warning, young lady, that if you're wasting our time there will be serious consequences for you,' and he'd stare at me very hard, without smiling. And quite often when I got to that point I couldn't continue, so I'd get up and run out of the room and go home. Occasionally, I'd force myself to go further. I'd tell him: 'Well I believe my mother, who used to be Miss Agnes Higgs but is now my father's wife, Mrs Harry Lang – that is Mrs Harry Lang the Second, because she is not our mother. Our Own Mother died.' And the Sergeant would say, 'Get on with it, Miss.' So next I'd tell him, 'Well I believe my stepmother knows something about the missing young women.' And he'd look very fierce and say, 'This is a most serious accusation for a child to make against her mother, even if she is her stepmother. Tell me why you think this.' And I'd start to count the reasons on my fingers: 1) She locked me in our cellar – same as the kidnapped girls; 2) She has a sister who lives in Beeston, which is where the first girls were kept; 3) I heard her tell the Verger at our chapel that she knew where the missing girls were; 4) She came home late one night with some possessions that must belong to one of the missing girls, Miss Mildred Blessing. It was rare for me to get this far in the scene, counting on my fingers, but every time I did – before I had uttered a word to the Sergeant – I had to come out of it, because even though I knew it to be true, I could see that this was not going to get Miss Higgs locked up; especially when I have a reputation for being a troublemaker and even my own dear sister Beatrice, who loves me, thinks I am mad for believing it.

So after playing this encounter through many times, in which it always came out the same, I decided I would not go to the police station and accuse Mother of kidnap. But I resolved that if the police came to our house to question Daddy, I would inform them that they were making a mistake and it was Mother they ought to be suspecting. But the days passed and no policemen turned up, and although I continued to sneak a look at the newspaper every day when Maisie threw it on to the pile for wrapping the ashes to go down to the ash-pit, there was never any mention of Miss Blessing.

But I knew I must tell Beatrice what I had discovered. One evening, about ten days after the incident of the Bag, we were reading in the sitting room in front of a big, bright fire. Our parents were out. I was desperate to hang on to the new Beatrice, the Beatrice that had taken me into her confidence, my partner in crime over the saving of Nana but who, since the failure of that adventure and the disappearance of Miss Blessing, seemed to have retreated into the old Beatrice who still regarded me as an irritating little sister.

'Can I talk to you?' I began.

'Not really.' Beatrice was engrossed in *The Youngest Girl in the Fifth*. She didn't look up from her book.

'Ple-ease, Bea. It's important.'

'Is it, Annie?' She glanced at me over her spectacles with that slightly misty, short-sighted look.

'It's about what's happened,' I hissed.

'About Nana?'

'No. You know. Miss Blessing ... missing.'

'Annie, there's no point wasting time on that. We don't *know*.'

I closed the book on my knee carefully and studied my black stockings, one of which had sprouted a hole in the toe. 'A peculiar thing happened a few nights ago,' I told her.

Beatrice sighed. She closed her book and reached over to the coal scuttle for the poker.

'*Listen*,' I said. 'Mother came home really late, in the middle of the night, and she had this bag which she hid in the broom cupboard—' The words came tumbling out in a rush. 'And after she'd gone, I looked inside and there were some books and things, and some photos.' I stared at her anxiously. She was listening now, the poker in mid-air. 'One of the photos,' I took a deep breath and paused.

'Go on,' she prompted.

'One of the photos was of Miss Blessing's sister, Edwina. Another was of her as a little girl, my age sort of, with Miss Blessing – Mildred.'

'What are you suggesting?' asked Beatrice with a menacing calmness.

I shrugged and stared at her. 'Well,' I said. Did I have to explain? 'Don't you think it's odd?'

'In what way?'

'Beatrice, Miss Blessing disappears; the family does some kind of midnight flit' – I was counting the oddities on my fingers again – 'everyone's wondering what's happened, and our mother turns up at midnight with a bag of things and a *photo* of the missing girl!'

'You think she knows where they've gone?' Beatrice was frowning.

I sighed heavily. 'Come on, Bea. She must know! She must have had a hand in it!'

Beatrice prodded at the fire, shattering a lump of coal in a shower of sparks. 'What d'you mean?'

'I don't know, do I? But in some way ... like, she could be keeping her!'

'Keeping who, what?' Beatrice put the poker back in the coal scuttle with a clatter. She had her *I'm finding this really annoying* expression on.

'You know ... *keeping* her ...' I dropped my voice to a whisper: '*prisoner.*'

'What?' She sat back on her heels on the hearthrug and glared at me.

'Locked up. If you were keeping someone *prisoner.*'

'Annie, you're being ridiculous!'

'Beatrice, I swear.'

'Where were you, anyway? How d'you know about this bag?'

I took a deep breath and tested out my story. 'I – I couldn't sleep and I went down for a drink of water. When she'd gone, I opened the cupboard to see what she'd been doing and it was there.'

'Well, she was probably looking after it for Mrs Blessing, or something.'

'*In the middle of the night*? The Blessings aren't parishioners. Why would she? She doesn't even know them. And why' – I remembered something else – 'why didn't she put the electric light on, Bea? She turned up the lamp, then turned it down again and crept upstairs in the *dark*! It was ... furtive. She didn't want anyone to see.'

'And where is it now?'

'It's gone! Two days later.'

'So you're saying Mother has been abducting girls and keeping them prisoner in some dungeon somewhere. Is that it?'

I hung my head. Put like that, it did sound preposterous. 'But where did she get those things? They must belong to the Blessings and if she's got the bag, she must know where they've gone!' Then I remembered something else I hadn't told my sister: '*And* I heard Mother tell Mr Wilkinson she knew where the kidnapped girls were. I heard her say it, Bea, ages and ages ago, before Miss Blessing even disappeared!' I enumerated the other suspicious circumstances, which I knew by heart now, from having repeated them so often (in my imagination) to the police.

But Beatrice is too down to earth for any of this. She just shook her head and said seriously, 'Annie, I'm with you all the way over Nana and I try and stick up for you with the grown-ups. But when you come to me with these insane fantasies you make it very difficult.'

'But I—'

'Be quiet and listen,' she went on fiercely. 'If this is some idiotic scheme in your head to somehow get Mother removed from our house so that Nana will be safe, then you can forget it, Annie. It's just plain wrong for a start. It's also immoral. And it'll get you into so much trouble that you won't care about Miss Blessing or Nana or any of it. D'you understand?'

I can honestly say that until that moment it hadn't dawned on me that if we couldn't find Nana a new home, the other solution would be to remove Mother. Even to me, this sounded mad and I was ashamed that Beatrice should think it of me – ashamed, too, to have to write it here. But then, a couple

243

of days after that, I didn't have to wonder any more about whether Mother really could be the abductor, or whether I ought to report what I knew to the authorities – because the police made an arrest.

# EIGHTEEN

## *1926*

On the day the abductor was caught, the news was all around school like a wind.

'Did you hear?'

'They took him to the police station in a Black *Maria*.'

'He was wearing a mackintosh.'

'He had a limp.'

'Ivy in the kitchens saw it.'

'She never, but her husband's a policeman. *He* saw it.'

'It must be true.'

Marjorie caught up with me in the playground at break. 'They didn't come for your dad, then?'

'Of course not!' I felt my face turn red and glared at her. 'It's not funny, Marjorie.'

'I think it is! Had you rattled, didn't I!'

'You wouldn't like it said about *your* father.'

Marjorie shrugged. 'Wouldn't bother me,' she said, "cos I'd know it wasn't true.' She threw me a dark look.

'*I* knew it wasn't,' I retorted.

She laughed. 'Wouldn't have mattered anyway,' she said. 'My dad could have saved your dad.'

'What d'you mean?' I asked.

'They're 'Masons, stupid!' She looked at me as if I was being exceedingly thick. 'That's what 'Masons do: they help each other.'

Her father wasn't a policeman; he was something at the Players factory. I couldn't see how that would help, but I didn't want to talk about it any more, so I said nothing.

Besides, I was uncomfortably aware that for all I knew, 'they' might have come for Daddy; he hadn't appeared at breakfast. I hurried home after school and was relieved to find the house seemed reassuringly normal.

'Have you seen Daddy today?' I asked Maisie, trying to keep my voice casual.

'No, duckie, he went to Derby with Mr Gibson, your mother said.'

And I had to be content with that.


Feeling listless, with the butterflies again, which I didn't know why I should be feeling them, I wandered into the front room and sat down at the piano. From my seat on the piano stool I could see our front path, and as I practised the Chopin prelude I was learning, I found myself sneaking a look for the paperboy, who was surely late today.

Mother put her head around the door. 'Annie, have you taken Nana out yet?'

'No, Mother.'

'Well don't leave it too late, will you?'

'I'll go when I've finished this,' I promised (and once the *Evening Post* arrives, I added silently). No sooner had she left the room than the familiar squeak of the front gate announced that here it was. When I sensed the coast was clear

I darted out into the hall, scooped it off the mat and retreated to the front room again.

The story was not on page one, which surprised me given its importance all around our school, but a large headline on page three announced, 'Man Arrested in Missing Girls Mystery'. Four young women, it said, had been

> discovered last evening at a house in the Meadow Lane area and a 47-year-old man arrested at the address. The girls, whose names have been withheld at the request of their families, are said to be recovering at the City Hospital where they are under-going medical tests. One of them has been missing for two-and-a-half years, another for 14 months; these two were thought to have been kept in Beeston for some time. The remaining two were taken more recently. Their eager families are expecting them home as soon as doctors are satisfied they are fit to leave hospital. The man is helping police with their inquiries, but at the time of going to press no one has been charged …

Well that ruled out anyone in my family, then. We lived nowhere near the Meadows, which I always thought sounded lovely but the others said was a foggy slum near the River Trent. Anyway, if Daddy was at the police station then he couldn't have gone to Derby with Mr Gibson, could he? I felt better – or thought I would very soon. I was sure one of the released young women must turn out to be Miss Blessing. That would be wonderful news indeed! Feeling rather smug at knowing something not revealed to the general public, I played the Chopin prelude once more for luck, picked up my coat and went to collect Nana from the yard.

When I returned from our walk, I was relieved to see Daddy's coat and hat hanging on the hall stand. Well, of course he was home. Why on earth would he not be? I went upstairs to wash my hands and tidy my hair. At tea, I waited for an opportunity to find out more, though the arrest of a man for kidnap and abduction was not the kind of subject generally discussed around our family tea table. First, I asked Beatrice if she had read the paper that evening. She looked at me oddly.

'*No*,' she said, screwing up her face in an *are-you-mad?* sort of way. 'Why, should I?'

'Everyone in our class was talking about those girls today,' I said. 'You know, the ones who disappeared.'

Mother looked up sharply. Beatrice bit her lip.

'We'll have no tittle-tattle around this table,' Daddy cautioned. I looked at him.

'But Daddy, it's good news, they've found them!' I thought it would be all right if the news was good. 'They're going home to their families soon.'

'Of course they're going home,' said Mother. 'As I've kept saying ever since the first girl was taken, I've always known where they were – safe in the arms of Jesus. I never had any doubts'

Beatrice threw me a scornful look: *Trust you to pick up fag ends,* it said.

This annoyed me so much, Mother's smugness and Beatrice's scorn, that I couldn't help myself: I looked from Mother to Daddy. 'D'you think Miss Blessing could be one of them? Do you know if she's safe?'

Mother turned pale. Beatrice's head jerked up, as if she'd seen a ghost. Daddy went icy still, his blue eyes drilling into me. Then he threw back his chair, its legs screeching on the floor. 'Didn't you hear me, Annie? We won't discuss it.' I had never heard this voice before. I thought he might come round the table and hit me. There was an awful silence.

Then Mother said, 'More tea, Harry? Pass your cup.' And Daddy's eyes flicked away from me. He drew his chair back in to the table and pushed his cup and saucer across to Mother. I watched as she filled it with thick brown tea and then went slowly back to my egg. No one spoke. Then Daddy looked over at Beatrice and grinned. 'Good weather for the Robin Hood trail tomorrow,' he said. I daren't catch Bea's eye. We finished tea in silence.

When it was over, I ran upstairs. I didn't want to speak to anyone, but Beatrice was at my heels muttering, *How many times have I told you?* I was in tears, and shaking, as she pushed me into my bedroom and shut the door carefully behind us both.

'But how am I to know what I'm not supposed to say if no one's told me *why*?' I gasped between sobs.

'I've told you *never* to utter the name of Mildred Blessing in this house. I've *told* you that.'

'But he himself talked about her after I'd seen them in the street!'

'That was then.'

'Well why not now? *What's happened,* Bea?'

That was when my all-knowing wise sister collapsed on to my bed in tears. 'I don't know, Annie. I don't know. I just know we mustn't.' We clung to each other. Beatrice crammed the eiderdown into her mouth to stifle her own sobs. For a moment, I felt it was me who had to take care of *her,* but after a while, she quietened and sat up. 'I must go downstairs. Stay here: do your homework. Just keep out of their way tonight.'

*

This was typical of rows in our family: people may get punished or sent to bed without supper, but if you tried to write *down* these rows, nothing would actually have been *said*. So the argument-that-never-was would be squashed under layers of whatever happened the next day, and the day after that, until it would be a tight, cold mass in the pit of your stomach and the middle of your brain that would never go away.

Over the next few days, I searched my family for clues. You had to become expert at this, or there would be no chance at all of discovering what on earth was going on, or how anyone felt about it; but I was almost eleven now and good at spotting them. What I observed was as follows: Maisie returning the bottle of calcium lactate to its place on the top shelf of the kitchen cupboard, so Mother must have been having one of her headaches; Daddy missing his Masonic evening and going off somewhere else in different clothes – highly unusual; Mother herself planting bulbs, pressing them down into the earth as if she were trying to put their eyes out; and Beatrice absent-mindedly singing grim hymns around the house, when it was not even Good Friday or anything:

> *O Sinner, lift the eye of faith*
> *To true repentance turning:*
> *Bethink thee of the curse of sin,*
> *Its awful guilt discerning . . .*

These dismal hymns depressed me more than I could say, because they also signified a drawing-back from my newfound closeness to my sister. And just as Beatrice had seemed to be standing up for herself and even defying the Mission – why, she had actually told a lie to get Miss Blessing's address! – Mother suddenly announced on Beatrice's fifteenth birthday that she would be baptised the following Summer. I think this was quite young to have the total immersion because you're supposed to do it from a position of wisdom and stuff, but it must have been Mother's idea of a special birthday treat. I felt sorry for Beatrice because it's a bit of a disappointment, when you could be getting a visit to the ballet or a Fair Isle jumper, but Bea turned pink and lowered her eyes and looked quite holy, so I didn't dare make a joke about it.

And later, when I ventured to tell her I thought it was a bit mean because she must have known she'd be baptised sooner or later, it became clear that Beatrice didn't see it like that. She said she was happy because when you're baptised it means you'll be saved.

This confirmed some of the doubts I'd been having. 'D'you mean that until I've had the total immersion I'll go to hell?'

'Well you will have it, won't you,' she reassured me. 'So it won't arise.'

'But supposing I died tomorrow? I thought we were saved *anyway* because of the Mission and all the punishments and everything?'

Beatrice seemed hazy about this. I told her she'd better get it straight because I needed to know. 'If that's true,' I went on, 'do you have to go absolutely under the water, every bit of you, for it to count? I mean, supposing your finger doesn't go under, does it mean your finger's not saved?'

Beatrice frowned. She obviously thought this was irrelevant, so I shut up, but it was an unsettling thought. It would be like Elise and the Swans: Elise had to weave shirts out of stinging nettles in order to break her wicked stepmother's spell and turn her brothers from wild swans back into human boys; but she didn't have time to finish the final shirt, so her youngest brother, the one who took most care of her, always had a swan's wing instead of one arm. Elise could make it better, but she couldn't take away the evil completely.

A short while ago, when we were plotting to save Nana, we might have had a reasonable conversation about this, but that's what I mean about Beatrice sort of closing down again. Now she was getting baptised, I realised miserably that I just could not expect to talk to my beloved sister about all this any longer. And the worst of it was that even though we had joined forces for those few brief weeks, we hadn't saved Nana. With the mystery of Miss Blessing, we simply hadn't had time to worry about our poor dog. Perhaps we had been lulled into a sense of false security because Mr Holley and his gun had not appeared. But the danger was just as real, and time was passing: we had failed to come up with a rescue plan, and at any moment we could lose her.

On the nights it felt safe enough to collect Nana from the kennel and stow her in her secret bed underneath my own, I took to sleeping on my tummy so I could reach down and cradle one of her ears. Sometimes I would wake in the morning still clutching it and, bless her, she never protested. I felt as if Nana and Little Sid were the only loyal people in my world, and I was getting too old to depend on Little Sid. Well, Beatrice was loyal too, of course (most of the time), and Fred when he was there.

After one of these nights I awoke in the dark as usual and sensed it must be time to return Nana to the yard. We crept downstairs, the same as all the many other mornings, and across the kitchen to the back door. I was just about to fit the key into the lock, feeling for the keyhole in the dark as I always did, when to my horror the lock slowly turned on the outside and the door swung open. I had to jump back to avoid it hitting me, but there was no possible chance of escape. Frozen to the floor I waited for the electric light to switch on, fearing it would be Mother again. But it was Maisie.

'Lord save us!' She clapped her hand over her mouth. 'Annie, what on earth—' Then she looked down and saw the dog. Nana wagged her tail uncertainly, then stopped. We all sensed the seriousness of this moment.

Maisie was the first to recover. She nodded slowly. 'I knew it,' she said. She held the door open. 'Get that dog out of here, Annie, *now.*'

I gave Nana a little push and after looking up at me, as if wondering whether I needed protection, she trotted out.

Maisie shut the door. I stared at her. I couldn't speak. 'You look as if you've seen a ghost,' she muttered. 'As well you might.' She glared back at me. I could tell she was angry. I had a sudden vision of what would happen now: Mother told. A punishment to end all punishments. And – worse than anything – Nana destroyed. This must be certain.

'Maisie—'

'Be quiet and listen.'

Maisie was breathing hard. She unbuttoned her coat and went to hang it carefully on a hook by the back door. Then she removed her hat, patted her hair, took down her pinny, placed its loops over her head and tied it deliberately behind her. Moving to the stove she picked up the kettle and filled it at the tap over the sink, placing it with a clang upon the burner and lighting the gas. I watched her, feeling faint. 'Sit down, Annie,' she instructed at last. 'I need to talk to you.' We moved into the breakfast room. She turned up the lamp and I sat numbly at the table, scraping the chair with a teeth-on-edge noise upon the tiles. She glanced anxiously at the clock and went to face me across the table. She remained standing.

'There isn't much time,' she began. 'So you're not to interrupt. I'll only say this once.'

I nodded.

'I blame myself in a way, because of course I've known for months this has been going on. How did you think you could smuggle that dog upstairs night after night and not make a mess with her hairs under the bed? Elsie spotted it when she was cleaning. I went and checked. I didn't know what to do. What makes me so angry, Annie, is that you put me in this impossible position with your stepmother. If I wasn't going to tell her, I was living a lie.'

'I'm so sorry, Maisie,' I whispered. 'I didn't know.'

'That's what I told myself,' she said. 'You're only a child. You weren't to understand the consequences. And I also know other things that go on ... well, never mind that. But I discussed it with Mr Brown at home. He's a soft touch. He loves animals. I knew what he'd say. To be honest, I was more worried about what would happen to you if *she* ever found out.' Maisie tailed off. We both knew who 'she' was. 'But now—'

'Maisie, *please*,' I implored her.

'I said you're not to interrupt. And if you're going to ask me to do nothing, Annie, then *don't*. Because that's not possible after ...' She spread her hands. 'Not after this morning.'

I had been trying to stay calm, but at this the tears just started to run down my face. I tried to wipe them on the sleeve of my dressing gown. I was almost choking in an effort not to cry outright. Maisie watched me for a moment, then she took a clean handkerchief out of her pocket and handed it to me. Almost to herself, she said, 'Bless you, duckie. You love that dog to pieces, don't you.'

I couldn't help it then. I put my arms on the table and howled. In between sobs, I told her, 'Beatrice overheard something. Something about Mr Holley.' I didn't dare mention the gun. 'We've been trying to find Nana a new home. We wanted to save her. I took her down to Miss

Blessing's mother's house in West Bridgford – she's our Sunday School teacher – but that's when I discovered they'd gone.'

'They have, have they?' Maisie looked grim at this news (did she know the Blessings, then? This was peculiar in itself). 'Well that's as maybe. But you can't continue like this, Annie. *I* can't, knowing what I know.'

'But Mr Holley . . .'

Maisie paused and thought for a moment. 'All right,' she said. 'Dry your eyes. One thing to put your mind at rest: Reg Holley is an old friend of Mr Brown's. He's not a bad man, Annie. He just does odd jobs for your father. Mr Holley doesn't have a telephone, so if anyone here wants to get a message to him, it goes through me. D'you understand?' She paused, watching me as this sank in.

'And had they asked you . . .?'

Maisie didn't answer this. 'So I've been talking it through with Mr Brown, and now this has happened I think we'll have to stop talking and just do it.'

I looked up at her.

'Nana is getting on Mrs Lang's nerves, and heaven help her she's got more than the dog to worry about now. I said to Mr Brown, the only way to solve this is for Nana to come to us.'

I gazed at her in amazement.

She went on, 'I'll take her with me when I leave on Monday nights and bring her back Saturday mornings. That way Mrs Lang doesn't have to have Nana's smelly old rug in the yard, but you can still see her at weekends. So Mr Holley doesn't have to come into it, and she can live in our house and sleep in our kitchen weekday nights. She won't have to live outside. How's that?'

I stood up. 'Maisie!' I was round the table and wanted to give her a hug, but we don't do that, so I grabbed her hands.

'Oh Maisie, it'll save her life. Thank you! Thank you *so much*!' I burst into tears again.

Maisie gave my hands a quick squeeze. 'All right, well don't get overexcited about it. I'll speak to Mrs Lang this morning. See what she says. She may not agree to the weekends, mind, but we'll give it a try.' She patted my shoulder. 'Now run along and get dressed, it's almost breakfast time and you're making me late. And Annie—' I was halfway out of the room. I turned and looked at her. 'Not a word about what happened this morning. D'you understand?'

'Of course,' I promised her. 'Beatrice doesn't know about me and Nana coming indoors, anyway, so I couldn't even tell her.'

'Good. Mum's the word,' said Maisie.

Maisie wasn't able to let me know what Mother and Daddy said that day, but when I got home from school in the evening, Nana, her lead and her old tartan rug had gone. I had no way of knowing whether I'd see her at the weekend – or indeed would ever see her again – but when on Saturday morning I looked anxiously out into the yard, there she was, sitting where she always sat. And that's how it went on. Nana went to live with Maisie and Mr Brown, and we had her at weekends – which was heaps better than if she'd gone to live with the Blessings. But just like the appearance of Nana's kennel in the first place, and like everything else in our family, the matter was simply never discussed.

After a few days I did tell Beatrice it had been Maisie's idea, though, and Bea said, 'You spoke to Maisie about it? Why didn't you tell me?'

I fidgeted and looked down at my fingers.

'Well it was a really sensible thing to do,' said Beatrice warmly. 'Well done, Annie. I should have thought of that.

I'm afraid I've been a bit distracted with the baptism classes. We should have asked her earlier, instead of going through all that West Bridgford palaver.' I felt bad I couldn't tell her what had really happened, but all the same it was like the sun coming out to be praised by Beatrice.

Throughout these days there was no word of Miss Blessing; whether she had been found safe or not, I had no idea – and of course I could no longer ask. The *Evening Post* named one of the girls, whose family gave an interview to their reporter, but the others remained anonymous. Then the following Sunday came a genuine clue – and not so much a clue as a boulder dropping from the heavens into our congregation.

If you haven't realised it so far, I should explain that at the Golgotha Mission we do not indulge in pageantry; in fact any demonstrative behaviour would be completely out of place. We have no symbols, no rituals, no processions, no fanfares of any kind at all. We have hymns and the harmonium, of course; we have prayers and sermons, but any kind of drama would be considered unholy, even sinful. The baptism by total immersion, when discreetly before the service the wardens take up the grating and reveal the short staircase going down into the mysterious bath which they fill with kettles from the vestry sink, is as dramatic as life ever gets at the Mission.

So it was entirely within keeping when, at the time of notices, which generally comes before the final hymn, Pastor Eames straightened his back, gazed out at his flock, and announced that there would be a bring-and-buy-sale in aid of our fellow Mission and the school at Tai Yuan-Fu in Shansi Province, China, on the last Saturday in February, to which we were all invited to contribute. And he reminded us that since this school was presided over by our sister, by which he meant his niece, our Auntie Frances Eames, we had a particular duty to support it – the ladies, especially, to bake cakes. And that the collection from our services the previous month had raised a total of six pounds, fifteen shillings and eightpence which, in his view, fell short of the sum he would like to have been able to present to the God's Purpose Overseas Mission for the provision of Bibles to our friends in Ethiopia. In recognition of this, he had invited Mr Gloom of the G-Pom to deliver a lecture on Friday fortnight (his actual name was Mr Bright, but Fred and I knew better: we had heard him lecture before). The subject of this one was to be Coptic Christians and the Conversion Question and we were all urged to attend. Grandfather Eames paused and peered at us severely over his steel-rimmed spectacles as if to say this was not so much an invitation as a summons, to make up for the poor level of collections the previous month. Then he put aside his notes and said:

'The soul, the divine part of man, needs refreshment, just as the body does, and Jesus is the only One Who can supply that. While I know from experience that we can draw continuously on Him, I find my greatest uplift in life is when I go to the House of Prayer. But that House must remain Pure if it is to benefit the body and soul of its congregation, and it is therefore meet and necessary to remove the tares that may from time to time take root in its fertile earth . . .' I was thinking about the way he said Pure – he pronounced it, '*pyaw*' and I was repeating it over to myself experimentally when suddenly his words jolted me back to the present: '. . . Therefore it is with sorrow I must announce that our former sister Miss Mildred Blessing shall henceforth, and permanently, be excluded from this congregation, let us pray.' He said it in the tone of voice you might use if you were running through a shopping list to yourself – *half a pound of lard and some damson jam* – yet as the words sank in I sensed a wave wash through the rows, an exchange of glances and raised eyebrows under-cover of rheumatic knees being lowered on to hassocks and overcoats catching in upturned heels. I vividly remember I was sitting between Mother and Beatrice. I dropped to my knees, aghast, sending the chair in front scraping forwards and earning a fierce look from Daddy, two seats to my right.

The sermon that day had come from St Paul's letter to the Corinthians, 'When I was a child . . .', those verses about children only half-understanding the grown-ups, and how we had to work out what God was up to 'through a glass, darkly'. But at that moment – and I have thought about this a good deal since – I knew that whatever Miss Blessing's transgression, however appalling and unpardonable even by the Good Shepherd (who is supposed to forgive *all* His lost sheep, isn't He?), I didn't believe a word of it. And I resolved that one day I would find out what it was, and put it right.

# Part Three

1932

# NINETEEN

**Wednesday, August 3**

I'm following Staff Nurse Jennings down the corridor from my usual ward to the ward where Millie Blessing is a long-term patient. We stop halfway at a heavy barred gate. Nurse Jennings selects a key at her belt and we pass through. Before locking it behind her, she looks at me anxiously.

'Do you have shoelaces, Miss Lang?' She glances down at my feet. 'A comb, perhaps, or a mirror?'

'I left my bag in Sister's room,' I assure her, wondering what on earth could befall a comb on the long-term ward. 'I have a hanky.' I take it from my pocket to show her.

'Anything else in your pockets?'

'Nothing.'

'No pencil, notebook?'

I say nothing, but hold up my empty hands.

She hesitates a moment longer. 'I know it must seem odd,' she says. 'But when you've been working with them as long as I have, you learn never to be too careful.'

We continue down the corridor towards a second barrier;

this one is of solid metal. Instead of unlocking it, Nurse Jennings pulls a bell lever and sets off a jangling on the far side. A small flap opens and a man's face appears.

'Who is it?'

'Staff Nurse Jennings with one visitor.'

There is a noise of a key in the lock; then a bolt slides back with a squeal and the door swings open.

'Go in quickly,' says the nurse. We enter and the person who unlocked the door now locks it again behind us. On the inside we're in a kind of cage, and through its bars I can see a long ward, similar to Fred's, except that its high windows are protected by thick iron mesh which blocks out much of the light. Beside every bed there is a small locker and an upright chair. One or two of the beds are occupied but most are neatly made. A long table runs between the two rows of beds. Some women are sitting at the table; others by their beds; a few move around the room. There is a strong smell of carbolic, but what hits me is the noise: it is a kind of undertow of groans and calls that bounce off the ceiling and tiled walls. Some of the women appear to be speaking into a void; others to be rocking within themselves. No one seems to have noticed us. The attendant comes forward and now unlocks the cage and we go through into the ward.

Nurse Jennings starts across the vast room towards a door halfway along one side. 'Come,' she instructs me, over her shoulder. 'Don't worry. They won't bite. But it's better if you don't catch anyone's eye.'

I follow her. As I pass one of the beds, a woman snatches at my skirt. 'Miss – miss —'

I turn and smile, but I pull my skirt away and keep moving.

'Hey, miss. You new here, miss?'

'Hello,' I say.

'Not now, Hodgkins,' orders Nurse Jennings.

The woman throws her head back and cackles. 'Not now, Hodgkins! Not ever, Hodgkins!'

'That's enough now! You don't want to go back in strips, do you?'

'Don't care was made to care. Eh, Nurse? 'Ere, duck, new girl, they'll eat you for breakfast in 'ere!'

'She's not stopping,' says Nurse Jennings. 'Don't get your hopes up, Hodgkins.'

'Not stopping,' the woman mimics. 'They never do stop in 'ere, do they, Nurse, if they're decent and *sane*. And if they're mad or bad like we are, they stop for ever an' ever.'

We've reached the door halfway up the ward. It gives on to a side room with a thin Turkey carpet, half-a-dozen stained-looking armchairs, a well-stocked bookshelf and, in one corner, a piano at which Mildred Blessing is sitting in her grey shift. She is practising scales. A second woman, seated on one of the armchairs by an empty fireplace, is weaving something on a card with a blunt wooden peg instead of a tapestry needle and singing along to the music. She stops, peg in mid-air, to stare at us. Miss Blessing stands and comes forward; her face registers no recognition and no greeting.

'Well, Blessing,' says Nurse Jennings, 'We've found you a piano player. This is Miss Lang.'

Mildred holds out her hand and I take it. The fingers are cold and dry. 'How do you do, Miss Lang?'

'Very well, thank you, Miss Blessing.'

Nurse Jennings stands back. 'Hmm. Well, I've to leave you now. Some of us have got work to do. You'll be all right with Blessing, Miss Lang. She'll make sure you're not bothered. I'll come back in half an hour or so.' She turns on her heel and notices the woman in the armchair. 'You all right with her?' she asks Mildred.

'Ivy is fine,' says Mildred. 'Leave her be.'

'Aye. She's no trouble, is she?' Then with a sharp look, Nurse Jennings adds, 'See to it – you know.'

Mildred nods. 'Don't worry, Nurse. And thank you.'

'I can lock you in, if you want to be left in peace?'

'We'll manage. It's fine.'

'Ta-ta, then.' Nurse Jennings leaves the room, shutting the door firmly behind her.

Miss Blessing smiles for the first time. 'I'm so glad it's you,' she says. 'I hoped it would be. I knew you'd volunteered. I thought there was a chance they'd let you in here, but they wouldn't, of course, under normal circumstances. I should have guessed.'

'Well, I'm here anyway,' I say, though now I've got what I've been working for, I feel awkward and at sea.

'Don't look so shell-shocked,' she says. 'You'll get used to it.'

I blurt out, 'I just don't understand what you're doing here . . .!'

'No.' Her face seems to close down for a moment. 'But I'm here. So. We'd better get on with it. Haven't got long.' She turns away to the piano and picks up a pile of music. 'The choir are singing some C.V. Stanford and Hubert Parry in Part One. In the second half it's extracts from the Mozart *Requiem*. The Parry is *Songs of an Ending*.' She pulls a face. 'Written in the Great War and all about death.' I remember that her father died in the war. 'The good news for you is that it's unaccompanied. All you have to do is give them a split chord at the start of each one. The tricky accompaniment is the Mozart.' She hands me the music, frowning. I realise she's as nervous as I am.

I look it through. 'This'll be all right, as long as I can take it away and learn it now.'

'These copies are for you.'

266

I tell her I'm hoping to do Grade Eight next year, if Mother will let me.

'Then it won't be too difficult,' she says, clearly relieved, but she doesn't take the opening to ask me anything about myself.

We're speaking rapidly in low voices. The other woman, Ivy, seems impervious; she is concentrating on her weaving, tongue clamped between her teeth. But I don't want to be talking about the music. I want to know about *her*. Why did she vanish so suddenly? How long has she been here? Where is her family? And why is she shut away in this place?

I look up at her. 'Miss Blessing—'

'Millie. Please.'

'Millie, you know just after I last saw you—?'

But she interrupts me. 'How's your brother?' She asks. 'I was so sad to see him in here.'

I hold her gaze for a moment. She says, 'I'm sorry. I can't. I hope you understand.'

So we talk about Fred's breakdown. I tell her that in some ways I'm finding it easier to have conversations with him in Mapperley than I did before. 'He's having this treatment. Perhaps it's something to do with that.'

'He's having the intravenous Cardiazol?'

I nod. 'Sometimes it gives him a stiff neck or a bad back.'

'That's the convulsions.' She shudders. 'I was with one patient who broke a rib; another lost a tooth. Sorry. I shouldn't be telling you this, should I? They don't know how it works, or who it's going to help. It's just the latest thing, so they give it a try on most people. It really does seem to help some of them.'

'Have you had it?'

'No. My situation was different. But I've been with people who have. I doubt if that's what is helping him talk to you.'

She is silent for a moment. Then she says, 'He's probably just getting better, Annie. I'm sure seeing you and having you there will be helping. Talking is the thing.' She breaks off.

'But you can't?'

She shakes her head. She can't meet my gaze. 'I haven't seen anyone from outside for so long, I've forgotten how to speak of myself. And too much has happened. I'm a completely different person from the one I was before.' Her eyes have filled with tears and she checks herself and turns away.

'But you still play *Sheep May Safely Graze*.'

'Music is the only thing . . .'

And that is about all she can tell me. When Nurse Jennings returns, I take the sheaf of music and prepare to leave, disappointed for both of us, with the sense of an afternoon wasted.

'Did you sort it all out then?' asks Nurse Jennings.

'Yes, thank you, Nurse,' I tell her.

Millie Blessing nods. She is looking distracted and for the first time I can see something like panic in her face. I hope it's because our interview is over and she's said none of the things she may have wanted to say. Suddenly emboldened by this possibility, I turn to the nurse again. 'Nurse Jennings, I am going to go away and learn the music, but then I shall need to come and practise it with Miss Blessing,' I tell her. 'And I'll need to rehearse with the choir; it's the only way this will work.'

I catch Millie's brief expression of relief and know I've guessed right. 'Shall I speak to Sister Jones about it?' I ask. 'Sister Jones sings in the choir, doesn't she? I'm sure she'll understand . . . And before we get to that stage, I'd like to go through the music again *here* with Miss Blessing once I've learnt it, please; it will save a lot of time in rehearsal.'

Nurse Jennings looks from one of us to the other. 'Very

well, Miss Lang. I can't play the piano for toffee-nuts, so if that's the way it works, and Sister Jones is happy, it's all right by me.'

And that's how we leave it. I'm to come back at the same time next week. Miss Blessing's grip is a little stronger when she shakes my hand goodbye.


## Wednesday, August 10

As soon as I enter the long-term women's ward for my second visit today, it's clear that something is wrong – or more wrong than usual: raised voices and high-pitched screams are coming from a little knot of patients further up the line of beds. Staff Nurse Jennings instantly breaks away from escorting me and shouts for assistance as she runs towards the scuffle. 'Go in there, Miss Lang,' she instructs, 'and close the door!'

Suddenly, there are running feet behind me as a posse of attendants and nurses come scurrying in her wake. Millie Blessing appears in the doorway and watches, expressionless, then pulls me through, closes the door and leans against it. She's very pale, but all she says is, 'Flo can be violent.' She explains that this patient, Flo, is having a bad day, being obstreperous and shouting. Earlier, one of the less experienced nurses had threatened her with the strip-cells, and this sent her into a wild, flailing attack on the nurse. A few patients had tried to pull her away and a fight broke out. Things had quietened down for a while, but it all flared up again just as I arrived. Millie explains that the strip-cells are in a separate corridor segregated from the main ward by double doors so no sound can escape. Each cell is bare but for a light bulb behind a wire-mesh guard and a mattress on the floor. Sometimes women ask to be segregated because they're feeling desperate and want a bit of peace, or because they think they might do something stupid; but if it's a disruptive patient, as in this case, she is usually bound into a straitjacket, given a sleeping draught whether she wants one or not, and left there until her attack has passed. Millie explains prolonged attacks are called 'psychosis'. Then she says, 'That's what I had – after the baby.'

We're sitting side by side on the long piano stool in the room off the ward. I turn and look at her, but she's staring at the piano keys.

'What baby?'

'Oh Annie, did you not know? I thought the whole congregation of the Mission knew.' She bows her head.

'You were going to have a baby?'

She nods.

I don't know what to say, but the shame is burning off her: I can't keep silent. 'That must have been ... so worrying for you.'

'Utterly shameful,' she says in a very low voice. 'It is the worst thing ... it goes against everything we learn as Christians, but also against ... trying to live our lives as good people.'

I don't contradict her. This must be the greatest transgression, the greatest taboo in the whole Mission; so great that it is simply never spoken of. I have a sudden vivid vision of myself, with all my imperfections rolled into a ball but amounting to nothing, *nothing*, in comparison with the appalling stain of – unmarried motherhood. 'I'm so sorry,' I breathe. 'And yet—' I turn to her. 'You are not a bad person, Millie. It can't be right to think it.'

But she's having none of that, and somehow it unleashes her tongue and she's talking. 'Oh Annie, it *is* a sin. In the eyes of God and the Mission and the pastor and the congregation it is a most heinous sin – yes, in my own eyes, too! Think of my poor mother; thankfully my sister was already in Canada, but Mother – can you imagine? – had to leave our home in secret without telling anyone and go to another town where nobody knew her.'

Of course, from my adventure with Nana I already knew they had left home in a hurry, though not the reason why. I'm silently thankful I missed them: if the drama with Nana had taken place just before all this happened, the additional burden would have been unthinkable for them.

Miss Blessing is explaining her mother had to pay double rent for leaving without notice. 'It gave her severe money troubles – we're not well off – and for a while we lived in one room, she and I. I was in such a confused state, what with having to leave school just before my final exams and being publicly expelled from the Mission, that for a while I was no help to her. We lived from day to day; I got a little cleaning work, but we were outcasts – it was no less than I deserved, but my poor mother deserved none of it.' She breaks off, flushed and breathless.

'Could your brother be of support?' I ask her.

She looks perplexed. 'My *brother*? I don't have a brother, Annie.'

This is very odd. 'I thought you did.' I try and remember who told me about him.

'No, I don't know what gave you that idea – unless it's because we call my sister Edwina "Eddie"? It's just Edwina and Mother and me. Luckily, Eddie managed to send money after a few months and Mother joined her in Canada. She wanted to stay in Mansfield with me – that was where we'd fled to – but we persuaded her it would be for the best to make a completely new start. The idea was for me to join them when I . . . after the baby . . .' She lapses into silence again.

So she was all alone at this terrible time. 'If only we had known!' I say. 'Couldn't we have helped in some way?'

'Ah, but you did, Annie.' She still can't look at me. 'Your father did, and your stepmother, too.'

'Daddy?' I stare at her. 'What did he do?'

She's silent for a few moments. 'As the time approached, I needed to go somewhere – to be somewhere – to have the baby. Mr Lang found me a place – it was a sort of a home, a mother and baby home – to do with one of the charities he supports. In the end, that's what persuaded Mother to go to Canada. I was to be looked after for the lying-in and after-wards—' She breaks off.

'He never spoke of it,' I say, feeling suddenly proud of my generous-minded father, and a little surprised as well. 'When the Mission could only think about keeping their nose clean and expelling you into outer darkness, he stepped in.'

She nods slowly. 'And your mother went to our old lodg-ings and rescued some possessions we'd had to leave behind in the rush.'

The heavy bag! I'm embarrassed to think how wrong I was to have seen it as evidence of Mother's guilt, when in fact it was Christian charity: Beatrice had been right, as usual.

'I was grateful to them both,' Millie was saying. 'In fact . . .' She hesitates. 'Your – your father is still paying for me to stay here.'

This jerks me into the present. 'He pays for *this*?'

She says softly, 'Well, where else would I be now?'

I can't help myself. I grip her arm. 'You'd be out in the world, Millie, leading a normal life! You must leave this place. You don't belong here!'

She shakes her head. 'You don't understand, Annie. I could no more live out in the world now than you could survive in here.'

'Why not?' I ask fiercely.

'Because I'm sick. You have to understand this. My doctor here, Dr Squires, has told me I must stay here for my own protection, you see. He's very advanced in his thinking: he believes in being completely frank with his patients and he has told me that I will not recover.'

'How can he know that?' I burst out. 'Millie, you're no more sick than I am! There's nothing wrong with you. And they must realise, too, if they let you play the piano for the choir, and the harmonium on Sundays!'

'Ah, but that's it,' she explains sadly. 'If you knew Dr Squires you would understand. He's a really enlightened man, Annie, a brilliant psychiatrist – and he's choirmaster of the choir. It was all his idea I should play for them, and play at Sunday services, too. It's safe for me to do that, he says, because the chapel is part of the hospital and I can be protected there. He can see I need some stimulation in my existence here and has gone out of his way to make life as pleasant for me as it's possible to be. D'you know, he even arranged for this piano to be brought in? He's so kind. Well, you'll understand for yourself when you meet him at the rehearsal.'

I gaze at her. 'Mildred – Millie,' I say. 'Of course I'm just a girl. I know nothing, and he's a doctor. But, well, maybe you *were* really sick when you came here. But I don't believe you're sick now. I just *can't* believe it.'

She sighs. There is a silence, punctuated by muffled noises from the ward outside. 'There was one nurse in the home,' she says at last, 'who took pity on me after my little boy was born. He had been removed at birth, of course, because that is how they do it, but she – her name was Joan – worked nights when most of the staff were off duty and many of the mothers asleep. I was having pain' – she lays her hand on her breast for a moment – 'and Joan went and fetched him from the nursery where the babies slept. She brought him to me, secretly. I fed him. I nursed him. I cuddled him for a few precious hours, my lovely son.' Her voice is breaking, but she doesn't cry. 'Oh Annie, I can't let myself think of it.' For a while she's silent, pleating and re-pleating the grey fabric on her knee. I lean forward and rub her back at the top of her spine as Beatrice used to do with me when I was small. After a while she gives a long shaky sigh. 'This went on for three precious nights,' she says. 'Little fellow. He never betrayed me by crying. It was as if he knew we had to be very quiet. But on the fourth evening, Joan was no longer on duty and the new nurse didn't bring him.' She breaks off again. 'I never saw him after that. In fact, I never really saw him at all because it was always dark, but I feel I knew his face. I learnt every bit of it by touch, to keep safe for the future. And in spite of everything that happened later, I was glad and grateful that I had spent this time with him.'

'They never let you see him?'

She shakes her head. 'They weren't being cruel. They said it was kinder that way, that it would be easier for both of us, but I don't believe it. At least I knew him for a little while and he knew me. Maybe somewhere deep inside he may still know his Mummy loves him. Anyway——' She shakes her head; says in a falsely light voice, 'I'm sorry, Annie. That's quite enough. We must get to the music!'

Reluctantly, I open the Mozart *Requiem*, which I've been learning at home, and she listens to me play. 'Slower here,' she says, indicating an *allargando* I've missed. I nod and circle it with the pencil I've been allowed to bring this week. We work on through the movements that the choir are going to sing.

'You have a very nice touch,' she says – something that

under normal circumstances would make me glow with pride, just as it did when Mother said the same all those years ago.

But I'm not interested in the music today. Time is so short and I want to know what happened next. My fingers tail off along the keys. 'How long did you stay in the mother and baby home?' I ask her.

'Maybe a month? They took him after five days, though. When Joan came back on nights she told me he had gone. It was very quick. A good thing really, as he needed a mother to hold him tight—' Her voice breaks on the final words. 'But it was difficult, left in that place with the mothers who still had their babies.'

'Where did he go? How could they take him from you?'

She says gently, 'I always knew it would happen. It was explained to me when I went there. And part of it is that you must never be told where he is to go, or who will bring him up. It would have been impossible, of course, to keep him. They didn't have to remind me I was destitute. I was a fallen woman!' She looks at me shyly. 'It was only fair he should be given a decent Christian upbringing. It seemed completely logical at the time.'

'But you were his mother!' I, who lost my mother when I was six, feel the pain of it sharply. 'He should have been with you, no matter what. You weren't going to be a fallen woman for ever, were you!'

She laughs. 'But I was, Annie. I *am*. And I'd no means of support.'

'My father would have understood! He could have given you an allowance or a job at Roebuck's, or something.'

She sits very still. She takes a deep breath. 'I'm afraid it doesn't work like that. He was doing his Christian duty. He was seeing to it that the child would be given to good, loving parents. I'm sure of that. But it wasn't his duty to keep supporting me. It wouldn't have been ... respectable.'

I look at her, exasperated, 'But he still *is* supporting you, if he pays your keep in here!'

'That's different,' she answers quickly. 'You see, after they took the baby away, I became very sick. It was a depression that mothers do sometimes get, but in my case – as I began by saying – it was a psychosis. It was extreme, and I'm afraid I let myself believe that I was to blame: for having spent that forbidden time with my baby, you see. I had learnt to love him and I must pay the price. The home couldn't keep me; I was raving mad, Annie!' She smiles ruefully. 'I suppose that's why I don't get upset by Flo out there' – nodding towards the door – 'I was so desperately sad, just as she is really. And I was angry. I'll admit I had very unchristian thoughts about the Mission and all it stands for!'

'I'm very glad you did!' I break in. 'How dare they make your situation so much worse? What's Christian about that?'

'Well, they are bound by their own strong principles,' she says. 'I broke their rules. So I don't blame them, and I don't feel anger now. But I'm not a believer any more – well, that's another story.'

I say nothing. This isn't the moment to tell her I'm not a believer, either: she has far more cause than I do.

'Anyway, your father arranged for me to come to Mapperley,' she continues. 'I suppose he kind of got stuck with me because I was ill. And if I hadn't come here I wouldn't have met Dr Squires, who really did save my life – I do believe that, Annie. So I was very grateful, once I had calmed down and my acute illness had passed.'

'Did Daddy come and see you in the home – or here?' I ask. 'Does he still come?'

She shakes her head. 'Never. I would not have expected it. It would not have been proper.'

But I have a thought forming in my head: 'If he came to see you *now*, Millie, he would see that you are well and that he's wasting his money keeping you in this place. You're young: you can take your LRAM and become a piano teacher, just as you said you wanted to be! I can bring him to see you!'

A sudden look of alarm crosses her face. 'Annie, I've told you before: you mustn't ever mention to him that we've met in here! You must *never* say it! Please, I mean this from the bottom of my heart. I beg of you. Promise me. It will be the end of me if you do.'

I look at her in astonishment. But she is in such deadly earnest I immediately say, 'I promise, Millie. I swear to you I won't ... But I also swear I'm going to help get you out of here. You can't waste your life in this place! I promise I'll find a way!'

She looks at me sadly. 'Annie, please. There are things you don't know ...'

It's at this moment Nurse Jennings returns and our meeting is over, though not before I arrange to attend the next rehearsal of the choir so I can see how she works with them. It will be difficult to continue our conversation there, but I will manage it somehow. For now, I need to get away and think. She must be set free from this place, and Daddy – who has been so generous towards her in the face of the Mission's disapproval – must be the key to it. She's making my job unnecessarily difficult by forbidding me to speak to him: if he's paying for her to stay there, what is it that's so terrible he can't be told?

I return home, my heart overflowing for Millie and her lost child. As I pass through the yard I notice, as I always do, the dark stain where Nana's kennel touched the ground. I cannot know what it's like to lose a baby, but as I squat down within the cramped rectangle, my eyes fill with tears for our faithful dog. She belonged with us, should have lived out her life with us, just as poor Millie's baby boy belonged with her. Nana died two years before I went away to France. She died when Fred was having his first breakdown, boy and dog sick of a broken heart. No, that's nonsense. Nana had lived a good life with Maisie and Mr Brown, and she surely wouldn't have minded not seeing us after Mother said she didn't want the dog coming home for weekends any more. But we always loved her. Fred and I used to sneak off during the holidays and take her for walks, then, when Nana was older and frail and Fred couldn't go to college, he would just disappear to Maisie's. She never mentioned it, but I know that's where he used to go. I've always been very grateful to Maisie for giving him and Nana sanctuary in her home. But now I weep again for our beloved Nana. I wonder what secrets she knew, that she could never tell us.

# TWENTY

**Friday, August 12**

Normally at this time of year we would be setting off on our annual family holiday to Mablethorpe. I have a picture of us three children and Nana crammed into the back of Daddy's car; one of the two Agnes Langs with Daddy in the front, and buckets, spades, fishing nets, umbrellas and galoshes in the boot. There is a photo in the family album – stuck in with photo-corners, so it must predate Mother's death – with me in a swimsuit, paddling, Beatrice holding my hand, and Fred digging in the sand at the water's edge. Nana is not in the picture, but she was there: you can see the end of her tail.

This year, there's been no mention of Mablethorpe and I'm relieved not to have to go: anyway, I'm far too busy solving the mystery of Miss Blessing.

My first dilemma is how much I can say to Fred of what I've discovered. I wonder if he knows about the baby. Quite apart from his illness, I feel it's improper to speak to my brother of such things, or tell him Miss Blessing's private business, but she said herself that the whole congregation knew, so maybe it is not such a secret. My chief concern is not to tell Fred anything that could make him worse, for the truth is he has started to get better. He recently won his 'ground parole' and is allowed to work in the gardens; so when I visit him now we can walk there together, past other patients weeding the shrubbery and dead-heading the annuals in the circular bed.

'Well', he says when I see him today, 'what's the news?'

I frown. I still haven't decided how much to let on, so I try stalling. 'We're definitely not going to Mablethorpe,' I tell him. 'Mother said last night she won't be missing any of the summer Bible circles, so that means we aren't going away.'

'And?'

'Beatrice has bought a new handbag. She got it really cheap in the sales in Marshall and Snelgrove.'

Fred gives me a look. 'Come on, Annie. Did you go and see Miss Blessing again?'

'I did,' I say emphatically. 'There was a patient called Flo who was in a bad way. You're right about the strip-cells, you know. Miss Blessing says patients sometimes want to go in there if they're feeling poorly, but Flo didn't want to go. I think they had to force her.'

We walk on in silence for a few moments. I've realised I won't be able to avoid the subject but can still not decide how much to divulge. 'Miss Blessing did say a bit about why she's in here,' I begin. 'She wasn't well, Fred.'

'Did she say why?'

I look at him. Something in his expression tells me he already knows. 'She was in trouble,' I say, testing the water. 'Wasn't she?' And the phrase suddenly makes me think of that long-ago afternoon walking home from hockey with Marjorie Bagshaw past the Kingdom Hall of Jehovah's Witnesses, two figures up ahead in earnest conversation.

Before Fred can answer, I stop and touch his arm. 'Fred, I've just remembered something: about her brother.'

'I never knew she had a brother,' he says, stopping too. 'I thought she had a sister.'

'That night, Daddy came home early. He said he'd been talking about her brother.'

'What night?' Fred is baffled.

'He said her brother had failed to get an apprenticeship at Roebuck's and he was going to look into it.'

'So? When was this?'

I suddenly feel cold. 'I met them,' I say. I realise my hands are half covering my face. 'Marjorie and I bumped into them in the street.'

'You look as if you've seen a ghost, Annie. Who did you bump into?'

'Daddy and Miss Blessing. After hockey. We were on our way back to school.'

Fred is lost. 'What's this got to do with anything?'

'Don't you see? He had to explain what he was doing. He came home at teatime and told Mother we had all met in the street. He said he was talking to Miss Blessing about her *brother* and the apprenticeship at Roebuck's. He even told us his name: Eric. That's why I thought she had a brother! I remember now.'

'So she probably does, then.'

'No.' I shake my head. 'Yesterday I mentioned her brother and she said . . . Fred, she said she doesn't have one!'

'Daddy said she did?'

I nod.

'Well, he probably got the wrong end of the stick.'

I say nothing. My brain is struggling to make sense of it.

Fred frowns. 'And this is . . . how long before she disappeared?'

'I don't know. Not long. It was when all those girls were being kidnapped, d'you remember? We thought she was one of them, but she wasn't.'

Fred knows nothing of this; he was away at school. 'So, shortly before she vanished?' he asks.

'Must have been . . . just four days.'

Fred thinks for a moment. 'Actually, that explains a lot,' he says. 'I think I understand.'

Now it's my turn to be puzzled. 'Well I don't!'

'You said it yourself, Annie. She was in trouble. Everyone at the Mission knew.'

'And he was helping her!' I said. Perhaps it was all becoming clear. 'Fred, he was so generous: the Mission just kicked her out, but Daddy was helping her in secret! You'll never guess – he – he—' I'm about to say he paid for the mother and baby home, but I'm still not sure if what Fred means by *trouble* is that Miss Blessing was going to have a baby. I don't want to be the one to tell him if he doesn't know.

'I should hope he jolly well did help her!' says Fred.

'How d'you mean?'

'Well, it was his fault, after all!'

'*Daddy's* fault she was kicked out of the Mission?'

'Miss Blessing was going to have a baby!' he says. 'Isn't that what she told you?'

'Yes, yes.' This is a relief. 'And Daddy paid for the mother and baby home.'

'It's the least he could have done!' Fred explodes. 'It was his baby, after all.'

I don't remember much more of the afternoon. I still can't believe it. Fred says he's been wanting to tell me all along, but he couldn't talk about it. It stayed in his mind and haunted him. When he came home from school and realised something terrible had happened, he got the truth out of Beatrice – so this is the thing that everyone knew, and Bea knows, too. He says I was too small to be told (but I was eleven by that time and it wasn't fair they kept it from me). I think I explained to him Miss Blessing hadn't told me about *why* Daddy had been helping her. It sounds as if she wasn't being straight with me, but I'm not surprised: who would have had the effrontery to tell *me*, of all people – his daughter? Now I'm worried that bringing it all back will make Fred worse and I've promised to give Mother the slip and go and see him again tomorrow.

I bitterly regret I ever dug into this. Sometimes the truth is better untold. If Fred becomes ill again, I shall never forgive myself. As for Miss Blessing, what could have possessed her? Why ever did I go in search of her in the first place? And I've foolishly made her a promise to help her escape from Mapperley. You must never break a promise, but how am I going to keep it, now I know this?

### Saturday, August 13

As soon as I see Fred today I realise I didn't need to fret about making him worse: he's positively cheerful, which I find odd to begin with. But gradually I understand it's a relief for him that I know our bitter family secret. The second thing I realise is that the real reason I needed to see him today is for my own sake, not his.

'How *could* she?' I ask, as soon as we're away from the main path in our habitual garden walk. 'A married man old enough to be her father – with three children practically her own age! She even *knew* us, Fred. She taught me Bible stories!'

He looks at me quizzically. 'Lining up with the Mission now, are we, Annie? That'll be a first!'

'I – well, *yes* – sort of.' I scowl at a bed of pelargoniums. This is not comfortable.

'All her fault, then? She's a scarlet woman. Is that it?'

The vision of scarlet woman scarcely fits our Sunday School teacher. But then I think of my father. 'Well, whose fault is it, if it's not hers?'

Fred throws me a look. 'You don't know anything about it,' he says shortly.

'Whatever it is, it's disgusting!'

Fred shrugs.

I want to say something in defence of Daddy, but all that comes to mind are Marjorie Bagshaw's innuendoes about him back in our schooldays. 'You're different since your illness,' I manage at last. 'You're sort of, I don't know, on the outside looking in.'

We walk on for a few paces. Then he says, 'I suppose I just don't belong with you all any more.'

I turn and stare at him. 'Belong with *us*, with the family?'

'The family. The Mission. The whole shebang!' He's speaking in the sarcastic, offhand voice I heard for the first time when he was really sick.

'You mean you've lost your faith, too?'

He shakes his head. 'I didn't say that. I just don't care about our family and what it stands for. It's all . . . rotten.' His voice is thick now, as if he might cry.

'Since *this* happened, you mean?' I really need to understand. 'Fred, is that the reason you're so angry with Daddy?' I wonder if he's even aware of the terrible things he said about our father on my first visit.

'There's no point discussing it, Annie. You obviously think differently from me. But . . .' He hesitates. 'It was just never the same after I found out. I mean, in here.' He taps his head.

We're back at the main subject. He turns to me: 'And you:

what do you really think about the Mission throwing her out?'

My mind is still reeling from what he's just said (let alone what he told me yesterday). I say, 'I think it's shocking and awful about Daddy and Miss Blessing. I can still scarcely believe it. But if you're part of a Mission that's supposed to be practising the forgiveness of sins, it's a bit *off* to kick someone out because they've sinned. Isn't it?'

'I see,' says Fred.

I wonder what he means by this *I see*: is he agreeing with me or disapproving? My new brother is hard to read. We walk on in silence for a while. 'So it's a good thing that Daddy is still helping Miss Blessing,' I say. 'Isn't it? At least he's being a proper Christian.'

Fred says nothing.

'Fred, d'you think he still loves her?' I stop in my tracks. 'Is that why he's doing it?'

Fred doesn't reply. We walk on.

'Fred!' I stop again. 'The baby. That little boy . . .'

'What about him?'

'He's our brother!' I've only just realised this.

'Half-brother,' says Fred, so promptly that I know he's already thought about it a good deal.

'Well . . . shouldn't we find him?'

'How would that help?' Fred asks drily.

'He's part of our family!'

'No, he's not.'

'But he sort of *is*, isn't he?'

Fred ignores this. Then he says, rather pompously, 'The child will have been adopted by a good Christian family. Daddy will have seen to that. He is much better off without the shame of being the illegitimate son of our family, and we're better off without having him as a constant reminder.'

I look at him. 'You feel ashamed. Don't you?'

No answer.

'Well, I don't,' I say. 'It's not your fault, or my fault. It's definitely not the poor baby's fault – or anyone's, apart from *theirs.*'

We've reached the furthest corner of the hospital gardens, bordered by a high wall with pieces of broken glass stuck on the top. Fred says, 'We'd better be getting back.' He turns and starts to walk away.

I remind myself that the reason I'm here today is to make sure he's all right – and he clearly was, to begin with – but I've upset him again by raising this.

He quickens his pace and we rejoin the main path. 'Oh Fred,' I say, thinking that perhaps to ask his advice will cheer him up and pull him out of whatever dark place has reopened in his head. 'I've gone and made a promise to Miss Blessing.'

I wait for him to respond. 'What promise is that?' he asks at last, sounding rather bored.

'I promised I'd help her get out of here.'

'That was rash, wasn't it?'

I take a deep breath and push on: 'It was before I knew Daddy was, was . . . you know. Do I have to keep the promise, Fred?'

'That's entirely between you and your conscience.'

This is a hopeless sort of answer. I'm so angry with Miss Blessing, I don't want to help her escape: I want him to say it's all right to break my word.

But he doesn't. 'If you've promised, you've promised, haven't you? Though heaven knows how you'll get her through all those locked doors!'

We hurry on. 'I thought, actually,' I explain rather breathlessly, 'that if Daddy could see how well she is, he

286

might agree it's no longer necessary to keep paying for her to be here. He might be able to get her a job outside, or something.'

Fred doesn't respond. We're now almost running along the path. I put my hand on his arm to slow him down. 'Please, Fred. I need your help.'

He looks around at me and stops. 'What for?' he demands.

'She says I mustn't tell Daddy we've met – on pain of death, almost!' I try and make light of it.

'Then you mustn't tell him, must you?'

'But how else will she ever leave? If he doesn't know she's better!'

'Why should she leave? She's got a roof over her head, hasn't she? You don't seem to get it, Annie,' he adds harshly. 'It's not her choice any more: her life is finished.'

I blink at him. 'Fred ... she's, what, twenty-four years old? You know what it's like! On her ward ... with those poor women, she's – she's a prisoner—'

'I'm not saying I agree with it,' he interrupts. 'I'm saying that in the eyes of the world, she's better hidden away and forgotten.'

'Oh, and then there's her psychiatrist,' I tell him. 'Have you heard of Dr Squires?'

Fred thinks for a moment. 'Nope. Can't say I have.'

'This Dr Squires has told her she's never going to get better. And she believes him!'

'So she must be more sick than you think, then, mustn't she?'

'But you've seen her – she's not sick at all! Surely no one would want her to stay there for ever! Not her doctor. Not even the Mission. And certainly not Daddy.'

Fred just looks at me. Then he turns and strides on back towards the hospital.

Tonight, it's time for me to go and meet the choir. For this rehearsal, Miss Blessing will still be playing for them. I'm there to observe. Relieved as I am, now, that there will be almost no opportunity for us to speak in private, I feel embarrassed at seeing her again. How can I look her in the eye, knowing what has passed between her and my father?

To make things worse, she throws me a brief but warm smile as she files into the chapel, like a meek child, on Doris's arm. I gaze back at her coldly but she probably thinks I'm just being cautious. I suppose I ought to go and speak to her, but I hang back and take in the scene. The chapel has an odd air of being got up as something else tonight, a domestic parlour, and the effect is a little incongruous. The stained-glass windows have receded into the shadows; a baby grand piano has been wheeled into the place previously occupied by the harmonium, and a standard lamp with a modern fringed shade throws light on to its keyboard. Miss Blessing settles herself quietly, adjusting the stool a little and sorting through her music. Members of the staff choir drift in, laughing and chatting together. I can't help noticing they all ignore her. No one even says hello; she might as well not exist. A couple of young nurses arrange chairs in three semicircles one behind the other, and a man appears with a small rostrum and a music stand for the conductor. Doris waits until most of the choir have arrived and then slips away. I wonder if she will reappear at the end or whether one of the choir members will take Miss Blessing back to the ward.

As I'm absently weighing the possibilities for smuggling Millie Blessing out of the hospital, and getting nowhere, Sister Jones arrives – she to whom I had first applied as volunteer accompanist. 'Ah, Miss Lang!' she sees me sitting facing the choir and bustles up in greeting. She has removed her starched headdress and hairpins are bursting out of her bun like spines on a hedgehog. 'My dear, I'm so pleased to see you. Have you been introduced?' Then, without waiting for me to reply, she turns towards the choir and claps her hands for attention. 'Everyone? Quiet, please! Can I introduce Miss Lang, who is kindly going to play for us at the concert.' I stand awkwardly and try to smile at them. I can't bear to glance at Millie Blessing. How must she feel to have me usurp her position, without a word from any of them or the least expression of thanks? But when I do steal a covert look at her, she is sitting calmly, staring at her music, neither smiling nor disgruntled but … accepting her lot, perhaps. I think of what Fred has said about her life being over and despite my complicated feelings towards her, I can't resist a shiver. However evil or misguided, no one should deserve to be wiped off the map as if they had never lived.

The members of the choir are smiling and greeting me now and I feel I must say *something* that will include their true accompanist. 'How can I be useful tonight, Sister?' I ask. 'Would it be a good idea to turn the pages for Miss Blessing, perhaps?'

'A splendid idea,' says Sister Jones. 'She will be very glad of it—' Spoken without a glance in her direction.

I carry one of the chairs over to the piano and align myself firmly with Miss Blessing, who says in an undertone, 'Thank you, Annie. That's kind.'

Then the choirmaster, Dr Squires, walks briskly into the hall with his music and a baton under his arm, and the buzz of conversation ceases immediately. I am agog to see Miss Blessing's saintly psychiatrist. I already have a mental picture of him as plump and kindly, despite his rather brutal practice of telling his patients they will never recover, and am therefore surprised to see that he is tall, lean and rather formal-looking, with a military bearing and a dark brown pinstriped suit, the uniform I recognise as worn by the hospital's consultants. He certainly has presence and I can understand Miss Blessing being in awe of him. His movements are as economical as his smile, which he seems to ration as if perhaps he doesn't have many up his sleeve. But I have to remind myself that this is the man who took the trouble to find his patient a piano. He must be a kind man, at heart.

'Good evening, everyone. We've a lot to get through so I hope you're already warmed up.' He looks around at them over his spectacles, challenging any dissent. The nurses titter a little and adjust their caps, as though this will help them sing.

Millie Blessing whispers to me, 'That's a shame. They do so much better with a few scales.'

Dr Squires places his music on the lectern in front of him and opens the second piece in the pile. 'We'll begin tonight with . . . Parry. "At the Round Earth" . . . number five.'

While the choir settles down and finds the place with a flurry of coughs and fidgets, Millie murmurs, 'It's the most difficult thing they're singing. Watch for the sopranos going flat.'

'Are you still playing for them?' I ask. This piece is unaccompanied, with piano for rehearsals only. I haven't had to learn it.

She nods. 'Probably.'

As if on cue, Dr Squires glances for the first time in our direction. 'We'll start with the piano,' he instructs.

Millie waits, her hands over the keys. He raises his baton, she gives them a D-major chord, and they're off.

Halfway through the rehearsal, there's a break for tea and most of the female choir members produce thermos flasks.

Dr Squires is about to walk out when he is waylaid by Sister Jones, who tugs him over towards the piano. 'Dr Squires,' she says, 'May I present Miss Annie Lang, one of our volunteers, who has kindly agreed to accompany for us at the concert.'

Dr Squires looks at me with more attention than I would have expected. 'Miss Lang? Miss Annie Lang, you say?'

I stand, unsure whether he will want to shake my hand, but he doesn't offer his own. 'How do you do, Dr Squires?' I enquire, as politely as I can, looking into his face. His skin is waxy, as if he spends too much time in the hospital, and behind the spectacles his eyes are rather piercing. I wonder if all his patients find him as charismatic as Miss Blessing seems to do. Neither of us knows what to say next, so he mutters something like, 'I hope the music will not be too challenging for you, Miss Lang ... All well, eh, Blessing?' and turns on his heel without waiting for an answer and with barely a glance at his patient; they might be strangers. Then he leaves the chapel with an air of urgent business to attend to.

I sit down. This is the moment I've been dreading; the only opportunity for any kind of talk with Miss Blessing, but Dr Squires has at least broken the ice. 'Well,' I can't help saying. 'I don't know if he's a bit more friendly when you see him as a patient, Millie, but he's not someone *I'd* find easy to talk to!'

'Oh,' she says, 'but you know he can see all sorts of things going on that you're not even aware of!'

'I'm not sure I'd like that,' I tell her.

'Well,' she admits, 'I don't meet with him very often these days: he's such a busy man. But whenever I do, he seems to have a very clear idea of how I am. He's remarkable.'

After this beginning, I'm at a loss for words and Miss Blessing may have sensed I don't quite share her admiration, because she, too, suddenly seems to feel constrained. For several minutes we make polite conversation about the choir and the performance, which is not too bad, to my way of thinking. The singers are already starting to return to their seats, when Millie suddenly blurts out, 'I'm afraid I may have said too much at our last meeting.'

'Not at all,' I reply hurriedly, hoping we're not going to have to discuss it.

'I wanted to apologise,' she continues. 'I probably shouldn't have said as much as I said.'

I stare ahead of me, at the piano keys.

'It must have come as . . . as a shock, if you didn't already know it.'

*Not as much of a shock as what you* didn't *tell me*, I think to myself. But all I say is, 'I hope it didn't upset you too much to speak of it.' I can't turn and look at her.

'It was. . .' she falters. 'It was the first time for a few years I had allowed myself to dwell on it – in any, you know, detail.'

I nod.

There is an awkward pause.

'I hope . . .' she resumes, hesitantly; she is clearly struggling with herself. 'I don't want you to think badly of me, Annie.'

I shoot her a glance at that.

She continues, 'I would hate you to misunderstand. It is more complicated . . . as I think I said, there is more—'

'I know,' I tell her hurriedly. I can't bear it if she's going to confess to what Fred has already told me.

But she says, 'There are things I cannot speak to you about, though I wish I knew of someone who could.'

'Please,' I say, panic probably audible in my voice, 'you have told me enough. I mean, you mustn't upset yourself any more.'

There is another uncomfortable silence. She says diffidently, 'You made a promise.'

'I did.'

'Annie, I don't want to hold you to that promise.'

Into the chapel sweeps Dr Squires again. 'Hush,' I tell her. 'We can't talk now.'

But she repeats in a fierce whisper: 'Without your knowing the whole story, I cannot hold you to it, and I won't. Do you understand?'

I realise this is what she set herself to tell me tonight. Having been less than frank last time, at least she has the grace to set me free from any commitment to help her. And she's burning her boats because I must have been her only hope of getting out of here. For the first time since learning the truth from Fred, I feel a flicker of admiration for her. When the singing resumes, I see her fingers are shaking uncontrollably over the keys.

# TWENTY-ONE

**Wednesday, August 17**

During these weeks I've been visiting Miss Blessing and working on the music, I have also continued to volunteer on the short-term women's ward. It's after a particularly arduous session today, when I've had to deal with an outburst from one of the patients who mistook me for her maths teacher from thirty years ago, that Daddy suddenly raises the subject of the hospital choir during tea. Mother has been detained with an emergency visit in the parish, so at least I don't have to suffer interrogation from her; but of course, the choir is a dangerous subject. I simply don't know how much Daddy follows Miss Blessing's progress; I hope not at all.

'I hear you have taken on an extra duty at the hospital,' he says.

I wonder how he knows. 'Yes,' I tell him. 'They were asking for an accompanist for the choir, the staff choir, for their next concert. It's a job I was happy to volunteer for, as you can imagine.'

Daddy frowns. 'Don't they have a resident pianist, then?'

I decide to misunderstand the question. 'Oh yes. But with it being holiday time, he's away for this concert.'

'So does this person, who's away, play for all their rehearsals?'

'Um, no,' I say, wondering where this is leading. 'How do you know about the choir, Daddy, is it something the Mechanics' is involved in? Actually, they're rather good. They're singing some quite complicated music: the Mozart *Requiem* and some Parry ...' I can hear myself gabbling on.

'So who usually plays?'

'Oh, I think a few people ...'

'Patients?' He is looking at me intently.

'Possibly.' I shrug. 'I don't know much about it, to be honest. I've only been to one rehearsal so far.'

'So who played for the other rehearsals?'

'A patient, I believe.'

'You *believe*? Didn't you meet this person?'

'*Dad-dee*!' I push my chair back and go to the scullery to fetch more hot water, with an attempted throwaway, 'Why the third degree?' It's meant to be teasing but it sounds a bit desperate. 'I never knew you were so interested in Mozart!'

Before he can answer, the door opens and Mother comes in. 'What about Mozart?' she asks.

'Oh Mother, how are you?' I greet her, thinking I was never so relieved to see her in my life.

'Better now than I was,' she says. She adjusts the scarf at her neck and pats her hair. 'The doctor didn't want to come out, but I spoke to him on the telephone and he did come eventually. He managed to persuade the hospital to take the poor child.'

'Why, what was the matter?' I suddenly have a keen interest in the plight of these parishioners: anything to change the subject.

Mother is feeling pleased with herself, as well she might. 'It was a rash. Children get them, after all, and the doctor thought the mother was making a fuss. But when he saw the baby he agreed with me that this was almost certainly scarlet fever.' She goes into the scullery to wash her hands. 'The Lord be praised for opening the doctor's eyes,' she adds, when she comes back. Poor Mother: she must never let herself take credit for anything.

'The Lord be praised that you were there to persuade the doctor!' I say pointedly. 'Here you are. I made a fresh pot ... Will the baby be all right, d'you think? Do I know the family?'

'You would know them,' Mother replies tartly, 'if you spent more time in St Ann's where you belong, and less at that hospital.'

Daddy says, 'She's got a new duty at the hospital, Agnes. She's playing the piano for their concert now.'

Mother looks up at me. 'This is the first I've heard of it, Annie. Did your father give permission?'

'No!' Daddy protests. 'The girl's out of control! I had to hear it from someone at the Lodge last night.' So that's how he knows. I imagine one of the tenors or basses must have recognised my name.

'Daddy! Mother!' I say, holding out my arms to calm them both down. 'Please. It's only for a few weeks, and it's only a part of my other volunteering, which you do know about. I thought you'd be glad!' I turn to Mother. 'After all, it's excellent practice for me.'

Mother grunts and takes a sip of tea. 'You know what I think about performing on stage,' she says tartly. 'And, indeed, what I think about your persisting with your piano studies at all, Annie.'

There's a pause.

Daddy says, 'Well, Dr Squires tells me the music is difficult enough, so it will certainly be good for you.'

I freeze. If Dr Squires is his informant from the Lodge, then surely he will know about Daddy's connection to Miss Blessing, and Daddy will almost certainly guess that she is the patient I'm replacing as accompanist. So Daddy *must know about me meeting her.* Why, then, is he asking me all these questions? Is he trying to force me into some kind of admission?

I concentrate supremely on not reacting to the name of Dr Squires, even while I'm trying to work out the awful implications of what's just been said. All right, so Daddy knows I'm taking over the piano for the concert but that's all he knows; because Dr Squires himself only met me and heard my name for the first time two nights ago – it was clear from his reaction, which I now understand. So he doesn't know I've been visiting Miss Blessing on the ward, or anything about our conversations, of course. And she won't tell him. I must remain calm.

But then Mother is saying something, and it's not what she says, but how, that brings me back to the present: 'You told me he'd moved up north.' She is staring at Daddy intently.

'I don't think so, Agnes.' He is frowning. 'Pass the pickles, will you?'

But Mother is not to be deflected. She reaches for the bowl of pickled onions and cucumbers and hands it to him. She says, 'You told me they had both gone.' Her voice is low and intense. 'That because he had moved up North, she ... is ... *no longer there.*'

He is staring at her as if she's slapped him in the face. His expression is terrifying. I look at her in alarm; she, too, seems to realise that whatever she has said is in some way unacceptable. She holds his gaze, but I see something in her eyes I've never seen before: it's fear.

There's a moment of dreadful silence and then he says, 'Rubbish. You're mistaken, Agnes. *Not for the first time.*' He spears an onion with the pickle fork. It bobs around in the vinegar and he stabs at it again.

I look from one to the other. This is a mystery to me. My father's cheeks are darkening. 'Dr Squires is still in the Basford Lodge, and still at Mapperley,' he says softly, concentrating on the onions. 'Tell her, Annie.'

'I only met him two nights ago,' I say quickly. I don't want to get dragged into this. 'He's the choirmaster at the hospital, that's all I know, Mother.' I turn to my father. 'Fancy him being in the Lodge, Daddy.'

My father ignores this. He looks up at Mother again; his blue eyes drill into her, icy cold.

She has turned as pale as he is flushed. 'You assured me, Harry,' she mutters. 'You promised.'

This is very odd. My parents never air any of their private communications in front of us. What on earth does my stepmother know of Dr Squires?

His eyes narrow, transmitting a signal: 'You must be thinking of old Palmer,' he tells her. 'Moved to Preston last year.'

Mother seems to recollect herself. She drops her gaze. 'That's probably it,' she says quietly. She finishes her cup of tea and leaves the room. She's had nothing to eat.

Retreating upstairs, I have sat down to write this immediately and get some kind of order into my head. Whatever it is that bothers Mother about Dr Squires, I have some serious thinking to do about him and Daddy. Of course, I realise the Freemasons come from many professions. It's no surprise, as soon as I think about it, that they should know each other through the Lodge, and I suppose it follows that Miss Blessing should be in Dr Squires' care, since – what was it Marjorie

told me all those years ago? – *Freemasons help each other* ...
But what are the consequences of Daddy knowing that I've
found her?

Later, I lie sleepless in bed, wondering why my father
might have told Mother that Doctor Squires had moved
north? What did she mean by 'you told me *they had both*
gone'? My mind is running in wild circles of its own: does
Dr Squires know about Daddy's affair with Miss Blessing?
Is that what's upsetting Mother? I tell myself not to be so
fanciful – anyway, I can't waste time on that when I have to
work out if I've lied by omission in not telling my father I've
met Miss Blessing. I'm afraid I *have* lied, and because I didn't
let on about meeting her, he may guess I've discovered his
guilty secret about the baby. I feel I'm walking over a ravine.
One slip and I'm finished.


### Thursday, August 18

Next morning, I see Mother leave the house early with her
visiting-the-sick basket on her arm. She is out for hours; small
wonder she gets so tired. I am trying to read André Gide, *La
Porte Étroite*, from my course reading list. It's a dreary story
of self-denial, in which the heroine of the book gets drawn
into the heretical doctrine of Jansenism, thereby ruining
everything: my attention wanders constantly.

After lunch, which as usual is just Mother and me, she folds
the tablecloth and puts it away in the drawer with great care.
I'm about to leave the room when she says, 'Sit down, Annie.
I want to talk to you.' I have the familiar rush of nerves, wondering if she'll always make me feel like this, and sit sideways
in the chair, poised for flight.

She's silent for a moment, staring at her locked fingers as

if recalling a prepared homily. Then she looks up at me and says, 'If you've time to spend evenings at the hospital with this choir business, then you have time to spend days in the parish. You can start by visiting the Bagshaw woman – at least you know the family.'

'The Bagshaws?' I can't take this in. 'But – but they're not parishioners, are they?'

'Your school-friend Marjorie's sister married Ernest Wilkinson,' Mother explains. This is the verger's son. I remember Marjorie telling me Iris was friendly with him, but . . . marriage? 'It's their baby girl has scarlet fever, as I was saying last night,' she continues. 'The mother – what's her name? – is taking instruction.'

I can scarcely believe my ears: it's odd enough about a Bagshaw girl marrying into the Mission, but the idea of Marjorie's sister Iris taking instruction to enter our church is odder still. 'Oh,' I say. 'You mean Iris Bagshaw, as was?' (Just wait till I tell Beatrice!)

'Iris. That's it,' Mother confirms.

'Right. I'll gladly visit them, Mother.' The prospect seems suddenly much more intriguing than the miseries of André Gide. 'I'll go this afternoon, if you like.'

'She's up at the hospital this afternoon,' Mother says. 'I was with her earlier. You may go tomorrow.' She nods, to dismiss me.

*La Porte Étroite* goes better this afternoon.


## Friday, August 19

Mother sends me on Mission errands this morning, so it's not until after lunch I set off to visit Marjorie Bagshaw's sister. The family live in the grid of cobbled streets at the heart of

St Ann's, with a lavatory and a washing line in the back yard and a front door straight on to the pavement. As I knock and wait, I'm aware of being scrutinised by an elderly woman in carpet slippers sitting out on her front step two doors away. I say hello, feeling (as I do when I make the awkward rounds with Mother) that not much goes unnoticed around here, and she gives a curt nod back. Then the door is answered by Iris herself, whom I remember as a bosomy girl whose curves never fitted her gymslip, now large and imposing with combs in her hair and a shawl, which gives her an air of the exotic.

'Oh my!' she exclaims, looking somewhat alarmed. 'I knew you were coming, but I didn't know it would be as soon as this!'

I blink at her, wondering what Mother's gone and said. 'Hello, Mrs Wilkinson.'

She seems to recollect herself and breaks into a broad grin. 'Oh please, duck – Iris. You know me as Iris, Marjorie's sister, and I know you as Little Orphan Annie Lang, Beatrice's sister. Come on in.' She holds open the door. 'Given your stepmother the slip this afternoon, have you?'

'We were so sorry about your baby,' I say. 'Mother asked me to come and see what the news is and how you are.'

The door opens straight into the front parlour, two brown armchairs on either side of the empty fireplace. Newspaper is crumpled into the chimney to stop the soot falling. A hearthrug bears the scars of spitting coal, but the room is cheerful with a polished brass warming pan hanging on the wall, a playpen and a teddy bear in one corner, and books on a shelf. I see a large family Bible, presumably Ernest's.

'We were up at the hospital first thing and the doctor, the specialist on the children's ward, says German measles.' She shrugs. 'Well, I don't know, do I? Is he right? Is he wrong? So they got her out of isolation and she's on the ward.' Iris gives me a significant look. 'If our doctor's right and the consultant's wrong, and they all get it – well, heaven help the other little mites!'

'But this is good news, isn't it?' I say. 'I mean, I'm sorry, no one wants to be in hospital at all, of course, but German measles is good to have, isn't it, and hopefully it means she can come home?'

'Aye,' Iris agrees, 'if that's what it is. Well, obviously we're very relieved. I'll be back up at visiting time.' She glances at the clock.

'I don't want to hold you up,' I say and make to stand, but she motions me to stay where I am.

'No, you're all right yet awhile, duck.' She chuckles. 'It's nice to see you. How's Beatrice doing? I don't like to ask your mother, it seems like prying, but I heard she's working in London.'

'Yes. For the G-Pom.' Iris's eyes narrow; of course, she's not yet familiar with the lingo! 'That's the missionary society that Golgotha is part of. It's a good job. She loves it.'

'Is she going to be a missionary, then? Goodness me! Dedicate her life to people on the other side of the world?'

I shake my head. 'I don't think so. She says you have to be called to do that. Chosen.'

'Crikey. Who chooses you?'

I can't help smiling. 'Um. God, I think.'

'Oh yeah. Yeah.' She absorbs this. 'You'll have to forgive me, Annie. This religious stuff is all new to me!'

'Mother says you're taking instruction. Are you going for the total immersion, then, Iris?'

She laughs. 'Can't say I fancy it.' She shudders. 'That bath, when they take up the floorboards. Bloody freezing. And I mean, you don't know who's been down there before, do you? And wearing a white nightie an' all.'

'I suppose they change the water before the ceremony?' I suggest.

'Well, you'll have done it yourself, I shouldn't wonder?'

I shake my head. 'They didn't make me before I went to France, and no one's mentioned it since I came home. I hope they forget!' I add with feeling.

'Ooh, I don't blame you. I told her, your stepmother, I was doing the instruction just to keep her quiet, really. I think she was a bit shocked I were married to Ernest. But, you know, you don't think of all these things when you're in love, do you? I didn't realise I'd be taking on all this. Ernest, bless him, he'll not force me. Like you, I think I'm hoping it'll all go away in time.'

'You shouldn't do it unless you really believe,' I tell her seriously. 'You can always say you're having a problem with a bit of scripture. It's a good stalling tactic.' I grin at her. 'I'm working on it myself!'

''S all very well for you,' she says, 'with your book-learning and college an' that, but I don't think they'd believe me, do you, if I started arguing about the scripture?' She throws back her head and laughs.

I ask her about Marjorie and she tells me her little sister's doing an apprenticeship at Boots the Chemist in town. 'She was that glad to get it: they're so good to them, Annie. You wouldn't believe the trouble they go to. She works in the shop and goes for training on day-release. And there's all these extra-curricular activities, sports events and all sorts. And,' she confides, 'they get staff discount. Imagine!' She rolls her eyes to heaven. 'My, what that saves me on stuff for the baby. It's a godsend. Aye, we're right proud of our Marjorie. I was quite envious myself when she got the job, but of course, being married, it's out of the question for me. And I wouldn't swap our Ernest for Boots the Chemist, not even for the staff discount.'

I decide I rather like this straight-talking, jolly woman and wonder why Beatrice was so down on her at school. After chatting some more about Marjorie and her mother – the powerful Mrs Bagshaw, whom I remember all too well from the dreaded outing to Goose Fair – Iris confides they're a bit bemused that she's married to Ernest and is on the road to joining the congregation of the Golgotha Mission. I can sort of see their point: she's not exactly Mission material.

But Iris is frank about this, as she is – one imagines – about most things. 'To be honest, Annie, I'm not bothered about the *believing* side of it. If they say He's up there and we're going to be saved, that's fine by me. Well, of course there's the pledge.' She pulls a face. 'Have you had to sign the pledge?'

I nod. 'We all did. But I didn't mind because I don't drink anyway. Well, except a bit of wine in France.'

She bursts out laughing. 'Well, that's you damned, for one, then!'

'It was mixed with water, mind,' I say, laughing too.

'Oh Annie, you are a one! No, it's none of that. With the drink, I can take it or leave it. It's actually, it's . . .' She hesitates, not laughing now. 'I don't know how to put it.'

I wait.

'It's the gap,' she says, 'between what people say and what they do.' She looks at me. 'I suppose you'd call it the hypocrisy. There, I've said it now. I didn't ought to tell you that, did I?'

'Why not?'

She twists her hands in her lap. 'Well, I mean, it's your family, in't it? Not the pastor, your grandfather – I'm sure he's a good man. Oh, I don't know what's got me into this, Annie. I'm in deep water now.' She breaks off, biting her lip.

'Please, Iris,' I prompt her. I suddenly very much want to know what she's going to say.

'Well, you know, it's your father, really.'

'What about him?' I can feel the butterflies beating at my stomach wall.

'I know he was very much upset when your poor mother died. I were only a nipper then, of course, but yours is a big family in the area and you made friends with our Marjorie when you went to school, so I do know your family a bit. But then, much later, after I was with Ernest, I heard about that poor girl. Millie Blessing. The one they threw out of the Mission.' She can't meet my eye. She's looking down at her hands.

I can think of nothing to say. It's clearly true, then: everyone knows.

'I mean ...' She's addressing her left foot. 'She got the heave-ho from the congregation. But he got nothing at all. When he'd been, you know—' She stops.

'What? He'd been what?' I ask. 'Were they having an affair? What happened, Iris? I want to understand.'

She looks up at me. 'Of course, you weren't told. You were too little, and even if you weren't too little it's not a proper thing for a girl in a nice family to know ... that her own father is having ... relations ... with a young girl.' She pauses and takes a deep breath. 'And it's not the young girl's choice ... Because it wasn't, Annie.' She's watching me, unsure how much to say.

'Go on,' I whisper.

'I'm sorry to be the one to tell you this, but you're a grown-up now and you should be told the truth, because it's your family.' She pauses. 'That girl, Millie, wanted to say no, but she couldn't, Annie. She was only a kiddie. He kept finding her out. I think he was a bit ... funny about her, really. She was trapped.'

I stare at her. 'I can't believe it,' I say.

She looks up at me, her eyes full of sorrow. 'Our Ernest's mother was involved in trying to intercede with the elders, or whatever you call them. That's how I know. And it wasn't just once or twice before he got her – you know, with the baby. It went on for some time.' She stops, biting her lip, looking at me uneasily. 'Well, for three or four years, as a matter of fact.'

'It can't have,' I breathe. 'She's not a lot older than Beatrice!'

'I know, duck. But I'm afraid it did. They didn't find out about it for a long while, but Ernest's mother told me she found her one day, sobbing in the vestry, and it all came out. So then my mother-in-law, who was the verger's wife, of course, and a couple of the other women in the congregation spoke to their husbands – because, obviously, a woman can do nothing. And *they,* the men, went to see Mr Lang about it. But the trouble is with these people, Annie, they don't call a spade a spade. I mean you know them ... *I* would have come out and said it, because that's the way I am, but that lot are so sort of *polite* and *respectful*, it's my opinion they probably didn't rightly tell their husbands what was going on! They probably just complained he was being, you know, as some middle-aged men are with attractive young girls. Anyway, nothing changed. And in the end, well, we know what went down. *He* was the pastor's son-in-law and sort of untouchable really. *She* had no father to stand up for her. Poor girl. The Blessings left town. I suppose the baby was adopted. *He* should have seen to that, at least. I hate to think what's happened to Millie now.'

'Oh my God,' I say. There is a long silence. I look at Iris Wilkinson and she looks at me.

'And that's why I can't go for all this ... religious stuff,' she finishes quietly.

'Does my sister know?' I ask.

She shakes her head. 'I haven't told her, anyhow. I haven't told anyone, in fact. Not me mam, nor Marjorie. I know it would put them off Ernest too much – and, bless him, it's nowt to do with him, is it?'

I'm feeling dizzy and short of breath. I need to get away and think, but I'm not sure my legs will take me anywhere.

Iris seems to understand. 'Bless you, Annie, and here's me not even giving you a cup of tea. Stay there a moment, duckie. The kettle's hot.'

'No, I—' I grip the arms of the chair and try to stand, but she jumps up ahead of me and sits me firmly down again. The tea, when she brings it, is strong and sweet. Sugar for the shock, I remember from somewhere. We talk a little more about Marjorie as I drink it, though my mind is spinning and the cup rattles in the saucer.

Then she says, 'Actually, Annie, I was thinking out there' – she nods towards the kitchen – 'that there's one more thing I ought to tell you. It's about your stepmother.'

'Goodness, Iris, d'you think she knows about this?'

Iris looks at me, straight, as if weighing something up. 'Mrs Lang knows all right.' She hesitates. Then she says, 'Left to myself, I wouldn't have said this, you know. It's not my place, and we barely know each other, after all.' She smiles for a moment. Then she says, 'It was she asked me to tell you, Annie.'

'She? *Who*?'

'Mrs Lang. Your stepmother.' Her worried gaze is searching my face.

'What?'

She nods.

My mind's reeling. 'When? When did she ask you?'

'She asked me yesterday.' Iris twiddles the ring on her finger. 'She said she'd send you to see me. That's why I was a bit shocked when you turned up the very next day!' Then looking up in alarm, 'Don't you go telling her I said that!'

'Of course not!' My mouth is dry again.

'She's known about your father and that poor little girl a good while, so I believe. To be honest, I think she's had it up to here.' Iris raises her hand briefly and lets it drop. 'Of course, she didn't say owt, but I could see she were at the end of her tether. What it must be like, living with that. . .'

But I can't understand how they were even talking about it – Mother who abhors gossip! I look at her, speechless.

Iris guesses what I'm thinking. 'It was when I said my maiden name was Bagshaw, she asked if I were related to Marjorie, your school-friend. I told her I was at school with Beatrice and she – she – it was odd, really, but she said there was something weighing on her mind – something she'd just found out, apparently.' Iris is frowning as she tries to get it right: 'She said that girl who was expelled from the Mission is still paying a high price; and she was bothered about whether in the eyes of the Lord you've committed a sin if you do it *without consent*.' She waves a hand. 'Or some such. Anyway, "consent" was the word she used.'

As the shock starts to sink in, the second feeling to wash over me is shame. 'How – how could she have said all this to you, Iris? She never . . . allows herself to say anything to us about her feelings!' I'm thinking we never give her the chance.

'Oh, but you must have done this – well, maybe you're too young,' Iris says, with a smile. 'You find yourself confessing things to a stranger you'd never say within the walls of your own home. Then . . . I suppose she thought I'm a good person to tell you really, with knowing about what happened through my mother-in-law, and knowing you and Beatrice. When you think of it, I'm one of the few people who *could* tell you. And, well, we were talking about babies, weren't we, with my sick little one.' She glances at the clock again.

I put down the empty cup and manage to smile at her. 'You must go, Iris. Thanks so much for the tea.'

She looks at me anxiously. 'I'll need to be getting back up there before too long, but I can't just throw you out, Annie, feeling like you do. Not after a shock like this.'

'No, I'm fine now. Honestly.' This time I do stand. 'I so hope your baby is better when you get there.'

'Bless you,' she says. She leaves the room for a moment and returns with her hat and coat. 'Here, I'll walk you up the road a bit. It's on my way.'

We walk in silence. When we part, she says, 'I'm sorry it had to be me to do it, Annie. I wished she might have told you herself. But, she couldn't. It wasn't in her nature, I suppose, yet she said it was time you knew. Poor Mrs Lang.' She sighs. 'So I promised her I'd see to it. How could I refuse?'

I don't know how I got home after that. I'm sitting here upstairs after tea, my head bursting with doubt and arguments and questions. Bea has said Iris Bagshaw is not reliable. Is Iris telling the truth about this? I must speak to Beatrice, immediately, this very weekend, but that may not get us any further. What's certain is that I can't tell this part to Fred, for surely he cannot know it himself.

Thankfully, my father is out at a meeting; I don't have to face him over tea, and Mother is on her way to Bible Circle, so our meal is businesslike and short. She doesn't even ask me if I've seen Iris, and I can't tell her. I know I am in shock, but I must make plans. I have to talk it all through with Beatrice. Next, I must somehow find out if this really happened: though who apart from Millie Blessing herself can ever confirm it?

If Iris's version of events is true, I can't begin to know what it means for me – for all of us, our father's children. I think it will change our lives very much. There's an *abyss* inside me that I can't go near, a gouging-out and soiling of goodness; and that's all I can say for now. I long to discover that Iris is wrong, and none of this is true.

Then I remember the cellar, and I strongly suspect she is right.

# TWENTY-TWO

**Saturday, August 20**

Beatrice and I are facing each other over a table covered in a stiff white linen cloth. She has taken me to tea in Dickins & Jones. My fingers of toast spread with Gentleman's Relish are going soggy on the plate in front of me.

'Come on, Annie, it's all the rage!' says Beatrice.

I smile wanly, feeling sick, pick up a slice and bite into it. Actually, it's good. I finish the whole slice; at least it puts off the *moment*.

'Anchovy!' says Beatrice proudly.

'Ooh Miss Lang,' I put on my best East Midlands accent. 'So sophisticated. You and your London ways!'

'I discovered it because I had to send some out to the Reverend Richardson,' Beatrice explains. 'Six jars dispatched by sea to Peking! They do like their little refinements, my ministers. Anyway, you know from Auntie Francie how rarely they get home on furlough.'

This intriguing detail of Beatrice's working life triggers a whole inquisition on my part as to what else the missionaries out in China and Africa ask her to send them. She counts the shopping list off on her fingers: ink and cocoa powder to Ethiopia, a hairnet to Rhodesia, Marks & Spencer's knickers (they were for *Mrs* Richardson in Peking), sweet pea and lettuce seeds, a hot-water bottle ...

'*Hot-water* bottle?'

'That was for southern Sudan.'

'But it's *Africa*!'

'Juba's a desert town. Freezing at night.' Beatrice is proud of knowing these things. 'Annie, of all the places they go to, I would so love to be in that desert ...' She sighs. 'Oh yes, and they wanted charcoal biscuits for their dog.'

'That's sweet,' I say wistfully. Then, 'But Beatrice ...'

'I know. You didn't come rushing down to London to hear this.'

I sit on my hands. I stare at my plate. How can I do to her what Iris Bagshaw did to me? It's just a day ago, but it has changed my whole life.

'Come on, girl. I'm all ears!'

So I take a deep breath and tell her the version I've rehearsed: how I stumbled across Miss Blessing at the hospital when I volunteered to play for the concert. (I don't say how much plotting and planning it took.) How Miss Blessing told me about the baby and Fred told me whose baby it was. And finally I tell her about Iris Bagshaw, now Iris Wilkinson, and how it seemed to be that our father Harry Lang had – had—

Beatrice cuts me off before I can finish the sentence. 'I know,' she says.

I look up at her in alarm. 'You *knew*?'

Beatrice puts her elbows on the table and her head in her hands, which she would never normally do in public, and whispers, 'I saw them. And Annie, I think you saw them, too. *That night*. You know.'

I stare at her. Beatrice's face has gone white and she looks sort of hollow and suddenly older. 'I . . . came upon them, one night when I was walking home from Junior Fellowship—'

'Where?'

'Right by the house.' She shakes her head. 'What does it matter?'

'What were they doing?'

'For goodness sake, Annie! It was dark. She was . . . sort of, crying.'

'Did they see you?'

'I don't think so. I didn't understand what I'd seen. I just knew I had to get away fast. Then later, when you saw it too, I realised it was something very wrong. It was only all that time afterwards, when it blew up at the Mission, I understood what it was.' She drops her gaze. A tear splashes on to her plate. After a moment or two she says, 'And it changed everything.'

'What d'you mean?' I ask.

She doesn't answer.

'Did you tell anyone?'

She looks up at me from behind her tear-stained spectacles. 'Are you crazy? Of course not!' And then, more gently, 'Who would I tell? Fred was away at school. You were too small. Mother . . .' The word hung over the table between us. She went on, 'I would have gone and told our own mother in her grave, but I didn't want her to know. Actually—' A sob breaks from her. She stifles it. 'You'll think I'm mad. The only person I could tell was Nana.'

Now I'm very close to crying as well. I'd have told Nana, too. A woman from a table across the aisle is staring in our direction. I glare at her and she quickly looks away.

'I still have nightmares,' says Beatrice.

I want to give her a hug, but you can't in Dickins & Jones.

All I can do is sit there like a prune. I reach across the table and put my hand on hers.

She raises her head and smiles wanly. Then she rummages in her bag for a hanky and blows her nose. 'Afterwards, I mean when I was old enough to understand more, I thought I should have done something.' She is gazing down at her empty plate in agony. 'I *should* have done something. I did nothing, Annie.'

'Bea, you couldn't have. If people like the Wilkinsons and all those Mission folk couldn't stop it, what could *you* have done? I mean, when was this?'

She thinks for a moment. 'Well, it was a few months after Millie Blessing came to the Mission, so I was eleven, maybe, when I saw it – fourteen when I realised what it was.'

'There you are, then. Who'd have even listened?'

I wonder what I'd have done. Would I have gone to the police? In my head, of course, I'd told them about Mother – but that was make-believe. Could a child actually go to the police about her own father? *My father*! Unthinkable. I say, 'But now we *can* do something about it, Bea – sort of, make amends.'

Beatrice doesn't answer. She gets out her compact and powders her nose. I look around for the waitress. I was eight when Mother shut me in the cellar, so Millie Blessing was fifteen. And Beatrice had seen them when Millie would have been a year younger. My head is pounding. We need to get out of here.

We're walking arm in arm along Oxford Street, without even a glance at the shops and sights around us. I've never known Beatrice like this. My sister always knows what to do; is always what Auntie Vera calls *poised*. Not today.

Suddenly she says, 'You see, that's why I can't be a missionary, Annie.'

I'm thrown by this. 'I thought you said God hadn't called you yet?'

She sighs. 'No, and He won't call me. Because I'm not fit.'

'What d'you mean, you're not fit?' I stop in the middle of Oxford Street and force her to look at me. A lifetime of having to fish around for arguments from all over the Bible sometimes comes in useful and Beatrice and I are old hands at it. 'Deuteronomy,' I say.

'Exodus!' She flashes back.

Of course I knew she'd come out with that 'third and fourth generation' business, but I'm not having it, because it's barmy. Wasn't it to stop the Children of Israel worshipping idols in the wilderness? I tell her she needs to forget it, because otherwise it will blight her whole life. Besides, I remind her, in the next breath God says He will love those who love Him. And as quickly as it flared up, the row is over because she knows I'm right: *The fathers shall not be put to death for the children, neither shall the children be put to death for the fathers: every man shall be put to death for his own sin.* Deuteronomy got it right ... I hope.

As we walk on, I'm wondering what Deuteronomy would have to say about the fact that thanks to creepy Mr Wilkinson and all those other men at the Mission, our father would never be brought to justice for his own sin, while my dearest sister Bea might well pay a lifetime's penance for it.

'Our father ...' It has become more difficult since the revelations of Iris Bagshaw to call him Daddy, and I'm at a loss as to what I can possibly say about him.

Beatrice squeezes my arm. 'Poor Annie. I'm sorry you had to find out about it at all. You didn't need to know. I'm cross with Millie Blessing for ever telling you there was a baby.'

I start to explain that it wasn't Millie who said whose baby it was. I want to tell Beatrice how Miss Blessing is a prisoner, and how the only way we can make up for some of what our father has done is to get her out. But this is not yet the moment.

Then Beatrice says, 'I wonder if Mother knows?'

I take a deep breath. 'It was Mother who asked Iris Bagshaw to tell us.'

'*What?*' Beatrice is as nonplussed as I had been.

I nod, breathlessly. 'She must have known for years, Bea. And now she wants us to know.'

'You mean – she *knew* what Daddy was up to? And she stood by him – with this major sin!'

'Not just a huge appalling *sin*,' I burst out. 'It was a *crime*, Bea, too! But like those others at the Mission, *she* knew and *they* knew and none of them did anything to stop it. They just let it happen!'

'You said they spoke to Daddy about it?'

'Iris said some of the men did. But she reckoned they hadn't taken it seriously.'

'Mother must have taken it seriously,' says Beatrice.

'Shouldn't *she* have gone to the police, then?' Far from feeling sorry for Mother, I'm just angry. 'Here's you feeling guilty, aged fourteen, for not doing something to stop it, but none of these grown-ups lifted a finger. And – *oh my goodness!*' I stop stock-still and tug at Beatrice's arm. 'I've just realised even our own grandfather did nothing: he was the founder, the pastor, the head of it, wasn't he? How could he not go to the police?'

Beatrice says, a little too quickly, 'He can't possibly have known. Well, he must have known she was pregnant, of course, but they probably kept the rest of it from him.'

'He knew enough to throw Miss Blessing out of the Mission!' The possibility that the saintly Pastor Eames, our own flesh and blood, had allowed such a crime to go unpunished is deeply chilling, and we wander on towards Bloomsbury in silence, each sunk in our own grim thoughts. I'm thinking how remote our grandfather has been all our lives, and how little we know of him; while we thought we did know our father, when in fact we knew nothing at all.

Eventually Beatrice says she supposes Mother would have felt she couldn't be disloyal to her husband. She explains that's what it means to be married. Then she'd see it also as a betrayal of the Mission – so to *tell* would destroy the two most important things in her life. 'She must have felt completely trapped,' says Beatrice.

'Iris seems to think Mother's a victim too,' I tell her morosely.

Beatrice nods. 'Well, she is in a way.'

'Not as much as Millie Blessing,' I retort. 'Or that poor little boy.'

'What little boy?'

'Millie Blessing's baby. He must have started school by now.'

'I've no idea,' says Beatrice. Like Fred, she clearly doesn't want to think about him.

'Our brother!'

'No, Annie. Don't say that.'

I stop and look at her. 'D'you suppose his new parents go to the Mission? Perhaps we might even know them?' I haven't considered this possibility before. I try and remember who in the Mission congregation has a six-year-old boy.

'No,' says Beatrice firmly.

'How can you be so sure?'

'*He* will have seen to that.'

Back at Beatrice's digs, we spend the rest of the evening talking and talking. It's a relief for us both to speak about our father and what he has done. Beatrice tells me more – and small mysteries from our childhood begin to fall into place. She reveals, for one thing, that she overheard a conversation between Mother and Maisie that made her strongly suspect there was something bad with poor Elsie, the maid. Elsie left so suddenly: I think back to that day at the tea table when I asked about it. From what she overheard, Beatrice believes that the reason was not of Elsie's making, whatever Mother and Daddy said at the time. (Maybe this is why I get the feeling Maisie knows more about our household than she would ever say.)

Then I tell Beatrice about Dr Squires, his connection to our father and his mysterious attitude to Millie. 'Fancy telling her she'll never get better!' I explode. 'When he must know she's not very ill, because he lets her play for the choir.'

Beatrice sees no contradiction in this. 'Just because she's well enough to play her music, it doesn't necessarily follow she's fit to leave the hospital,' she points out.

'Yet they keep her on a *locked ward*? With poor women who are in a completely different state of mind from her? And he tells her she'll never get better, so she's come to believe it!'

Beatrice shrugs. 'Annie, that doctor has done years of training. Don't you think he might know a little bit more than you do about how well or unwell Miss Blessing is? She's on that ward for her own protection. It sounds as if she was awfully mad after the baby.'

'Yes, I'm sure she was – *six years ago*.' I look at her fiercely, wondering if I can test out the theory that's been nagging at me ever since I discovered all this. Well, knowing me, I'm going to tell Beatrice anyway. 'Listen,' I begin, 'Fred thinks that when someone does something like Miss Blessing has done – you know, become an unmarried mother – she has sort of burned her boats in life. She's an embarrassment to her family. No one wants her around.'

320

Beatrice says, 'Do Mrs Blessing and her sister think that of her?'

I shake my head. 'I don't know. I truly hope not – but they're on the other side of the world. They can't see what's going on. They've been told she's too sick to leave the hospital and of course they have to take the doctor's word for that. But . . .' I hesitate. I don't quite know how to say the next bit because it sounds so far-fetched. 'There are others for whom it's more than just an embarrassment: it's a – a threat.'

'You mean the Mission?'

I nod. 'And particularly for Daddy himself, because of the . . . way of it.'

'Yes,' says Beatrice softly. I know she is thinking of what she saw.

'So isn't it kind of . . . *useful* if Miss Blessing is thought to be mad because, if she should ever tell, no one will believe her?' I look at her steadily to see how she takes it.

She doesn't hesitate: 'Honestly, Annie, I don't know how you can even suggest that!' She thinks for a moment. 'For a start, it's not just down to him, is it? He'd need her doctor to agree. And anyway, Daddy would never dream of such a thing!'

'But Bea, look at what he has *done*. Our father might do . . . *anything* now.'

'It's not our job to judge,' Beatrice says. 'We just don't know all the facts.'

'We know enough, don't we?' I explain that I believe Mother asked Iris to tell us because of that strange conversation a couple of nights earlier. I think he must have fobbed her off quite a while ago with some story about Dr Squires leaving the hospital, and Millie no longer being there. So it would have come as a shock to Mother when he let slip that his friend Squires was still at Mapperley. 'I was there,' I finish. 'She reacted really oddly, and he was furious with her. I didn't understand why – but now I think I do. She knows Millie Blessing shouldn't be locked up. That's why she went and told Iris to tell us, isn't it?'

Beatrice is frowning. 'I've no idea, Annie. You can't just jump to conclusions like that!'

But I'm sure I'm right. 'It all makes sense, Bea. And now it's our job to help Millie get out of that place. We have to! It isn't just saving *her* life, you know. You said yourself it's made you feel you can't be a missionary. I don't know if Fred knows everything Iris told me; but even as much as he does know is enough, I shouldn't wonder, to have sent him off the rails in the first place. This is something to help us save *our* lives, too – yours and Fred's and mine!'

By the time we fall asleep in the small hours of the morning, Beatrice and I have the outline of a scheme to get Millie Blessing out of the hospital and away to a new life.

# TWENTY-THREE

**Monday, August 22**

There are four enormous holes in our plan, to which I need to find a solution. First, and most importantly, I must persuade Millie to come away with us. Secondly, even if she agrees, our scheme depends on her being at the concert and I have no guarantee at all that she will be allowed to attend.

With barely three weeks to go, I take my courage in both hands at tonight's rehearsal and approach Sister Jones as soon as she walks into the chapel. 'Sister,' I say, squatting by her chair as she unpacks her music, 'please may I ask you a favour?'

Sister Jones looks at me, expectantly. I know she likes me because I've done a good thing for the choir, but I think she also likes me for myself, and I her. 'I wanted to ask . . .' I falter. Supposing she just says no?

'Spit it out, Annie! I won't eat you!'

So I ask that Miss Blessing be given permission to come to the concert – that is, listen from the vestry. When Sister doesn't immediately answer, I rush on, 'No one would know she was there. It just seems such a shame—'

'Yes. Yes, I understand.' Sister Jones is frowning. 'The trouble is that it's a Saturday night and Doris and most of the other assistants are off duty. We can't spare the ones that are left on the ward.'

I take a deep breath and make my all-important suggestion: that my brother Fred could do it; Fred who, as a voluntary patient, is nearing the end of his stay; who knows the ropes and knows Miss Blessing, 'And you know yourself that Miss Blessing is – is not a patient who is likely to give any trouble,' I finish. I believe that if Sister Jones is as humane as I feel her to be, she must surely agree, deep down, that Millie Blessing shouldn't be on a locked ward at all.

What I'm saying seems to be hitting some kind of nerve. Her face contorts as she tries to work out whether to allow this unorthodox thing. 'Your concern for her is touching, Annie,' she replies carefully. 'But I don't know if Blessing even wants to come to the concert. She might find it distressing to be surrounded by the general public.'

'Oh, I think she would like it very much!' I say. I so badly need her to agree that I'm almost imploring her. 'And it won't be as demanding as when she plays the harmonium for the service on Sunday mornings, will it, Sister?'

Sister Jones seems very uneasy about this. She twists her fingers in her cape and considers it. 'No, the two occasions are not comparable,' she insists at last. 'The chapel service is strictly for staff and patients, not for people from outside. I can see it would probably not be a security risk ...' She sighs. 'But it's not a judgement I can make, I'm afraid. I will have to ask her psychiatrist who, as you may know, is our very own Dr Squires.'

'Oh, Sister!' My heart sinks to my boots, but I try and maintain an optimistic tone of voice. 'If you would be so kind? I do hope he agrees.'

*

The third unknown in our plan is whether Millie's sister Edwina will make the long and costly journey to take Millie back to Canada. I have already asked Millie to bring Edwina's address to this rehearsal so I can write to her, but I haven't yet said why: it's too dangerous to put in a note. However, she may guess well enough, and there is more of a spring in her step than usual when she enters the chapel tonight. For this rehearsal, I am to play for the first time; she is only here for the *a capella* pieces. As we take our places at the piano, she produces from her pocket a folded page torn from a notebook and pushes it into my hand: Edwina's address in Canada. Then she looks around carefully before bringing out a second, larger sheet, folded in four and closely covered in handwriting. She whispers that she's taken the opportunity to send a separate letter for me to enclose with mine: the chance to write without the fear of being censored has allowed her to tell them for the first time what life in the hospital is really like. She adds, not meeting my eye, 'And also to say things they didn't know before.'

Encouraged by this spirit of rebellion, I draw her away from the piano and launch into our plan as soon as Dr Squires breaks for the interval. But Millie is incredulous. 'I can't possibly *leave*!' she whispers rapidly. 'I could not survive it, Annie. You don't understand!'

I'm thrown by this, having almost convinced myself she is ready to go. I start to tell her as gently as I can that I want to write to her sister and suggest she takes Millie to Canada.

'Then I must ask Dr Squires,' she says at once. 'He will know what to do.'

'No!' I burst out, rather more sharply than I intended. A couple of the nurses sipping coffee nearby stop their conversation and look at us. I smile at them nervously. 'No,' I repeat, turning back to Millie and keeping my voice low. 'I don't think that would be a good idea.' I've rehearsed this many times in my head. I take a deep breath, but somehow in this place, and with the urgency, it doesn't come out as it's meant to. 'Millie: Dr Squires and my father know each other.'

She looks at me, puzzled.

'Listen,' I press on, 'I know my father did you a great evil.'

She recoils in horror – it's the first time I've revealed that I've discovered what my father did. She starts to ask a question, but we haven't time to discuss this now and I raise my hand to stop her. 'I'm sorry. Never mind how I know. But you would be justified in taking steps against him for that.'

Millie is clearly in shock. 'I – I don't understand. What steps, Annie? What do you mean?'

'You could go to the police, for a start!'

She looks at me in disbelief. 'How could you possibly think I would do such a thing? After all this time? How could you *think* it of me?'

'Listen, Millie!' She has misunderstood completely. 'Please. That's not what I meant at all!' I can hear my voice tight with alarm.

'I would never hurt your family! Anyway, who would believe me?'

'No, I ... that's not what I'm saying. I'm saying you would be *justified* in accusing him.'

She gives a little cry and pulls away from me.

'Millie, please, let me explain ...'

Sister Jones is moving in our direction. 'Is everything all right, you two?' I can hear a note of concern in her voice. This display of fright on Millie's part is not going to play well with my request to let her come to the concert.

But Millie, used to years of dissembling to authority, pulls herself together and withdraws behind her mask. 'It's nothing, Sister. Annie was just telling me a – something rather surprising!'

Sister Jones is frowning. 'Annie,' she says after a moment. 'Will you step this way, please.'

I follow her to a place in the shadowy nave of the chapel, wanting to kick myself for making such a mess of this delicate conversation and conscious that the short coffee break is ticking away, my only chance to say to Millie what needs to be said. Sister doesn't read me the riot act; she merely tells me she hopes I now understand that Millie Blessing is not 'normal', as she terms it, and cannot be treated as such. 'I expect,' she goes on, 'that you were telling her something quite harmless, were you not?'

I don't know how to answer this. If I say yes, it will confirm the fact that Miss Blessing is 'sick' and cannot stomach even harmless things. I say, 'It was something more . . . unexpected for her, really, Sister,' adding that I am terribly sorry for my thoughtlessness.

She looks at me critically. 'I could ask what it was you actually said, but I won't intrude. Just remember, Annie, that poor Blessing isn't as used to being shocked by things as the rest of us. I hope you now fully understand that her mind is very fragile.'

I nod, miserably.

She looks at me for a moment, then says in a softer voice, 'Don't worry: I shall still speak to Dr Squires about her coming to the concert, but I hope this has taught you a lesson.' Then she turns on her heel and goes back to her seat.

As I hurry up the aisle towards Millie, the nurses around us are starting to pack up their thermoses and coffee cups. I sit down beside her, my mind in tatters as to how I'm ever going to speak to her about these things now time is so short.

She looks at me expectantly. 'Did you get into trouble? I'm terribly sorry. It was just a shock – what you said.'

'No, *I'm* sorry,' I tell her, groping for the words I need to continue. 'Millie, I was only trying to tell you that my father might fear you could at some point accuse him.'

'That's over,' she murmurs. 'It's in the past.'

'Listen.' I take a deep breath and return to my theme that for this reason, he and Dr Squires may believe it's perhaps *safer* to keep her in hospital. I look at her anxiously, wondering how she will take this. 'I'm afraid they may want you to believe you're more sick than you really are, Millie, so you don't think of leaving.'

She shakes her head. 'It can't be so, Annie. It would be too cruel.'

I say fiercely, 'My father has already done the cruellest thing!'

'But Dr Squires is good and honourable. He found me a piano. He has entrusted me with this privilege of playing for the choir. I can't betray his trust.'

I feel I'm sinking again. 'It's very difficult,' I agree. 'I would find it as hard as you. But—'

She breaks in, 'It would be dishonest of me to run away, Annie.'

'But I'm afraid he's not being honest with *you*, Millie. You know you're not as ill as the others. You shouldn't be in this horrible place. You don't belong here.'

'I don't belong anywhere else!' We're speaking in whispers, but her voice is bitter, her face angry.

The choir are moving back to their places. The break is over. There's one thing I still urgently need from her tonight. As we sit down side by side at the piano again, I ask, 'Will you at least let me write to Edwina about this?'

Millie looks down at her hands and out into the shadowy

chapel. 'How can I disobey Dr Squires? Why won't you let me speak to him?'

This is what I've been dreading. I try to say it calmly, but my words are stuttering and jumping. 'Because I'm afraid that if you do, he ... If you let him know you want to go ... he will lock you up further. If he fears you may leave, we will miss our only chance!'

It sounds so melodramatic, I don't know if I'd believe it myself – yet I'm sure it's true. She is staring at the piano keys. Poor Millie: it seems brutal to be trying to undermine her trust in the one person who has encouraged her – and after all, I may be wrong! Seeing her face so strained, I suddenly feel very uncertain I'm doing what's best for her. 'You're not betraying him by going to Canada, Millie,' I point out, as much to reassure myself as her. 'You're simply seeking a – a second opinion.'

Dr Squires, who as usual has left the chapel during the break, now returns to the rostrum and taps his baton on the music stand to bring us to attention. It's my turn to play for the choir now – for the very first time – and I have never felt less capable of doing so, my whole being jangling with the sense of a mission not accomplished. I stumble on two notes in the opening introduction, aware of the intense figure of Millie sitting beside me. She is turning the pages, but I know her mind is in turmoil, too.

At the end of the rehearsal she stands up rather awkwardly as Doris approaches to lead her away. 'You may write, as we discussed,' she murmurs, her voice distant and formal. 'But for myself...' She gathers up her music then drops her voice so Doris can't hear. 'I'm not ready yet, Annie. I need to think.'

## Sunday, August 28

The great event of this week is that Fred was given weekend parole last Friday and has come home for a whole three days! He looks around him with a sense of wonder, as if not quite believing he's no longer on the ward, and we walk up the Oaks arm in arm as if he's afraid to walk unaided, his confident striding around the hospital grounds quite forgotten. I remember what he said about no longer belonging to our family; it seems to be written in his face as he watches us having our mundane conversations at mealtimes, his eyes moving from one of us to the next, without apparently being able to take part himself. When I raise it with him, all he says is, 'You've all got smaller – the house, everyone.' And later, 'None of it's real, Annie.'

In an effort to involve him in my own all-too-real adventures, I tell him, on that first walk, about our plans for Miss Blessing.

'You've changed your tune, haven't you? The last time we spoke,' he reminds me, 'you were four-square behind the Mission and all its works. What happened to that?'

'I understand more about it now,' I say stiffly. 'I've changed my mind.'

'And Miss Blessing has agreed to this?' he asks.

'She's thinking about it.'

'Ah. Thinking.'

'I'm sure she will come round to it,' I tell him, with a confidence I don't feel.

'Are you? And what about her sister? Will she play ball? It's an expensive journey from Canada. Does she want the responsibility of a mental patient on her hands? Can she even get away to come and collect her?'

'I'm waiting to hear,' I tell him. 'But if Edwina

understands what's really going on, I believe she will come somehow.'

'And what *is* really going on, Annie? Explain it to me. What's changed? Why does Miss Blessing have to be set free?'

'Because …' I glance at him, unsettled by his tone. 'Because, actually, of something you said about her life being over.'

'I didn't say that,' he protests.

'You did. You said that having broken the rules, she must pay the price – which is that she's expendable.'

'In the view of some people.'

'All I can do is help her, Fred.' I'm conscious I mustn't get riled on account of his state of mind. 'What would *you* do if someone were incarcerated in that place for ever, and you kind of owe it to them?'

'Do you owe it to her?' he asks. He sounds surprised rather than sarcastic.

I hesitate. I haven't mentioned the revelations of Iris Bagshaw. 'The circumstances are more complicated than they seem,' I say at last. 'I have heard it and Beatrice knows it.'

'Are you going to tell me what they are?'

I'm thinking of Fred's own words many years ago: on the night I was locked in the cellar, Nana must have known the wearer of the blue shoes well enough not to bark. Beatrice says she saw Miss Blessing with my father near the house even before that. Has Fred always known, perhaps, the way things were between them? But no, I can't risk telling him: it's far more important that Fred recovers and gets out of hospital himself.

'I'll tell you one day, perhaps, when you're not being so grumpy!' I give him a dig in the ribs, hoping he will take a teasing in his present mood. 'But you've met her; you know she's no business being on that locked ward. Don't you think we should help her get out?'

'It's down to her doctor, really, isn't it?'

We walk on in silence. There is a voice screaming in my head; it's Marjorie Bagshaw's again, from when we were children: *Freemasons help each other.* Dare I suggest my Dr Squires theory to Fred? I wonder if I've taken his support too much for granted. If he disapproves, he could easily betray us. We talk about other things as we continue our slow walk around the reservoir, but my mind is racing. I say: 'D'you feel up to going to the Arboretum?'

He stops to catch his breath. Then he says, 'Why not?' And we continue on, instead of turning back to the house.

Only later, when his mood has softened in the fresh air and he's almost his old self again, do I return to the subject of Miss Blessing. 'You know the choirmaster is her consultant,' I tell him. 'Dr Squires.'

'Yes, you asked me about him before,' Fred says. 'Means nothing to me.'

'He's in the Lodge with Daddy.' I try and say it as neutrally as possible. 'Isn't that a coincidence?'

Fred stops in his tracks. This is clearly news to him. 'No,' he says quietly. 'No, it's not.'

We walk on in silence for a full five minutes till we're almost home, but I can sense something in him has changed. 'So . . .' I venture, 'coming back to my earlier question, are we right to get her out?'

He turns and looks at me. 'How can I help?' he asks.

As he leaves on Sunday evening to go back to Mapperley – Daddy has gone to bring the car round to St Ann's Hill – Fred places his hands on my shoulders and looks at me seriously. 'Annie, you don't have to protect me. I know it all.'

"'The dog that didn't bark in the night'?'

'Yes. I've known for a long time.'

I wonder how, but there isn't time to ask.

'I want to say, I support you all the way,' he tells me. Gone is the sarcasm now. 'If I wasn't stuck in *there* . . .'

'Fred!' Our father's voice up the back steps.

'You'll be home very soon.' I give him a hug, but he isn't used to it. He stands stiffly with his arms stuck out at an angle. 'You're better, Fred,' I tell him, pulling back. 'You've got your part to play. We need to know you're with us. We couldn't do this without you.'

'I wish I could do more,' he mutters.

'*Fred*, are you coming?'

Mother enters the kitchen. 'Frederick, what are you loitering around for? Can't you hear your father?'

He looks at her over my shoulder. 'I'm off. Goodbye, Mother.'

He hesitates. It is an awkward moment, as it always is in a family that never touches. She waves him away. 'Get along with you. I'll remember you in my prayers.'

He stays a moment longer, squeezes my hand, and is gone.

### Tuesday, August 30

I cannot say how heartened I am by Fred's support for our plan, because – as the day approaches – I have become less certain we're doing the right thing. I'm feeling more and more uneasy about forcing poor Millie out of the one place where she feels safe and dispatching her across the world just because, according to some notion of mine, I feel she must be set free! Of course my family are right: I'm no doctor. My father may have committed a terrible crime but can he be the monster I'm taking him to be? And Dr Squires is a respected *psychiatrist,* not an evil demon. Who am I to know better than all of them? There is a part of me (I have to admit it) that hopes Edwina Blessing will write back and tell me not to be so fanciful, so I'm forced to drop the whole hare-brained scheme. But then Fred's endorsement brings me back to the reason for hatching the plot in the first place: my father *is* a monster. And so doubt and determination wash over me in contradictory waves.

It's too soon to have heard yet from Canada, but every lunchtime I imagine it is morning in New Brunswick and that my letter is reaching Edwina and she is reading it at the breakfast table. What will she say? Will she be shocked and angered by what she reads and resolve to rescue her sister? Or will she dismiss me as a hysterical, meddling girl? Will she respect my request for secrecy, or report us to the hospital authorities?

There is a silent player in all this, and I'm conscious I haven't mentioned her since my meeting with Iris Bagshaw: I could almost say that Mother has been avoiding me. Our conversations at mealtimes have been perfunctory and she has neither set me Mission tasks, nor suggested any further visits to the sick of the parish. Sometimes I have the feeling she is watching me, an instinct so strong that I dare not turn and look at her for fear of catching her at it. I still can't fathom what she's up to, sending me to see Iris, and I certainly don't want to discuss it with her; the very idea would be horrifying. So her sudden appearance in the room today while I'm practising the *Requiem* makes me physically jump. I can feel my shoulders tense and in an effort to shut her out I lean in to the keyboard, peering at the music as if I've never seen it before.

She stands by the door until I finish the passage, and then advances towards the piano. I fold my hands in my lap and look up at her, waiting for her to speak. 'It requires a particular skill to accompany singers,' she says. I brace myself for the criticism that I'm sure is coming next, for of course – unlike her – I have no experience of this at all. But she continues, 'You took over from … whom, exactly?'

'A patient,' I say. I watch her face warily, willing her not to ask if it's Miss Blessing, and wondering whether I'll tell a lie, if she does.

She nods. 'A patient. Yes. The accompaniment is not easy.'

'No,' I agree. I wonder where this is going.

'Whoever plays it needs to have their *wits* about them. Wouldn't you say, Annie?'

I nod. Is this a macabre joke about the patient's state of mind? But Mother is not breaking the habit of a lifetime: she means it literally.

'However, you are taking over for the concert, after all.' She smiles a thin smile, turns and leaves the room.


Tomorrow is the penultimate rehearsal and I'm jumping with nerves. I should at least get Dr Squires' answer from Sister Jones about whether Millie can come to the concert. My brain tangles up whenever I try to imagine what our strategy will be if he has said no: *Sufficient unto the day is the evil thereof* (Matthew 6:34). As to Miss Blessing's own decision about whether she wants to be rescued, the answer has to be yes! No other decision will do.


**Thursday, September 1**

Dr Squires has given permission for Millie to attend the concert, as long as she stays in the vestry. I said when we hatched it, our plan had four big holes and since last night, this one is resolved. The second is Millie herself, but I cannot push her for a decision. The third is Edwina: I believe that if Edwina makes the journey, Millie will agree to escape – so we are both waiting for letters from Canada. The final unknown is Maisie. We cannot free Miss Blessing without her help, but I've no idea how she will react when I tell her what we're doing. I can't put it off any longer; but it's the most enormous risk.

Ever since Maisie kept her word and never told Mother about Nana and me, I've felt I could trust her with my life; but of course Beatrice never knew that particular secret, so I can't tell her now. She's unhappy about Maisie for a different reason. 'You can't ask her to defy her employer,' she argues. 'Maisie could lose her job, and her references.'

This is true, and it worries me. 'What about Iris Bagshaw, then?' I suggest. 'We could ask her.'

'And have it all the way round the Mission?' says Beatrice.

I don't think this is fair; in the matter of Millie Blessing, Iris would be solid. I haven't had any further dealings with her since our one encounter, though I know her little girl has recovered and is out of hospital. She would probably agree to help us.

'But she'd have to tell her husband!' Beatrice points out. 'It's too risky.'

So Maisie it is. We'll just have to make sure she's not caught.


**Thursday, September 8**

Time has dragged this week. I started to believe Edwina had found it necessary to tell the authorities, and when I reported for my normal volunteer shift I fully expected to be hauled into Matron's office and dismissed. It was a huge relief, of course, when this didn't happen; but since then I've been fretting dreadfully about what to do if we haven't heard from Edwina by the concert, which is now just two days away: our one chance – lost.

Then, this very morning, we're sitting at the breakfast table when Mother enters with the first post. She gives my father two or three letters and keeps one to herself. I can see it's an airmail envelope. She is surveying me critically.

'This letter is for you, Annie.'

I don't doubt it. I take a sip of tea to try and disguise the fact that my cheeks are flaming.

'I wasn't aware,' says Mother, 'that you have correspondents *overseas.*'

Naturally, I have my story prepared. 'That'll be one of the girls from Bordeaux,' I say as lightly as I can.

'But this letter isn't from France.'

'Oh, it must be Françoise from La Réunion. Or maybe one of the French Canadians,' I tell her, and hold out my hand. 'Please may I see it, Mother?'

'I'm not sure. Who is this person? How do we know she – if indeed it *is* a she – is suitable?'

Stealing a glance in my father's direction, I'm relieved to see he is deep in his own letters and paying no attention. 'Mother, the students I knew in Bordeaux are all from good families,' I reassure her. It's meant to sound like sweet reason, but it comes out wheedling and prissy.

'The writer has withheld their name and address from the envelope, a fact I find suspicious. I may need to read the letter first.'

The dismay in my face must be plain to see. For us to founder on *this*! I want to say, *May I ask you, please, that you don't? I'm not a child any more. At least give me credit for choosing suitable companions!* But I can say nothing. Mother's chipping away at me over the years has done its work. Our plan will fail, of course; foolish of me not to realise it earlier. With my whole being I want to scream and snatch the letter from her bony hand, but all I can do is stare at her helplessly in silence.

Mother, her eyes never leaving my face, takes the butter knife and slits open the envelope. To my added horror, I realise Daddy has finished his own correspondence and is looking at us curiously. Mother glances at the address, and then turns the letter over to read the signature. I see her lips purse, a momentary hesitation . . . then, to my utter shock, she pushes letter and envelope at me across the table as if they're on fire. 'Very well.' She can't meet my eye. Now it's her turn to conceal her own confusion. Does she understand, then, whom it's from? I cannot read it in front of them. I take up the letter and fold it back into the envelope with shaking fingers. Somehow we continue with breakfast.

Edwina asks a hundred questions; she needs more convincing. She's worried about what will happen to Millie if I'm wrong, and she does need to spend the rest of her life in an asylum. But she understands the urgency and the brief opportunity and, on the gamble that I'm right, has agreed not to alert the authorities 'or anyone'. She is coming to England for the first time in six years and will meet Millie in London. Provided she agrees her sister is well enough, they'll travel back to Canada together. This is wonderful news! Edwina says she's written by the same post to tell Millie, so everything is ready now.

Beatrice will be home for the weekend and arrives tomorrow evening: my father and I are going to meet her train. (The long-awaited Wolseley has been delivered and he's keen to show it off.)

## Friday, September 9

Ever since my visit to Iris Bagshaw, I have been steering clear of my father, except for family mealtimes when I can't. So I'm sitting uneasily in the passenger seat of the new car, breathing a strong smell of leather upholstery and varnished wood. My father is exceedingly proud of it. 'Very smooth, isn't she?' he comments as we glide into Woodborough Road. 'Very smooth ride.' He puts his foot down and we shoot forward. At a cross-roads he scorches up behind another car and brakes abruptly. The movement is making me feel sick, like being on a boat. I just want to get to the station. I want to be with Beatrice.

'So this concert, Annie,' he says, glancing over at me. 'Important night for you, isn't it?'

I frown. 'Important night for the choir,' I tell him. 'It's not about me.'

'Sometimes,' he says, 'I worry about you, Annie. You need to own up to your achievements.'

I say nothing. Whenever I try doing that, I get squashed by Mother. Which is it to be?

'Well, it's true, isn't it?' he persists. 'Bright – and beautiful, with it.'

He gives me a sideways look.

I shrink further towards the window. I really don't want to talk about this, or about tomorrow. I don't want to be in the car at all.

'Well I'm proud of my little girl,' he says. He reaches over and pats my knee. 'So proud, let me say, that I've half a mind to come and see you perform!'

I'm aghast. 'No!' I say. I move my legs away and look around at him. 'No, you can't!'

'Why ever not?' His blue eyes turn towards me in innocent surprise. (Is this how he plays it with the girls?)

I haven't even considered in my elaborate planning that he might turn up at the concert. I fumble for a reason. 'You'd hate it, Daddy!' I splutter at last. 'You know you detest choirs. And – and Mother wouldn't like it!'

'Well Mother doesn't have to be there, does she? That's settled it now. I'm coming, and that's that!

# TWENTY-FOUR

**Saturday, September 10**

I can't read. I can't eat. I pack and repack the things I must take with me. Outside, the weather has broken and there's a whiff of autumn around the yard: this is satisfactory, as I must wear my long mackintosh to the concert, a vital part of Miss Blessing's disguise. Terrified of meeting my father coming home early from wherever he's gone to this Saturday afternoon, I pick up my music case and the all-important bag for Millie and slip down to the kitchen. It's far too soon, but I can take no risks. Maisie is standing at the stove. Dear Maisie, when I finally plucked up courage to tell her our secret, listened carefully, elbows on the kitchen table, hands pressed together. When I finished, she said, 'I worry for you girls, I really do. I hope you know what you're letting yourselves in for.' She paused for a moment and muttered, 'It's high time something were done,' so, as I had guessed, she knows more than she would ever say. 'In that case ... yes, duck, you can count on me. And good luck to you.'

And today, our Maisie has come in on her afternoon off to wish us God speed. 'Here, Annie,' she says when she sees me. 'I've done you a bacon sandwich.'

'Ah Maisie, no!' I protest. 'I feel sick. I can't eat anything.'

'Nonsense, duckie, you can't play the piano *and* the knight in shining armour on an empty stomach! Mr Brown says there's never an occasion when you can't find room for a bacon sandwich.'

She cuts two thick slices of bread and lifts the rasher out of the pan. 'There you are. I've done it crispy, as you like it.'

I put down my bags reluctantly and sit at the table. 'He might come ...' I murmur.

She looks at the clock. 'Mr Lang only went out after lunch, Annie. He'll not be home yet. And even if he did walk in, you tell him you've got to get up to the hospital in good time.'

'He'd want to drive me ...'

She pats my shoulder. 'Don't fret, love. He won't come. You eat now. It'll calm your nerves.' She pours me a cup of tea and, of course, I'm grateful; it's what I need.

Just as I finish, licking my fingers, Beatrice appears. 'You off already, Annie?'

I nod. 'You're wearing my coat, aren't you?' I ask her. 'I'll look odd walking out without one.'

'I am. Don't worry.' Beatrice has her little blue costume to wear under my coat; we're to swap at the chapel. Everything is planned. 'You've got the hat?' she asks.

'You girls,' Maisie laughs. 'You're both as bad as each other.' She looks at us seriously for a moment. 'I'd just like to say, though, how much I admire what you're doing. You're good, brave girls. Mr Brown and I are right proud of you both.'

'We couldn't do it without you, Maisie,' Beatrice tells her.

'Oh, it's nowt to do with me,' Maisie says. 'Glad to be of assistance. She'll be safe with us, don't you worry.'

I stand up, put on the mackintosh, pick up my two bags and turn to them for inspection. 'Do I look odd?'

'You'll do very nicely,' Maisie says. 'You look just like a lady pianist going to play in a concert!'

'Good luck, Annie!' Beatrice gives me a quick squeeze. 'Will I see you in the interval?'

I shake my head. 'Not with Daddy around: he might follow you. I'll have to stay with her. Drop the coat in before it starts. Oh Bea!' I'm seized with sudden fear. 'Supposing she's decided not to come with us!'

Beatrice throws up her arms in an elaborate shrug. 'Then we bring it all home again quietly and no one will know there was ever a plan!'

The hospital is quiet as I walk in with my bags: it's the late-afternoon lull before the bell rings for first tea. My smart shoes, not the ones I normally wear here, click–clack down the tiled corridor and the sound makes me feel conspicuous, though not a soul is around to see me. I enter the chapel, pass the rows of chairs set out for the choir in front of the altar, the rostrum for Dr Squires and the piano, pulled forward for me. With barely a glance at them, I make for the vestry and push open the door.

Someone is inside. I jump, startled. It's a nurse, and I realise to my shock that I know her: she's my enemy from my first visit to the chapel, the time I first met Millie Blessing after the service. She is stacking hymn books.

'I'm sorry!' I say. 'I wasn't expecting anyone.'

She turns and looks at me. 'Nor was I.' She comes forward a few paces. 'I know you, don't I? What on earth are you doing here?'

343

I'm seized with nerves again, standing with a bag in each hand, feeling guilty. 'I'm here for the concert,' I tell her.

'The concert starts at seven-thirty. Can you leave?'

'No. I'm – you see, I'm playing for them, Nurse. The piano.'

'*You*?' She looks at me in disbelief. 'Are you good enough to play for the choir?'

I decide to ignore this. 'I'm a volunteer, you see. I'm here—'

'Who are you, anyway?' She cuts across me.

'Annie Lang.'

'Well, I don't care, Annie Lang. You've no business in my vestry. Go away and come back at the proper time.'

Nurse Bleakley: that's her name. I remember her well.

'I need to practise, Nurse Bleakley.' I look her in the eye, trying to sound assertive.

'Too late for that. You should have practised before. Just get out.'

'Sister Jones said it would be all right.' I hesitate. 'Will you be coming to the concert, Nurse?'

Nurse Bleakley regards me with a mix of hostility and frustration. 'I'll be coming to the concert because it's my job,' she says grandly. 'But Sister never consulted me. She knows I'm in charge of the chapel.'

'I'm sorry, Nurse. I didn't realise. I wonder if I might stay, now I'm here?' I take a step back with my bags in tow, intending to keep everything safely by me at the piano. I don't want her prying.

Deep in the building, the tea bell rings. Thankfully, it seems to summon the nurse.

She twitches. 'Well, I have to leave now, anyway,' she says. 'Stay if you must. But don't make too much noise. Remember this is a place of calm reflection.'

I assure her I will play very quietly and back out of the vestry in my mac, with my bags. After a minute or two, Nurse Bleakley bustles past me as if I'm not there and I hear her shoes squeak away down the corridor.

To be on the safe side, I play through the 'Introit' and then, when I'm sure she has gone, I tiptoe back into the vestry. First, I place my mackintosh over a chair. Then I take from my bag the small hat with a net that Beatrice has found in her cupboard. She modelled it for me last night, pulling the veil down as far over her face as possible, which is not far enough for our purposes.

'Great for disguising spots,' she observed drily.

'I hoped it would cover more than that,' I said.

So next we found some of Bea's old spectacles, a pair with heavy frames from which she expertly slipped out the lenses. Then she added a bright red lipstick. 'This'll do the trick,' she said.

I tried on the hat, the veil, the specs and the lipstick and turned back to the mirror: a transformation! 'Excellent!' Beatrice cried. 'She'll be unrecognisable.'

I certainly hope so now, as I unpack each item and conceal them on the chair under the mackintosh. Then I take out the dress I've brought – one of mine that folds up small. She will have to make do with her own stockings and shoes. *Oh Millie,* I think. *We've done everything we could. Please trust us! There will never be another chance like this!*

When there's nothing more to do, I realise I have indeed come much too early. I play through the remainder of the Mozart and then settle down quietly in the vestry with my thumping heart, to wait.

At ten to seven, the choir starts to arrive in dribs and drabs. Gone are the uniforms, the starched nurse's caps; they are dressed in black, the women in long skirts and blouses, the tenors and basses in dinner jackets. Conversation is muted. I feel their nerves, and after venturing out of the vestry to let Sister Jones know I'm here, I retreat again. My own fingers are clammy as I practise phantom scales on my knee. I check and re-check the turned-up page corners of my music. At seven, the chapel doors open and the audience begins to drift in. I can see them through the crack of the vestry door, talking and smiling with not the remotest suspicion of the drama playing offstage.

Then, at ten past seven, the vestry door opens wider and Fred enters. He is dressed in his hospital garb but his hair is neatly combed and flattened – I suspect with water – and he has managed somehow to look smart. He grins at me nervously. The hall is filling up now and I wonder if Beatrice and my father have arrived. I look at my watch: it's gone 7.15 and I start to worry that something has happened, a crisis on the ward perhaps, or that Miss Blessing has lost her nerve at the last moment and may not come. A few minutes later, Beatrice slips into the vestry, my coat over her arm. It's the first time she's seen Fred in weeks and she gives him a silent hug. They exchange a few words of greeting before she turns to me.

'Good luck, Sis.' She never calls me that. I look at her in surprise. 'We're bang in the middle; good place to keep him stuck in his seat for as long as possible.'

'Can he see the vestry from where you are?'

'Not if he doesn't know what he's looking for. Is she here?' I shake my head.

Beatrice glances at her watch and pulls a face: it's gone twenty past. 'Is there another way into this place?' she asks.

'Yes. We can do a quick exit.' I nod to a small door I've found behind the robing screen. 'You hang back quite a while with him. I just hope she turns up before it starts – though Fred will stay in here. She won't be alone.'

As Beatrice turns to go, the door behind the screen opens and Miss Blessing enters rather breathlessly, accompanied by an attendant I don't recognise. She comes hesitantly round the screen and I jump to my feet, resisting the temptation to clasp her hands and wish her well. She is looking pale and scared beneath the now-familiar veneer of impassivity.

'Welcome, Miss Blessing,' I say, and to the attendant, 'Thank you. I'm so glad you could come.'

'We almost didn't!' says the attendant tartly. 'Another patient kicking off – and I can't stay.'

'We quite understand,' I tell her. 'My brother is here to sit with her. My sister will be in the audience, too.'

Everyone shakes hands. Beatrice says, 'I must dash! Miss Blessing—' She touches Millie on the shoulder, mindful of the attendant who is still hovering beside her. All she says is, 'Enjoy the concert.' And she goes. The attendant leaves a moment later by the opposite door.

I smile at Millie with a confidence I don't feel and raise the corner of the mackintosh to show her the elements of her disguise laid out beneath.

She barely examines them, but nods and sits on the next chair. Does the nod mean she's agreed to leave with us, then? There's an expectant hush outside, and I'm too scared to ask. 'Good luck, Annie!' she says. For a moment, the tension leaves her and she raises her head and smiles at me with sudden warmth.

I thank her, and then it is half-past and Dr Squires is on the rostrum. I take my seat at the piano and the concert begins.

We start with Stanford's *Three Latin Motets*. Someone has thoughtfully laid a programme on the piano stool and once

I've given them the chord to begin, for the first time I can read the translation: *'Justorum animae in manu Dei sunt . . .'*

> *The souls of the righteous are in the hand of God,*
> *There, shall no torment or malice touch them.*
> *In the sight of the unwise they seem to die,*
> *But they are at peace.*

Miss Blessing versus the *insipientium,* the 'unwise': it's like a prediction for her future. I look out over the audience and spot Daddy and Beatrice in a sea of upturned faces. After that, I stop feeling nervous.

The interval seems to drag on for an age, while members of the choir hand out cups of coffee to the audience. I dread Daddy barging into the vestry, but Beatrice is clearly steering him away. Perhaps he has met some more friends from the Lodge. Perhaps he has met Dr Squires! I feel a sudden rush of nausea. Fred, Millie and I sit in an agony of waiting, not wanting to talk. Then Millie says, 'The sopranos didn't go flat in the Parry, did they?' And we all giggle. 'They get the energy from their nerves, I suppose.' I feel my fingers damp and puffy. How can I contend with Mozart when all I want is to bundle her out of the vestry right now and not stop running until I've got her safely on the bus to Maisie's? As the interval ends, I nod to Millie and she raises the mackintosh again, softly collecting each piece of her disguise. Once she puts them on, there'll be no going back. I watch her. Our eyes meet. Then the audience falls silent again and I leave the vestry.

The choir is more confident with the piano accompaniment than singing on their own. They seem to have relaxed and our performance of the Mozart goes well. We stand for the applause and then Dr Squires gestures for the sopranos to lead off into the auditorium, where they will be reunited with their friends. I slip away on the other side and walk sedately towards the vestry. Behind me I hear a rising babble of voices.

We need to leave at once; not before the audience itself, but before the arrival of the young soprano nurse who has been ordered to take Millie back to her ward. I sincerely hope she has friends and parents to greet before fulfilling her duties. Fred and Millie are waiting. She is sitting stiffly, straight-backed, the small bag of her worldly possessions on her knee. As I enter, she stands and I look at her face. The hat is pulled well down, the veil reaches just far enough over her nose. Beneath it the spectacles seem to change the shape of her face and below it the lipstick glows redly. It doesn't look absurd, as I had feared it might, but the difference is almost shocking. 'I would never have recognised you,' I murmur as I stuff the music into my music case, and behind the veil I see her eyes briefly gleam with relief. Fred is ready with my coat and as I fasten the buttons, he goes to the little door and looks out. People are starting to move back down the corridor. I hesitate, torn between leaving too early and being spotted, and getting out before anyone comes to find us.

'Let's go,' says Fred.

I put my hand on his arm. 'No. Wait a moment longer.'

'They might come!'

'We'll be too conspicuous if we leave now!'

'We might bump into Daddy if we wait!'

'No. Beatrice knows to keep him back a while.'

These are agonising seconds of indecision. After the initial exodus, the corridor has gone quiet again. Millie stands behind me, peering over my shoulder. Then, thankfully, another surge – this time a larger one. Fred leads the way into the corridor so as to peer backwards towards the hall doors. After a few moments, he says, 'Now!' and we shuffle out into the crush, eyes to the floor, or fixed on each other, anything to avoid the gaze of people crowding around us. Millie clutches my hand: I realise this is her first experience in more than six years of a press of strangers around her. Our progress is horribly slow; the concertgoers are laughing and chatting, in no apparent hurry to get home. It's like one of those nightmares where you are running from danger but slowly, slowly, through treacle. I briefly worry about what Sister Jones will think when she realises I've left without saying goodbye, but on Monday I will return the music and take my leave properly, as long as no one connects me personally with the disappearance of Miss Blessing.

We're almost back at the flight of stairs where Fred ought to leave us and return to his ward when I hear a shout from behind. 'Miss Lang! Annie Lang!' For a moment, I wonder if I can ignore it but someone is coming through the crowd towards me. People are turning to look and then looking back at me. 'Take her to the main hall!' I instruct Fred. 'Stay with her. I'll meet you by the front door – inside or outside. Do whatever you have to, but don't leave her!' Then I turn and raise my arm. 'I'm here,' I call. 'What is it?'

It's the young nurse, Gladys, who is supposed to collect Millie. 'Thank goodness I've found you!' she says as she pushes through the last of the crowd. 'I was to take Blessing to the ward, but she's gone! Sister Jones said you and your brother were looking after her.'

'Does Sister know she's gone?'

Gladys shakes her head. 'I was too scared to tell her! I only stopped a moment to say hello to my mother and my Auntie Dorothy. I knew I shouldn't, but Auntie wanted to talk ... I couldn't believe it when the vestry was empty, so I thought I'd try and find you first.'

'Don't worry,' I say. 'Another nurse took her, I think.'

'Another nurse? Who?'

'Um, I think it was that nurse, you know, the one who looks after the chapel? Is it Nurse Bleakley?'

'Nurse *Bleakley* took her?'

'Yes, I'm pretty sure,' I say. 'I was packing up my music but I saw them, and then when I turned round again they'd gone.' I cross my fingers and cling to my music case, wondering how this will sound in the cold light of day.

'Oh Miss Lang, I hope you're right!' Little Gladys – she must be my age – is looking relieved. I feel very bad about this, but in the end it will be my head on the block, not hers. (About Nurse Bleakley, I have no qualms at all.) 'What should I do now, d'you think?' asks Gladys.

I make a quick calculation. To make her way back to the chapel and report to Sister Jones will take barely five minutes. I need longer than that to collect Miss Blessing from the front hall and get to the nearest bus stop.

'Well,' I suggest. 'You might want to go and check the ward before you report to Sister Jones?' That should buy us a little more time, given the crowds, the corridors and the security gates, and I can't see it would get Gladys into any more trouble than she's in already. She's lost precious time coming to find me.

'Oh, I'll do that. Perhaps it will be all right.'

'Well,' I reassure her, 'If she did go with Nurse Bleakley, that nurse is very efficient.'

Gladys raises her eyes to heaven. 'She certainly is,' she agrees with a laugh. 'I'm sure I'll find her, Miss Lang. Thanks for your help. Goodnight.' And she starts to move back through the crowds, which I see, to my satisfaction, are as thick as ever. I feel wretched on Gladys's behalf, and deeply guilty on my own: under normal circumstances I would never, of course, leave a patient until her escort arrived. But then I remind myself that I haven't left her, have I? As Maisie says, you can't make an omelette without breaking eggs. And recollecting that my father must be somewhere close behind now, I wade through the departing audience as fast as possible towards the front hall. We have very little time.

I find them again by the front door as the crowds shuffle past; Millie has wisely turned her back on everyone and is deep in conversation with Fred.

'She wants to stay,' he announces, as I reach them. 'She thinks she'll get you into trouble.'

'Nonsense,' I tell him. 'We'll all be in trouble if they find us. Let's go. Fred, thank you for everything. I'll see you very soon.'

He picks up the urgency in my voice and holds out his hand to Millie. 'Goodbye, Miss Blessing. Annie's right. I wish you all the luck in the world.'

Before she can protest, he shepherds us both through the door. I take her firmly by the arm and we begin to walk up the drive. There are plenty of people milling around us and for the journey to the hospital gates I feel far less conspicuous than I normally would. As well as knots of people, a few cars edge past at a snail's pace; in their headlights, I'm reassured to see that the walkers are just silhouettes. We move on steadily, Millie still gripping my arm.

But as we approach the gatehouse, the crowd slows down and becomes a queue: something is happening at the front. It's now a good ten minutes since we left the chapel; time for Gladys to have raised the alarm. I can see the cars are being directed around the pedestrians, but each one is made to stop at the gate. As we get closer, it becomes clear that everybody leaving the hospital grounds is being checked.

Millie has realised it too. 'They're going to find us,' she whispers. 'They must be looking for me.'

I try and force myself to think: this is not something we envisaged, Beatrice and I, but we did agree an emergency identity for Millie if anything should go wrong. 'Listen,' I tell her. 'Your name is Ida. Ida Rowbotham. Can you remember that?'

She looks up at me fearfully. 'Ida? Who's she?'

'She's another volunteer – like me. She's away at the moment. She won't be here, but they'll have her name as someone with a right to be in the hospital. We'll get you through.' I pat her arm. 'Don't worry.'

'Ida Rowbotham?'

'Yes. She's about your age, your size,' I reassure her. 'You work on Ward Three. You've been at the concert. They won't know her on the gate.'

'Are you sure?'

'The doormen have no idea who any of us is, but they'll have a list.'

'Won't they want some proof?'

'Well,' I smile, 'I haven't any proof of who I am. You'll be fine. They've never asked me for proof before.'

'Hadn't I better just tell them the truth, Annie, and have done with it?'

I look at her seriously. 'If you do, we'll both be in trouble!'

She is silent for a moment. 'Ida Rowbotham?'

'Yes.'

'All right.'

We move slowly towards the front of the queue.


But just before we get there, a car stops beside us: a Wolseley. The window rolls down.

'Annie?'

It's my father. 'Hop in!' he says.

I want to scream and cry and tell him to leave us alone. 'I'll be fine, Daddy.' I try and sound calm.

'Don't be ridiculous!' he argues. 'Get in, girl. What's the matter with you?'

'I said I'd see a friend home.'

'Well, you can't do that with this going on. Get in. Both of you.'

I feel Millie stagger beside me. Is she going to faint? I look at her urgently and tighten my arm through hers. Then Beatrice leans past Daddy and speaks through the window, enunciating each word: 'Annie, just as we were leaving we heard a violent patient has escaped from the hospital. The police have been called. They're going to be combing the streets: it's not safe for you to be hanging around at bus stops. This patient's out there somewhere. You might get attacked.' She's pulling meaningful faces at me that Daddy can't see. She must have a plan.

'All right,' I say reluctantly. 'We were just nearly at the front of the queue, that's all.'

'You'll be quicker with us,' Daddy says. 'Anyway, wouldn't you rather have a lift?'

As we turn towards the rear door I mutter to Millie, 'Remember: Ida. And you've lost your voice.' I push her, half-fainting into the rear passenger seat and run round the other side before Daddy can start asking her questions. 'Oh Daddy,' I say as I jump in. 'This is Ida Rowbotham. She's another volunteer. She went to the concert but she's not well, so I said I'd see her home.'

Daddy asks her, 'And where is home, Ida?'

'Hyson Green,' I supply quickly. The plan is to go to Maisie's house in Hyson Green where Millie will stay the night. It was all going to be so simple.

Daddy is adjusting the mirror so he can get a good look at her. Millie shrinks into the far corner and turns her head away.

'She's feeling really ill, Daddy. Don't start talking to her,' I say sharply.

'Poor little Ida,' he responds with mock sympathy. 'What's the matter with her then?'

'Laryngitis,' I tell him. 'She can't speak, so don't try and make her.'

'Ida the mystery passenger!' he muses. He's still searching for her face in the mirror. He thinks he's being funny. I want to hit him over the head.

'Watch out,' says Beatrice. 'We're next.'

I'm relieved to see there's no policeman at the gate; it's just one of the hospital doormen and he *is* checking a list. We tell him our names, and I give Ida's. 'You won't have our names on your list,' drawls my father. 'I'm Harry Lang. My daughter was playing at the concert. My elder daughter and I went to see her.'

'Ida and I are volunteers,' I chip in, leaning forward. 'Our names will be there.'

'That's no problem, Mr Lang,' says the doorman, ignoring me. 'I'm sorry to have delayed your journey, sir. Goodnight.' He touches his cap.

I lean back in my seat, seething with a mixture of relief that we're through and anger at the ease with which my father has controlled the situation. He's the one they should be arresting. Only the good get caught. I reach across and give Millie's hand a reassuring squeeze; she doesn't respond but I can feel the terror radiating off her. As we move away, a couple of police cars with blue flashing lights draw up at the hospital gate. Beatrice did the right thing to make us go with Daddy: we wouldn't have made it alone.

'So Hyson Green it is,' announces my father, putting his foot down on the accelerator. 'Which street?'

'Just make for the sports ground, Daddy,' I tell him. 'We'll direct you from there.'

I know Maisie's house quite well from having visited Nana there and realise that my next problem is how to persuade him to drop us off without it being obvious where we're going. Luckily, Beatrice jumps into the silence as I try and work out what to do, gossiping about the concert, the performers and asking questions about the music. This passes the journey which, with Daddy at the wheel, is a great deal swifter than the bus would have been.

'Ida, my dear,' he says as we draw into Hyson Green, 'you're going to have to break your intriguing silence and tell me where you live.'

She throws me a desperate glance and whispers, 'I can't speak, Mr Lang. Annie knows.'

He's delighted, of course. 'Ah!' he cries. 'She has a voice, and a very attractive, husky voice if I may say so!'

'That's because she's got a throat infection!' I snap at him. I can't bear to think what effect this behaviour is having on poor Millie. 'Take the next right.'

'"Please, Daddy"!' he prompts. 'I don't know what's happened to your manners tonight, Annie. I think this concert's gone to your head.'

'I'm sorry, Daddy.' I need to try and behave.

'Actually' – his eyes search for mine in the mirror now – 'you were jolly good, darling.'

'Thank you, Daddy.'

'You *were*,' echoes Beatrice. 'Wasn't she, Ida?'

'Yes,' rasps Millie.

We have almost reached Maisie's. I guide him one block past the turning and say, 'That's fine. You can drop us here.'

'Well where is it?' he asks.

'Just along there.'

'Hang on. I'll take you.'

'No, that's fine.' I insist.

'*If she's so ill . . .?*' He turns and looks at me. There's a challenge in his eyes.

'Didn't Annie say you have rather strict parents?' suggests Beatrice helpfully to 'Ida'.

Millie looks at her. She doesn't know what to say, but I do. 'They wouldn't want anyone driving her home,' I tell him. 'They'd ask awkward questions.'

'What's awkward about it?' He looks from Beatrice to me, but I'm halfway out of the back seat. I flap my hand at him. 'Oh, you know. Don't agree with cars and things . . . *Jansenists!*' I knew *La Porte Étroite* would come in handy for something. Then I'm running around to open Millie's door.

She turns, but she can't look up at him. 'Thank you,' she whispers awkwardly.

'The pleasure is all mine.' He is gazing at her with a puzzled expression. 'I just wish you'd let me take you home!'

But I almost yank her out of the car and pick up the bag, which she has been hugging on her knee. 'Don't walk too fast,' I mutter as we start off in the wrong direction to throw him off the scent. I take her arm again, and sling the bag over my shoulder. As soon as we're round the corner, we break into a run; fifty yards on, we double back around a second corner and reach Maisie's from the opposite direction, breathless but elated.

She opens the door and looks from one to the other, as we stand there spluttering and laughing. Or at least, I'm laughing. Millie is just shell-shocked. 'Annie!' Maisie cries. 'Well, look at you both! What's gone on?'

'Oh Maisie, this is Millie Blessing. We've had such adventures. Daddy drove us here!'

'Mr Lang? Here?' She darts around me, looking anxiously up the road.

'Two streets away! Don't worry, Maisie. He doesn't suspect a thing. Millie will explain. I must run. I'll see you tomorrow, Millie. It's all going to be fine now. I promise.' I wave goodbye and walk off briskly back towards the car.

At the junction of Gregory Boulevard and Mansfield Road, a fleet of police cars and a Black Maria whizz past us, bells ringing. I suddenly feel very tired.

# TWENTY-FIVE

**Sunday, September 11**

I sleep badly, my head full of police cars and anxious slow escapes, and when I wake up I have to disentangle nightmare from reality; it's a while before I truly understand that our plan has worked: under the nose of the authorities, we have spirited Miss Blessing out of the hospital. Not all the city's police could surely track her to Maisie's and today will be the simple part. We just have to get her on to that London train. It ought to be a triumph, so why do I feel so uneasy?

Normal life must continue, of course, and I have to go with Mother and Beatrice to morning service at the Mission. Beatrice and I barely exchange a word: I can tell she's as apprehensive as I am. The service drags even more than usual; Grandfather Pastor Eames delivers a long sermon on the Last Judgement, which does nothing for my failing spirit.

Over Sunday lunch we converse, to my mind, like automatons, as if we've each been wound up and left to speak clockwork sentences, while our real selves, tangles of mental torment and fractured nerves, have been left in the wardrobe.

For the first time I understand how it must feel for Fred outside the goldfish bowl. As soon as Beatrice and I finish doing the dishes, we race upstairs for a quick conflab in Beatrice's bedroom. I throw myself down on to her bed. 'Why do I feel so bad?' I ask.

She shrugs. 'Because we've done wrong, perhaps?'

'We haven't done wrong!'

'We have, sort of. In the eyes of—'

'*Who*, Beatrice?' I turn on my elbow to glare at her. I can't bear it if she's going to say the Lord!

She shakes her head. 'I suppose we've been brought up not to flout authority.'

'Perhaps,' I agree. I think about this. 'But when authority's as wrong as all the grown-ups around *us*' – I wave my arm in the air – 'flout away!' Once upon a time this would have had us in giggles, but not today. I bury my face in Bea's eiderdown. I want to shut out the possibility I've made a terrible mistake.

'We just need to hold our nerve and finish what we've started,' says Beatrice. 'You've done brilliantly. My part is only just beginning.'

'It doesn't feel brilliant,' I tell her. 'It feels a mess. I thought I'd be on top of the world, Bea, getting her out of that place, but it's really shaken me up. Heaven knows how poor Millie must feel! I can't face going back in there tomorrow and having to lie to Sister Jones and the rest of them – they're good people. They trusted me and I've let them down.'

'It was the *right thing*, Annie! You'll see it through, and you'll be fine in a day or two.'

'Once I know she's safe with Edwina!' I admit. 'When is it she arrives?'

'This Friday in Liverpool.' Beatrice knows about sending telegrams, so she's in charge of the travel arrangements.

'Edwina's done well to get such an early sailing. It's not long for Millie to have to wait.'

'I hope she'll be all right in London on her own. I wish I could come with you, but they'd smell a rat.'

'I'll be with her every evening. It's only a few days.'

We lapse into silence. Then I have another thought: 'Supposing it all unsettles Millie so much that Edwina thinks she's too ill to go to Canada? Then what do we do?'

'Sufficient unto the day . . .' Beatrice reminds me.

'I know,' I say. 'I know.'

'It *is* the right thing, Annie. You're the one who's said it all along.'

'That's what's worrying me! Suppose I'm wrong?'

'Well, you've got university in a couple of weeks. Think of that.' Whenever Beatrice mentions the university, there's a wistfulness that makes me feel worse.

We're both silent for a few moments. 'You'd better get going,' she says. 'Buses not so good on Sundays.'

I sit up. 'Should she wear the disguise, d'you think?'

Beatrice groans. 'Not today, surely. They won't be watching the station. Will they?'

We haven't considered this. We look at each other in consternation.

'I'll get her to wear the hat,' I decide. 'Not the specs.' I'm starting to feel better. 'They don't exactly know who they're searching for; the hospital people won't recognise her in the hat. She's so different in ordinary clothes, anyway.'

'So: ten minutes before the train?' Beatrice instructs. 'You'll need to buy her ticket first.'

'I can do that. See you—'

'—by the departure board,' she finishes. 'Twenty-past five.'

I jump off the bed, straighten my frock, give my hair a quick brush with Bea's hairbrush and go downstairs to get my coat. I'm about to leave the house when, as if on cue, Mother comes out of the sitting room, shutting the door carefully behind her. Daddy will be dozing in his armchair by now.

'Annie.'

'Mother.' I wait. We look at each other for a few moments.

'I heard at the Mission this morning' – her voice is even more clipped than usual – 'that the woman, Miss Blessing, has disappeared from the hospital.'

I say nothing. There's a kind of boiling in my head. I wonder what I'm going to do to her if she tries to stop me leaving the house.

'I don't know what you've been up to all these weeks in that place,' she says. 'But if you have anything to do with her disappearance. . .'

She pauses. If she understood who my letter was from three days ago, she will know that I do. But it is not quite a question and I don't answer it.

'Then,' she continues, 'I pray you get her away, Annie. Get her right away. I don't want to know. Just get that poor creature away from here.' Her voice is shaking, her eyes bitter, but she says nothing more.

I want to say *I will, I promise,* but I can't trust her. Instead, I say, 'I have to go now, Mother.'

She looks at me a moment longer. Then she murmurs, 'It's more than I could do.'

Maisie opens the door in her Sunday pinafore. 'Oh Annie, I'm glad to see you.'

'How is she?' I ask.

'She's all right.' Maisie steps outside for a moment, pulling the door to behind her. 'Tell Beatrice,' she says, 'she's got to go easy on her. She's very nervy. I wish she could stay here and not go to London. We'd look after her till her sister comes.'

362

I suddenly very much want this to happen, too, but it's not safe. 'You'd be at our house all day,' I point out. 'Mr Brown wouldn't be here. They could come at any time. If Daddy ever realises who he had in his car last night, he knows where he dropped her.'

'I know, Annie. You're right.' She looks anxious. 'I just worry for the poor lamb. Six years is a long time to be locked up: she'll need looking after. This morning she barely dared get out of bed. I took her up a cup of tea and she jumped like a scalded cat.'

'Beatrice's landlady is kind, and Bea will be there every evening. Edwina will collect her in five days.'

'Well, that'll be a mercy. 'Cos I worry for you and Beatrice, too, you know, while she's still in the country. Now come and have some tea before you go.'


On the bus to the station, Millie sits very straight and still. She says, 'I can't believe I'm really going to see Eddie again!'

I glance at her. Something has been bothering me and I haven't had a chance to ask her. This is hardly the time, but there will be no other. 'Millie, when Edwina comes to London ... she does know, does she? The truth about my father when you were a girl?'

Millie nods. 'She does. Now. I couldn't let her come without telling her.'

'You mean, she didn't know before?'

'That letter you posted for me. That was my chance to tell.'

'Only now?' I am shaken.

She looks down. 'I couldn't, before, Annie. I couldn't say it.'

'So all these years they've never known?'

'Later, when I felt I could perhaps tell them, I had no way to do it – until you took that letter for me. Then, just the

363

day before yesterday, I had a reply from Eddie. She couldn't say anything much, of course, but it's quite clear that it was after reading my letter she decided to come. She's going to support me, whatever happens. I think it was *that* that finally gave me the courage to leave.' She turns to me and smiles. 'Something else to thank you for.'

So Millie's letter, not mine, has persuaded Edwina; and Edwina's letter has persuaded Millie. And I realise that's as it should be.

We arrive in good time for the train. As we turn the corner into Station Street, I cast an anxious glance around the fore-court, looking for police cars, but there's nothing obvious.

I haven't told Millie about our concern that the hospital authorities may be looking for her and, whatever Maisie says, she seems a little calmer today, with the courage to gaze about at her surroundings. 'It's like seeing everything for the first time!' She tells me. 'Breathing fresh air again, the colours – I feel so out of things, Annie – but it's wonderful, too.'

At Sunday teatime, the station is not crowded; I imagine the rush will come later. A few people bustle towards trains after a weekend visiting friends and family. Some carry bunches of dahlias from late-summer gardens; others have knapsacks with maps tucked into the side pockets, on their way home from hiking in the Peak District, perhaps. I guide Millie to the ticket office and buy her a single to London.

'Cheaper if you get a return, Miss,' says the ticket clerk. 'It's valid for a month.'

'She won't be back,' I tell him.

'Very well.'

I hand the ticket to Millie, who puts it carefully in the purse I've given her. We make our way back into the main station and head for the departure board, which is above a sort of bridge that spans the platforms. The London train will leave from platform one in twelve minutes' time. I look around for Beatrice, who is generally early for trains, but she's not here yet.

Millie says, 'Annie, I don't know how to—'

'Please don't, then.' I smile at her. 'We did it for us, you know, as well as for you. It was something we needed to do, all three of us.'

'There was no need,' she says gently. 'But you did it anyway. I can't tell you how it helps – not just physically, of course: I'm here, after all! But it helps . . .'

'It was the least we could do.'

'I just hope *you* don't get into trouble!' she says seriously.

'Millie,' I take her hand. 'I'm about to start a whole new life. My future is not in that hospital. Whatever happens, Beatrice and Fred and I will be fine. I just long to hear that you're safe and well in Canada, and you must write and tell me everything.'

'I will. I promise.' She smiles, her eyes glistening.

And then I see Beatrice. She is almost upon us. Her distress is palpable. She is actually wringing her hands. She says, 'I couldn't warn you. I so wanted to warn you! There was nothing I could do.'

A few paces behind her, my father.

For a moment, I freeze. I wonder if they would make it to the platform if they ran now. But they don't. I walk towards him. 'Daddy!' I put out my hand. He pushes it off.

'I thought as much.' His pale blue eyes are looking at Millie. 'Ida Rowbotham, indeed!'

Millie shrinks away. Beatrice puts her arm round her to support her.

'Daddy,' I say. 'You have to let them go.'

'I shall do no such thing, miss. Don't you tell me what to do!'

'Listen!' I fasten my hands around his forearm to restrain him. 'Listen to me. You will hear nothing of her again, I swear. She is going to Canada. Her sister is taking her away for ever.'

'Oh no, she's not!'

'Why does it matter to you?' I challenge him. 'What's it to you if she leaves the country?'

'She's a sick woman, Annie. She's going nowhere!'

'She's not sick!' I am speaking urgently but low, close to his face. If we make a scene of this, we're all lost. 'You know she's not sick. Your doctor friend knows it. You're keeping this woman a prisoner, adding to the appalling harm you've already done her!'

'Harm? I'm her guardian! I saved her from ruin, didn't I?'

'You shut her up in that place!' Beatrice is speaking now, soft but insistent. 'You thought if you said she was mad you could keep her there for the rest of her life.'

'Daddy,' I tell him. 'This is the only decent thing: let her leave.'

'Go and sit in the car, Annie. I'll deal with you later.'

'No,' I say. 'No. You don't tell me what to do. You don't have the right.'

'I'm your father!'

'And Beatrice and I are atoning for your sin – your *crime*!' I am staring deep into his vacant eyes. I wonder if he even understands what I'm talking about.

'I'm no sinner. You're the sinner, you deceitful, lying girl, and after what you've done – I'll tell you this for nothing – you will not be going to the university.'

He wrenches his arm away and lunges for Millie. Beatrice moves deftly between them.

'Daddy!' I have him by both arms now, pushing against him with all my strength. 'Listen to us. We know what happened. I'm not talking about the baby. We know what happened when she was sixteen, fifteen, *fourteen*. Listen to me, Daddy: we saw it. I did. Beatrice did. I believe Fred saw it too. Millie *knows* it. And were there others, Daddy? Was Elsie another one?'

For the first time, something seems to get through to him. He hesitates, but only for a moment. 'And who'd listen to you? A bunch of children?'

'Daddy, Mr Wilkinson's wife saw it!' I have no idea if this is true, but it's worth a try.

'And who on earth is she?'

'Mr Wilkinson, the verger at the Mission? They all know at the Mission!'

For a moment his eyes narrow. Bea understands what I'm up to; seizes her moment. 'Mother herself saw it!'

He's rattled at last. 'She never saw anything.'

'You don't know what she saw. She *told* me!' Beatrice insists. 'You ruined her life. You've ruined Fred's. And mine!'

'And mine, Mr Lang.' Millie speaks quietly but clearly. She has detached herself from Beatrice and is standing closer to him. 'But if you leave me be and let me go to Canada, you'll not hear from me again. I give you my word.'

The loudspeaker wheezes into action: 'The train approaching platform one is the five thirty-three for London St Pancras, calling at Loughborough, Leicester, Kettering . . .' The rest is drowned by a whoosh of steam and a screech of brakes as the train hisses and grinds into the station.

'Six witnesses, Daddy!' I yell at him over the racket. 'You let Millie Blessing go to Canada. And I *shall* go to university! You don't deserve it. You're a very lucky man!'

A gush of smoke billows over the parapet where we're

standing. I feel him draw back a fraction. 'Run!' I shout at them. 'Run for it!' And in the steam and the confusion, they do. Beatrice picks up Millie's bag, waves her ticket at the inspector at the barrier and drags Millie to the iron steps leading down to the platform. I stand and watch through the smoke as they reach the bottom and join the last passengers climbing on board. I relax my grip on my father's forearms, for the strength has left them. I wait beside him as the announcer finishes announcing and doors slam. I watch the guard with his whistle and his green flag check up and down the line. I see the signal rise at the end of the platform and the whistle blow and the train begin to chug slowly, then faster, as it starts on its journey south. *Each a glimpse and gone for ever.*

Through my tears, I watch my father turn and make his way out of the station. And in the slump of his shoulders as he goes, I see the possibility – though for now I can put it no higher – that he may not pursue Millie to London or prevent me from starting my degree. So perhaps, after a long while, Millie might become a music teacher in Canada; and Beatrice find her vocation, whatever it is; and Fred break free from the demons in his head; and Miss Higgs make peace with her own conscience and with the man to whom she's bound for ever. And me? Well, that perhaps I may be all right, I suppose. If I believed in any god at all, I would pray we may all be all right – in the end.

# ACKNOWLEDGEMENTS

I would like to thank my publishers, Sarah and Kate Beal, for their faith in this novel, and David Reynolds, without whose thoughtful insight it might never have found them. I'm most grateful to the notMorley writers who sat through the first draft and gave me wise criticism; to Elinor Bagenal, Michael Bailey, Elizabeth Byrne and Lesley Toll for their invaluable advice; and to all my colleagues, friends and relations for their endless tolerance and support while I was writing it – particularly Penny Hayman, Barbara Mitchell and Jennifer Potter.

The book is dedicated to the memory of my mother and my dear Auntie Joyce. This is in no way their history, I'm thankful to say (apart from the incident of the long combinations), but their spirits may inhabit the story.

# A NOTE ON THE AUTHOR

Ros Franey grew up in the Midlands, where this book is set. She began her career in television just as her first novel was published and became a maker, and later an executive producer, of award-winning documentaries, many of them around issues of social justice. *The Dissent of Annie Lang* is her second novel. She lives in North London.